Also by Boman Desai

PORTRAIT OF A WOMAN M

An unhurried but immersive tale of ambition and love.
—*Kirkus Reviews*

A splendid foray into the initiation rites of the modern fearless woman—brimful of erudition, some age-old wisdoms and a more recent one that everyone seems to have forgotten: the meaning of gender equality.

Tara Sahgal, *India Today*

Desai's intimate novel digs into pressing themes of love, marriage, divorce, education, and feminism as it weaves the threads of its determined protagonist's quest for independence.... Desai invests such telling detail and engaging context into the telling, that readers of novels about women in the world will remain immersed, caught up in descriptions that are simple and beautiful.

—*Booklife*

A remarkable feat ... an erudite and literary novel which is also a potboiler.

Bapsi Sidhwa, *Fezana Journal*

A complex tapestry of marriage, love and betrayal.

Prasenjit Choudhury, *Deccan Herald*

A deliberate and skillful construction of a well-paced and cadenced narrative.

Sundeep Sen, *The Hindu*

Extremely readable.

Firdaus Gandavia, *Parsiana*

Delightful and entertaining.

Gopali Bandyopadhyay, *8th Day*

A GOOGLY IN THE COMPOUND: a novel of the Raj

This engrossing chronicle of a complicated family builds to a stunner of a conclusion.
—*Booklife*

A family's long-simmering tensions boil over during a trip to the old homestead in this literary novel.... The result is a wide-lensed meditation on power dynamics—within countries and within families.
—*Kirkus Reviews*

The tiger cub grows as dangerous as the British Raj for India. Both have tasted blood and both demand more. Desai spins a fascinating story of Parsi bloodlines, romance and intrigue, counterpointed by the events that made WWII such a watershed in the history of both India and the world.
Anjana Basu, *The Statesman*

The bare bones of the plot don't do justice to the theme, but the structure of the novel is fascinating. The entire story is wrapped around a single breakfast which takes place at the Sanjana residence at Navsari. The progress of the breakfast is broken into five sections each titled 'Day of the Tiger.' Desai skillfully closes each section with a particular character who then narrates his or her story.
Firdaus Gandavia, *Parsiana*

Boman Desai's novel pulls the reader in and doesn't let go till the end. A family secret lies at the heart of the story, but the periphery is no less exciting. Two lovers escape Stalin's Soviet Union to India and a soldier meets with tragedy during the Kut-al-amara campaign of the Great War in Mesopotamia.
Afternoon Despatch & Courier

A "class" act of historical proportions, [the novel] rips into the conventional class hierarchies between British and Indians, upperclass Indians and lower.
Prasenjit Chowdhury, *Deccan Herald*

TRIO: a Novel Biography of the Schumanns and Brahms

A *Kirkus Reviews* BEST BOOK OF 2016!
A riveting dramatization of musical history.... Desai has produced a magisterial work, which is clearly the result of astonishingly thorough research. Although the story revolves tightly around the three main figures, there are also fascinating cameos by such musical luminaries as Richard Wagner, Franz Liszt, and Frédéric Chopin, and he memorably depicts the ego-driven rivalries between them. Each has a unique personality, and the author does a lovely job of dramatizing their quirks.
—*Kirkus Reviews* (starred review)

Boman Desai has dramatized the story of the Schumanns and Brahms in the form of a novel, citing their original correspondence among his sources. He writes so compellingly that it is like discovering the story anew. The great composers of the age make appearances when their lives intersect those of the trio, and I was glad to see that Desai presents them to us, warts and all, with the deepest sympathy and understanding. Bravo!
  Zubin Mehta (Music Director: Los Angeles, Israel, and New York Philharmonic Orchestras)

I finished reading your novel, TRIO, and found it compelling and illuminating. Would that the American (or Canadian) reading public could appreciate such a story as well told. It's a story that Tolstoy might have told in similar terms, and I do hope that it eventually gets the recognition it deserves. It is surely a tour de force.
  Vernon A. Howard (Former Co-Director, Philosophy of Education Research Centre, Harvard University)

I loved and admired this book.
  Diana Athill (Author/Editor: *Instead of a Letter*, *Stet*, *Somewhere Towards the End*)

I loved your book. You completely transported me. I read it through at a gallop. The love & feeling you have for the subject comes through—you disappeared & they appeared on the page, in the flesh, & I could *hear* their music. Congratulations!

> Sooni Taraporevala (Screenwriter/Photographer: *Salaam Bombay, Mississippi Masala, Parsis, Yeh Bombay*)

In portraying the lives and loves of the Schumanns and Brahms in his novel, TRIO, Boman Desai accomplishes a remarkable feat. Exhaustively researched, charming and readable, I was loath to put the novel down. It is a massive achievement and I recommend TRIO wholeheartedly not only to music lovers but to all those who love to read.

> Bapsi Sidhwa (Author: *The Crow Eaters, Cracking India, Water*)

Boman Desai approached his sprawling novel, TRIO, a dramatized history of the Schumanns and Brahms, as a biography for people who hate biographies and a novel for people who hate novels. Desai does a wonderful job describing the music. The language of TRIO is so vivid it makes one want to explore the composers' repertoires which get some evocative descriptions. So do the performers themselves: Clara's meticulousness, Liszt's power and bravura, Brahms's perfection at the piano as a cocky young virtuoso and sloppiness as an old man, Mendelssohn's spot-on imitations of Liszt and Chopin. Like the music, the book is meant first and foremost to be enjoyed—and on this account, it does not fail.

> Chris Spec, *Quarter Notes*

THE MEMORY OF ELEPHANTS: a novel

A big book with a baroque design. By an interweaving of narrative voices, a brilliant picture is drawn not only of individuals, but of a whole upper-class Indian family.

> *Punch*

India comes to life with great vividness and humor. Added to that are rewarding insights into the alien wisdom of exiles. The writing is never dull. The observations are acute; you sense a generosity of spirit in Desai's way of looking at the world and at people.

> *Yorkshire Post*

Fantastical though the framework, the book is neither a fantasy nor science fiction, but a vividly realistic presentation of three generations of Parsis. A variety of strikingly life-like characters, drawn with a warm feeling of kinship, yet with much humor, and often with a penetrating satirical observation, give the novel a vibrant sense of reality.

The Indian Post

The characterizations are vibrant. The writing has so much drive that, once started, it is almost impossible to leave this book unfinished.

The Statesman Literary Supplement, India

DANCING ABOUT ARCHITECTURE
(a Songwriter's Guide to the Lennon-McCartney Catalog)

A close look at the 162 Lennon-McCartney collaborations from "Love Me Do" to "The Long and Winding Road" unearths nuggets yet to be mined from their catalog. Rock music, generally speaking, is judged less for its musical value than for its performance, packaging, and delivery—less for the distribution of notes on the page than for their impact on the listener. Matters of taste cannot be questioned (those are personal), but matters of quality not only can be questioned, but must be questioned and objectively asserted. That is the business of music criticism, also the business of *Dancing About Architecture*.

It is widely known that Paul McCartney requested sole credit for just "Yesterday" from Yoko Ono (who holds Lennon's rights to the song). The song had blossomed fullblown one morning after a good night's rest, so complete in its first incarnation that Paul found it necessary to play it for others to assure himself that it was a new song. He had no lyrics and used "Scrambled eggs / Oh, my baby, how I love your legs" to sound out the melody. Yoko denied the request, but for the wrong reason. John's contribution is undeniable (as the book reveals), but Yoko doesn't know what it is, and Sir Paul himself may be amazed to find this tip of the hat to his longtime, longdead, longlovely friend. Roll over, John Lennon, and tell Paul McCartney the news!

THE ELEPHANT GRAVEYARD
(A *Moby Dick* for Elephants)

BOMAN DESAI

Winner of the Dana Award for Best Novel of the Year (2014)

Copyright © 2022 by Boman Desai. All rights reserved.
For information please contact boman@core.com
Library of Congress Control Number: 2022901625
ISBN: 9798794281354

All characters and events in this book are fictitious and any resemblance to real characters, living or dead, is coincidental—except for historical characters and events.

Book designed for Amazon KDP by Word-2-Kindle (www.word-2-kindle.com)

DEDICATION

Henry "Hank" George Zimoch is 2 days short of 2 years younger than me, but for many years—decades—he played the role of my older brother more than my younger, my older brother more than my friend, even my parent sometimes more than my friend, though neither of us seemed aware of it for the longest time. As an immigrant from Bombay to Chicago, 19 years old, knowing nothing, imagining I knew everything, I was a babe in the woods, boy in wonderland, new kid on the block. He was 17, feet firmly planted, comfortable in his skin, as much part of the landscape as the air. He played homesteading American host to my pioneering Indian guest, as curious about our differences as I was solicitous about finding similarities between us, as happy to show me around as I was happy to be shown. We seemed bonded by differences as much as similarities, both of us budding archies at the Illinois Institute of Technology, high on Mies van der Rohe and Frank Lloyd Wright, looking to find our own places in their wake. He also seemed older for having his own car, job, and girlfriend—and I, growing up with servants in a middle-class Indian family, the younger for rarely needing to lift a finger to get what I wanted, practically helpless in DIY Chicago. He got me my first job at a dry goods store where he also worked, and then proceeded to do my chores in addition to his own, driving me around as we made deliveries.

Almost from the start our vocations diverged. He had risen to the profession, never doubting he wanted to be an architect; I had fallen, encouraged by my father, a civil engineer for whom I'd done drawings while still in Bombay, for whom I'd earned a diploma in architecture through a correspondence course, for whom I'd studied at a part-time school of architecture for 3 years before jetting to the US. I was too seduced by the difference that was America, the welcomingness as much as the overwhelmingness, to be sure of what I wanted. Two events began my irrevocable and inevitable slide: (1) I won the Lewis Prize (creative writing) during my freshman year (a story about an executive who gave up job, marriage, and lifestyle to find another way); and (2) a reading of Plato's Apology, which created a lifelong admiration for Socrates, leading to my choice of philosophy as a major for my junior year at the Bloomsburg State College in Pennsylvania. I wanted to decipher the meaning of my life. Professionally and geographically Hank and I were moving in different directions, but personally we remained in touch. (I still have a letter from him, sent to Bloomsburg in 1971, asking if I needed money!)

No surprise, my fall from architecture set off explosions in Bombay (my grandmother said she had heard about Socrates, he had died a poor man)—but this is not about that. Even as I fell, Hank continued to rise.

He married, fathered 2 daughters, became partner in an architectural firm. After making a mess of marriage, many false starts, and much desperation, I published my first novel (I was 38), but fell down on my second (declined by my publisher). He continued steadily upward, not without roadblocks, but taking 2 steps forward for every step back. I took 2 back for every step forward, but the friendship never faltered. He continually called, we'd attend movies, visit new restaurants, sometimes 2-3 times a week, sometimes just a quick sandwich for lunch when he'd drive to my place (after I started working part-time to gain time to write) and off we'd go.

A falling-off was perhaps fated; a close friendship is not unlike a marriage, and like a marriage requires continual tenderness. I had long wanted to show him Mumbai (as Bombay came to be called) as he had shown me Chicago, and invited him to join me during a visit, only to have the first fissures appear in our mosaic. For the first time in our association I was in the driver's seat, I was finally truly 2 days short of 2 years older, finally his older brother and parent, but I drove us into a ditch. It would not be fair to either of us, nor to our friendship, for me to be more explicit—nor to rationalize nor self-justify what happened.

Returning to Chicago the fissures germinated in Mumbai multiplied when I found my dream job. I was 57. I had refused offers of fulltime jobs paying a living wage to write novels barely paying for my pride. I had just returned from another visit to the home country to confront another series of depressing part-time jobs, when someone I met at a dinner party introduced me to the concept of low-residence universities. With a published book and Masters in English I was eligible to teach writing. My presence would be required on campus twice a year, 5-10 days each in January and July. I would need to be prepared with seminars, readings, and workshops, the rest of the year to communicate with students via email. These were not plentiful jobs, but my good angels were out in force. For the first time ever I had a job that I loved that paid the bills, attentive students who read my books, and the luxury of time to continue writing.

Friends wondered at the change in me, commenting without fail, I looked brighter, happier, in love, a circus in my face. I even took better photographs! I'd had better-paying jobs, but none that engaged me so seamlessly—but the chasm between Hank and me continued to widen, providing the substance of a book that will never be written. We were incommunicado for a few years, each of us dealing with more slings and arrows, but taking arms against the sea of troubles we made it up. It's true what the song says, "Love is lovelier the second time around"—and, as I realized, the second time around could as easily be with the same person as with another, in this instance one who made a large and lovely difference in my life, the dedicatee of this book: Henry "Hank" George Zimoch.

Hank with a beefeater teddy in Bath during our trip across the pond. For reasons I have never understood I am the only person never to call him Henry.

ACKNOWLEDGMENTS

To paraphrase John Donne: *No man is an island. Every man is a piece of the continent, a part of the mainland. If a clod is washed to the sea, Europe is the lesser. The same might be said for the loss of a promontory. The death of any man diminishes me because I am part of Mankind. Ask not for whom the bell tolls. It tolls for you and me.* On a less exalted stage, the paraphrase also works as a thank you to the many who stood by as I filled these pages, all of whom make me so much more than an island, more than a continent, more even than the oceans which gobble the islands, among them Ronnie Desai (poet, producer, brother, blessing), the Dadabhoys and Darkis (Porus, Zerin, Abdul, Darius & [Dina & Amir for their continually fabulous Thanksgivings]), Tata-Colchesters (Shirin, Giles, Farah, & Peter), Weils (Richard & Zarine), Limbeck-Siegels (Kevin & Wendy), Suerth-Ernsts (Frank & Susanna), Diller-Ernsts (Lois & Ron), Gulyases (Stephen & Norma), Katrak-Karkarias (Kamalrukh & Cyrus), Ghadialy-Karanjias (Rashna & Rohinton), Mehtas (Hosi & Kim), Coopers (Farobag & Ashees), Kennedietsches (Bill & Jeanne), English-Kellers (Jim & Emily), Wisnowski-Profumos (Jim & Ally), Davers (Manek & Dilly, Minoo & Dina), Tarapores (Erach & Silloo, Shenaya & Pirzad, Phiroz & Soraya), Chokseys (Vera & Farhad), Tatas (Jimmy & Farida), Godrejes (Pheroza & Jamshyd), Chibbers (Homi & Maki, Percy & Yasmin, Darius & Ranjana), Taraporevalas (Kamal & Kai), Del Sestos (Xun Mei & Tony), Engineers (Rustom & Yasmin), Mistrys (Jangoo & Arnaz), Bapsi Sidhwa (& Noshir), Lalas (Sharookh & Zenobia), Mittals (Vijay & Priti), Mirzas (Parveze, Noshir, & Meher), Piloo Tata, Robin Blench, Marcia Nueske, Tess Daniels, John Striegl, Tom Gross, Tim Spadoni, Vispi Cooper, Steve Marmur, Cheryl Dority, Aban Rustomji, Aban Mukherjee, Jonathan Hollander & Anand & Nandita Mehta, Dolen Perkins-Valdez & Breena Clarke (for help with Blackspeak), Jim & Barb Carter (for Circus lingo & logistics), Linda & Paul Koptak (for the most comfortable armchair ever), Mary Elizabeth Parker (for the Dana Award), Dr. Shailen Petigara (for kindnesses through the years), Nawaz Merchant (powerhouse writer in her own right), Steve Barron (more than a gifthorse, a godsend), Barry Birnbaum (more than a godsend), Mom & Dad (of course)—and, again, always, Diana Athill.

All Nature is but Art, unknown to thee;
All Chance, Direction, which thou canst not see;
All Discord, Harmony not understood;
All partial Evil, universal Good;
And, spite of Pride, in erring Reason's spite,
One truth is clear, Whatever is, is right.
And if the World to us doth seem unfair,
Then take up Arms we must against Despair;
But failing that, and Only failing that,
Accept we must what seems unjust thereat.
     Alexander Pope
     [with apologies for
     the final quatrain]

... a far, far better thing ...
     Charles Dickens

THE ELEPHANT GRAVEYARD
(A *Moby Dick* for Elephants)

CONTENTS

PART ONE / SPIKE
WINTER 1947-1948

THE BLACK ELEPHANT
1 / JUST A JUGGLER / 3
2 / THE JOEY, BROWN E / 10
3 / JILL HAZEL BAILEY / 13
4 / ELBO DE BLEU / 17
5 / NIGHT FLIGHT / 23
6 / THE MOUTH OF THE ELEPHANT / 26
7 / PRINCESS ADA / 35
8 / MASTER AND MAN / 41

THE DYING ELEPHANT
1 / ON THE BACK OF THE ELEPHANT / 49
2 / THE BACKWARD BACK / 54
3 / JACK AND JILL / 56
4 / A SKIPPING PEBBLE / 65
5 / THE SHIMMY SHIM SHEBANGO / 73
6 / ELEPHANT MEMORIES / 77
7 / THE FIRST SON / 85

HATHI MINAR
1 / THE PR GAMBIT / 97
2 / ABOARD *THE GARDENIA* / 103
3 / PANTHER AMONG LIONS / 107
4 / ARRIVAL IN BOMBAY / 115
5 / 3RD PASTA LANE / 121
6 / SURROUNDED BY MIRACLES / 132
7 / THE CHAMBER OF ELEPHANTS / 138
8 / ELEPHANT GRAVEYARD / 143
9 / A JEZEBEL, A DELILAH, AND A PANDORA / 147

PART TWO / SIMON
SUMMER 1971

PSYCHEDELIC ELEPHANTS

1 / TWO PINK FAT FUCKIN' PIGS / 159
2 / BODYPAINTING / 167
3 / ON THE BACK OF THE ELEPHANT / 173
4 / WHEN BLACK WAS NOT SO BEAUTIFUL / 177
5 / A CURIOUS CHILD / 182
6 / TRIPTROPPING / 187

THE GHOST OF THE ELEPHANT

1 / ARRIVAL IN BOMBAY / 197
2 / NANDI / 204
3 / JACK AND JILL / 213
4 / HIS MOTHER TONGUE / 218
5 / UNDER THE MOSQUITO NET / 222
6 / HALFLIFE / 226

THE IVORY TRAIL

1 / OAK PARK / 233
2 / HURRICANE MERCEDES / 243
3 / MYRTLE AND THE ELEPHANT / 255
4 / THE BRASS FLOOR / 259
5 / DINNER IN THE PENTHOUSE / 266
6 / OPHIOPHAGUS HANNAH / 284

AFTERWORD / 295

GLOSSARY / 303

EXCERPTS
The Memory of Elephants
TRIO
A Googly in the Compound
Portrait of a Woman Madly in Love

BAILEYS AND BLUES FAMILY TREES

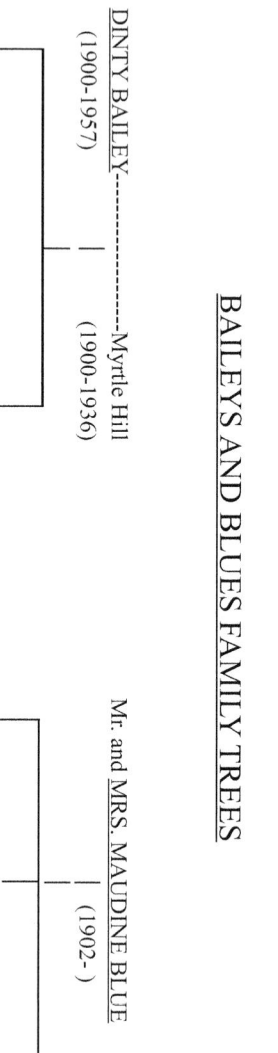

DINTY BAILEY
(1900-1957)

——Myrtle Hill
(1900-1936)

DANIEL "SPIKE"
(1932-1948)

JILL HAZEL
(1918-)

ROYALE
(1919-)

SIMON
(1950-)

Mr. and MRS. MAUDINE BLUE
(1902-)

Elbo
(1929-1948)

Prize
(1929-1947)

PART ONE / SPIKE
WINTER 1947-1948

THE BLACK ELEPHANT

In its early days the circus gave young, awkward America a view of the glamorous outside world; indeed, it was almost the only entertainment our grandparents had to watch. In its later, greater days between the two World Wars the circus provided perhaps the most popular entertainment available to all the people.
                                    LEONARD V. FARLEY

ONE   JUST A JUGGLER

Call me Spike, everyone did, but my name's Daniel Patrick Bailey, and a Bailey I am to my bones, descended from Mr. James Anthony Bailey of Barnum & Bailey, who was once an orphan named McGinness, who changed his name to Bailey when he apprenticed as billposter to Fred Bailey, a circus agent who claimed descent from Hackaliah Bailey of Somers, New York, best known for owning Old Bet, America's first circus elephant, back in 1815.

Now that's a lot of Baileys, and this is not about them, colorful though they were, not even about Baileys at all, except incidentally, Bailey though I am—and there were also differences: James Anthony was an orphan, I was half an orphan (still living with Pa and Sis); James Anthony ran from his sister's home to the circus, I ran from the circus to India; James Anthony was eleven when he made his run, I was circus-born—but this is tittle-tattle about fiddle-faddle, confessing what's trivial to avoid confessing what's not: My plunge into the graveyard.

Let me speak plainly. I am what you'd call a spook, but no spook as you know spooks, no woman in white turning the screw, no Nosferatu in the night, no haunted headless horseman, just a rattling of bones, dust and ash in a box in the graveyard, my limbo for twenty-three years. I hate to confess it, but there's no sidestepping, no sugarcoating, no silverlining the story. The sooner I get it out, the sooner I'll get it over. I killed a man—accidentally, but as surely as if

I had rent his limbs, thrust the knife to the hilt and twisted the blade, the deed which opened the gate to the graveyard, sorry miserable wretch that I was, shiteating shithead, bloodletting loon—but let me just get on with it.

Look at me the way I was before my damnation, my incarceration in the graveyard, a wiry runt of a 16-year-old kid, skinny as a snake but swaddled in a baggy coat, hair pale and thick as straw peeking around the motheaten edges of a beret, the very reason I was called Spike except by my ma, who had called me Danny, but she was long dead—an accident, I was told, nothing more, but the accident was palpable in my face. Look at my eyes, slits in the sun, brimful of water in the shade, muddy green and glazed, drooping at the corners, the sorrow of a man in the face of a boy, seed of the knifetwisting loon soon to be loosed in the world.

Look at me boarding an early bus to Toledo, Ohio, on a Friday (payday), with Monks "Moley" Moran, one of the dogboys, and Padraic "Paddy" Murphy, one of the propmen. Monks was his real name, but those who knew what he could do with his hands called him Moley. Paddy's chief talent was his eternal readiness for a cashgrab, for which he'd taken more than one ride in the paddy wagon—named, by the way, for the number of its besotted guests named Paddy. Respectable they were not, but their coats were cut from respectable cloth for the occasion, borrowed from the circus wardrobe, their faces shaved, shoes shined, heads sporting fedoras. Each of us carried a sack, mine full of apples, oranges, tennis balls, and bowling pins, theirs empty and invisible, buttoned into the linings of their coats.

It was November, end of the trouping season, the busiest time for agents routing the new season, contracting for grounds, parades, feed, water, and billposting, but the gloomiest for troupers, propmen, roustabouts, and butchers, the end of a party, end of summer, end of childhood, Moley and Paddy among the ranks of the unemployed. The dismantling of the circus, storage into winter quarters, was like the funeral of a friend, leaving in its wake orphans all. Suddenly, and until the following April, many of us were without prospects and many dispersed the same day with our final pay, some to Salvation Army centers, some to ride the rails, but even the more foresightful among us, who had lined up indoor engagements elsewhere or saved enough for the lean months ahead, left just as abruptly, just as dejectedly.

Some stayed, blacksmiths, carpenters, and wardrobe men, making repairs for the next season; skinners, cage hands, and bullmen—meaning us, Baileys, the elephant handlers. All elephants are bulls, even the cows, and all handlers bullmen, even the women. I, my big sister Hazel, and our pa Dinty rented a room in a flophouse, the Abbott Hotel, close to the winter quarters of the Great Frank Bros. Circus in Kendall Green, Ohio, for which Hazel held herself accountable with savings and wages waitressing at Salt'n'Peppah, a diner. What Dinty did was a mystery even to Dinty, and I did what I did for love, but I was sixteen, young enough to confuse lust with love. Love paid you back, lust made you pay. Love was its own reward, lust exacted punishment. Love gave you wings, lust made them wax. I soared for a brevity on the wings of an eagle, soon to be turned to wax.

The woman was Mary Eileen McDonnell, billed the Girleen from Ballaghaderreen, outfitted in glittering green when she took her turn in the ring, a girleen for her size more than her age (thirty), but an equestrienne supreme, at the peak of circus aristocracy, ahead of (in descending order) aerialists, featured stars, wirewalkers, acrobats, animal trainers, and joeys (as clowns were called after Charles Dickens edited the memoirs of Joseph Grimaldi, the famous English buffoon, which sold more quickly in its first edition than *Oliver Twist*).

As juggler and tumbler I might have been counted among acrobats, but as a bullman not even among joeys. I was barely above ponypunks and dogboys in the circus dungeon, while Eileen hovered among clouds drifting past turrets and towers. Each of us did flips and tumbles, but mine were on the broad back of Hero, the blackest elephant in the world, and hers on the thundering rump of her Andalusian, Andromache, the difference between performing in the middle of a plain and the middle of an earthquake—and differences there were more and plenty.

First, little women with large animals are a greater draw than little men. Second, Eileen leaped from tanbark to bareback, Andalusian at the gallop, and back again, and back, a stunt not even a kangaroo could have managed with Hero. For my star turn I maintained five bowling pins in the air while Hero lifted me to a pedestal—but my turn was little more than a prelude to Hazel's, and once again the little woman with the big animal outclassed the little man, her white spangled virtual nudity contrasting sharply with Hero's craggy black hide. Third, Eileen, in love with the smooth streamlined gloss of horses, forelock to fetlock, hated the ugly untidy mass of elephants, their rough wrinkled epidermis, their smell—and, I was convinced, their handlers. Fourth she was a celebrity, flashed on the posters, tycoons gave her diamonds, beer barons gave parties in her honor. I couldn't compete.

As luck would have it I didn't have to compete. She knew better what to do with coals smoldering in the basement than I did. She invited me into her trailer one lazy Sunday afternoon in Wilmington, Delaware (we played different towns every day of the week, resting on Sundays). I lacked grace, I lacked gravity, I lacked authority; I lacked emeralds and other glittering flowers; I lacked the means to make them available; but though my face was as smooth as a girl's my appetite was more rapacious than that of the most heavily bearded man, my stamina that of a stallion. I marveled at my fortune, the girth of her thighs, each thick as a hydrant. I appeared and disappeared at her pleasure, asked no questions, and said little, not because I had little to say but because I didn't want to reveal how little I knew about the world, how littlesuited we might be for each other.

She had engagements in Europe for the winter: Lisbon, Barcelona, Strasbourg, Frankfurt, Prague, Cracow, Budapest, Salzburg, Milan, Zurich, Paris, The Hague, London, to mention only the most prominent. I studied maps, tracing her itinerary, planning to send perfumes, purses, scarves, stoles, sachets, flowers, and candies to her as often as possible, to as many of her destinations as possible, culminating in a bouquet of red roses in London; also to have a photograph accompany each gift, of myself, her trailer, the winter quarters, landmarks in Kendall Green, the horses she'd left behind (she'd taken only Andromache), culminating in a bouquet of photographs, again in London.

We chose the business district that day in Toledo. I drew a wellheeled crowd, letting my hands (and beret, belly-up, on a bench) do the talking. Moley and Paddy kept tabs (locations of wallets, quantities of cash). Paddy stumbled into the marks, smiling and apologizing while steadying them, backing them into Moley. Moley let his hands do the walking (the burrowing for which he was named), talking to distract the men, brushing breasts and thighs to distract the women, smiling and apologizing all the while no less than Paddy—but this is the moment of the ugly truth, the beginning of my end, the birth of my death, my key to the graveyard, ignominious, shameful, brutal, vile. Despise me if you will, I would think less of you if you didn't, but you couldn't despise me more than I despised myself. I'm sorry it happened, sorry to be revealing it, sorry for every miserable thing I've ever done, sorry for the wretch I was, my head too full of hammers even to know I was swimming in a sea of shit—but here's what happened. I miscalculated—hugely. I didn't account for the unaccountable. A burly man, chest like a barrel, in bowler and vest, rummaged suddenly through the pockets of his coat and pants, and yelled. "WHOA! I BEEN ROBBED!"

Moley and Paddy were at the periphery, I was at the epicenter. The burly man's gaze latched onto my skinny sunbrown face, framed in arcs of whirling fruit, pumped by two blurry whirring arms. I was clean, but the burly man's insinuations, the involvement no doubt of police, the commoner's mistrust of the carny, would entail an expenditure of time and explanations I had no wish to indulge. The fruit flew magically into my bag, cash from the beret on its belly to my pocket, the beret on its belly to my head, and—shame of shames, ugliness of uglinesses—I turned to a young negro, not quite twenty, crouched at my feet, as mesmerized by the disappearance of the fruit as he'd been by the incredible spinning wheel, and shouted as loudly as the burly man. "HEY! WHERE'D THIS NIGGER GET THIS WATCH?"

The crowd became a cyclone of activity.
"HEY! THAT'S *MY* WATCH!"
"HELL'S FIRE! WHAT'S GOIN' ON!"
"TARNATION! MY *WALLET*'S GONE!"
"CHRIST ALMIGHTY! SOMEBODY CALL THE POLICE!"

The watch was mine, a small price to pay. The crowd pounced like a panther and I disappeared like a rat into the night. On the bus back, I sat as we had planned apart from Moley and Paddy exchanging discreet winks, puffing on cigarettes. They had been jubilant making their escape, judicious in their movements and cautious as professionals, but I shudder now to see myself in my blackest moment. A woman of the palest complexion sat on one side talking to a boy with tomato hair, someone mentioned Truman, someone else the Brown Bomber, someone else hummed "Nature Boy." I didn't know it, but I was already a ghost, already a man without a country, already dead among the living. Look again at the face, closely at the eyes. You can pull the wool over the eyes of others, you can pull a mask over your face, but you can't mask the eyes, and mine were crying dry tears.

It was dark and drizzly when the bus pulled into Kendall Green. Moley and Paddy separated, shucking coats, unbuttoning linings, removing fedoras, sloughing shoes, taking separate routes to Moley's room where I joined them. Paddy picked up Johnny Walker on the way. We were cautious dividing the money, quiet not to attract the attention of the walls. Moley and Paddy couldn't stop smiling, blowing smoke rings, lifting glasses. I aped their faces and gestures, but the cloud shadowing me from Toledo had settled like a shroud on my shoulders. My horror was plain: my smile a grimace, my face a sea of wrinkles, my expression of a man haunted (hollow cheeks, wide white eyes, head of hard white bone).

Moley nudged my elbow. "C'mon, Spike. He was jus' a nigboy, y'know."

Paddy grinned. "Even nigboys good f'somethin'."

The two laughed like a murder of crows, but I couldn't laugh.

Moley struck my shoulder: "Y'did whut y'had to do. He'll get a good drubbin', thet's all."

Paddy nodded, still grinning: "Yeah, he was jus' a nigboy. Why're we even talkin' about 'im?"

"B'sides, when they see he got nothin' they'll let'im go. Thet'll be the end o'thet."

I hoped thet'd be the end of thet. What was done could not be undone and there was work yet to be done, the sweetest part of the job, the hill of purses and wallets to be divided among us, the evidence burned. "Yeah, I bet you're right. They'll just let'im go. C'mon, let's get busy."

We parted later in the evening congratulating one another on a job well done. Not only were we richer by almost fifty dollars each, but one of the wallets belonged to a gentleman from India, and I kept his business card:

PREM W. GUPTA, ESQ
IMPORT/EXPORT MERCHANT
HANDICRAFTS OF INDIA
PRAKASH MAHAL, 3RD FLOOR
3RD PASTA LANE
NEAR COLABA CAUSEWAY
BOMBAY, INDIA

The card was a rubious shade of ivory, the inscription gold, two embossed tusks crossed in a gothic arch. I held it by its edges, not wanting to smudge it, and examined it under a lamp as a paleontologist might a fossil, a jeweler a diamond. It was a contact, a sign I was destined for a new beginning. I recalled a short dark man in the Toledo crowd for the difference of his features, of his color, of a mark on his left temple which might have been from an attack of chicken pox, shaped like a crescent—or a tusk.

Our mahout, Srinivasa Koodalattupuram Kuttichidambaran, Siri for short, brought from what is now the state of Kerala in southern India, had enthralled me with stories of Keralan wildlife (herds of elephants, barking deer, wild dogs, warthogs, monkeys, bison, even tigers spied at waterholes from the safety of an elephant's back). No less enthralled was I by Frank Buck's accounts of trapping in India, Burma, China, Ceylon, and Malaya. I had read all his books—*Bring 'em Back Alive*, *On Jungle Trails*, *Fang and Claw*, *Wild Cargo*—promising myself someday to see it all firsthand.

Jonas Frank had acquired Siri alongside Hero when he'd purchased the Griffin Bros. Circus during the depths of the Depression. You can tell the worth of a circus by the number of its elephants. You could count the clowns instead, but masked in clownwhite and constantly moving they're too easily miscounted. You could count the railcars, you could measure the spread of the canvas, but few circuses still travel by rail and fewer still exhibit under a tent. You could count the peanuts, horses, wagons, tents, trailers, trucks, but ... well, I'll let *you* determine the drawbacks. You could, of course, astute though unimaginative accountant that you may be, look at the ledger—but the elephant (slow, large, unmistakable) will provide a dependable count and a dependable measure.

The Griffin Bros. Circus had just one elephant, Hero, an Indian—no ordinary elephant not for his appearance, nor for his performance, but he was still just one elephant; the blackest elephant in America, possibly in the world, black as pitch on a starless moonless night, none of the sorry stippled pink pigmentation you've seen on the brows, trunks, and ears of many of his siblings, with three foot tusks, shining white arcs against the glossy black hide—unforgettable, yes, but still just one elephant.

A single elephant was not unusual for circuses during the Thirties; the Depression followed by the shortage of manpower during the war had left circuses reeling no less than the rest of America, biting the sawdust by the score; the Ringling Bros. and Barnum & Bailey Combined Shows, though still billed the Greatest Show on Earth, belonged to the bank, and John Ringling, last of the brothers, had died in 1936—but by 1945 the country was regaining its feet. Ironically, the truck shows came into existence during this decade, marking the end of the rail shows, which had marked the end of the mud shows (horses drawing wagons through field and stream before the days of roads). The beginning of truck shows also marked the beginning of the Frank Bros. Circus. By 1948, the circus had acquired five more elephants. Siri slept with them in the stalls, but was sibling only to Hero.

TWO   THE JOEY, BROWN E

What Quint did to the elephant, the elephant did to Quint. Taking ivory from the elephant, Quint had the ivory taken out of him. Taking Quint from a woman-in-need, Mercedes herself became a woman-in-need. The quality of mercy, like the qualities of kindness, sacrifice, selflessness, are all twice blessed, blessing giver and taker, but not the quality of karma. Karma is a killer as much as a deliverer, twice cursed as much as twice blessed—but I get ahead of myself, much too far ahead of that clammy night in Kendall Green when so many strands of the story came together.

I had no sooner returned to the Abbott from our Toledo misadventure than the joey, Brown E, waited under a streetlamp in the drizzle for Hazel outside Salt'n'Peppah. All joeys have two faces: God gave them one, they gave themselves the other. It's an unwritten law, no joey may copy the face of another, and all joeys know all other joeys by their clownfaces. When John Jack Lewis (his baptismal name) wore his clownface, his frown, carved like a gash into his face, was hidden behind a big red smile spread like a heart around his mouth. His ripe tomato nose was straddled by the fat blue fish of his eyes and thick black glistening boomerang brows. Orange wings of hair were topped by a derby white enough for a wedding, but too small even for a doll. Even so, under the clownface, you could see the sad sack of the man he was. A white jumpsuit large enough for a gorilla and flat shoes round as tennis rackets completed his outfit. The suit sported, front and back, his trademark, a huge brown "E."

Devoid of clownwhite he was a handsome man, his jaw a firm isosceles, his nose as perfect in cross-section as a rightangled triangle, eyes as green as Eileen's, brow swept by long fat wavy goldenbrown locks. In another era, in another country, his appearance might have placed him among the King's musketeers. In his own era and country he could have been Errol Flynn but for one shortcoming: he was not swashbuckling. The green in his eyes didn't sparkle like Eileen's, the brow under his locks was as lined as a clerk's, matching perfectly the anxiety in his eyes. His only major act of insubordination had bled him of insubordination for the rest of his life. He'd run from his Illinois family farm in 1930 at the tender age of fifteen to sell apples from the family orchard for the price of a ticket on the circus lot—and stayed, not to be missed, the eighth in a poor family of nineteen.

Standing under the streetlamp in a trenchcoat, homburg over his brow, rain dripping from its brim when he bent his head, he was identifiable as neither Brown E nor as John Jack Lewis, no more than a shadow in the glistening night, but his fortunes had improved immensely in the three years since he had made the acquaintance of Mr. Donald Wilson Cuddihy II, proprietor of Cuddihy & Sons of the garment industry, when the great man had attended a performance with Edna, his five-year-old granddaughter. He had enchanted Edna, fishing brownies out of her ear, snapping photographs of her with his Brownie, not to mention honking her august grandfather's nose while squeezing a rubber horn in his pocket—and, enchanting Edna, he had enchanted her grandfather, winning subsequent invitations to perform at posh parties for Edna and her friends in the Cuddihy mansion on Park Avenue in New York.

Get thee back. Thy soul is too much charged with Bailey blood already. The words in his head brought a sad smile to his face. He found comfort quoting the Bard. It made him more than just a joey, it linked him to joeys of the past who had answered questions from the audience with quotations from Shakespeare, the most famous of whom, his hero, joey of joeys, the American Grimaldi, was Dan Rice.

No clownwhite for Dan Rice, no harlequin outfits, no pantomime. Whiskered like Uncle Sam, he was just as revered. In the days of the single ring a large tent could hold four thousand and a strong voice could hold every patron. Three ring circuses killed the talking clown, but in his time Dan Rice walked tightropes, danced jigs, rode bareback, caught cannonballs on the back of his neck, trained an elephant to walk a tightrope, and monopolized every circus he worked. He could lick any three men on the frontier, trade witticisms with audiences and ringmasters alike. He could banter with backwoodsmen and philosophize with professors. He counted Abe Lincoln, Robert E. Lee, and Jefferson Davis among his friends, and at a thousand dollars a week made more money than the President of the United States. In those preTV, premovie, preradio days, the stars of traveling circuses were celebrities as big as Lucy and Valentino and Murrow.

Get thee back, he muttered again, expecting Hazel any moment, debating still the wisdom of waiting for her, *thy soul is too much charged with Bailey blood already*, but still he waited until he saw her, scarfed head bowed against the rain, huddled under a blue rainjacket too short to cover white shirttails like aprons front and back over blue jeans, trotting down the street. He wished he'd brought an umbrella, but heaving a sigh he stepped forward to walk alongside. "Hello, Jill." He was the only person to call her by her first name, imagining serendipity in their names.

Her head turned sharply, her chin rose. "Jack! What're you doin' here?"

"I was waiting for you."

"In the rain?"

"It wasn't raining when I set out."

Her voice softened. "You shouldn't have, Jack. You're sweet, but you know how it is."

"I came to say goodbye."

She put her head down again, eyes on the ground. "I know. You told me you were leavin'. Mr. Cuddihy?"

"Yup. The bus leaves early in the morning. I'll be back in a month. I'll write."

"It's only a month, Jack, but you can do what you want."

"Don't be so hard, Jill. I'll miss you."

She maintained her pace, but paused before she spoke. "It's rainin', Jack. I don't want you catchin' pneumonia for me. I've done enough damage already."

He smiled again, his sad smile, as if she'd made a joke. "Don't be silly. I didn't want to leave without saying goodbye, that's all."

"That's nice of you, Jack, but I do wish you'd take better care of yourself. You know I mean well by you."

"I know."

It was a ten-minute walk to the Abbott. The conversation remained desultory, Hazel fielding Jack's conversation more tenderly, knowing what he had endured in her behalf, knowing what she had put him through, even kissing him lightly at the doors of the Abbott. "Now go home and dry yourself off. I'll be mad if you don't."

He smiled again. "Right you are—and, oh, by the way, Spike borrowed my Brownie. Tell him it's his. He can keep it."

"What's Spike want with your Brownie?"

Jack winked. "I think he's taking pictures to send Eileen."

Under different circumstances, Hazel might have smiled complicity, but her relations with Jack were too complicated. She only turned away.

THREE   JILL HAZEL BAILEY

It was midnight when Hazel got home from her shift. I'd been unable to sleep and sat curled in a couch reading *On Jungle Trails* by Frank Buck, rereading rather as you could tell from the cracked spine and dogeared pages, of Buck's boyhood beginnings in Dallas, Texas, where he'd responded to a newspaper ad and received a standing order for shipments of rattlesnakes to Rochester, New York (rattlesnake oil was used to cure rheumatism), Prem Gupta's business card like a talisman on the lampstand beside me. I'd been damp from the drizzle, returning to the hotel, but I'd been more mindful of the card than of the money I'd made that day, packing it carefully to keep it crisp. Hazel was damp from the drizzle herself, removing her jacket and boots. "Hey."

I didn't look up from the page. "Hey."

"Lovely weather."

I said nothing.

"Brown E's headed for New York tomorrow."

Everyone called him Brown E, even she unless she was talking to him directly. I said nothing.

"He said you could keep his camera."

I said nothing.

"Aren't you gonna say something?"

I knew he did it for her more than for me, sap that he was around her. "Brown E's bats."

Hazel paused, eyebrows rising. "Oh, I get it. He gives you a camera— and that's all she wrote."

"I mean it, Haze. I didn't ask him for it. I took it. When I asked him before he said *I can deny thee nothing. My soul is too much charged with Bailey blood already*. What the hell does that mean? It was easier just to take the damn camera than to ask. He talks Shakespeare so much he's got me doin' the same thing."

I expected Hazel to defend her clown, but she shut down again like a door, headed for the bedroom, and returned in her robe. "Where's Pa?"

"I don't know."

Her face wrinkled. She looked out the window. She was mother and father to Dinty as much as to me and hated to think of him in the rain. He needed help, but she couldn't grasp that he was beyond her help. There was a basin in a corner of the room where she brushed her teeth. "Hocoom yostilloop?"

"What?"

She spat in the basin and removed the brush from her mouth. "How come you're still up?"

"Just readin'."

Her tone got ironic. "Why?"

"'Cause I wanna, okay? Geeze, Haze!"

She rinsed her mouth, dried her face, and picked up the business card. "What's this?"

"Give it back! It's mine!"

Her jaw dropped. She raised her eyebrows, shaking her head in disbelief. "Holy smokes, Spike! What's the matter with you? Why're you so jumpy?"

"It's mine! You got no right to take it. Give it back!"

"We'll see about that. First, tell me where you got it."

I'd never been able to lie convincingly to Hazel, but kept my voice down, my eyes in the book. "If you got to know, I found it on the street, okay? If you absolutely got to know, I found it on the street."

She put down the card. "What street? Where've you been all day?"

"Around."

"I don't think so. I'd a hunch you might've gone to Toledo."

The room was suddenly arctic, my skin tightened, my throat contracted. I didn't know how she knew, but I shook my head, rolling my eyes. "Well, geeze, Haze, if you knew, why'd you ask?"

"I didn't know. That's why I asked."

"Well, how'd you know to ask?"

"What's the matter, Spike? What're you hidin'?"

"Nothin'. I'm just sick and tired of answerin' your dumb questions. I just wanna go to bed."

"I thought you wanted to read."

"Aah!"

"So, what were you doin' in Toledo?"

"So, how'd you know to ask?"

"I saw your itinerary lyin' around—Miss Hot-to-Trot's itinerary."

"Don't call her that."

Hazel laughed. "Touchy, touchy. What's the matter with you, Spike? I don't mean no harm."

I said nothing.

"I saw your weather report next to it. What the hell're you up to, Spike? You gonna be a meteorologist?"

She'd seen me by the radio console in the downstairs lounge the day before, listening to the weather report, making notes. I'd wanted to be sure we wouldn't have a snowfall. "Aah! and what the hell does that make you, Haze? snoopin' around my stuff? Seems to me we should call the FBI. Seems to me you'd make one helluva snoop."

"Spike, what's the matter with you? I wasn't snoopin'. It was just lyin' there. If you don't want folks lookin' at your stuff you shouldn't leave it lyin' around."

"Oh, right, I forgot. In my father's house are many mansions. I shoulda kept it locked up in *my* wing of the palace that Pa built."

She knew I was hiding something, but was too tired to ferret it out. "Don't talk about Pa like that. I don't see you helpin' out any. He'd appreciate it if you'd help out now'n then, y'know. It'd make him feel better."

"Why should I, Haze? What's he ever done for me? He don't give a damn about me. He don't even talk to me. Why should I do anythin' for him?"

"Pa gives a damn, Spike, but he don't always show it. You don't know what he's been through."

"Well, whyn't you tell me if you know so damn much? Whyn't you tell me what he's been through? Nobody ever tells me nothin', and everybody just shuts up if I say anythin' about it."

She got suddenly quiet. It was always the same. I could see her withdraw, and frustrated as I was there was nothing I could do.

"You're doin' it again, Haze. I can see you shuttin' up. I can see you shuttin' up jus' like a door."

She looked startled. "It's not the right time, Spike. I don't know what else to tell you."

"So when's it gonna be the right time?"

"I don't know."

I was no longer upset, suddenly sorry for her. She was tired, she worked hard, I loved my beautiful big sister, and I wanted to make things easier if I could. "Aah, Haze, I wanna do what I can. I jus' don't know what to do." I pulled a tenner from my pocket and held it out. "Take it, Haze. I mean it. I wanna help. I jus' don't know what to do."

She took the bill. "That's a lot of money, Spike. Where'd you get it?"

"I worked for it. Let's jus' leave it at that."

"Spike, I don't wanna tell you what to do. I don't even wanna know if you don't wanna tell me. Just don't do nothin' dumb. We can't afford it."

"Aah, Haze, it's no different from when the boys were peekin' at you in the trailer. I didn't hear you say nothin' about doin' nothin' dumb then."

"That was different. They were payin' for a service, and I was deliverin'. I just hope you're deliverin', Spike, whatever it is you're promisin'."

During the season we were in the peepshow business. I herded about a dozen boys from the midway between shows and took them to our trailer window where Hazel gave them a show, lying around starkers in bed, smoking a cigarette, reading a magazine. Once, reading *Movieola* in bed, Marlene Dietrich on the cover, I'd convinced the boys that she was Marlene Dietrich herself. They looked alike, short blond hair, penciled eyebrows, scornful eyes. It was true what Barnum said, the public loved to be fooled. He'd posted a sign in his museum, "This way to the Egress," hung it alongside the signs leading to the lioness and tigress, and when an unsuspecting visitor found himself in the street again he had to pay a second admission fee to get back in. "I'm deliverin', Haze. I'm deliverin' all right. Don't you worry none about me."

I went back to my book, but she rubbed my head. I brushed her hand aside, but she kept at it and when I got up she followed me into the bedroom, tickling me, wrestling with me, until I was grinning. Hazel was all right.

FOUR ELBO DE BLEU

In that same damp drizzly November of the soul from which I had escaped, through which Hazel had rushed, in which Dinty still wandered, loped yet another Kendall Greener, a boy of eighteen, most prominent for his gait. Camels and Great Danes shared his gait, moving left legs together, followed by right legs together, instead of left foreleg with right hind and right foreleg with left hind, as do most animals and humans—but this boy strode like camels and Danes, left arm and leg together, followed by right arm and leg, giving the appearance of a soldier continually out of step with his regiment, continually struggling against gremlins in the mist.

His name was Elbo de Bleu; Elbo, because he had poured into the world elbowfirst from his mama's womb, covering his head, and as for the family name, it sounded as if it had been truncated midsyllable and no one, not even the family itself, could pronounce it correctly. They were the Blues of Bronzeville, and 34 Cumberland was the House of the Blues. It was simply easier than de Bleu with which many had lost patience, which most had now forgotten.

Elbo was glad for the drizzle and mist. It kept folks indoors, folks who would have recognized him, questioned him, pointed fingers, raised eyebrows, shrugged shoulders. It kept him invisible. He'd taken bread and cheese from Sam's Market on the corner of Grace and Main, and he'd been caught. Worst of all, when the police arrived he'd fainted—with shame, he insisted, not fear, shame for his mama, not for himself. They had held him for three days, and returning now to the house on Cumberland Street he felt the shame again in varying degrees, for stealing, for getting caught, for fainting.

His older brother by ten years, Royale, was a lawyer in Chicago—and his twin, Prize, short for Surprise (for tailing Elbo into the world to everyone's surprise, most of all their mama's), had followed the lure of big city money to Cleveland, abandoning the bosom of the family despite their mama's tears running like water from a tap, her rain of recriminations. Elbo had almost run with Prize, but chosen against doubly decimating their mama, only to find himself now a veteran of the Blue Eagle Jail, newly a man with a record.

Elbo was no criminal, but a philosopher. He would have asked why it was wrong for a man to steal when he was hungry and without resources—why, when a white man was arrested the big white world never stopped turning, whether friends and family rallied or not, but when a colored man was arrested the tiny colored world stopped so suddenly the colored man might as well have fallen off. Fingers pointed in all directions as if to escape the shadow of shame spreading to catch them all. Family and friends were first to make the colored man an outsider in a race of outsiders. He had seen it happen with Prize: the mama had said to erase the son, and the son had been erased. Prize was no more.

The streets grew as narrow as alleys, as riddled with junk and refuse. The frame houses appeared less sturdy as the streets grew narrower, their windows more cracked, their posts more crooked, their paint more chipped, their yards more unkempt. Elbo found himself backpedaling a step for every three forward as he approached 34 Cumberland, then every two, and at the gate he rocked back and forth on the balls of his feet, a step back for a step forward, bobbing to the two-step rhythm of a distant combo.

Had there been no mist you would have seen Elbo as an occasional silhouette in the dim scattered nimbuses of streetlamps—tall, lithe, lanky, hair cropped close, damp shirt clinging to his back, baggy pants dripping from the drizzle, scuffed boots squelching with water, sharp handsome features marred by perpetual mistrust. Had there been no mist you would have seen the sheen on his cheeks, hair, and arms, laminated by the drizzle. Had there been no mist, you would have seen him shiver though he could not have said himself whether from cold or apprehension. Had the drizzle been heavier you would not have heard the creak of the rickety swaying chipped fence, the squeak as he unlatched the gate.

Elbo stood with one hand on the gatepost as if for support, the other bobbing with his rocking rhythm, staring at the house, surprised by the brightness of the front room in the window as if it were on display. He could distinguish hairs in the straightening comb on the sofa, stitches where he'd ripped the upholstery years ago during a scuffle with Prize, stitches in GOD BLESS OUR HOME which his mama had embroidered and framed on the wall, buttons on Abe Lincoln's coat in the picture his mama had ripped from a newspaper and mounted next to her embroidery, writing on the crates they used for chairs, RYBERG STEEL, covered partly by cloths embroidered again by his mama. Most surprising, the windowsill showcased food in cracked dishes: biscuits dripping with butter, two fat smothered porkchops, blackeyed peas and collard greens, a slice of apple pie. He stared for a minute like a Brementown musician before smiling. What else could it be? His mama loved him, it was his homecoming, it took a crisis for folks to mend their ways, she was sorry she had driven him to stealing.

He bobbed immediately forward, making the stoop in two bounds, no longer shivering, and knocked jauntily on the door. When he heard nothing he knocked again, even more jauntily. Shortly after, he heard his mama shuffle from the backroom and saw her shadow cross the front room. "Yes?"

Elbo smiled at her caution. "It's me, Mama."

"Who?"

"Me, Mama. Elbo."

"Who?"

"*Me*, Mama! *El*bo! Yo' *son!*"

Her voice was flat, as if she were reading something she didn't understand. "I don't know what you talkin' about. I got a son in Chicago, a lawyer name of Royale. I don't know what you talkin' about."

Elbo shivered, cold again, afraid again. He was being erased as Prize had been erased. Nothing had changed and he was mad at himself for assuming too much too quickly, dreams came true only in dreams. His voice softened, rose in pitch. "Mama, it's me, Elbo. I'm also yo' son."

Her voice came back, the emphasis more chilling than the flatness before. "I know *who* you are, but I don't *know* you."

Elbo was proud of his voice. He'd been thirteen when it cracked, descending directly to a basso profundo, making him the overnight jewel of the school choir—but you would not have guessed it from his words trembling like a child's. "I cain't help it, Mama, if I ain't Roy. I cain't help bein' me." There was no immediate answer. "You *made* me what I am, Mama. You *made* me. I'm *yo'* son."

There was a pause during which Elbo heard a quick intake of breath. He knew how she would look behind the door, tall and skinny like himself, head in a scarf to keep her hair straight, grey housecoat thin and smooth and shining from too many washings, longboned arms, hands in fists in her pockets, lips of leather thick as thumbs meeting in a thin line. "You watch what you say, boy. I did *not* raise my boys to steal. I did *not* raise my boys to be niggerish. You ain't welcome till you learn how to behave decent."

Elbo wasn't aware of tears, but you could tell even against the sheen of his drizzledamp face he was crying. "I'll behave, Mama, I'll behave decent. Please, Mama, I'm cold. I'll behave. Please, Mama."

"I cain't do that. I cain't trust you. It's gone be a while before I trust you again."

"You can trust me, Mama. Please let me in."

"I cain't. I cain't trust you after what you done, not just yet."

"Then when, Mama, when? How much longer's it gone take?"

"As long as it take you to learn yo' lesson."

"Mama, I done learned my lesson, I swear it. I been in jail learnin' my lesson, Mama."

"If you done learned your lesson like you say, you wouldn' be swearin' at me."

"I'm sorry, Mama. I won't swear."

"You been in jail 'cause you ain't learned your lesson. If you'da learned your lesson you wouldn'ta been in jail."

"I was hungry, Mama. They put me in jail for stealin' food. What was I to do?"

"Now you sayin' it was my fault."

"No, Mama, that ain't what I'm sayin'—but I cain't get a job 'cause you won't let me work Sundays, 'cause that the Lawd's day, an' there ain't no jobs with Sundays off—an' if you won't let me work, an' if you won't give me food, then I got to get it somehow. That's all I'm sayin'."

His voice turned bitter with the unfairness of his situation, but his mama didn't seem to notice. "If I didn' give you food it was to teach you the value of food. How you gone learn the value of anythin' if it always gone be gifted you?"

"You right, Mama. I'm sorry."

"If I didn' give you food it was to teach you a lesson—not to have you stealin'."

"I'm sorry, Mama. I won't steal."

"And now you sayin' it's my fault. It's what everyone sayin' 'cause of what you been sayin'."

"I never said it, Mama. I never said that. All I said was, if you gave me food I wouldn'ta stole. That's all I said."

"You ain't gone trick me, boy. I know you seen the food in the window, but that ain't for you. That's so folks can see we got food. That's so folks can see we don't got to steal."

"Mama, I stole 'cause I was hungry. That's why I stole."

"That was yo' punishment, to be hungry, to stay hungry. Ain't you man enough to take yo' punishment?"

"My punishment for what, Mama? What'd I do to be punished?"

"A man's got to be punished. It's how he learns to be a man."

Elbo could think of nothing to say.

"An' it was a elegant punishment. I coulda whupped you like a nigger—but we ain't niggerish. We elegant. You know that."

He knew what she meant. She kept house for the Springers, a lawyer and his family, and when the Springer children misbehaved they were sent to bed without dessert—but she sent him to bed without supper, not even a crust. There was no way he could convince her he'd have preferred a whupping. His voice returned to its natural pitch, but only because he'd given up, dipping so low he was almost talking to himself. "Mama, I'll do anythin'. Please, let me in."

"I ain't givin' you nothin'."

Elbo sat down on the wet stoop. He was tired but that was not why his knees were suddenly rubbery. He couldn't have said exactly why he couldn't stop crying, but the trouble went beyond what had happened the week before. He couldn't compete with Roy, skin of ginger, hair of peach, eyes of amber, not to mention the firstborn, class prodigy, valedictorian, not to mention ten years old by the time Elbo had elbowed his way into the world, pulling Prize on his tail, both unwanted since their pa had died a month before their birth in an accident loading freight at the docks. She made steady money working for the Springers in the Garden, Kendall Green's fashionable neighborhood, and the Springers had always been kind, which was how Roy had first imagined himself a lawyer; Mr. Springer had even occasionally taken Roy to witness trials in court; but she'd been working too long.

It wasn't her fault. She loved him, but she was too tired to show it. Life had made her halfcrazy, thinking she was white like Mr. Springer and his family after Roy had passed the bar. It happened when you were tired all your life, it made you angry and you put your anger where you could because you couldn't put it where it belonged. She'd been going wrong for a while, but had nothing left to give and he was done wanting what had never been there. She was still talking when he left. "I ain't givin' you nothin', boy, till I see you learned your lesson. I ain't givin' you a red cent."

The drizzle had stopped, the wind had dropped, but Elbo was cold from his damp shirt in the night air, walking back the way he had come, heading for the Union Bus Station (no more than a parking space outside the Imperial Hotel on High Street). He would go to Cleveland, he would find Prize, he'd heard Prize worked in a steel mill. There was no one and nothing for him in Kendall Green, but in Cleveland he could start again. Prize would help him. He would find money for the bus, maybe a job for a day or two. He'd find shelter for the night, a doorway, an alley, a shed. The point was to act upon what was in his power, to leave what was not. Not for nothing had the streets been his Yale College and Harvard.

FIVE　　　　　　　　　　　　　　　　　　NIGHT FLIGHT

Kendall Green, Ohio, lies on the south shore of Lake Erie, closer to Cleveland than to Toledo, close enough for Kendall Greeners to joke that Cleveland is their backyard. In 1948, the town boasted a population of 60,244, four hotels, three movie houses, two railway stations, two bus stations, one golf course, one college, and there was talk of building an airport to rival Cleveland's. Clevelanders paid no heed. They knew Kendall Greeners liked to talk, talk was what they did best, but even Clevelanders would have admitted Kendall Green is among the larger shipping ports on the Great Lakes, largely a labor town, fueled by steel mills, coaldocks, paperworks, breweries, fisheries, and packing houses.

The town (Kendall Greeners call it a city) hugs the shore for ten miles, and wanders four miles inland into Cuyahoga County. Ten times smaller than Cleveland, it hosts large numbers of Polish, Irish, and German immigrants, as well as a sizeable negro community owing its roots to an Underground Railway station. It's divided by Broad Street running north and south and High Street running east and west almost into Bronzeville, Elbo's neighborhood, one of three negro neighborhoods east of the tracks.

The Elephant Graveyard

Elbo loped back along Broad Street, his crazy camel lope, back the way he had come, a solitary shadowy figure in the mist, back past 17th Street and the Blue Eagle Jail and beyond in less than half an hour. The buildings grew successively larger as he left the neighborhoods, and reaching downtown he imagined they were alive, watching him like giants looming above.

The drizzle had stopped, even the mist was rising, but Elbo had never stopped being tired, and had a bed appeared before him he would have tumbled gratefully in, but while he walked it was easier not to resist the momentum from blocks of walking. He remembered old Satchel Paige's dictum: *Don't look back, something might be gaining on you.* Old Satchel knew how to handle himself. Not for nothing was he a Cleveland Indian.

You would think he would have heard something before he realized he wasn't alone, but it was a testament to his exhaustion. Someone dashed into view around the corner of the cross street ahead, skidding sideways on one foot like Chaplin eluding the Keystone Cops, and rushed almost directly at Elbo, finally cutting off Elbo's momentum. Something fell with a clatter as they almost collided. Elbo, caught off guard on one foot, maintained an arabesque for a second, before spinning a complete circle on the ball of his foot like a ballerina and coming to a halt—but his partner in the dance, almost out of sight, never slowed. Elbo bent instinctively to pick up what had been dropped. He waved the object in the air with a yell. "Hey! Hey, Mister! You dropped somethin'! *Hey!*"

Suddenly, the night erupted. Shouts of "Stop, Thief!" sprang from around the corner. Elbo imagined in the pursuant footsteps a herd of bison thundering across a plain in primal America. The object in his hand fluttered like a banner with his heart, ice in his veins paralyzed him, and his legs turned again to rubber. His head grew lighter, his face hotter, and he panicked, afraid he was going to faint again, afraid he was going to jail again—and dashed like a runner at the crack of a pistol after the fugitive himself. Another of old Satchel's dictums was to avoid running at all times, but Elbo was running on instinct. He couldn't have said whether he ran to return the object he'd picked, to apprehend the fugitive, to escape attention, to escape the law, or simply to keep from fainting. He knew only that a nigboy's word was worthless, he had to run, and the fugitive gave him direction.

Even from the distance Elbo could tell the fugitive was a small man, but with the drumming of the herd close behind him he narrowed the distance so rapidly the small man appeared to inflate like a balloon. So great was Elbo's fear of recapture that despite his exhaustion, despite his crazy camel legs, despite his lightheadedness, he appeared not to be running as much as bounding, even flying in a single mighty leap, descending like Achilles with watermelon thighs on hapless Hector circling the walls of Ilium. You would not have imagined, watching him hurtling down the avenue, that he'd been seconds from fainting. You would have sworn his momentum would carry him past his quarry to Cleveland, but turning the next corner as perfectly as a ricocheting bullet he found himself alone and stopped as if a frame had been frozen in a movie.

Elbo didn't know it, but he suffered from a fibrillation of the heart which occasionally provided extra beats, occasionally took some away. By itself it meant little, but when the occasional flutter was yoked with stress his plumbing went on strike and the valves of his heart danced to the tune of a distant brain, draining his head of blood. He suffered no pain, only the shame of appearing womanish, but he had no more control over the fibrillation than over strange men rushing at him along dark deserted avenues. Fortunately, for the present, his fibrillation was past and he was operating on automatic pilot, surprising even himself, senses, sinews, and thews as alert as a falling cat's. A scrambling sound directed his glance toward a gateway in the fence lining the side of the building. Through the gateway, ten feet upward, he saw his quarry again, disappearing over the ledge of an open window. Pitching the object still in his hand unerringly through the window, Elbo pitched himself like a human spider at the wall, clambered to the ledge, and across the sill.

No sooner was he across the ledge than he ducked out of sight, breathing in spasms, but no sooner had he taken a breath than the smell made him want to vomit, reducing him to dry heaves. His veins turned icy again, his head hot and light, as between heaves he tried to regain his breath—but the smell, of meat left too long in the sun, was so strong he might have been in a charnel house. Compounding his terror was the sound of large bodies in motion and deep relentless rumbles, one of which erupted into a roar as if the earth were cracking, and others followed primeval as a carnival of dinosaurs. Lying on the floor like a foetus, Elbo was too scared even to look, but he heard the men outside as they rounded the corner:

"Sonovabitch! What the devil was that!"

"Damned if I know!"

"Damned if I wanna know!"

"Damned Beelzebub himself!"

"Let's get the hell outta here!"

Elbo's head rattled against the floor as he trembled. Minutes later, after the roaring had subsided, after his breathing had resumed a semblance of normality, he opened his eyes. There was no light. His eyes grew accustomed to darkness, but he could not understand what he saw: two hovering rows of eyes, one on his left, one on his right, convex jets of orange and yellow flame in the blackness, tiny in the distance, larger as they got closer. He tried to absorb what he could just rolling his eyes, not moving his head, from the far side of the room to where he lay. The distance remained shadowy, but closer at hand a huge striped beast rose on its hindlegs, eyes large and shining as radioactive rats and descended roaring like a jackhammer. There was no other explanation: Elbo was sure he had died and gone to hell, but dead or not his trials appeared to have mushroomed, and fibrillation or not you could not have blamed even a brave man then for fainting as he did.

SIX   THE MOUTH OF THE ELEPHANT

Elbo awoke to velvet paws dangling over his face. He recognized the paws from Tarzan movies, but they were close enough for him to distinguish a bug on one of the pads, each paw as large as his head. It had dawned on him by morning that he wasn't in hell. He knew of the winter quarters, he'd even visited the circus once, a long time ago, thanks to the munificence of the Springers, his mama's employers, Roy's benefactors, who had also sometimes taken him to the cinema, but his curiosity had since abated. His own life had begun to preoccupy him.

He didn't move, but could see from where he lay on his back that he was at one end of a long room with cages on each side mounted three feet above the floor. A doorway stood at the far end of the room and he prayed to reach it safely, prayed the cages were locked, but couldn't find the courage even to move. He felt safe only as long as he didn't attract attention. Even behind bars, the tiger on high, chin tufted in a Vandyke, one gleaming fang overhanging a furry lip like that of a crocodile, appeared as regal and menacing as a sphinx, as if he could reach Elbo anytime he chose by extending one dangling paw. Elbo could have lain there until someone found him, but he was no more enthralled about the prospect of another term in jail at the end of his adventure, and plucked courage finally to slide on his back, imperceptibly as possible, toward the door.

The first move, the most difficult, attracted the most attention. Something touched his knee and he kicked reflexively sending it clattering as loudly as a motorbike through a mausoleum, the object he had picked and tossed through the window, a blowtorch. The tiger erupted with another jackhammer roar, three inch claws raking the air inches from his face, other cats nudging the bars of their cages, grunting and growling and puttering like tractors. Elbo would have been no more terrified had the Great Sphinx itself cracked out of its stone death to roam the plains of Ghiza. Had he not been on his back he might have fainted again, but when the tiger failed to touch him he slid again toward the door, moving in infinitesimal increments, as if he were running a gauntlet between the cages, as if he were on a tightrope though there was plenty of space between the cages along the center of the room.

It was a high room, at least twenty feet and appeared higher as he wriggled wormlike across the floor. The doorway was arched to a point, fifteen feet at its apex, and the hallway outside appeared higher than the room because it was narrower and darker. The house might have been built for giants.

He breathed more easily in the hallway, thankful to leave the room and its smell behind. To his left the hallway stretched interminably with giant doorways similar to the one he'd crossed. To his right the hallway turned in an elbow. Elbo chose the elbow, but couldn't stand. His legs were paste and he scrabbled along the hallway on stomach, hands, elbows, knees, whatever would hold him, like a jellyfish.

Turning the corner he was dismayed to find another long hallway with more giant doorways, but the doorways were all on his left and the hallway was bright with morning light from windows on his right. He knew he was on the first floor and guessed the windows faced the street. Had his legs been able he would have jumped from a window and run, but convinced the front door couldn't be far he continued his crawl into the hallway, confident of success in the light and silence after the caterwauling of the cats, confident the rooms ahead would either be empty or full of caged animals.

He tried again to stand before passing the first doorway, but couldn't. Even his elbows felt weak and he flattened himself on his stomach before inching his head cautiously ahead for a peek. It was just as well he was on his stomach. What he saw might otherwise have caused him once more to buckle. The room was deep and at the far end were elephants, massive and chained, about half a dozen, but Elbo imagined an army ready to converge on him. That would have been enough to keep him moving, but he saw the army only secondarily. In the foreground a woman faced him from the far side of yet another elephant, the biggest and blackest of the lot. Elbo was sure the woman had seen him and motion was no longer his, not even to crawl on his belly like a worm—but as the moments ticked by he realized he was wrong. Her gaze, fixed with concentration, wasn't fixed on him.

She wore a dirty yellow sweater, baggy jeans cuffed midway to her calves, and loafers, not unlike hundreds of blond white girls he'd seen who all filled him at once with fear and longing—but this one was different, uncannily different, for her situation.

The elephant was no less uncanny, for his blackness even more than his bigness, blacker than the rest, an upright individual living shadow of an elephant, glossy with oil under the lights, highlights gleaming in midnight blue, in sharp contrast to its tusks, white as oysters, also gleaming with oil, curved like scimitars, and its eye, the only one Elbo could see from where he lay, red and narrow and tiny for so large an animal, no larger than his own—but with outsize lashes, frondlike and drooping like willows.

Hero was in his prime, six thousand and fifty pounds, nine feet at the shoulder; and he would grow larger yet, his tusks longer. Elephants are entropic, so are their tusks, neither ceasing to grow until death, but they appear more fatigued with age, the everincreasing burden of the tusks (the longest of which have been measured at almost twelve feet in an African, and the heaviest weighing in at almost 230 pounds) is telling even on the broadest neck—but their heads are otherwise lighter than they appear, honeycombed by passages of air to compensate for the weight of the tusks, a third of which are invisible, borne within their sockets. Hero's tusks measured three feet, but he was barely twenty-five. They might grow yet to twice their present length.

There was another woman on the near side of the elephant, skinny and straight as an obelisk, barefoot, black hair flowing past her shoulders, wearing a grey sweater, baggy jeans, but her back was to Elbo and caught in the spell of the first woman he barely noticed the second. She steadied the elephant with an ankus edged by a metal claw. When she prodded the side of the elephant with the claw it raised its trunk, lowered its head, and opened its mouth. Elbo couldn't see the first woman anymore because the second had stepped in his line of vision, but he scrabbled along the floor for a better look.

The first woman moved slowly, placing her head sideways in the elephant's mouth, lifting her arms until she held them aloft like the transom of a cross to signal readiness. The second woman prodded the elephant again and the elephant closed its mouth, lifting its head, lifting the woman into the air. She dangled for a moment, a foot above the floor, before raising her legs like a plane raising its wheels into its belly on takeoff.

Hazel knew Hero's mouth better than any mouth in the world, better than her own, from the grey whiskered trowel of his lower lip, past the pink lubricious slug of his velvet tongue, past four stained molars, to his deep dark gullet. She knew the dark wet pink cavern better than a rabbit knows its warren, a hound its kennel, a child its pen, a murderer his dungeon. She knew where the grey of his outer cheek turned gradually to pink, where the whiskers in the skin gave way to wrinkles in the flesh and finally to ridges on the teeth. She knew his tongue well enough to give it a name, Eel, sightless inhabitant of the unsightly cavern.

Ironically, an elephant not killed for its tusks may die of starvation because it runs out of molars with which to masticate; an elephant may die of starvation surrounded by the lushest, most luscious, vegetation. Through its seventy odd years it runs through six sets of four molars, each of which is pushed out of its mouth by the succeeding set. Born with the first set, it develops a second by its second year, a third by its fourth, a fourth by its tenth, a fifth by its twenty-fifth, and a sixth by its forty-fifth which lasts another twenty-five years. You can tell the Indian from the African by the shape of the ridges on their molars, the Indian's are parallel, the African's shaped like lozenges, and the upper set bears down on the lower like the blades of a pair of scissors. Hazel had known Hero only during his fourth set of molars, but she was aware of its progress through the years toward the front of his mouth from which they would simply fall off.

By your teeth, your bones, and your organs, are you known. German shepherds might more closely resemble wolves, but are more closely related to dachshunds. Elephants might more closely resemble hippos and rhinos, pachyderms all, but are more closely related to hyraxes, superficially resembling rodents—and to dugongs and manatees superficially resembling seals and sea lions—related by the bifid apices of their hearts, partially crossed bones of their forelimbs, also by their stubby digits, flattened carpals, incisor tusks, treadmill teeth, testicles retracted into their abdomens, and two breasts on their chests like humans, not two rows of breasts alongside their bellies like bitches or sows. Dugongs and manatees, cows of the sea, sirenians, in the habit of standing upright in water and staring, were mistaken by sailors too long at sea, for sirens and mermaids (the prettiest manatees, the ugliest mermaids). Ironically, elephant seals (despite their names) and walruses (despite their tusks) belong to the seal family—but you get the picture: in the animal kingdom, as in the human, appearances are deceiving.

When still with the Griffin Bros. Circus, Hero had performed dance steps and pyramids with the other elephants, but after he became a solo act Jonas had wanted something more spectacular, and Dinty had obliged. He had encouraged Hero first to hold a dummy in his mouth, then added weights until it was about Hazel's weight—after which Hazel had taken the place of the dummy.

The Black Elephant

Hazel inserted her head sideways, at the tip of Hero's tongue, cushioned within the soft wet V of his lower lip, beneath the underside of his trunk, between the tusks (the upper incisors of the elephant). She didn't have to watch out for lower incisors, elephants have none, and no canines either, just the assembly line of molars. Once clasped in Hero's jaws, Hazel lifted her legs and, groundless, arms aloft like wings, acknowledged unwavering waves of applause while Hero curled his trunk, touching its tip to the vast doubledome of his forehead, salaaming acknowledgment.

An elephant's mouth may appear benign relative to a carnivore's, but the feat was hardly less dangerous. If spooked into clamping its jaws shut Hazel's head would become mush, her spine would snap like a twig, her body dangle like a puppet, the slightest sudden twist of the elephant's neck levered through its jawbone and skull would have fulcrumed Hazel's neck a hundredfold, leaving her as lifeless as if she'd been mauled by fang and claw. Ironically, in the circus, where every entertainment becomes a playground for an exotic deathtrap, more roustabouts are injured than performers—but that's a tribute to troupers more than a rebuke to roustabouts.

Hazel made her performance more than a performance. She made it penance for her part in her ma's accident: her pride, her prayer, her meditation. Hero's mouth was her shrine, her performance was her worship, and she liked the early morning best when the winter quarters were quiet as a temple. Some swallow pills, some shoot needles, some take to the bottle, some seek multiple orgasms, some go to church, to shrinks, to lovers, to friends, to family, some leave the country, but Hazel put her head in the elephant's mouth. When recriminations got too sharp she put her head in the elephant's mouth; four and five and six times a week she put her head in the elephant's mouth; during the offseason, while troupers perfected new acts, worked at other jobs, and tended other businesses, she put her head in the elephant's mouth. She lived to put her head in the elephant's mouth.

Had he been able, had he thought of it, Elbo would have applauded the orchideous sight, but he was in awe of its Biblical grandeur and gravity. He'd seen frogs snapping bugs from the air, hindlegs of the bug bicycling, head already mealy. Pythons swallowed deer, headfirst and whole, antlers, teeth, and bones, he'd seen pictures in a *National Geographic*. He remembered Jonah driven into the belly of the whale for dodging the word of the Lord—but, unlike the others, this woman appeared to seek the belly of the beast, making herself a martyr, a sacrifice, a St. Joan of Kendall Green.

The second woman prodded the elephant again and the animal began, carefully, to walk, one lumbering foot following the other. Elbo stood not knowing he was standing. Regaining possession of his senses he realized he needed to withdraw, but couldn't withdraw. Once the woman's eyes, staring from the elephant's mouth, found his, he was a chicken mesmerized, its head on the chopping block.

The woman's eyes held his as she lowered her arms, signaling the second woman to prod the elephant into lowering her. Elbo debated whether to run, but though he was standing, able again to run, he stayed where he stood, lost in reverie until the exotic accents of the second woman brought him to his senses. "Where did you come from, you blackie boy? What are you doing here? Get out, I say, you Sambo. Get out of here! Get Out!"

Elbo was surprised to see the woman was a man. He'd been fooled by his hair and his size from behind, but though he was blacker than himself he'd never seen a colored man with such hair, nor heard anyone, colored or otherwise, sound so strange. The man raised his ankus to strike Elbo, but Elbo remained motionless, too confused to protect himself, hardly glancing at the ankus, but the man was so sputteringly ridiculous, no more than a broomstick, that Elbo may also have perceived no threat. The receding hairline made him seem wise, but the highpitched indignation made him a boy of ten.

The blond woman picked up a towel from a nearby stool and yelled without taking a step toward him. "Siri, quit your yappin'! Lemme handle this."

The man's face remained livid, but the arm with the ankus dropped to his side.

The woman wiped her face as she took leisurely steps toward them and Elbo trembled, debating again whether to run. She was the archetypal woman, blond venus, blond bombshell, blond goddess, all in one. He'd lusted after her in the movies, but turned his head when he'd seen her in the drugstores. She was forbidden; there were people who would kill him for talking with her, even just looking at her. Suddenly, the police seemed less hazardous, but still he stood his ground, wanting her to see him.

"What're you doin' here, boy?"

Her voice was flat, demanding more than curious, her eyes the palest blue, almost white, like a Norwegian fjord reflecting mountains mantled in snow, and as cold. They could have chilled the blood of a polar bear or frosted a skating rink. They could have frosted Kansas in August. He shook his head, unable to say anything.

"Talk, you blackie boy, or it will be the worse."

Elbo didn't look at the strange man, but continued to shake his head.

"How did you get here, boy?" The eyes remained cold, but curiosity crept into her voice.

Still Elbo shook his head, but though his skin crawled, each pore a claw in miniature, he wanted to trust her. She was a white woman, but like no woman, white or black, he had seen. She was St. Joan of Kendall Green, who'd protect him if necessary, or so he wanted to think.

"Why're you here, boy?"

Elbo began nodding his head.

"Why are you here? Talk, blackie boy! Talk, I say, or I swear it will be the worse for you."

The woman spoke warningly, but without looking at the man. "Siri!"

Elbo ignored the man, but found his tongue and addressed only the woman. "Please, ma'am, I want a job. I want a job is all, ma'am. I'm lookin' for a job."

The woman looked at Siri, weighing what Elbo said, wondering if he were telling the truth. When she spoke again, she looked again at Elbo. "Tell me first how you got here."

Elbo couldn't think of lies enough to cover himself, and he might otherwise have said nothing, but he wanted to trust the woman as much as he wanted her trust. He pointed down the hallway. "From over there, ma'am, through the window, where you got the lions an' tigers."

The woman looked at Siri again who shook his head self-righteously. "Lies, all lies! Princess Ada is shutting the windows. All lies." He turned to Elbo again. "No more lies, Sambo, no more lies, I'm telling you, or it will only be the worse."

The woman said nothing, but looked at Elbo raising penciled eyebrows.

"No, ma'am, I ain't lyin'. I swear to you I ain't lyin'. The window was open. I followed someone. The police was behind us."

"The police?"

The man began a dance of excitement. "I knew it, Hazel! I knew it! He is a robber! He came in the night to rob us! He is a liar and a robber!"

The woman looked sharply at Siri, a warning as sharp in her voice. "Take it easy, Siri! He ain't lyin', and he ain't a thief. He wouldn't mention the police if he was a thief—and he sure wouldn't lie about the police." She turned again to Elbo. "Who were you followin'? Why were the police after you?"

Elbo told her the night's story leaving out only that he had returned from jail and saying no more about his mama than that there was trouble at home. When he was finished, Hazel was thoughtful. Dinty had returned late and tired and fallen asleep almost immediately. She looked at Siri again. "See if the blowtorch is where he said. Hero needs his shave."

Hero's hairs, thick and silken as nylon threads, were concentrated around the eyes, ears, and chin. Not for nothing is an elephant called a pachyderm, thick skin, though the skin is thin as paper inside the ears and around the mouth and anus, but where it's thick the skin is cracked like the bark of redwoods, like parched earth, to retain moisture from mudbaths since elephants have no sweatglands. The skin appropriates as well the color of the mud—and Africans, with less accessibility to water, develop deeper cracks in their skin than Indians.

Siri left the room. Hazel ignored Elbo while they waited. Hero spread his hindlegs, raised his tail, and released nine round footballs of shit, spattering into pancakes on the ground, accompanied by piss gushing like a fireman's hose. You might imagine an elephant eats like a pig, but you would be wrong. He eats more than a pig and more elegantly. He uses his trunk, his hand (the Indian has one finger at the tip of the trunk, the African two), his hath (the Hindi word for hand), from which you get hathi (the Hindi word for elephant), and Hastinapura (the city of elephants in the Indian epic, the *Mahabharata*), but the trunk is also his snorkel, his smelloscope, and showerhead. A trunkful can carry two gallons of water, a single drink can amount to more than fifty gallons, and a day's supply to more than a hundred. He also has a penchant for the harder stuff.

Elbo marveled at the quantity, marveled that Hazel appeared unfazed, oblivious, walking toward the elephant, heedless of splatter.

While we're on the subject, let me steer a whimsical course: the digestive cycle of the elephant lasts a day but is among the least efficient systems. Forty percent of its food remains undigested—but Brahma creates, Vishnu preserves, and Shiva destroys. To put it scientifically, matter can neither be created nor destroyed. In the wild, seeds in the elephant's diet pass intact and, distributed with shit, germinate more vigorously, shells softened by enzymes in the elephant's entrails. Baboons and other animals scavenge the shit for seeds and fruit and insects which can also pass intact. Dung beetles, scarab beetles, scatter the shit, roll it into balls, into nests for eggs, food for larvae, and bury it at discrete intervals, recycling nutrients. Iguanas and honey badgers scavenge the shit looking for the young of the dung. You get the picture: circles within circles of life.

SEVEN   PRINCESS ADA

Let me steer a still more whimsical course for a moment. Columbus, in days when the earth was presumed flat, risked the edge aiming for India, reaching America instead. Let me also risk the edge.

Wooing Spain for eight years before securing the backing of Ferdinand V and Isabella I to sail for the land of spices (India's west coast rich in pepper, the black gold of its time, a pungent peasized berry, not to mention cardamoms, cashews, cloves, cinnamon, ginger, and nutmeg among others, over which the mightiest European powers crossed swords and volleyed muskets), Columbus reached the Bahamas instead, on October 12, 1492, saving India from European civilization for another six years when Vasco da Gama arrived at Calicut to establish Portuguese power. If Vasco had traveled a hundred miles south inland he would have found Alleppey, the town of Siri's boyhood, where four and a half centuries later a scout for the Griffin Bros. Circus purchased Hero at an elephant fair a mile from Periyar where he'd been stockaded.

The scout had brought Siri to America with Hero. Siri's father, a mahout for one of the temple elephants, had been killed by an elephant in musth (testosterone overdrive, sperm count rising like mercury over a flame, a condition recognized by the sight and stench of a thick dribble from the temporal gland, a head held high above the shoulder, and aggression toward all)—after which his ma had lost her mind. Siri had been adopted by a Christian orphanage, nuns taught him English—and Hero, separated from his ma at about the same time, became the only family he recognized. The scout had made a shrewd calculation: Siri had the elephant's affection, but he was also an attraction on his own, another Sabu the Jungle Boy, providing the Griffin Bros. Circus with two attractions for the price of one.

Hero was Siri's only link to the land he'd left behind: Kerala. Gilded with beaches, laden with lagoons, canopied with coconut trees, honeycombed with estuaries, this strip of a state, occupies the southernmost lap of the Malabar Coast, micrometers on the map from Kanniyakumari at the southernmost tip of India. In Kerala, the world's first freely elected Communist state, you could be Marxist by conviction and Hindu, Muslim, Christian, or Jewish by faith. No surprise, then, that black Siri called black Elbo a blackie boy as if he himself were no less black. As a minority of one among the troupers, he needed to ally himself with the majority; but he also needed to feel better about himself, and there was nothing in America better than a black boy to make him feel better about himself. Prejudice is at large in the world at large and Siri had caught it like a virus in the wind even in the middle of the polyglot polycultural world of the circus. His scowl of self-righteousness deepened as he turned the elbow in the hallway toward the room of cages muttering imprecations to himself about bloody blackie buggers, so immersed in his black study that he didn't see Princess Ada until it was too late.

Ada had been a real princess, of Dromania, an eastern European province since swallowed by the Soviet Union. It was hard to tell but she was almost sixty and had been handling big cats almost as long, first as pets in her own zoo, and with the fall of Dromania in European circuses until she and the Griffin Bros. had discovered each other. She wore a pink velor robe over a pink nightdress, pink slippers, a pink scarf, and her face and hands were pink and white from long hours indoors. Siri guessed she had come directly from her hotel on waking that morning, but didn't dwell on it because she was advancing rapidly with a raised blowtorch. The pink monster spoke five languages, French, German, Hungarian, Dromanian, and English, but her accent was as much a trial for Siri as was his for her. She spat like one of her Bengals, thrusting forward the blowtorch like a dagger. "Vhat this is doing here? In the middle of the floor, I see it. How it came, this, your thing, in the middle of the floor, in the middle of the night?"

Siri didn't have to understand what she said to know what she meant. Someone was always threatening him, all the Baileys, even Hazel thought nothing of telling him to quit his yapping. He was everyone's punching bag because he was an easy target. He threw up one arm, shrinking as if she'd struck him. "Don't be hitting me, you witchy woman. I am not a dog. My name is not Rover."

The princess threw the blowtorch on the floor at his feet. "Aaah! Tchaaah! Stupid boy! I not hit you. I not hit childrens." She shook her head disgustedly, pointing to the blowtorch. "But this is your thing. How it came, in the middle of the night, here?"

Siri picked up the blowtorch. "Why are you asking me? How should I know?"

The princess put her hands on her hips. "If you do not know, vhy you are here? Vhat you are doing here?"

"Hazel sent me. She said to look here."

The princess's eyes flashed like lightbulbs. "Vhy here?"

Siri was afraid he'd said too much. "It was missing. She said look everywhere. I was looking everywhere. That is all."

The princess advanced again as if she might have walked through Siri. "Vhere is Hazel?"

Siri cringed. "With Hero! She is with Hero! We were practicing! That is all."

"Vhe shall see, shall vhe not? Vhe shall see. Vhe shall talk to Hazel."

The princess strode into the hallway, around the elbow, and beyond. Siri grabbed the blowtorch and ran after her shouting, "I have got it,

Hazel, I have got the blowtorch," meaning to warn her—of what he couldn't have said, but the blackie boy was nowhere to be seen when they got to Hazel, and Siri was relieved he'd said nothing about him to the princess.

The princess thrust herself against Hazel as she'd thrust herself against Siri, but drawing herself to her full height Hazel stood her ground, appearing to Siri like a mother defending her young. He still missed his ma, but the last time he'd seen her she'd jabbered like the loon she'd become and thrust him aside like a stranger. Hazel, confronting the Pink Monster, was the mother of his dreams and for a moment he envisioned her, not unlike Elbo, as his savior, his St. Joan of Kendall Green.

"Hazel, vhat means this? Vhy is your thing in my room vith my kitties?"

The two women were so close they might have licked each other, the princess gesticulating, Hazel with arms crossed. "I don't know what you're talkin' about, Ada."

"Your thing was in my room vith my kitties. All of last night I cannot sleep. Something tells me something is wrong in the room vith my kitties all night. I rush in the morning to look, and vhat do I find? I find your thing. How it came, in the middle of the floor, in the middle of the night?"

The princess's face grew larger with her anger, like a face on a balloon being blown. She had stared down Siberians and might as easily have stared down sabertooths had they sprung around them. Siri quailed standing behind her, Elbo quailed hidden behind a column, but not Hazel. She had faced elephants in musth, and might as easily have faced mammoths, mastodons, stegodons, and deinotheriums, all in musth. Her pale blue eyes bore glacially on the princess, her breath was an icicle as she spoke, slowly, as if to a child, making dramatic emphases without raising her voice, hissing. "*Lis*ten to me, Ada. *Lis*ten *care*fully. It ain't my *thing*. It's a *blow*torch. You should *know* what to call it. You are *old* enough to know what it is. You are *old* enough to know what *ev*erything is."

The princess hated being addressed familiarly, without her title, especially by Hazel whom she considered a child. She hated being reminded of her deficient vocabulary and of her age. She knew she couldn't bully Hazel, but refused to concede her ground. Instead, she spoke as if to a child herself, but placatingly. "Hazel, now enough! I do not care vhat you call your thing. If I have to go to Jonas I vhill go to Jonas. If I have to get him to finish this business I vhill get him to finish this business. All I vhant is you should tell me how your thing got in my room in the middle of the floor in the middle of the night."

Siri gazed upon Hazel with awe, ready to prostrate himself at her feet. Hazel didn't retreat, but didn't bother anymore even to look at the princess. "I don't know and I don't care. If that's all you got to say you better leave. Siri and I got work to do."

Hazel may not have known everything, but the princess was sure she knew more than she was telling. She was just as sure she would get no more out of her, but was unwilling to leave. "Tell me, Hazel. How you knew to send your little boy to my room to look for it? How?"

Siri, courageous in Hazel's presence, spoke contentiously. "I am not a little boy. I am thirty-one years old. Thirty-one years is not a little boy."

Both women ignored him. Hazel kept unblinking eyes on Princess Ada. "I didn't send him. We were rehearsin' the act. Hero's whiskers were ticklin' me. I said he needed a shave. I said to find the blowtorch when we couldn't find it on the shelf. The next thing I knew you were shriekin' down the hall like a bat outta hell, loud enough to wake the dead."

Sputtering his indignation, Siri interjected the first thing that came to his mind. "In India we have bats. Yesyes, vampire bats, bigbig vampire bats, squeakingsqueaking, loudly enough to wake up the dead."

The princess looked at him. "You, little boy! You are an idyot!" She turned abruptly then, leaving without a backward glance. "I vahn you, Hazel, this is not finish of the business. You vhill hearing about this more. This is not finish."

Seeing her ebb, Siri's courage flowed. "Yesyes, oh, yesyesyes! And what about you, you old woman? You are a batwoman! Yesyes, you are a batwoman!"

He looked at Hazel after the princess had disappeared as if they had been partners in the rout, but Hazel appeared otherwise occupied. She spoke as if she were at a cocktail party, bells in her voice as if she'd enjoyed her encounter. "You can come out now."

Elbo stepped into view from the column behind which Hazel had pushed him when she'd heard the princess coming. "You still want a job?"

"Yes, ma'am."

Hazel spoke without humor. "The only job we got is shovelin' shit, cleanin' up, general stuff. There'll be more in the spring, when we're tourin' again. You can help the roustabouts then, but for now shovelin' shit is as good as I can do—and there's a lot of it as you can see. You want it, you got it."

Elbo wanted to grin, but he was too tired. This was better than working with Prize in Cleveland, and guaranteed past the spring. "Yes, ma'am, sho' enough, I want it. That'll do me just fine."

"You'll sleep with the elephants, like Siri here. Don't worry, they won't hurt you. You'll eat what we eat. If anyone asks, you tell 'em I picked you up in town lookin' for a job, you got that? I picked you up in the town!"

"Yes, ma'am, I sho' enough got it."

"Good, us troupers, we got to stick together."

"Yes, ma'am."

"And if the police come around askin' questions you tell 'em just what I said, you got that?"

"I got it, ma'am, sho' enough."

She nodded approvingly. Siri said nothing, but stared at her, shaking his head vigorously, frowning furiously. She grinned, turning to him. "This is Siri. He's your boss, you got that? He'll show you the ropes. He'll answer your questions. But anythin' he says you got to do it, you got that?"

"Yes, ma'am, I got it, sho' enough."

She nodded approval. Siri kept his frown, but raised his chin nodding approval as well, his frown assuming a new importance.

Hazel turned again to Elbo. "Good. I'm Hazel Bailey. What's your name?"

"Elbo Blue, ma'am."

"What?"

"Elbo—like your elbow." He indicated his own elbow. "Elbo Blue."

"That's a strange name."

"I was born comin' out elbowfirst, ma'am. It's what they tells me."
"Elbo what?"
"Blue, ma'am, like the color."

Hazel grinned, scratching her head. "Well, I guess I've heard worse. Welcome to the circus, Elbo Blue."

EIGHT   MASTER AND MAN

There is an elephantheaded god in India, Ganesh, son of Shiva and Parvati. Ganesh wasn't born with an elephant's head, but he was born fullgrown, sans babyhood, sans childhood, sans youth, during Shiva's absence, and when Shiva appeared, the day after his birth, to venture into Parvati's bedchamber, Ganesh, a man of one day, stood in his way warning him that he was the son of Shiva. Shiva laughed, saying he knew his sons, and when Ganesh continued to stand in his way he cut off his head and flung it over the Himalayas—only to replace it with the first head he could find, the head of a sleeping elephant, after Parvati had verified their headless son's story.

Why did he not replace it with the original head? Could not great Shiva have summoned the disembodied head back from the icy wasteland? Clearly he was too distraught to think clearly. Besides, we would then have had no Ganesh as we know him, no elephantheaded god, no god of wisdom and success, no god as adored and as adorable, no god to invoke blessings on new ventures in art, commerce, science, and the like for which Ganesh was invoked.

Late in the day though it may be for invocations, with all respect, with all humility, I invoke the blessing of great Ganesh for my endeavor, this document you hold, a moment please of silence, hands joined, brow bowed, invocation sotto voce, shantih, shantih, shantih.

DINTY WAS EASILY RECOGNIZED AS MY PA, as much a wiry runt of a man as I was a wiry runt of a boy, as much a senior hobo as I was a junior for the outsize overalls he liked to wear, the boots too big, the unruly thatch on his head, the chip on his shoulder the size of the Big Top. He had muscular arms, a thick waist, had once been a contortionist, but a spinal injury had concluded that chapter of his career. His fingers had twitched, strumming a guitar in the air, when he'd received the summons from Jonas, and twitched again as he entered Jonas's suite in the Imperial Hotel.

Jonas had come to Kendall Green from Dundee in the old country (home of marmalade and Dundee cakes), a lad of nine, with his parents, Junious and Merilee Frank. When rail shows had been replaced by truck shows in the Thirties and Junious Frank's trucking business had languished, the Griffin Bros. Circus had been put on the market with little to offer other than Hero. Jonas, Junious's oldest son, had negotiated a price the devil would have envied, and continually imagined scenarios in which he pulled Roy Rogers and Gene Autry and Hopalong Cassidy like rabbits out of a hat to match Ringling's Frank Buck and Gargantua the Great Gorilla.

Jonas lay in a reclining chair as plush as the pile under Dinty's feet, his own feet on a footstool. He wore black satin slippers and a black satin robe which parted midthigh revealing powerful legs, red and hairy, and red and white striped satin boxers. He took particular pride in the black silk top hat he wore in the ring rubbed gently everyday with a clean cloth soaked in beer. He was a Beau Brummel more than anyone Dinty knew, the Equestrian Director, better known as the Ringmaster, but there was a difference. The Equestrian Director conducts the show, the Ringmaster conducts the horses, touching a left shoulder with a whip for more speed, under the belly for less, to maintain an even pace for riders pirouetting, somersaulting, and tumbling from one horse to the next.

Dinty was late, a point not lost on Jonas who looked at his watch in reproval. Dinty couldn't see what difference it made. It was midmorning, but Jonas had just awakened, his hair still tousled, his face still creased with sleep, and he showed no sign of amending his routine for Dinty. Dinty had hurried through breakfast, a toasted ham and egg sandwich at a grill on 12th and Broad Street, gobbled whole, washed with black coffee scalding his tongue and throat, but he was not in the habit of saying anything to Jonas unless Jonas spoke first and he said nothing.

Janet Frank, in a white bathrobe, had let Dinty in without a word, hate glinting like metal in her eyes. Her glint was a habit, appearing whenever he appeared. He'd seen her smile on occasion, apparently gay, until she saw him, and the smile would surrender to the glint. The success of the years since the Depression might have softened her, but he seemed to have lodged a chancre under her skin deep enough to require surgery. Fat as she was, fingers like sausages, she reminded him of Jack Spratt's wife who could eat no lean. Depression or no, she had waxed as the country had waned.

She was also the spur to her husband's success. Had he been judicious with his time, she was convinced they might have rivaled the Ringlings, but he was too beholden to his past—burdened by his past. It showed in his drooping eyes and lips, and Dinty was one to whom he felt beholden. He never doubted Janet was right about Dinty, but he was indebted to Dinty for the act with Hero which had saved the Griffin Bros. Circus in its incarnation as the Frank Bros. Circus and for his role in the accident that had killed his wife.

He lifted his feet from the stool and heaved himself into a sitting position, tucking his robe between hairy red knees as demurely as a schoolgirl. Before the death of his wife, Myrtle, Dinty had suffered the death of his brother, Alf. In 1934, the year in which Jonas bought the Griffin Bros. Circus, unpaid employees were tossed off trains between stops when the payroll ran short, an old circus practice called redlighting (tossed within sight of a trainyard's red lights they could find their way to town, but they were more often tossed into the indiscriminate maw of a lightless night). During their last journey by rail to Cincinnati, Dinty had stayed in his bunk in Hero's car with Myrtle, Hazel, me (babe in arms), and Siri (Siri and Hazel on blankets on Hero's back). Alf had been with the roustabouts, all of whom had been redlighted, but of whom only Alf had hit a telegraph pole before hitting the ground.

Sad sober tones matched the sad round eyes under the single grey and white caterpillar lining Jonas's brow. He spoke as he might to a child, which was how he saw Dinty, circus simple, working for the circus, not for money. Without the circus he was nothing. "Good morning, Dinty. I trust you've breakfasted."

Sure, he trusted, as if it made any difference, as if he'd ever meant to breakfast with him. "Yessir. Mornin', sir." The aroma of fresh coffee suffused the suite, there was a steaming cup of black on a table within

Jonas's reach, Janet no doubt had a cup of her own in the bedroom, but she had disappeared without offering him any. He could have asked, but wanted to be careful—at least, until he knew why he'd been summoned.

Jonas took a sip of his coffee. "All right, then, Dinty, I shall come straight to the point, I shall."

Dinty said nothing; the silken voice didn't fool him, especially not with his wife in the next room listening to every word. The tone was mournful, but not sympathetic. Even seated, Jonas was almost taller than him—and, itching from guilt, intimidated by Jonas's luxury, he couldn't stop his fingers twitching and thrust his hands into his pockets.

Jonas put down the cup. "I want to bring something to your attention, Dinty, something that was brought to my attention yesterday."

His voice remained languid, unaccusatory, but Dinty wished he were seated himself, at least standing alongside a wall or doorway he might lean against. He slumped, shifting his weight from one foot to the other, twitching fingers turning to fists in his pockets as he swayed, appearing stockier in his oversize coat. A voice rose from the maelstrom of noise in his head to ask for coffee, but he remained silent.

"What I want, Dinty, is for you to tell me what you make of it, of this incident."

Dinty wished he would get to the point, but he'd been in the circus long enough to know the buildup was half the show.

"Do you understand me, Dinty?"

"Yessir."

"Good. I want you to understand because that is what I want for myself. I want to understand what happened."

"Yessir."

Jonas took another sip of coffee. "Ah, this is good coffee. I must ask Janet to find out the blend."

"Yessir."

Jonas indicated his satisfaction with a deep sigh, speaking finally as if he had no other choice. "Well, Princess Ada was here yesterday. She brought me a copy of *The Afternoon Courier*." Jonas picked up a newspaper from the coffee-table next to his cup. "In fact, here it is."

Dinty had seen the paper and understood where Jonas was headed. His mind raced as his body ceased to sway, fists in his pockets tightened digging fingernails into his palms, and the voice in his head continued to demand coffee.

Jonas took a while unfolding the paper, turning to a specific page. "Ah, here it is! 'The Idjit Midjit of Kendall Green' it's called. Do you know about it?"

He was vaguely aware of Janet in the bedroom doorway. He'd read the article, but said nothing.

"Dinty, I asked if you knew about this article?"

He shook his head, but said nothing.

"What's that?"

"No, sir."

"No?"

"No, sir. I don't know nothin'."

Jonas shook the paper straight and folded it to read more conveniently. "Well, it says here that someone broke into Pat's Liquor Store the night before. It says here that it must have been a small man because the ventilator through which he broke in was quite narrow. Now, you are sure, are you, that you know nothing about this?"

Dinty shook his head. "No, sir—I mean, yessir, I'm sure I don't know nothin'."

"It goes on to say that this small man, this so-called midget, was not too bright. The register had been left inadvertently open, but he didn't even think to check it. What do you make of that, Dinty?"

Dinty allowed himself a ghastly grin. "He couldn'ta been too bright, sir. I can see why they'd say that about him."

Jonas nodded. "Not only that, Dinty, but he welded the safe shut instead of open—and he used a blowtorch. What do you make of that?"

Dinty kept his grin, rocking on his feet. "He couldn'ta been too bright, sir—for a certainty, he couldn'ta been too bright."

Jonas nodded again. "Now, Dinty, that's all and well as it is, but here's the part I don't understand."

"Yessir?"

"Princess Ada found a blowtorch, *your* blowtorch, in the middle of the floor of her cathouse. Do you understand what I am saying, Dinty? She knew something was wrong because she couldn't sleep all night, and early the next morning—yesterday—she found the blowtorch in the middle of the floor. It must have come in the middle of the night she said because she had not seen it the night before. Do you understand what I am saying, Dinty?"

Jonas stared so piercingly that Dinty looked away. "Yessir."

Jonas's voice fell to a whisper. "What am I saying, Dinty?"

Mr. Frank had occasionally been kind. Dinty wondered if it was to his advantage to tell him the truth before it was spelled out for him, but remained uncertain. "I don't know, sir."

Jonas quietly put down the newspaper, leaned forward, elbows on knees. "Dinty, the police chased a man from the liquor store to Willow Street where they say he disappeared, right off the street he disappeared, right outside the windows of our quarters, outside Princess Ada's cathouse where the blowtorch was found on the floor." His voice continued softly, but it began to tremble with anger. "Those are high windows, Dinty, which is why they weren't mentioned in the paper, but how long do you think it will be before they figure out that height is no obstacle for a trouper? How long do you think it will be before the police come to me?"

Dinty's grin thinned to a string. He moved his shoulders in a grotesque shrug. "I don't know, sir."

"Dinty, don't make me spell it out, man, don't make me do that. I'm trying to help you, I am. I will not give you up to the police, we troupers have to stick together, you know that, we do not have anybody else, but I want to hear it from your own lips, for my own satisfaction. What am I saying, Dinty? Tell me: What am I saying?"

Dinty might have confessed then, there was a droopiness about Jonas's eyes that wrested confessions, but there was a knock on the door, Janet let in room service with their breakfast trolley, cozies and covered salvers of stainless steel, racks of toast, jars of honey, marmalade, and jam, and he lost his urge. He watched as the cozies were lifted, salvers uncovered, revealing a steaming jug of milk, hot kettle of tea, steaming eggs, crisp bacon, and the piece de resistance, smoked kippers, a nod to Jonas's past in the old country, and he lost his urge. He looked at the Watteau and Fragonard prints on the wall, the heavy drapery around him, the thick pile under his feet, and he lost his urge. He was safe; feuds between troupers and townies were as old as the circus itself; and he didn't see after all that Jonas deserved the satisfaction he requested. His grin turned slowly genuine. "I don't know, sir. I jus' don't know."

Jonas nodded his head slowly, understandingly, rubbing a palm wearily across his brow.

Dinty's grin turned wider as he focused his eyes on the trolley. "Sir, if you don't mind, sir, I wouldn't mind a cuppa myself."

There was a brief silence as dark as if he had asked for his wife's honor, and for the first time Dinty had the satisfaction of seeing Jonas's drooping eyes rise to his forehead and Jonas, apoplectic, order him from the room. He bunched his hands in his pockets as he left, but skipped back to the Abbott, fingers twitching no more, decibel levels dropping from the voices in his head.

The same *Courier* brought greater worry for the son than for the father, a story on page seven titled NIGGER TRAMPLED TO DEATH IN TOLEDO mentioned a juggler and pickpockets. Brown E seemed to scream in my ear: *Then comes my fit again.* Hazel said nothing, but she knew: a wall rose between us as if we were strangers. The boy with the sorrow of a man in his face lost the sympathy of the world, tearducts turned to stone, the orphan had unmothered a mother. I was a madman in the making, maniac in utero, mopefaced monster. Forgive me if you can, forgiveness I need, though deserve it I do not. A helpless boy had been deprived of his life by a shiteating shithead, a bastard of mammoth proportions, a coward who would be a man, a killer in boy's clothing.

Oh, the places I have been, the things I have seen, starting with the circus, moving to the sea, following with Bombay and Nandi and Chicago—all the backdrops of my brief years of breath. I had paid for my great defiance with time in this dharamsala of a graveyard, this resthouse of the dead. There had never been any recourse for my condition except to give up the ghost, lay down my life, but I had done no such thing, not for a long time, not until I had found myself with Quint and Mercedes in the hannah-haunted penthouse in Lincoln Park—but yet again I get ahead of myself.

I was wary enough to push the assignations farther afield, as far south as Dayton, north as Flint, west as South Bend, and east as Pittsburgh. I cut down on the number of assignations, exchanged my beret for a fez, darkened my face and hair more closely to resemble an Arab;

but by night, every night, the charade ended. Brown E inhabited my dreams, wagging a fat white clown finger, his face swollen to monstrous proportions, chanting in a theatrical voice full of echoes, *Glamis hath murdered sleep, and therefore Cawdor shall sleep no more, Spike Bailey shall sleep no more*, and I would wake in a sweat, unblinking as a basilisk, the boy's face in my eyes, his mouth an O of amazement turning to terror.

THE DYING ELEPHANT

*Hidden away from the haunts of men, west of a
widespread Lake
Out of the scope of human ken, in tangled
thicket and brake,
'Mid arching trees where a foetid breeze ruffles
the ragged sky,
Is the sombre place where the vanishing race of
the Elephants comes to die.*

CULLEN GOULDSBURY

ONE   ON THE BACK OF THE ELEPHANT

It is no surprise that elephants eat more than other animals, not even that they eat less relative to their body weight. The smaller an animal the more it eats relative to its body weight. A rat may consume forty percent of its body weight daily in food, an elephant just eight—which still distills to a sizeable hill of greens, four hundred pounds daily for a five thousand pound elephant.

They also strip the bark from trees, some say for fiber, some for minerals (calcium, manganese, boron, iron, copper). They rake walls of deep dark caves with their tusks excavating for minerals (yes, elephants wander in caves); they rake the earth for salt and more minerals (yes, elephants eat dirt); and their calves absorb microbes for digesting cellulose from the dung of their elders (yes, elephants eat shit).

When they're not resting, elephants are eating. When they're not bathing, elephants are eating. When they're not drinking, you guessed it, elephants are eating. When they're not sleeping (and they don't sleep much, three hours a day will suffice), elephants are eating. They eat three times a day, morning, afternoon, and midnight, and when they're not eating, you guessed it again, they're eating. They eat seventy-five percent of the day, and if they ate like rats, forty percent of their body weight, they would be eating three hundred and seventy-five percent of the day, and if that were possible, you guessed it yet again, they would still be eating.

No surprise either, that entering an elephant stable we would find them at tiffin, gorging on trunkfuls of hay—nor that Hazel, pastmistress of the peep show when the circus was in town, lazed naked on her back on Hero's back, resting her head on her robe (bundled to a pillow), *Photoplay* in one hand, bottle of Coca Cola in the other. Siri, on lookout, appareled in a white loonghi, brow furrowed in concentration, sat crosslegged on Hero's head.

The routine had developed so naturally it would be difficult to say when or how it started, but Hazel spent free winter afternoons on Hero's back, Siri watching for intruders. It was cold though the stable was indoors, but Hazel welcomed wintry fingers like the fingers of a lover, it was just another way of putting her head in the elephant's mouth, just another penance—and Siri, sharing the cold, sharing the familiarity, was grateful for the sheer stark privilege.

Siri's watchfulness had kept them from discovery; the stall provided additional cover; but Siri now shared the loft with Elbo and discovery had become a greater hazard. Both Siri and Elbo imagined themselves rivals for Hazel's favor, Elbo finding any excuse to be in the stable with her, Siri constantly chasing him out. During his brief tenure with the circus, Elbo had never seen Hazel naked, but he had begun to harbor suspicions—of what, he couldn't have said, but all too often, coming upon them unexpectedly, he found Siri smug, Hazel smiling, berobed.

Hazel was amused, seeming at once to ignore and bask in their attention, but she was puzzled when black Siri called black Elbo a black Sambo as if he himself were less black. Elbo was different. He watched her at every opportunity as he might a divinity. If she returned his stare his eyes grew large and white before she released him from her stare. She accepted his surreptitious looks as tribute: she would not have called it tribute, no more than a compliment, but compliments are exchanged between equals and a blind man could have divined the reverence in Elbo's loitering looks.

The Dying Elephant

It was the strangest affair. It had taken Hazel a while even to recognize that it was an affair, but the dynamics were no different. Siri was jealous of the trust they shared and guarded her privacy like a eunuch, but wanted to be her only eunuch. She would have been as comfortable naked with Elbo as she was with Siri, she would have preferred it because with Elbo sharing the loft her opportunities became more restricted, but she was surprised when she tried to establish what would have been a chaste menage a trois, a luncheon on elephantback, *Déjeuner sur le dos d'un éléphant.*

It was rare that they were interrupted in the stall, but if Siri heard or saw someone approaching he would whisper, "There is someone," or "Someone is coming," and she would pluck the robe from under her head, fling her arms into its sleeves, and wrap it around herself. If Siri were in a playful mood, he would yank her big toe, whistle, and wink, and she would return his wink, smiling as she plucked her robe. On the day in question, he whispered, "Elbo is coming," his eyes wild with warning. She smiled and shrugged her shoulders, too immersed in *Photoplay* to care, an article on the samba, the new dance from Brazil, and the movie stars who were under its spell, imagining herself practicing with an imaginary partner: step, close, step, close, dip and spring, dip and spring.

She was surprised from her brief reverie by Siri suddenly pawing her breasts and shoulders while the *Photoplay* fluttered to the ground and the Coca Cola bottle flew into a hayloft. She would have misunderstood if not for the rage in his eyes and the hiss in his whisper. "You have got no shame? I said, no, Elbo is coming? Do you want him looking at you like this?"

He was grappling for the robe under her head. She understood him intuitively, but though she disagreed she was too astonished to resist his argument. Grabbing the robe she covered herself, shoving him so he slid down Hero's side and fell to his knees on the ground.

Hero's was the farthest stall, and though Elbo might have heard the scuffle, the frantic whispers, the magazine fluttering, the Coca Cola fizzing in the hay, Siri's HHHOOOOOOFFFF! as he fell, he was too late to see more than Hazel wrapped as tightly in a bewildered look as in her robe and Siri wildeyed on the ground, running at him, flailing his arms. "What are you doing here? I told you, no, to go to the store? We are needing things from the store. I told you, no, to go? Such a Sambo, you are."

Elbo stood his ground, amazed, hypnotized again by Hazel's gaze, staring at her through the haze of Siri's blows, shrugging them off like flies. Siri couldn't hurt him, he didn't know how to hit.

Siri's words poured like a stream. "What are you doing still here? I said, no, to go to the store? What have you got? mud or what in your ears? Dirty black nigger boy! At least, go and clean out your ears! Go on! Get out! Go clean out your ears! Get out the mud from your ears!"

Elbo continued staring at Hazel, as if for direction, until finally even Siri looked at her, eyes damp, humiliated by his futility. Hazel nodded. "Go on, Elbo. Go to the store. Do as he says."

Siri gave her a grateful glance, but Elbo ignored him. "What should I get from the store?"

Siri almost yelled. "Get a soap! We need a soap! Also a toothpaste! Get a toothpaste!"

Hazel nodded again. "Do as Siri says."

Siri barked. "Yes! Immediately! Right now! Go!"

"I don't got no money."

"I have got money! I have got money!" Siri rushed to his knapsack by the side of the stall, pulling out a dollar bill. "Here, come over here! Take this and bring a soap! Bring a toothpaste!"

Elbo stood his ground until Siri brought the money to him. "How much should I get?"

"What have you got? Boiled potatoes for brains? Boiled cauliflower for ears? Get what you can get for a dollar. Go now! Get out!"

Hazel nodded from her perch. "Go on, Elbo. Do as he says."

Siri waited for Elbo to leave the stable before turning to Hazel. "How you could do such a thing? What you were thinking? How you think it looks if he see you like that? Have you got no shame?"

Hazel didn't understand the difference between exposing herself to Siri and to Elbo, but she seemed to have locked herself into a room to which Siri believed he had the only key. She might have defended herself, but his face ran with tears like a delta and she lost heart. "Let's just leave it, okay, Siri? Let's not talk about it no more."

Siri shook his head, a smile on his damp face, as if he were her confessor. "Nonono! We *must* talk about it. You *must* be more careful. When I say someone is coming, then someone is coming. I am not only whistling Dixie music. You must promise me you will be more careful."

Hazel pursed her lips. "Don't be dumb, Siri. I ain't makin' no promises. Who the hell d'you think you are, tellin' me what to do?"

Siri was immediately contrite. "Sorrysorry. I did not mean to offend, not to offend at all." He prodded Hero's leg to give himself a legup, hoisted himself again to Hero's head, and prostrated himself, face hidden in Hero's back, hands clutching her robed knees. "So sorry. Please forgive. I am just an oolloo boy from India. What am I knowing? Forgive, please. Veryvery sorry."

She drew her knees away. "Siri, I don't know what came over you. You had no right. What'd you think you were doin'?"

Siri withdrew his hands. "Right, right, right you are. Righto! Right, you are. I had no right. I am sorry, veryvery sorry."

She shook her head, bewildered, sorrier for him than he was for her, and sighed. "It's all right. Let's just forget it. Let's just put it behind us."

Siri kept his face buried in Hero's back. "Behind, yes. It is behind. Already it is behind."

Hazel spoke more kindly. "Siri, look at me."

Siri looked up slowly.

Hazel smiled. "It's all right. Really, it's all right."

Siri's eyes widened with pleasure again like a child's. He wiped tears from his face with bony black hands. "Behind. Everything is behind."

Hazel nodded, glad to have cheered him again. Despite his strangeness he was family, he had no other family.

Siri smiled slowly, slyly. "Elbo is a tough cuckoo."

"You mean a tough cookie."

"Nono, I mean cuckoo. He is a cuckoo."

Hazel shook her head, but couldn't help grinning. "You're the only cuckoo around here."

TWO   THE BACKWARD BACK

I've said it enough that I'm a dead man, but not enough that I'm a trouper and proud. Once a trouper, always a trouper, even in this graveyard from which I speak. It gets in your blood the way the sea and the sky get in the blood of the sailor I was to become, the sawdust is as bracing as a wind of salt, and spangles in the spotlight as autumnal as a setting sun. More even than an elephant, the Big Top is a baggy monster; there's a ribcage in its struts, skin in its canvas, blood in the sawdust, and a heart bigger than a thousand elephants under the lights.

I see the empirical among you, statisticians and accountants, furrow your broad brows, shrug your narrow shoulders, scratch your pointy heads. What's the point of wisps of information in a world where increasingly only specifics have meaning. What's the heft of one elephant's heart, let alone of a thousand elephant hearts? About 35 pounds, since you must have specifics, and the heft of its brain a little over ten. Its small and large intestines reach a hundred feet in length, it takes 24 hours to digest a meal, shits two hundred pounds a day, pisses fifty gallons, ejaculates a quart at a time. Its erect penis reaches forty inches, has a diameter of more than six. The orifice is Y-shaped, the length of the clitoris sixteen inches, the genital canal 35. The vulva lies between the hindlegs, not under the tail as in a mare ... but I see the empirical losing its appeal, my more dyspeptic readers twirling their moustaches, curling their lips, tossing their curls. Why should we care about the heft of an elephant's heart? the length, breadth, and cross-section of its organs and their spillage? More picturesque to say an elephant's heart is a balloon of blood, a mandrill's blue and red head of blood, which dropped from the height of a tightrope would flood the ring with blood—and blood in the sawdust we soon shall have.

The principal rider poses, pirouettes, spins, and leaps over banners, through hoops of paper and fire while her animal trots, canters, gallops in the ring at a steady pace, never to be distracted, not by the blaring brass band, crying babies, butchers—little short of an earthquake would distract her. A principal rider also somersaults. The backward somersault is standard, face forward, somersault backward—standard but hardly pedestrian, not on the ground and emphatically not on the thundering rump of an Andalusian. Next in difficulty is the forward forward, face forward, somersault forward; you lose the momentum of your arms going into the somersault, and sight of your feet coming down. Finally, the most difficult, the backward back, face backward, somersault forward—and twist in the air so you land face forward. You also need to synchronize your descent with the descent of your horse's caboose, or the bumpity-bump of his rumpity-rump will throw your concentration, your balance, you.

The challenge for the Girleen from Ballaghadareen might have been intimidating, but the blood of troupers flashed through her veins. Challenges only invigorated her. There was little the McDonnells didn't know about equestrianism when they arrived in America in 1937, but a lot they didn't know about showmanship, and their act began to soar only after a timely introduction to Summit and Sons, Couturiers Supreme, but the challenge of her couture was long in her past, the challenge of tiaras and plumes and playing to a crowd. The challenge of the next somersault lay ahead.

The European tour had enhanced her prestige, widened the mantle of her fame, and the next somersault was as inevitable, as relentless, as the sun in the morning, the moon at night. She had me in her palm, but wanted only the next somersault. She had suitors by the score, lined by her door, but wanted only the next somersault. She had venues for the asking, in Europe and the US, but wanted only the next somersault. She had fame, fortune, power, grace, style, worship, adoration, but wanted only the next somersault. Head of the circus elite, the world at her feet—but, you guessed it, she wanted only the next somersault. She had mastered the forward forward, even the backward back, even without a mechanic (the harness suspending her in the air if she missed her footing)—but never before an audience, and she had committed herself to the backward back in Paris, at the Cirque d'Hiver, the posters had advertised the feat, the time was at hand—or so she imagined. She broke her neck on her first night.

There was a collective intake of breath, like a chug of steam from a locomotive, followed by scattered screams. She appeared to shrink in her progress from her powerful leap to her spreadeagle in the sawdust. The spotlight vanished, the band broke from a tremolo in strings to a brass polka, joeys collided on the tanbark, spilled from the sides, as if the world had grown suddenly merrier instead of mad. True to tradition, the tears of the joeys and other troupers remained unshed, at least in public. Solange Bontemp and her performing poodles commandeered the spotlight, but according to the story in the *Journal de Paris* the next day the eyes of Eileen's proud Andalusian, Andromache, were damp and swollen.

THREE JACK AND JILL

1933 was the worst year for John Jack Lewis, waiting in long lines for thick bread and thin soup, fighting over garbage in the backs of restaurants, sheltering in Hoovervilles where the homeless gathered in sheds of cardboard and scrap metal, covering himself nights on a parkbench with newspaper. Andrew Mellon, multimillionaire and former Secretary of the Treasury, said there was nothing fundamentally wrong with the social system; Dwight Morrow, a diplomat running for governor of New Jersey, said too much prosperity ruined the fiber of the people; *The Literary Digest* said that many a thoughtless wife who'd neglected house and husband had become more appreciative and tame.

Jack spent days foraging, nights keeping warm, and was never without his volume of *The Complete Works of Shakespeare* (solace by day, pillow by night). The new year also brought a new president: the old had refused to put America on the dole, the new gave America a new deal. The end of the year saw the end of prohibition, and the beginning of the new year saw the beginning of Jack's tenure with the Frank Bros. Circus, newly formed from the Griffin Bros. Circus. He celebrated with a fifth of Jack Daniels shared with a stranger. The New Year also ignited his romance with Jill Hazel Bailey.

Hazel, at seventeen, was too young to be more than impressionable, less than susceptible to Jack's abundant charms. She was also his first younger lover, by three years, also the first she'd pursued herself. His gentleness had made the difference. She'd caught him looking at her, but knew he wouldn't approach her—which was new in her experience. She hated her act with Hero, hated putting her head in his mouth, and her promiscuity was more likely related to her aversion—until she met Jack and poured her frustration into her new romance, but they'd been together barely a year before Myrtle's accident turned them both celibate, her out of guilt, him out of respect for her guilt, she dedicating herself to her act, he to whatever she wanted.

The years of mutual celibacy might have boosted Jack's confidence, created a bond between them, brought them closer, but he blamed himself still for what had happened and worried that she did too. He mounted the stairs to the room in the Abbott insured by the good news with which he hoped to change their lives, but felt familiar constrictions in his ribcage, spine, and skull. He'd planned what to say, rehearsed how he'd say it, but found himself losing resolve, forgetting what he'd rehearsed, holding his news as a weapon more than insurance. He should have written ahead, he should have called, but he hadn't wanted to give her time for reasons to refuse him.

He straightened his polka dot bow. He wore a new suit under his new winter coat, but he'd left his new homberg at home not wanting to be too overbearing. He'd worn a baseball cap instead, the polka dot bow for the same reason, and sneakers though his feet were frozen. He'd scraped the sneakers against the threadbare welcome mat downstairs, scuffed his feet against the bare wooden stairs on his way up, against the floor along the hallway, and pawed the floor with his feet standing in front of Room 305.

He sighed deeply and the breath he exhaled left his face looking like a party balloon the morning after, closer to fifty than his thirty-three years. He stood momentarily still, fist in midair, knuckles to the door. He could still leave and send her notice of his arrival, he would seem less desperate, but wanted now only to get it over. He rapped softly—and, when there was no answer, again, barely more loudly.

"Who is it?" Hazel's voice rang clearly through the door, annoyed as if she'd been interrupted. He swallowed and she called again before he could reply. "Who *is* it?"

He wanted to reply with the authority of church bells in his voice, but in his eagerness he almost choked. "Just me. Jack." A brief silence followed, but not brief enough for Jack who had to fill it to cover his discomfort, adding "Brown E" as if she might have forgotten.

A brief light appeared behind the peephole before it darkened again. There was no reply, but the latch was removed, the door swung open, and she stood before him again in a robe and slippers, drying her hands with a dishrag, her face impassive.

He held open his arms to welcome her in. "Hey, Jill!"

"Jack!" She seemed more surprised than pleased, there was no welcoming smile, and she ignored the invitation of his arms. Jack provoked a conflict the years had never resolved. She had led him down a garden path, but had neither the courage to push him away nor take him back. He stepped forward to embrace her and she submitted, patting his back like a child's. "Jack, whyn't you say you were comin'?"

He held her as if he might never let go though she was now drying her hands again with the dishrag behind his back. "I have good news. I wanted to give it to you in person."

"You could've still said you were comin'."

"Sorry, I guess I wasn't thinking." He let her go. It was going wrong already. He hadn't meant to apologize; he had nothing for which to apologize; and he should have been the first to let go. "It's good to see you again."

She wanted to comfort him, but not at the risk of encouraging him. His absence made her long for him, but his presence only muddled her. She smiled finally, slowly, hooking the dishrag by the sink. "I like your moustache. It's … mature—like you grew up or somethin'."

He began to relax. "Thanks. That was the idea. Mind if I make myself comfortable?"

"I don't care."

"Gee, thanks a lot." She looked at him sharply and he grinned as if the sarcasm were in fun, a lover's game, but wondered if she found him rude. She took his coat and hung it in the wall closet. Next to the closet was the door leading to the bedroom. Jack wondered if they were alone. A table by the window held dirty breakfast dishes and he became aware of a lingering smell of coffee.

She still smiled, returning from the closet. "You look such a swell, Jack, I'd never have known you. I'd've walked right by you on the street. Those threads must've cost a bundle—specially the cap and sneakers."

He grinned, tugging on his bow. "I kinda like the bow myself."

"You would."

"You know me." He was glad to be kidded, to find her more amenable.

"You want some coffee? We just had breakfast. I think we got a cup left."

There was a noise in the next room. He looked at her inquiringly.

She shrugged. "It's just Pa."

He nodded thoughtfully. "Can we go somewhere?"

"Why?"

"I want to tell you alone."

"Tell me what?"

"My news. My good news."

"You can tell Pa, specially good news. We sure could use it."

"I will—but it's kind of personal. I want to tell you first—alone."

This was not how he'd planned it. His voice thinned. She got warier. He spoke more hurriedly.

"We could get coffee at the Country Kitchen. We could get biscuits. You like their biscuits."

"Not for me. I just had my fill. Too much coffee gives me the heeby-jeebies."

She said nothing about the biscuits and he didn't repeat his offer. She might think he was bribing her and he wasn't sure he wasn't. "Oh, all right."

She appeared more thoughtful, lit a cigarette, and offered him one. He accepted gratefully though he didn't want it. She avoided his eyes, keeping hers on the closed door to the next room. "I think Pa's on his way out. Said he had a mission for the day—or somethin'."

"A mission?"

She shrugged as if it made no more sense to her, puffing on her cigarette.

He puffed on his own. "That's fine, then. I'll take that cup of coffee, after all, then."

He could hear Dinty in the next room while she got the coffee ready, grunting and swearing as if he were struggling with something. Jack guessed he was getting into his coat and he was right. Hazel had no sooner cleared a space for his coffee at the table by the window than Dinty appeared, still a small man in large clothes, wearing one sleeve of a coat which dragged behind him, reminding Jack of Charlie Chaplin. Hazel went to help him with the sleeve. Dinty pointed a finger at Jack from his sleeved arm as if they were in the middle of a conversation. "Did you know that? I ask you, sir. Did you know that?"

Jack nodded a greeting, smiling broadly. "Morning, Dinty! No, I didn't. I didn't know that. What're we talking about?"

Hazel gripped the cigarette between her lips while getting Dinty's other arm into his sleeve and he shrugged on the coat. "About Gargantua—the great gorilla. He had a twisted face. Everybody said he had a twisted face. Did you know that?"

Everyone humored Dinty, but Jack had a bigger stake than most. He nodded again. "It was a mean twisted face, Dinty. They said someone threw acid in his face when he was a baby."

Dinty's face lit up like a child's at Christmas, like the Christmas tree itself. "Yes! Yes! Exac'ly right! That's what I said. E*xac* 'ly what I said. Good boy, good boy. It made him look mean. It made him look orn'ry. E*xac* 'ly, e*xac* 'ly!"

"What're you talkin' about, Pa? What's this all about?"

His eyes widened with surprise that she didn't appear to know. "About Gargantua. What'd you think? I'm talkin' about Gargantua, the great gorilla."

Hazel spoke patiently. "I know, Pa—but what about Gargantua?"

Dinty shook his head irritably, his face darkened. "Ah, it don't matter, it don't matter. Never mind what I said. Never mind. I didn't say nothin', nothin' at all."

Hazel's eyes fluttered. "You feelin' all right, Pa? Would you like some more coffee?"

"Nah! I got a mission. I got to go. I'll be back soon, but I got to go—but I'll be back."

She made sure his coat was buttoned, kissed him goodbye. "When're you gonna be back, Pa? I worry about you."

The Christmas tree lit up in Dinty's face again. "I'll be back soon. I'll be back real soon, but I got to go. I got a mission."

Dinty appeared to have forgotten Jack as he left, but Jack said goodbye and he acknowledged him with a brief grim look. After he left,

Hazel shook her head, lips pursed. "I don't know what to do about Pa. He's been like that a long time. I just keep prayin' he'll get better."

Jack nodded sympathetically, glad to be included in the family trouble. "How's Spike?"

She had excised Toledo from her mind. She shook her head again, lips still pursed. "Spike'll be fine, I guess. He's shook right now 'cause of what happened to Eileen."

"Eileen? What happened to Eileen?"

"You don't know? We got a telegram almost a week ago."

He shook his head. "I got in just this morning. I just freshened up a bit before coming here."

Her eyes focused without smiling on his face again and he was sorry he'd revealed his eagerness, as if he had no life away from her—which was true, but it didn't help to let her know it.

Hazel blew smoke rings, following them with her eyes as if she hadn't wanted to see his eagerness any more than he had wanted to reveal it. "She was in Paris—broke her neck doin' the back-back. Spike thinks he's never gonna get over it." She looked at him again. "You know—young love, puppy love, you know how it is."

He nodded, but looked away, following his own smoke rings. She wanted his assent that their love had been no different, puppy love, it would have comforted her to have such an assent, it would have freed her to be his friend, but he couldn't give it to her. He grimaced. "I'm sorry to hear that."

She shrugged. "But that's not it. He's up to somethin'. I don't know what. We don't talk like we used to. I told him not to do nothin' dumb. We can't afford the trouble. He said not to worry—but I can't help it. I can't help worryin'."

"Of course not."

"So, anyway, what's the big news?"

He was disappointed. She spoke without excitement, just curiosity, even impatience. He took another sip of coffee, another puff of the cigarette, preparing himself for his moment, pasting on his smile. "Well, actually, it's a mixture of bad news and good. Maybe you heard—it must've been in the papers, even in Kendall Green."

Hazel knew she was being unfair, but resented the suggestion that Kendall Green was not New York. Jack hardly meant to be condescending, but he was, or so she felt—but she knew she resented the suggestion because she envied him. She wished she might have wintered herself instead in New York as the guest of a potentate. Her face flattened as she slowly nodded. "You mean about Mr. Cuddihy?"

Jack nodded.

"We heard—just what was in the papers."

"There's not much to be said. It was a heart attack, very sudden, very severe. They'd had dinner. He'd retired with Mrs. Cuddihy to the family room. He got up to stoke the fire and fell to the floor. He stopped moving in minutes, long before the doctor got there."

You would have thought from the way Jack shrugged off his response that he'd rehearsed his delivery, but Hazel stared coldly, her glacial ultramarine stare, though she knew Jack was not as callous as he appeared.

"I don't know how to say this, Jilly, 'cause on the one hand I'm sorry, Mr. Cuddihy was very good to me—but, Jilly, he left me fifty thousand dollars! He left me fifty thousand dollars in his will! Isn't that incredible?"

Jack's face was suddenly animated, green eyes sparkling as brightly as Eileen's, goldenbrown handlebar moustache spreading like a crescent across his face. He put out his cigarette in the saucer they'd been using for an ashtray as if he no longer needed it. He stared at Hazel so intently she had to look away. "What do you think, Jilly? Isn't that amazing? Isn't that wonderful?"

Hazel didn't understand the way she felt. Money meant power and Jack was suddenly out of reach. It wouldn't have mattered if she'd loved him, but she couldn't—and the wall of money between them complicating her feelings, made her angry. She drew heavily on her cigarette and spoke haltingly. "Oh, Jack, of course, that's wonderful. That's just swell."

Jack could read the anxiety in her eyes as easily as in a book, he imagined rightly that she was afraid of what was next in store for them, and his smile widened even further because he imagined that it made her more easily his. "I have plans, Jilly, big plans. I won't be trouping anymore. I want to set up in New York. I'm getting to know the ropes around there."

Hazel spoke coolly, without looking at him. "More coffee?"

"What? Oh, sure."

"I'll have to make some."

"Oh, don't bother then. It's all right."

"It's no bother. I'll make some."

"Jilly, you don't have to."

She stared at him, eyes brilliant and cold like diamonds. "Jack, I said it was all right. I'll make some."

"All right."

He said nothing while she made the coffee, suddenly less sure than ever. She spoke as if she'd read his mind. "You can talk. I can still hear you."

"I want to open my own store, Jilly: BROWN E'S CLOWN SUPPLIES." He held up his hands, open palms tracing a row of letters in the air. "Of course, I'll be selling clown accessories—but also circus accessories, guys, saddles, cages, anything that's needed, anything I can think of."

Hazel said nothing, no longer even pretended to smile. "I'm sure that'll be very nice for you, Jack, if that's what you want."

"It *is*. It's what I want, but I also want something else."

"What?"

Jack took a deep breath, fixing Jill with a more intrepid gaze, speaking more seriously than he had yet. "I want to share it with you, Jilly. I want you to come with me. I want you to marry me."

"What?"

"You heard me, Jilly. I'm serious. I think we could make it. All we needed was a chance and Mr. Cuddihy's given it to us."

Hazel found herself relaxing again. Money or no, she still had the power. She smiled again and her smile was genuine. She flicked ash from her cigarette, a note of triumph tinged her reply. "Jack, I'm touched, but you know that's impossible. You should know better'n to ask. D'you think it's money that makes the difference? D'you think that was the only problem between us?"

He noted the triumph and he noted an undertaste of bitterness. He was afraid he'd offended her, suggesting money made a difference. "I don't think you're saying the money wouldn't make a difference, Jilly, are you? That's not what you're saying, is it?"

"No, the money would make it easier—but that's not what I'm sayin'."

"Are you thinking about your ma?"

"How could I forget?"

Jack felt his moment slipping away. "Jilly, think a moment. Do you really think that's what your ma would want? Do you really think she'd want you to punish yourself for the rest of your life? Don't you think she'd want you to be happy?"

Hazel shook her head, confident again of herself. "That ain't it, Jack. It ain't a matter of what she'd want. It's too easy to say she'd want what I want. That ain't it. What I want is to do the right thing. For me that's all that's left. I got to do the right thing."

"Do you think it's the wrong thing for you to be happy?"

"To be happy with *you*, Jack, yes, I do—after the way things happened it'd be the wrong thing for me to be happy with you. I couldn't be happy with you, not really. I could only pretend."

Jack swept his hair back with his hand revealing his lined brow, his eyes lost their sparkle, his moustache drooped. "Jilly, what can I say to convince you? What can I do? I love you, Jilly. I'd do anything for you. We could help Dinty, we could help Spike. Think about it. Don't you think your ma would want that? We could all be happy—at least, happier."

She shook her head, keeping her confident smile. "I don't think so, Jack. Under the circumstances, I don't think we could be happier."

He clutched a clump of hair in his hand. "Jilly, you've got to stop blaming yourself. It wasn't your fault. It was no one's fault. Things happen. You've just got to carry on the best way you know."

"That's what I'm doin', Jack. That's jus' what I'm doin'." She was still smiling. She put out her cigarette, anticipating his departure.

He got up. If he'd stayed he might have cried. "Jilly, promise me you'll at least think about it. That's all I'm asking. Just say you'll think about it."

She continued to shake her head. "It ain't no use, Jack. I can't see it differently. It's too bad, but it's the way it is. I'll always *al*ways remember you as the sweetest man I'll ever know, the loveliest man, but that's as much as I can say. It wouldn't be fair to give you a hope that could never be."

He might have said more, but knew better. She meant to be tender, but not to encourage. At the door, after she'd given him back his coat, he kissed her goodbye and she kissed him back as fervently, limp in the circle of his arms, her own arms folded like wings against his chest. He kissed her face repeatedly, feverishly, holding her as if she might disappear. Her breath came in quick shallow gasps, she leaned into his arms, closing her eyes, holding up her face for more kisses. He kissed her face as if to memorize it with his lips. His voice was suddenly small. "At least say you'll call if you need help, if I can do anything for Dinty, for Spike, for anyone you want. At least give me that."

She cried, and blurred by tears his face appeared hazy, his eyes swam like fish. "Oh, Jack, my lovely Jack." She held his head in her hands, pushing back his hair, tracing his eyes, ears, nose, mouth, moustache, and jaw with her fingers. "My dearest, my love, my darling, I'm so sorry, I'm so sorry." She couldn't stop kissing him, but pushed him out of the door even as she kissed him.

She leaned against the door after she'd closed it, sliding to the floor, covering her face in her arms, and crying as if she couldn't stop. She couldn't have said what she minded more, losing Jack as a lover or as a friend.

FOUR   A SKIPPING PEBBLE

I cannot say enough about the hearts of troupers, big as Ferris wheels, whether defying gravity, soaring into the ether, or confronting mane and stripe and tusk, taking risks for all of us, twice daily during the season, not unlike priests wearing hairshirts for the sins of others. You watch to become for a moment bereft of breath, to share triumphs and thrills vicariously, drawn to feats for their daring as much as their beauty. You could argue that without daring there would be less beauty, pressure adding dimension to grace, pressure even exalting grace, and the pressure of an audience exceeding that of no audience—but you could also argue that the sound of one hand clapping provides more grace than the sound of hundreds of thousands, the act itself being of greater importance than the perception of the act, anonymity being more difficult to bear than glory, the pressure greater for unsung accomplishment, the conquest of vanity greater than the conquest of danger.

This is the dichotomy of East and West, whether to suffer the slings and arrows or take arms against a sea of troubles. Let me take my reader back for a moment to Paris, to the Cirque d'Hiver, to that wideeyed openmouthed crowd holding its breath when Eileen attempted the backward back on Andromache's back. Let me focus attention on that banker in the doublebreasted suit with the fleur-de-lis in his lapel, who smiled in the moment of Mary Eileen O'Donnell's misfortune while the audience gasped en masse, who was quoted in the *Journaux de Paris* saying, *Je ne me suis jamais senti aussi vivant que lorsque je la vis tomber*, "I was never so alive as when I saw her fall."

Later, the customarily sober banker insisted he was making a philosophical point—but let me also focus attention, before we congratulate ourselves too hastily on our own humanity, to others who smiled as well, among them the daintiest women with the rosiest skin (and was that a child? no more than ten years old? displaying a million milky teeth?), and let me suggest that there are as many who draw satisfaction from trouper defeats as inspiration from trouper triumphs, as many who damn as admire us for stepping where none have stepped before, daring to slip the surly bonds of earth. It's a risk attendant with attending circuses, confrontation with the macabre—also a risk on which circuses depend to attract audiences though few admit the fascination.

It is difficult to say how the confusion sorted itself in Dinty's head as he hobbled in boots too big from the Abbott to the Imperial, cigarette unsteady between his fingers. He had something to tell Jonas, but what it was, how the pieces fit, he couldn't say. His logic was more intuitive than rational. Gargantua loomed in the foreground of the images, the great gorilla with the twisted lip, the greatest attraction of the 1938 season. He chuckled, unable to tell whether the public liked to be fooled as Barnum had said, or whether the public was just plain stupid. Gargantua was

The Dying Elephant

vicious, but his sneer had been superimposed on his lip by acid and the public had never seemed to care about the difference.

Dinty was not an old man, turning just forty-eight that year, but his past had long loomed more heavily than his present. It was a fairytale tragedy, the story of his life, he lost his pa to the Great War, when he was seventeen, his ma shortly after, the same year, to grief. His pa, wanting more for his ma than the nomadic life of a trouper, had followed General Pershing to France. His ma, wanting only his pa, had lost weight, appeared to stop moving, to turn transparent, first to glassiness, finally to air when she got the news of his death amid news of American victories against the armies of the Kaiser.

The older son, Alf, had left the Griffin Bros. Circus years earlier (Dinty had been ten), sick of the family contortionist act, but returned like the prodigal, ready to mend his ways, too late for his pa and ma but determined to do well by his kid brother, Dinty—but his kid brother, he was glad to learn, had done well by himself, better than anyone might have imagined. He'd married Myrtle Hill, a waitress from Tunkhannock, Pennsylvania, and couldn't have been happier.

Myrtle was best remembered for her flamingo hair flaring into coral highlights in the sun complementing her rubious complexion, but Dinty remembered best her tenderness through his troubles, the spinal injury which had marked the end of his career even before it had begun when he'd been nineteen years old, their marriage barely two, Hazel just one. There would be no more contortions for Dinty, and Alf had been out of the game too long to take it up again, but vacancies beckoned for a bullman and roustabout. Dinty, showing aptitude with the bulls, had been elevated to trainer, and Myrtle had joined him in the ring, adding elements of grace and beauty which no one could have taught. Hazel had joined him in the ring later, and much later so had I. As roustabout, Alf did not find life much improved, but he was with family again, as Myrtle and Hazel proved to be—and me just two when he had been redlighted.

Dinty carried two mementos from his past religiously on his person, elevated to the status of talismans. The first was the last letter from his pa, received from the town of Wassy by the Marne, about 120 miles east south east of Paris, confessing their real name was Dooley.

David Warren Dooley married Pamela McGinness, the sister of James Anthony McGinness, who ran away from his sister's home when he was eleven to join the circus, and took the name of Bailey in honor of his mentor, the circus agent, Frederick Harrison Bailey. You guessed it, that made him James Anthony Bailey of Barnum & Bailey, the organizing genius behind Barnum's genius for showmanship. Dinty's pa was one of David Warren Dooley's nephews. The exact kinship doesn't matter, but he changed his name to Bailey imagining the name might avail him of Jim Anthony's luck if not his genius.

The second talisman was a photograph. Dinty had never been a large man, but in the photograph, standing with an arm around his wife, a hand on Hazel's shoulder, me in Ma's arms, he appeared almost a giant, at least five-seven. Yes, Ma had been a small woman, and Hazel and I just children in the picture, but the smile on his face was the smile of a big man, big in ways that couldn't be measured, bigvoiced, bighearted, bigsouled, every inch a bullman, never a contortionist.

That was the past he remembered, or preferred to remember, following which he preferred to remember nothing, and closer to the present it got worse. His mind skimmed his memory like a pebble skims a lake, skipping in tangents before it sinks.

He took a last puff of his cigarette before chucking it in the hallway mindless of the deep green rug, knocking on Jonas's door.

Janet opened the door as always. "What is it you're wanting now, Dinty?"

Clutching his hat in his hand, Dinty bounced on the balls of his feet to look over her shoulder for Jonas. "A moment, Mrs. Frank, just a moment with Mr. Frank."

"He hasn't got a moment, Dinty. You should be knowing that now, what with the new season upon us like a hurricane. You should be knowing that now."

Dinty grinned at the mention of the hurricane, his ingratiating grin. "That's very clever, Mrs. Frank. Like a hurricane, yes, e*xac*'ly, that's *jus'* how it is, a hurricane. That's very clever, Mrs. Frank."

Janet pursed her mouth, closing her eyes, shaking her head in exasperation. She could hear Jonas approaching from the bedroom.

The Dying Elephant

Dinty bounced on his feet, knowing from experience if he waited long enough Jonas would appear. "Just a moment, Mrs. Frank—just a moment is all I need."

She looked as if she might shut the door in his face, but she knew he'd knock again until it was reopened, she knew Jonas would insist on letting Dinty have his say. She took a deep breath, released a loud sigh, and turned from Dinty leaving him without an invitation, but leaving also the door open.

Dinty still grinned—and Jonas, sober of face and bleary of eye as always, beckoned him into the living-room. Still in his robe, showing an ascot of red chest hair, Jonas took his customary seat in the plush reclining chair, Dinty stood before him bouncing on the plush pile of the carpet, still clutching his hat. "What is it this time, Dinty? What is it you're wanting now?"

It wasn't quite noon, but the blinds had been drawn back and the room was full of light. Jonas looked out of the window as if there were no one else in the room, but Dinty's grin never wavered. "It's not about me that I'm here, Mr. Frank. It's about the circus, sir. It's about the circus that I'm here."

Jonas continued to ignore his presence, listening as if it were a penance, but he grunted, still looking out of the window, which was all Dinty needed to continue enthusiastically.

"Did you know, sir, about Gargantua? Did you know about his lip?"

Jonas spoke softly, as if he were being patient. "What ... about ... his lip?"

"It was acid, sir. They threw acid on his face when he was a baby. Did you know that, sir?"

Jonas nodded slowly. His tone remained modulated, but he turned his sad eyes once more on Dinty. "Everyone is knowing that, Dinty. *Ev*eryone. Not just troupers. *Ev*eryone. It's no secret."

Dinty held up a finger as if he'd made a point. "Yessir, *exac* 'ly, sir. Everyone knew, and did they care? Did they care that Gargantua was a fake? Did anyone care?"

Janet in the next room wondered at her husband's lassitude with Dinty. No one else rated the degree of patience he afforded Dinty, not even she. She knew about his guilt, but felt herself slowly gaining ground, particularly when Dinty behaved foolishly as he'd done attempting to rob the liquor store. If there was more foolish behavior it would hurt the circus and Jonas's primary responsibility was hardly to Dinty. She imagined Jonas's eyebrows rising patiently then and wondered what it would take for him to see he owed Dinty nothing.

Jonas could have argued that Gargantua was not a fake, but once an idea possessed Dinty it became an article of faith. Janet was glad to hear the first note of impatience in her husband's voice. "Dinty, will you get to the point?"

The impatience wasn't lost on Dinty, nor was Jonas's glare. He lost his grin. "Yessir, the point. The point is this. They threw acid in his face and everybody came to see him, everybody came to see him b'*cause* they threw acid in his face. He was the big attraction of the season."

Dinty stopped to measure his effect. Jonas continued glaring silently, and he continued hurriedly.

"If they came like that to see a gorilla with a lip like that, sir, think about it, how they would come to see an elephant."

Dinty stopped again, grinning again as if he'd discovered gold. There was a yowl from the bedroom. Jonas's eyes narrowed, his tone sharpened. "Dinty! Think, man! What is it you are saying?"

Before Dinty could speak, Janet was in the room. "You want to know what he's saying, do you? It's not plain what he's saying, is it? I'll tell you what he's saying, Jonas Frank, I will. He's saying he's going to ruin the circus, that's what he's saying, Jonas Frank. He's saying he's going to ruin everything you've worked for, he is, and if you can't hear it more plainly than that you're a sorrier man than I thought, Jonas Frank. You're best rid of him, you are. Can you not see that, not even now?"

Dinty stood with his mouth open. Jonas shook his head impatiently. "Is that what you're saying, Dinty? Is that what you're telling me?"

Janet screamed. "Who're you going to listen to, Jonas Frank? him or me? Who's it going to be?"

Jonas glanced at his wife. "Janet, I want to hear what he's saying. I want to understand him clearly." He turned again to Dinty. "What is it you're saying, man? Out with it. Speak plainly. What is it you're saying?"

Janet had shaken him and Jonas's insistence shook him further. His hat fell from his hands to his feet, his hands fell to his sides, twitching fingers peeking from outsize sleeves, voice trembling in sympathy. "Jus' what I said, sir. If they came like that to see a gorilla with a twisted lip, think how many would come to see an elephant."

Jonas stared penetratingly at Dinty. "With a twisted lip, I suppose, you'll be meaning?"

Dinty brightened to be finally understood. "Yessir, e*xac'*ly my meanin'."

"And, Dinty, where do you propose we get such an elephant? with a twisted lip?"

Dinty shrugged. "We make one, sir. We *make* one. It wouldn't harm him, not in the long run, and we'd have the greatest freak in the world, the freak of the century. Mr. Barnum was always doin' things like that."

Janet yowled again, rolling her eyes, raising her arms to heaven.

Jonas spoke as if he were weighing possibilities. "Has it occurred to you, Dinty, that an elephant's mouth is not like a gorilla's. An elephant's mouth is practically invisible, you see. His face has no mouth, you see. He has just half a face—the top half, so to speak. What would be the point of damaging the half of his face that no one could see?"

Janet stared at Jonas as if he were growing horns, but he ignored her. The pebble of Dinty's mind began to skip, his brow to fill with wrinkles. "I suppose, sir, it doesn' have to be his mouth. His trunk, his ears, his tail, anythin' would do."

Jonas nodded, his eyes had resumed their sleepy look, and Dinty imagined he'd convinced him, or at least got him thinking. Jonas's voice was slow and soft again as before. "I think I understand you finally, Dinty, and I disagree. I think you should pick up your hat and leave."

Dinty's eyes, blinking rapidly, turned to the floor. He stooped to pick up his hat. "Yessir." He turned to go, but Jonas stopped him.

"Not so fast, Dinty. I mean, I think you should leave the circus. Do you get my meaning?"

Dinty's eyes, still blinking, stayed on the floor. "Leave the circus, sir?"

"That's right."

He pulled his hat low on his head and thrust his hands turned to fists into the pockets of his coat. "But why, sir, Mr. Frank? Why?"

"I couldn't explain it to you, Dinty. If I tried for a hundred years I couldn't explain it to you. I'll see to it that you receive a handsome severance, but I think you should leave."

Dinty screwed his face as if he were considering an offer. "But where would I go, sir, Mr. Frank? What would I do? This is my home. The circus is my home. I know nothin' else."

"That's your concern, Dinty, not mine. I think you should leave in two weeks—by which I mean you should remove your belongings from the quarters. Do you follow me?"

Dinty nodded, heading for the door, turning back. "What about Hazel, sir? and Spike and Siri?"

"Siri stays with me. The rest are your family, Dinty. I think they should stay with you."

Dinty nodded again as if he'd concluded a deal. "Yessir. Thank you, sir." At the door, he turned again. "What about Hero?"

"Hero stays. He belongs to me."

Dinty nodded. "Yessir." The pebble of his mind skipped again. He was being redlighted like Alf. Jonas was redlighting him just like he had Alf. His voice trembled. "Mr. Frank, sir, you should look after your elephants. Elephants can come to harm."

Janet stood smiling, arms crossed. Jonas remained urbane. "What do you mean by that, Dinty?"

Dinty was thinking about the 1941 season when six of Ringling's forty-seven elephants had become violently ill and died in a day. Five more had died the following week. They had eaten grass sprayed with weed killer and died of arsenic poisoning. "I mean, sir, elephants can die easily. You got to look after them. They're expensive animals."

Janet spoke, bubbling with rage. "Is it threats you're resorting to now, Dinty? Is that what you're reduced to?"

Jonas narrowed his eyes again. "Are you threatening me, man, Dinty? Is that what you're doing?"

Dinty froze. He hadn't meant to say that, hadn't meant to say that at all, but he'd said it. He'd felt bullied, and he'd said it, and he said it again. "No, sir, I'm just tellin' you what's happened in the past. Elephants've died from arsenic. It's happened."

Jonas took a deep breath. "I think you should leave immediately, after all, Dinty. I see no need of you in the quarters at all after this—and under the circumstances I do not think a severance would be appropriate after all. Do you follow me, Dinty?"

Dinty nodded, appearing again to consider what he'd said. "Yessir. I foller you." He fixed Jonas with accusing eyes. "I'm to be redlighted, just like Alf. Yessir—oh, yessir, I foller you."

He gave a little bow, a nod to Janet, turned on his heel, raised the brim of his hat, and left with more dignity than he might have imagined possible himself. Jonas and Janet looked at each other, bewildered.

FIVE   THE SHIMMY SHIM SHEBANGO

Dinty's pa had attempted in his letter to trace their roots to James Anthony Bailey, but Hazel would have said that people who bragged about their ancestry were like potatoes, the best part was underground. She cared less about her roots than her branches: she had a life to live, she had work to do.

She guided Hero out of his stall to the center of the stable, commanded him to lift her in his trunk, scrambled to his head, stood on his back, and swayed to the strains of "The Shimmy-Shim Shebango" from the Jonas Frank Brass Band two halls away, tapping her toes, undulating limbs, contorting her body, providing an alphabet of forms with arms, legs, torso, and head. She wore blue jeans, white shirttails hanging over, slippers, and when she stretched, when she turned on her hands, when she contorted, either in a backbend or forward, her shirt slipped upward revealing a white belly, white back, white sides. The song was her current favorite, the band played it slowly, and she whispered the words as she danced:

> Everybody's doing it, shimmy shimmy shim-shim-shim
> Doves are bill-and-cooing it, wallabies are wooing it
> Woodpeckers tattooing it, the shimmy-shim shebango.

The song was also a favorite with the crowds. Eileen had left a hole in the equestrian act and the troupe was hardpressed to polish the rest of its performance to a brilliant shine: the liberty act, so called because the horses cantered around the ring without riders, apparently without cues, moving in intricate patterns, at liberty; and the *haute ecole*, the high school act, in which horses walked sideways and backward, galloped backward, galloped on three legs, and galloped in place, minuetted, waltzed, foxtrotted, and sambad, apparently to the music, but Hazel knew, as all troupers know, the music followed the horses, not the horses the music.

> Everybody's doing it, shimmy shimmy shim-shim-shim
> Produce are producing it, moose are not vamoosing it
> Geese of course are goosing it, the shimmy-shim shebango.

John Ringling North had commissioned a ballet for elephants in 1944 from Balanchine, who had commissioned the music from Stravinsky, who had obliged with a jaunty march concluding with a parody of the Marche Militaire. Hazel had trained Hero to two-step to the music. Dancing elephants are not as incongruous as might be supposed. Elephants have toebones but no heelbones, their heels are fibrous, padded with fatty tissue, providing bounce to each step. You might say their skeletons tiptoe like antelopes and ballerinas, born to dance; and you might say their heels, if not the entire elephant, were made for dancing. Ringling knew what he was doing: the sight of elephants nodding their heads and swaying their behinds, swinging their trunks and tails, had audiences applauding like trained seals.

> Everybody's doing it, shimmy shimmy shim-shim-shim
> Victorians are undoing it, and voyeurs are just viewing it
> And cows of course are mooing it, the shimmy-shim shebango.

Hazel had heard that the weight on an elephant's foot was spread through the tissue of its heel so that the stiletto heel of a woman's shoe carried as much weight proportionately—and these dancing feet also made puddings of heads. Death by elephant was once a form of capital punishment and death by white elephant divine punishment: criminal head set on its ear on the executioner's block, elephant foot on the criminal head, easy as stepping on a cockroach, putting out a cigarette with a gaily twisting toe.

> Everybody's doing it, shimmy shimmy shim-shim-shim
> Crocodiles use their wiles, and while they're boo-hoo-hooing it,
> They're also crocodoing it, the shimmy-shim shebango.

They still had almost thirty minutes to wait, but Hazel liked her perch on Hero's back, it changed her perspective, rarefied her atmosphere, raised her from cares as if she were on holiday; if putting her head in the mouth of the elephant were her penance, dancing on its back was her reward, one she could justify more easily than the comfort Jack offered.

> Everybody's doing it
> Cock-a-doodle dooing it
> Yankee doodle dooing it
> Shimmy shimmy shim.

A brief movement caught her attention. She guessed it was Elbo, and confirmed her suspicion peering from the corner of her eye: Elbo crouched in the stall behind. She was momentarily surprised, not that he was watching, but that she wasn't alone. She'd kicked a foot in the air imagining Yankee Doodle doing it with Cock-a-Doodle and the momentary surprise had dislodged her slipper. She grinned as the slipper fell and sang more deeply, developing huskiness, shimmying her shoulders, shimmying her hips.

> Everybody's doing it, shimmy shimmy shim-shim-shim
> Monkeys leer, but they're not monks, and deer fear, but they're not nuns
> And elephants can use their trunks, the shimmy-shim shebango.

She wondered where Siri was, but didn't care. An opportunity had presented itself, and the second slipper described a more graceful arc to the ground than the first as she sang about monks and nuns. She turned slowly in Elbo's direction, appearing oblivious to his presence, and began unbuttoning her shirt, still shimmying her shoulders.

> Everybody's doing it, shimmy shimmy shim-shim-shim
> Lambs come when rams use their rams to ram and bruise their ewes
> Doing it to lose their blues, the shimmy-shim shebango.

She couldn't have said what she expected, but the responsibility she felt toward Siri was getting increasingly onerous and her responsibilities to her family made a cell of her world. She wanted to be the ewe rammed and bruised by her ram.

> Everybody's doing it, shimmy shimmy shim-shim-shim
> Shrewd shrews are doing it and kangaroos who never rue
> Are jubilantly doing it, the shimmy-shim shebango.

Unbuttoning the last button, she pulled back her shirt, thrust out her chest, exhibiting a black strapless wired bra.

> Everybody's doing it, shimmy shimmy shim-shim-shim
> Mules are fools for doing it and cocks for cockatooing it
> But donkeys too are doing it, the shimmy-shim shebango.

She held her shirt open, framing her torso, slowly wriggling out her shoulders, rubbing her back with the shirt as if with a towel, before taking it off, swinging it in her hand, and flinging it at the foolish mules.

> Everybody's doing it
> Cock-a-doodle dooing it
> Yankee doodle dooing it
> Shimmy shimmy shim

Elbo stood up, staring openly, no longer in control of his actions, no longer even looking at Hazel. He lurched forward, staggered in a circle before falling, first to his knees, then slumping forward on his head, shoulders, and arms, settling finally on his side beside Hero's feet.

Hazel stared. She knew little about Elbo, she knew he came from Bronzeville where he'd lived with his mama, she knew he had a brother in Chicago, a twin in Cleveland, but nothing else, nothing about his jail term, certainly nothing about the fibrillation of his heart to which he was now succumbing—but she had just overcome her amazement, just gathered her wits to jump down beside Elbo, when Hero trembled beneath her, lurching back and forth before slumping to his knees, aping Elbo's movements before crushing him underneath.

Hazel lurched herself, balancing on the earthquake of Hero's back, eyes wide with horror. Too dumbfounded to jump she was thrown from Hero's back and landed on her side. Stunned by her fall she forced herself to her feet, but stunned by what she had seen, by what she continued to see, Elbo's clodhoppered feet splayed like a fan, a pool of blood spreading around them like a growing shadow, she was suddenly frozen. Comprehension was long in coming, but realization began to seep, and blame to descend like a monsoon. She'd been caught as before in the machinery of the gods—and, as unknowingly and irrevocably as before, *she* had set the machinery in motion, *she* had pulled the lynchpin sending bits and pieces hurtling into a milky way of madness, losing Elbo and Hero as she had years before lost her ma.

The brass band receded. In its place, in the otherwise silent stable, she heard a whimper, a long spectral moan, as Dinty entered the stall, fell to his knees, and curled like a grub on the ground, knees drawn to his face, arms around his knees. From the way he shook you would have said he had a fever. Her mouth opened to ask what he was doing, but screams issued instead as if to drown the engine of the world.

SIX   ELEPHANT MEMORIES

On the last of his seven voyages Sinbad interacted with elephants, but few remember the story. Legends have been supplanted by the harder currency of facts—a shame because laws, facts, statistics, the wisdom of accountants and economists, move in a sine curve, change with the weather, the political climate, their currency varying with their context,

The Elephant Graveyard

but myths, legends, stories, novels, tales, fables, epics of ages, factual lies if you wish, have survived centuries, providing the primal hum of the machinery of man, eternally true, eternally relevant, eternally profound. Wall Street surrenders to the weather, gods of money to gods of the earth. The earth endures us, not we it, but gazing through the wrong end of the telescope we know no better. We share the same disease, myopia, but let me make my point, let me recap the story.

Stranded on an island by pirates, Sinbad was captured by the island king. Commanded to shoot elephants from a tree with a bow and arrow for their tusks, he killed an elephant daily for two months. The king was pleased because he'd lost too many slaves to the elephants in his hunger for ivory. Finally, the elephants surrounded the tree, the largest plucked Sinbad from his perch, slung him on his back, and deposited him in a valley from which the herd departed. Regaining his senses, Sinbad found himself amid skeletons, hills of bones tall as pillars, arches of tusks like the ruins of gothic cathedrals: the fabulous graveyard! Returning to the king, he related his adventure. The wisdom of the elephants was recognized: with ivory readily available there was no need for killing, not of slaves, not of elephants.

I ask you now, does it matter that the story is fiction? that Sinbad may never have existed? that having existed he may never have voyaged? that having voyaged he may never have adventured? that having adventured he may never have found the fabled graveyard? that no such graveyard exists? that no animal could be so wise? no elephant Solomon? and does it not matter instead that the heart of the fable is truer than the fact? that when you give of your plenty you save yourself? that accountants and economists and politicians and historians would do well to keep such fiction in mind? but it is no fiction, no myth, no legend, no lie, that elephants mourn their dead. Elephants explore carcasses and skeletons of their dead with their trunks, they roll the bones with their feet to identify the bodies, sometimes even burying the bones. A dead animal's siblings will often stay awhile with its remains before following the herd.

The distress call of a dying elephant is a rumble. We may recognize some of an elephant's vocalizations, its trumpet certainly, like the triple tone cry of a rooster (tonic, dominant, tonic), maybe also its snort, bark, roar, and growl—but not its rumble. Not possessing subsonic audition, the ability to hear infrasound (the sound of shifting tectonic plates), which elephants share with the larger whales, we cannot hear the rumble; but the rumble (which penetrates walls, carries three to four miles, and is used by cows in estrus to summon bulls) has been recorded and heard when played back at higher freqencies, again a triple tone performance, rising and falling.

Ironically, we cannot hear the rumble, but we can see it in the bridge of the elephant's proboscis, in a vibration on the elephant's temple, the consequence of air passing through nasal passages beneath. The vibrations were visible on Hero's dusky brow, but Hazel missed them among his convulsions, flailing trunk, and the black blood pouring from his throat, as she hopped, skipped, and jumped out of the way of his sad collapse to the ground, the final movements of this large and noble animal.

The mammoth memory of the elephant is no less a myth, but it is sensory more than sentient: touch, taste, sight, smell, sound, burnt child fears the fire, that sort of thing, built into the skin (they have a great deal of skin) more than the brain, Bergsonian, an impending death precipitating the memory of other deaths, the ghost of a smell precipitating the smell of ancient ghosts, one memory precipitating others like a row of dominoes.

We've come this far, let us take a bold step farther, presume to step into the vault of Hero's memory. Down by the riverside would be a good place to start, the watering hole, where the elephants gather for a good time, where they own whatever ground they please. Wild goats of the Nilgiris, bands of spotted deer, all retreat, herds of gaur (the pumped bison of the Indian southwest), even the solitary tiger—and if you look closely you will see the crocodiles receding in the water. The sun is bright, but Hero is so small, four feet to the shoulder with a two-foot trunk, that you'd think he was a tapir, especially when he feeds himself and the hose of his trunk folds in two reaching into his mouth—but there are no tapirs in India.

There is a pudding of shit before Hero, pate for a pachyderm, but he appears to be having difficulty getting it into his mouth. He hasn't mastered the trick yet, packing it with his foot and trunk before conveying it to his mouth. His coordination's off, the packing's too brittle, or he drops his morsel midway to his mouth. Every mouthful he misses brings his mouth, eager with anticipation, an inch or two closer to his pate, until finally he dives Dumbolike, mouthfirst, ears back, tail in the air, into his dinner, gorging his mouth with pudding, the corners of his mouth curling upward.

Around him the family goes about its business: an aunt, a more skilled diner, flips bananas with the finger of her trunk from the ground into her mouth; another aunt balls the tip of her trunk into a fist and rubs her eyes; an uncle, a tusker, drapes his trunk over his tusks to pick his proboscis, inserting the tusk inches into one nostril, then the other; cousins stand in a circle, like stonehenge animated, swinging trunks in rhythm like jump ropes, knees wrinkled like baggy pants, behinds sagging like badly fitted hosiery; lovers caress one another's backs with their trunks; young bulls place their trunks on one another's heads, daring them to be displaced, tusks clashing like giant castanets, testing one another.

In the water, trunks break the surface like snorkels, periscopes, Loch Ness monsters in miniature, and when the trunks submerge tiny spouts of water fountain in their place like the breath of baby whales. They squirt one another, dunk one another, play tricks on one another, folding the finger at the tip of the trunk so water gushes unexpectedly from two sides.

A second family appears in the distance and the elephants rush, trumpeting, urinating, defecating, joyously toward one another, reaching to touch one another's mouths, faces, genitals, rubbing heads, rubbing bodies, clacking tusks.

Aunts greatly outnumber uncles, herds being matriarchal. The basic unit is mother and child, mother and daughter often together more than forty-five years, young bulls leaving the herd in bands of two and three and four, sometimes alone, returning when in musth, summoned by the rumbling of cows. A core group numbers fewer than ten, but families of more than fifty often converge and clans of more than a hundred. You will see elephants defer to the largest cow, the matriarch, also the oldest member of the family since elephants are entropic, as are their tusks, though Indian cows have none, and neither do some Indian bulls, called makhnas; but makhnas are not necessarily weaker than tuskers.

The mad rush gives way to a seemlier deportment, an orderly trek through deep brush, under a softer sun. The compound family, more than twenty elephants, moves to a new feeding ground, when downwind from them an Englishman in khaki shorts and sola topi fires an Enfield rifle in the air, the signal for a few hundred villagers, even a thousand or two, to flood the jungle with an umbrella of sound, clattering pots, clapping hands, sticks beating hollow trees, screeches and screams, whoops and hollers and halloos. The elephants panic, and as they rush the path narrows into a bottleneck, but they thrust and squeeze through. Hero's mother stumbles crying to her knees, something is wrong with her leg, but she gets to her feet, hobbles forward, shrill with pain, sweeping Hero ahead with her trunk like a broom. A brushfire erupts behind them, sealing off their rear exit.

The vanguard of the herd spills into a clearing, fans out, slows down. The center continues to gush through the bottleneck, Hero and his mother in the rear. The clearing is so large it is not discovered until too late to be a keddah, enclosed by flanged fences. Villagers swing a gate into the bottleneck and wedge the gate with bars. When the first bull recognizes his imprisonment he lowers his head and charges the fortress, others follow his lead, but the walls hold. Gradually, the herd quietens. Some begin to feed.

Five of the younger elephants are selected, but not calves and their mothers. Koonkies appear (tame elephants with mahouts on their shoulders) to take their places, fore and aft of each chosen elephant, one at a time, roping them, leading them out of the keddah into training cages, after which the remaining elephants are set at liberty—except Hero's mother whose leg is broken. She is shot, and Hero, the last, the smallest, the most easily taken of the selected elephants, the only calf, is led away trembling.

Next, there are discrete scenes, shorter scenes, elephants learning commands (sit, stand, push, pull, stop, go, give the mahout a leg up), hauling logs, bathing with individual mahouts, being fed, bonding, among them Hero, taken to a temple, where he meets Siri, newly orphaned himself, who sings to him for hours, sings to him for days, hugs, caresses, bathes, feeds him, becomes his mahout, exhibits him at the elephant fair, where the scout from the Griffin Bros. circus finds them. The rest we know, the long journey from Kerala to Ohio, to the Griffin Bros. Circus, to the Frank Bros., to pyramid acts with other elephants, dance acts, the solo act with Hazel in his mouth, oiled and billed the blackest elephant in the world—to the winter quarters in Kendall Green where the antics descended to the worst kind of circus.

The heap of Hero lying on his side, an unruly mountain of wrinkles and dust, sparked an image I could not resist. Elbo's remains had been cleared away, but Hero's would take more preparation. The fluids had been drained from the stable, but the ground remained slimy. Despite the wintry air, despite fans and fragrances, the stench suffocated like a blanket of filth, but I didn't care. I brought a prop, used during one of the clown acts, a backdrop of a jungle landscape, verdant and twisted with vines, and set it behind Hero's carcass so that cropped strategically a photograph would reveal Hero lying in a jungle. I attired myself in hunting togs, borrowed by Paddy the propman from the wardrobe, sola topi, khaki shirt and shorts, jungle boots, like a burra sahib, as I'd seen Frank Buck in pictures. I'd also borrowed a rifle, an unloaded Winchester, for verisimilitude, and I was posing for Monks the dogboy who held Brown E's Brownie in his hand.

Seated on Hero's shoulder before the jungle backdrop, I passed easily for a big game hunter, Hero's master in Hero's hunting grounds—but before Monks could locate me in his viewfinder Siri burst into the room. "You, Spike, get off at once! You have got no shame? Off, I say, get off at once!"

I gestured to Monks to hurry the picture, but he was too late. Siri bound onto Hero's shoulder, knocked off my topi, and grabbed the Winchester. I swung Siri at the end of the barrel lifting him off his feet (he was light as a monkey), but couldn't throw him without releasing the rifle myself. "Let go, Siri, you damn fool! Let go!"

Paddy appeared, apparently from nowhere, to grab Siri from behind, and it took both of us, Paddy pulling Siri by his wrists, me tugging the Winchester, to get him to release the rifle. Paddy pulled Siri off Hero and held him back by his wrists, but with difficulty, which surprised him: Siri was so skinny a hat would have weighed him down.

I picked up my topi, straightened my clothes, took my seat on Hero's shoulder again, and nodded to Monks to take the picture again, but before he could focus Siri thrust a bony elbow into Paddy's gut and bulldozed into me again, knocking my topi off again, knocking me off Hero again, and again grabbing the rifle.

"You black fuckin' bastard!" Paddy launched himself at Siri, pulling him from me, lifting him off his feet, throwing him to the ground, falling on him, and sitting on him to keep him down.

"Oooff! Spike, what are you doing? What are you doing? You don't know what you are doing?" He twisted under Paddy like a snake, but he'd lost his advantage. "Let me go, Paddy! You bastard, you bloody bastard, Paddy! Let me *go*, I say!"

Paddy slapped his face. "Shaddap, you! Stupid black nigger bastard!"

I got up again, picked up my topi yet again, mounted Hero's shoulder yet again, sat down yet again, and gestured to Monks yet again, who was finally able to take a picture, and another with me standing in front of Hero, another with my foot astride Hero's, another with me leaning on Hero's tusk, and so on until Monks finished the roll.

I got off Hero and nodded to Paddy. "Let him go."

Siri got up shaking. "You will pay, Spike! You think because Hero is dead you can do what you want, but his ghost will get you! He will not forget! Elephants never forget! He will get you!"

I wagged my hands in mockery. "Wooooooh! I'm scared. I'm really scared. I'm so scared I'm shakin'. Wooo-wooo-woooh!"

Siri turned, rushed to Hero, jumped on his belly, and sprawled on his shoulder, sobbing, reverting to his native Malayalam as he did in difficult moments. "Ayoo ennte sahodharan, ayoo ennte sahodharan," oh, my brother, oh, my brother.

I TREATED SIRI SHAMEFULLY, but he seemed never to mind, revering me instead for the circumstance of my birth, believing I was among the anointed. In 1932, the fallout from the Crash of '29 continued to blanket the country in an everwidening shadow. The Griffin Bros. Circus was finishing the season with two elephants (down from six), Dinty was head bullman, Myrtle Bailey eight months pregnant, and Siri asleep on Hero's back as always—when the elephant had sneezed. Siri had been tapped awake by Hero's trunk which had bobbed momentarily before arrowing rigidly into the air, filling the night with a trumpet blast, inducing Myrtle Bailey's labor and my premature birth, a runt of a babe at three pounds and thirteen ounces.

Siri had recalled the legend of Maya Devi, mother of Sakyamuni, the historical Buddha, Gautama Siddhartha, who dreamed one summer night that she had been transported to a palace nestled within the icy spires of the Himalayas where she had been approached by an elephant as white as the clouds of snow around them with a lotus in its trunk; and subsequently, and consequently, given birth painlessly on awakening to birdsong in a garden.

My mother's had been a similarly painless delivery; Siri had attributed her later accident, unfortunately aided by Hero, to the will of Shiva the Destroyer, one of the three pillars in the mighty Hindu triumvirate complemented by Brahma the Creator and Vishnu the Preserver. The elephant gave, the elephant took. Siri didn't bother to distinguish between Buddhist legend and Hindu any more than he bothered to distinguish between the Christian virgin impregnated by the dove of the holy spirit and the Buddhist by the trunk of a white elephant. Gods were many, with many names, but God there was but one.

I was no Buddha, but an elephant had no less catalyzed my birth, a catalysis Siri did not take lightly. Like everyone else, he treated me deferentially because, like everyone else, he knew everything and said nothing to me about my motherlessness. Still, I had treated him shamefully and the pictures were hardly the triumph I had envisioned. It showed most clearly in my eyes. Dried to glass by murder, they might have been gathering dust in the hall of a master taxidermist. They might as well have been dead. The eyes of a murderer are the eyes of the dead. The tragedy in Toledo hammered the first nail in my coffin, the photographs with Hero hammered the rest. My dreams had progressed from Brown E's wagging sausage finger in my face to captures by cannibals who tenderized me with hammers before immersing me alive and stirring me in caldrons bubbling with blood and flavored with bones. The greater the suffering, so said the cannibals, the more succulent the flesh. The killer was reaping what he'd sown, sauteed and skewered and spun on a spit as he deserved, his telltale heart telling tales in dreams and metaphors soon to be told in the light of day.

I dozed by day, unable to sleep by night, and imagined myself haunted by ghosts the rest of my life. Elbo bore an uncanny resemblance to the boy in Toledo (his twin, Prize, as I was to learn later), but recognized me no more than he did the Sultan of Zanzibar, and I was convinced he had died *twice!* I took Siri's malediction to heart: *His ghost will get you! He will not forget! Elephants never forget! He will get you!*

SEVEN   THE FIRST SON

For its 1934 season, the Century of Progress in Chicago set aside an island in Lake Michigan for a midway to be reached by bridges from the mainland. Frank Buck was asked to build a replica of his jungle camps to draw customers to the midway. He was allotted two acres on which he built buildings and animal sheds with materials brought from Malaya: bamboo, rattan, hardwood logs. He even had his Number-One and Number-Two boys, Ali and Ahmed, on the island, sleeping, cooking, and bathing. They might as well have been in Malaya, surrounded as they were by honeybears and gibbons. Buck said the camp was so genuine it made him homesick—until the music of the merry-go-round sounded and he was returned to the shores of Lake Michigan from the Straits of Malacca.

Jay Jordan Lumsden, scion of the drugstore magnate, Gordon Humphrey Lumsden, had been inspired to build a similar camp a hundred miles north of Mangalore in the South Indian state of Mysore, north of Siri's home state, Kerala. He had too much respect to encroach on Buck's territory (primarily Malaya, but also Calcutta when he contracted for Indian animals), and built his own reputation emulating Buck's work. Buck's expeditions took months during which he collected animals in a central camp. Lumsden followed Buck's formula, constructing his camp by a river at an altitude too high for flooding by the rains, and as Buck grew older and his interests diverged to books and movies and lectures and his private zoo in Amityville, Long Island, Lumsden's reputation grew as the new Frank Bucker, the new Bring-'em-Back-Aliver.

I wasn't thinking clearly after Eileen's death, but I'd long wanted to leave the circus, and with Hero's death and our expulsion from the circus the time had come. Starting a new life, I imagined I would leave my nightmares behind. Lumsden had sailed for Bombay amid fanfare three months earlier with contracts for animals for zoological societies and circuses that could have filled a book, and I was sure he would hire me if I made my way to his camp. I didn't want wages, just a chance to prove myself. My circus experience would stand me in good stead, but I didn't want to approach him except in person to make assurance double sure (as Brown E might have said). Besides, I'd saved almost five hundred dollars for my life with Eileen which would cover expenses until I reached his camp.

I was never without Prem Gupta's card. I had developed a fascination with the talisman out of proportion to its significance, ascribing to it mythical powers as if it were a beacon heralding the future. I was a kid who felt he had lost everything, I needed magic in my life, I wanted to make Frank Buck's India my own, I wanted to make the myth my reality.

I'd mentioned my plan to no one but Hazel, to work as a steward on *The Gardenia*, bound for Bombay from New York via London, Marseilles, Suez, and Aden, hoping she would encourage me, but her face had gone blank instead, her eyes had glazed. "Are you sure this is the right time?"

I was sorry I'd mentioned it, but the alternative had been to disappear saying nothing and Hazel didn't deserve that. "Sure, I'm sure. I've saved some dough. It's what I want. It's what I've wanted a long time. And now with all that's happened it seems the perfect time."

"What about Pa?"

"What about him?"

"He's in jail. You can't cut out on him now."

"But I *ain't* cuttin' out on him. I can't help him—but even if I could I don't see why I should. I don't give a damn, Haze. I don't care what happens to Pa. He's a bum."

"Spike!"

"It's the truth, Haze! There's nothin' you can do for him either. You got to help yourself. Can't you see how it is?"

We'd been in the room at the Abbott, it had been night, she'd slapped me, I'd said nothing, not even gasped, not even moved my hand to my reddening cheek. She'd flushed herself for slapping me, redder than my cheek, straightening her back, broadening her shoulders, showing no sign of apology despite what she said. "I'm sorry, Spike, but you don't know what he's been through."

A child would have recognized the irony in my answer. "Of course not—and I'm never gonna. It's always gonna be the same old story. I don't know, and you're not gonna tell me. No one's gonna tell me. No one gives a damn about me, not you, not Pa, and I'm damned if I can see why I should give a damn about anyone myself."

Hazel had deflated, as always when I challenged her, face shutting up like always—but I meant what I'd said: I didn't give a damn. She had shrugged. "Okay, then, if that's how you feel, do what you got to do. You're right. I don't give a damn about you if you don't give a damn about your Pa in a cell. Do what you got to do."

Her candor surprised me, hurt me, but also vindicated me. There was nothing for me in Kendall Green, nothing with the circus, nothing with Pa, nothing even with Hazel. I knew she didn't mean it, I knew events had sapped her resilience, I knew she cared—but she was too tired to show it, she'd been tired too long, and I carried less of the baggage of life than anyone she knew. I should have been more supportive. Yes, Eileen was dead, and she'd meant a lot to me, but I could hardly blame myself for what had happened to her as she blamed herself for what had happened to Elbo and to our ma, whatever it might have been. It was more important for her to make whatever amends were possible to Elbo's family, which was why she had chosen to seek out the Blues of Bronzeville. She knew no more than that he was from the neighborhood, but she hoped someone would direct her to his home.

Unfortunately, it was a cold Sunday afternoon, the streets were mostly empty, and the first three people she asked couldn't tell her where the Blues lived. She was hardly accustomed to luxury, but the disrepair of the neighborhood surprised her: cracked streets, shattered glass, rickety houses, a dinginess she couldn't define, sinking her deeper into her well of depression.

It had not occurred to her that she was the only white person on the street, the only white person in the neighborhood, already an object of curiosity among the residents who had seen her on the streets from their windows. Her initial plan was to check the names on every mailbox in Bronzeville, but some had no names, just numbers, so she asked whomever she met if they knew the Blues, sure that someone would be able to direct her once she was in the vicinity.

Four hours later she had crisscrossed the neighborhood six times, run through all her cigarettes, and found herself once more on Cumberland Avenue. She imagined she would have more luck at the post office, but she'd come too far to quit. She wondered if the Blues were being hidden from her for her sin. There was no one on the street, it was getting colder, windows were turning yellow with electricity.

Two faces peered from a window. She'd been aware of peering faces all afternoon, ignoring them for faces on the street, but the afternoon was long dead and the evening getting short. She walked to the house, through the unlatched gate, and rapped sharply on the front door. The porch creaked under her feet, joists slanted left to right, someone came to the door. "Yuss?"

She repeated the litany she'd recited all day. "I'm sorry to bother you, but I'm lookin' for the Blues family, Elbo Blue's family. D'you know 'em?"

"The who you say now?"

"Elbo Blue. He used to live here."

The door opened on a chain. A woman peered out. She wore a robe, her hair in curlers. She looked carefully at Hazel. "Who you?"

"I'm Hazel Bailey. I'm with the Frank Bros. Circus. I'm lookin' for Elbo Blue's family. Did you know him?"

She was no longer with the circus, but had derived too much of her identity and authority too long from the circus to know what it meant to be without. The woman looked her up and down carefully again, a second woman's head bobbed behind her in the narrow crack of the open door held close by the chain. Hazel could see she was younger, her hair done in corn rows. "The circus, you say?"

"The Frank Bros. Circus. Our winter quarters're on the south side."

The second woman nodded. "That so, that so. I seen 'em there."

The Dying Elephant

The first woman never stopped her appraisal, the second never stopped bobbing for a better look. After the longest scrutiny, the first spoke again. "You outta luck. Elbo don't live here no more. He been gone mebbe two months now, mebbe three."

The second woman bobbed forward. "Mebbe fo'."

Hazel's weariness vanished, she almost jumped. "I ain't lookin' for Elbo. I'm lookin' for his family. D'you know where they are?"

The first woman spoke. "You got news about Elbo?"

"Yeah."

"What news?"

"It's personal. I think I should tell his ma first."

The second woman spoke. "Ol' Maudine don't want no news about Elbo, that fo' sho'. She jus' 'bout give up on him."

"Naw, she ain't—not after what happen to Prize."

"Naw, she don't care—not now she got the Law-Yer visitin'."

"Sho', she do. He still her baby."

"Do you know where I can find her?"

"Sho' do."

Hazel waited, but the woman appeared to be sizing her up again. She asked again, flooding her plea with urgency. "Can you tell me, please? It's important."

The woman gave Hazel a final sweeping look. "Sho'. They jus' down the block, on 34 Cumberland. You cain't miss 'em."

"34 Cumberland!" Hazel knew the address, she had passed it four times. She'd noted it for the food in the window: a pie, a plate of collard greens, another of cornbread. As evening had spread over the neighborhood and tattered blinds were drawn, 34 Cumberland had appeared the more conspicuous for its blinds left undrawn, framing the food in the window. She'd noted also the maroon Ford Mercury parked outside, the only car on the block. She smiled. "Thanks. I know the place. Thanks."

"You welcome." The door shut.

Hazel walked down the block to 34 Cumberland in triumph, but rang the bell with trepidation. She didn't know what to expect, how much to say. The bell didn't sound and she rang again. When it still didn't sound, she knocked hesitantly, lightly, three times.

She was aware of moving shadows from the brightly lit room falling outside the window. A board creaked behind the door. "Yuss?"

"Is this the Blues residence?"

"Who wants to know?"

The voice was authoritative. Hazel imagined an implacable face. "I'm Hazel Bailey, with the Frank Bros. Circus. I got news about your son."

"You with who? the circus?"

"The Frank Bros. Circus. I got news about your son, Elbo."

"Elbo? I don't know what you mean. I don't know no one name of Elbo. My son here with me, name of Royale. You got the wrong place."

The voice never faltered. If Hazel had not spoken with the neighbors up the street she might have left, but she didn't. "Is this the Blues residence?"

"Yuss, but my son here with me, name of Royale."

"I'm talkin' about your other son, Mrs. Blue. Elbo. I got news about Elbo."

"An' I'm tellin' you I don't know what you talkin' about. I ain't got no son name Elbo. My son here with me, like I told you, name of Royale."

She spoke slowly, drawing the name out to three syllables, Ro-ya-le. Hazel was puzzled, but prepared to sit on the stoop all night if necessary, she had too much at stake not to see the charade through. She persisted, but mildly, careful not to offend. "I got news about your son, Elbo. You should know what happened to him. It's important."

There was a brief silence, more creaking of floorboards, a shushing sound, the rustle of a sliding latch, the squeak of a turning bolt, the hammer of a falling tumbler, and a man stood in the doorway. He wore a starched white shirt and pinstripe pants which still held the crease from the store. If he'd worn a tie he'd have looked like any of the businessmen she'd seen about town. He smiled. "Hi. I'm Roy Blue, Elbo's brother, and this is my mama. What can we do for you?"

Expecting Mrs. Blue, Hazel was surprised. "Oh, hi—Mr. Ro-ya-le Blue?"

"I prefer just Roy."

He spoke quietly, reasonably, and Hazel seized her advantage immediately, smiling to show she understood the reason for his preference. She held out her hand. "Of course. I'm Hazel Bailey."

Mrs. Blue stood behind the man, wearing a scarf and a long grey housecoat, both shiny with age, but pushed herself forward before the man could shake her hand and stood between them with her arms crossed, her face a mask. "You got somethin' to say, you say it."

Hazel dropped her hand. "I got news about Elbo you should know about. Can I come in?"

A scowl twisted Mrs. Blue's thin black face. "There ain't no more news about Elbo. How many times I got to tell you there ain't no more news about Elbo?"

Hazel turned her attention to the man. "It's important. Please, can I come in?"

The man held his mama by the shoulders, pulling her gently back. "Of course."

Hazel stepped in and the man led her to the living-room with the food in the window. It was a small room with a single tattered sofa, two crates alongside a wall draped with embroidered cloth, two frames on the wall, one enclosing the embroidered phrase GOD BLESS OUR HOME, the other a newspaper clipping of Abe Lincoln. The single naked bulb was brighter than necessary, perhaps to ascertain that the food in the window was visible.

Hazel looked at the man for traces of Elbo, but his hair and skin were a dozen shades lighter. He was also older, but most striking was his manner, formal but friendly in a way she had not experienced from colored men, not even from white men, not the cool grace borne of adversity, nor the dignity masking cynicism, nor the smile pasted over bitterness, but a confidence and ease as if she were a colored woman, or he a white man, or he didn't know the difference, or didn't care, which surprised her because it was new in her experience of colored men, most of whom were like Elbo, diffident and awestruck, or defiant and aloof. Even white men were sometimes uncomfortable talking with her, but Roy appeared like a brother, an old friend, whose manner invited all manner of confidences.

Mrs. Blue was different, bony chin pointing at the ceiling, eyes closed as if she didn't need to see where she was going, but Hazel recognized a tiredness in her that she recognized in herself in the way she carried her body, as if she'd left it in someone else's care, as if someone else were pulling her strings, and Hazel knew her movements as if they moved in the same skin. Her nose was patrician, long and narrow, unlike Elbo's, flat and broad, but Hazel recognized Elbo's leathery lips, and if she could have seen under the housecoat she would have seen Elbo's skeletal arms—and under the scarf Elbo's tiny ears. Her skin was lighter than Elbo's, but hardly as light as Roy's. In the bright living-room Roy appeared orange, skin and hair, but looking more carefully she could see Elbo's nose, Elbo's lips, Elbo's ears, Elbo's arms. He held out a hand in invitation. "Please, won't you sit down?"

Roy wasn't smiling, but if she had closed her eyes she might have imagined he was. If she had closed her eyes she might have imagined he was English, he had that kind of refinement, and it brought out the English in herself. She bobbed her head in a slow shallow nod as if he were George VI himself. "Thank you kindly. I think I shall."

She sat at one end of the tattered sofa, Mrs. Blue at the other, he sat on one of the crates by the wall and continued in the same measured tones. "So, you're with the circus?"

"Yes—with the elephants."

"The elephants! How interesting!" He raised his finger like a schoolteacher making a point. "I say that because I had elephants on my mind just this morning."

He still wasn't smiling, but Hazel felt comfortable smiling herself. "Oh, yes?"

"I was reading John Donne. He said the elephant was Nature's great masterpiece, the only harmless great thing, and I wondered if it were true. I'm sure there must be other harmless great things."

Hazel was astonished to learn a colored man read books. Jack was the only man she knew, white or colored, who read anything besides adventure stories, and she was flattered that Roy troubled to talk to her about what he'd read. She spoke in a hush, wishing she had something brilliant to say. "That's very interestin'. I have a friend who reads a lot."

"Really?"

"He's a joey."

Roy inclined his head. "A joey?"

"A clown. Us troupers, we call them joeys."

"Ah!" Roy nodded, then grinned. "He's a clown because he reads?"

Hazel blushed. "No, I mean he's a real clown—in the circus. His name's Brown E. That's his clown name. His real name's Jack."

Roy still grinned. "Sorry. I was kidding—couldn't resist. Let's just say it's the clown in me."

Hazel smiled, but seemed to realize only then that though Mrs. Blue had kept her silence she had been frowning all along, glaring at her wellmannered son—and dropped her smile immediately.

Roy clapped his hands as if to conclude the matter. "But that's not why you're here. Let's get down to business. What can you tell us about Elbo?"

Hazel hadn't prepared herself, imagining her main difficulty would be finding the Blues, but having found them she had difficulty finding words, and felt embarrassed for her chitchat when her news was serious. Mrs. Blue remained immobile, wide bony shoulders erect, but she no longer glared, her eyes narrowed to slits instead straying neither left nor right. Hazel looked to Roy for guidance, but it was Mrs. Blue who spoke instead. "I don't care what you got to tell us. Far as I'm concerned, Elbo's dead."

Hazel turned her head sharply to Mrs. Blue. "You know? How did you know?"

A brief deep silence followed during which no one moved. Mrs. Blue opened her eyes, pursing her lips tightly in a white line and Hazel knew she had not known, she had meant something else.

There was an intake of breath from Roy, but when she looked at him he was speechless and she became breathless herself. "I'm sorry. I'm so sorry." She looked at him, but he was no longer looking at her. His eyes were on the floor. He took another deep breath, and another, as if he could not stop, as if he might otherwise burst. Mrs. Blue closed her eyes again as if she were praying, but the muscles of her cheek trembled, and the corners of her mouth drooped so low the tight white line of her lips became a white horseshoe. Roy crossed the floor, sat between them, and put his arm around his ma's shoulders.

In the longer silence that followed Hazel wished for darkness, the bright light appeared obscene, some emotions were too private for exposure. She looked at the floor, hating herself for not preparing them better. When Roy spoke again she no longer recognized his voice—hoarse and guttural. "It's worse than you think. Elbo had a twin ... died in Toledo. You may know ... it was in the papers ... mob violence. We only just found out ... thought he was in Cleveland all this time."

The circuitry was slow in Hazel's head, the news horrible, the coincidence terrible, but worst of all was the image of her brother that sprang in the recesses of her consciousness, a geyser of blood high enough to incarnadine the sky. It was a word Jack had used when her ma had died. She didn't know what Spike had done and didn't want to know, his sin beyond the pale, but the word seemed apropos again.

She seemed to have gone into a reverie, but became conscious of Roy again, turning to face her, his arm still circling his mother's shoulders. His voice remained breathless. "How ... did it happen?"

What could she say? An elephant fell on him? She was so nervous she ground her teeth, clenched her fists till her knuckles whitened, dug her nails into her palms, but she couldn't hold back her giggles. She giggled so hard she cried. Roy stared as if she were mad. Mrs. Blue seemed locked in a trance.

She couldn't stop giggling, rocking the sofa. "I'm sorry. I can't help it. I'm so nervous. I'm sorry." She closed her eyes, clenched her entire body, sitting with her knees joined, her fists clenched on her knees, her head bowed, until she was in control again. "I'm sorry. I don't know what came over me. I'm jus' nervous is what it is. I'm jus' so nervous."

Roy nodded his head. "Just tell us ... what happened."

"He got in the way of an elephant." She no longer giggled, but found herself instead, suddenly and uncontrollably, shaking with sobs. "I'm sorry. I jus' can't do nothin' right no more. I'm sorry."

She was crouched on her side of the sofa, face buried in her hands, still except for her shaking shoulders while Roy stared.

"I wanna do the right thing, I jus' wanna do the right thing, but I keep screwin' up. I'm a danger to my friends."

Roy's voice was brusque. "Don't talk like that. Not many people would have troubled to bring such news." Not white people was what he meant, but he kept his thought silent.

Hazel shook her head, still crouched on the sofa. "I keep screwin' up. I jus' keep screwin' up. I should be locked up. I ain't no good to nobody."

Roy's voice was gentler. "Hush! Hush, now!"

Hazel quietened, but kept her position, hiding her face in her hands. "My pa's in jail. We been fired from the circus. I got nowhere to go. I don't know what I'm gonna do."

Roy took a clean folded handkerchief from his pocket, touched her elbow with one hand, gave her the handkerchief with the other. He couldn't have known, but his touch meant more than a dress by Dior, a night in Paris. She was only thirty years old, but her past had been slammed shut in her face and her future held no roadmap. She longed for kindness, someone to hold her, and she cried not only for her shame, but her life, her family, her future.

Roy brought her a glass of water, offered a cigarette, both of which she accepted. He sat again, his arm around his mama's shoulders, and she related the rest of her story: Elbo joining the circus; Jonas charging Dinty with Hero's death; but Dinty had been under enormous pressure himself, suspecting Jonas of redlighting his brother, and everyone sharing the responsibility for her ma's death, she most of all. It was the first time she had disclosed the story about her ma's death. Mrs. Blue said nothing throughout, eyes wide open but refusing to acknowledge anyone's presence. Hazel felt sure she heard nothing.

Roy was a lawyer in Chicago; he might be able to help, but they would have to move quickly. He was in Kendall Green for just two weeks, he'd come to persuade his mama to move with him to Chicago, but if the circus were ready to begin its season it might work to their advantage if they didn't make their own time constraints known. They would need to devise a strategy; they couldn't that day, not after what had happened, but he gave her the Springers' address, where his mama worked, and said he would meet her there the following evening.

Hazel was surprised. "Why can't we meet here, or in my hotel room?"

Roy, too, was surprised. "Folks would get the wrong idea. They would make trouble for you."

Hazel still appeared surprised. "Why would they make trouble?"

Roy hesitated, speaking delicately. "Well ... let me put it this way. You would have to be blind not to see the difference between us."

Hazel understood what he meant. "I don't care. Why should we care about that?"

"We should care because we don't want anything to get in the way of our objective—but the Springers are rich enough and respectable enough not to care—and, besides, my mama's their maid. It'll give folks less pause to think."

By then it was late. Roy would have walked her back to the Abbott, but couldn't leave his mama. It was enough that he might help Dinty. She left feeling lighter than she could remember in a while.

His mama didn't stir from the sofa all night, said not a word. Roy turned off the light and stayed with her. When dawn slid into the room she cleared the food from the window, began cleaning the house. She cleaned the house everyday for a month, scrubbing the floors twice daily, hoeing and sowing her puddle of yard, straightening her stoop, fixing her rickety fence and gate.

HATHI MINAR

Do not seek death. Death will find you. But seek the road which makes death a fulfillment.
                                        DAG HAMMARSKJOLD

ONE   THE PR GAMBIT

Going to see Jonas, Roy wore a red tie and grey suit. Hazel had never seen a colored man in a suit and neither had most others from the looks they got walking from the Mercury sedan to the Imperial. Skin of ginger appeared almost as startling in a suit of grey as it might have naked. He'd smiled in greeting, her welcome warrior: "Dressing right is half the battle." Mrs. Springer had rifled Hazel's wardrobe before taking her shopping for the occasion. When Hazel wasn't uniformed for Salt'n'Peppah or outfitted for the ring she wore jeans, shirts, and sneakers. Mrs. Springer bought her a pleated grey skirt and jacket, ruffled white blouse, white hat, black heels, and plain earrings, nothing fancy, just businesslike. Not even a clown suit could have obscured Hazel's allure and she didn't see the necessity for new clothes, but walking to the Imperial with Roy it became clear. She was undertaking a new role, for which her new outfit provided confidence, but walking in heels was more complicated than walking on Hero's back—and just plain silly.

Roy was accustomed to the looks though they were fewer in Chicago, but the looks were different than when he was alone and he knew they owed more to his company than his attire. They were an uncommon sight, even an inflammable sight, and he was careful not to touch her, to keep as much distance between them as possible without appearing rude, not even to talk with her.

Janet answered the door as always. Roy had called the day before, introduced himself as Mr. Dinty Bailey's attorney and said it would be to Jonas's advantage for them to talk. Janet stared longer than necessary, not expecting Roy to look as he did. From his voice on the phone she had imagined a swell from New York. Roy was polite, handing her his card. "Hello. I'm Royale de Bleu. Mr. Frank's expecting us, I believe."

He used his full name to confuse Janet. She stared a moment longer before staring further at his card, reading his name carefully. "Yes, of course, Mr. Bleeyu. Come right this way."

Hazel smiled brightly. "Hi, Mrs. Frank."

Janet seemed not to have noticed her. "Oh, hullo, Hazel." With Dinty behind bars she didn't know what to expect of Hazel, didn't know how to behave.

It was almost noon, the same time of day when Dinty had appeared to propose his scheme to disfigure Hero, but Jonas wasn't lounging in his robe as before, nor was he in his recliner but in a chair at the dinner table with paperwork spread before him, nor did he keep his visitors standing, rising to greet them in a business suit, hiding his surprise marginally better than his wife when he saw Roy. "Can I offer you some coffee or tea?"

Roy shook his head. "No, thank you, Mr. Frank. I know you're a busy man. I know the season starts in less than two weeks. I don't want to take more of your time than I have to."

Hazel poked the plush carpet with her toe, staring at the paintings on the wall, bouncing in the sofa across from Jonas as she sat where Jonas indicated, but Roy seemed oblivious to luxury. Jonas indicated the space next to Hazel for him to sit, but he chose another seat instead, a higher seat than the sofa. The telephone rang and Janet left the room.

Having momentarily satisfied his curiosity about Roy, Jonas took a seat next to him but turned his gaze on Hazel with an expression of pain. His eyes were deep and sad and sleepy as ever, his tone as sepulchral. "Well, now, Hazel, I know what this must be about. I know exactly. It's Dinty you're wanting, isn't it? You had only to come to me, Hazel. Didn't you know that? There was no need for getting foreign parties involved. You know how it is with us troupers. We resolve our own difficulties."

Hazel's jaw dropped. "Mr. Frank, I tried to talk to you, you know I did, but you said a man's got to do what a man's got to do."

Jonas sighed, looking at neither Hazel nor Roy. "Ah, Hazel, you should have known." He shook his head in regret. "It was a difficult time for me. You should have come to me again. An elephant is an expensive animal. I could not afford to be losing another and you know how Dinty is. I had to have him incarcerated for the safety of the animals, but you should have come to me again. You should have come to me of your own accord and Dinty would have been yours."

He turned his gaze on Hazel and she stared back. "That's what I want. I want Pa back, outta jail."

Jonas extended open palms. "He is yours, provided I have your assurance that he will be under your surveillance. I only wanted him held until we left, but he is yours if you assume the responsibility for any more such accidents. Am I clear?"

Hazel looked at Roy, feeling silly about how easily the matter was being resolved. "Of course."

Jonas joined his hands. "Then it is settled. I shall inform the police I no longer wish to press charges against Dinty and he shall be with you tonight."

Roy had said nothing, but he'd been observing Jonas. Jonas's eyes drooped, but missed nothing; his voice droned, but held power in reserve. Roy spoke with his customary confidence. "Just a moment, Mr. Frank. That is a part of what we wish, but there is more. We also wish Siri's release from his contract. He has made it clear he considers the Baileys his family. Do you have any objection to releasing him?"

Jonas appeared to consider, but responded with finality. "Yes, I do. He is an asset to the circus in his own right. Folks come to see him as much as the elephants. He is an authentic mah-hoot."

Roy nodded. "Right, and I understand that a mahout's lifespan parallels that of his elephant. I think, with Hero dead, you can understand why he may no longer wish to remain with the circus."

Jonas shook his head. "He is still my mah-hoot, and I have other elephants."

Roy leaned forward. "Yes, I see, and I'm sure you will correct me if I'm wrong, but my understanding is that he isn't paid what you would pay an authentic mahout. My understanding is that he's given room and board, but paid nothing at all. Is that not right?"

Jonas huffed. "That is right, but you are wrong to assume I paid nothing at all. I bought him when I bought Hero. I own him like I owned Hero. He is mine as much as Hero was mine."

Roy spoke incisively. "Let me understand you correctly. You own him, then, like you would own a slave. Is that what you are saying, Mr. Frank? You must know that there are laws against such possessions."

Jonas spoke more quickly. "No, I do not mean that at all. I do not own him like a slave. I own him like an act. There is a difference."

Roy responded even more quickly. "I fail to see the distinction. He is a human being, no different from all the other human beings who perform acts for you."

Jonas took a deep breath. "Mr. Bluey, if you will give me the chance to finish, please?"

Roy sat back. "Sorry. My mistake. By all means, finish. Take your time."

Jonas sat back again, took another breath, spoke slowly again. "What I was going to say was that in light of Siri's consanguinity with the Baileys, I would be willing to release him from his contract."

Roy said nothing, but nodded slowly.

"Will that be all?"

Roy continued nodding. "Almost."

"Yes?"

"We also wish custody of Hero's tusks."

Jonas blinked slowly. "His tusks?"

Roy nodded again. "Precisely, his tusks—not for pecuniary reasons, I might add, but for Siri. You see, he considered Hero his brother. In losing Hero, he lost a brother. This would go a long way toward mending a man's heart, Mr. Frank. We wish Hero's tusks for Siri."

Jonas sat up straight again. He'd had Hero's tusks appraised, combined length of nine feet, combined weight of sixty pounds. He could get fifteen hundred dollars in Hong Kong, as much as three thousand perhaps in Japan. "Mr. Bluey, you would do well to bear in mind that it was not me but Dinty who poisoned Hero. It was not me!" He slapped his chest in indignation. "This is not a matter for debate. This is a matter of fact. He confessed his crime to the police. It was sheer good fortune we found the poison in the stable before the other elephants. Now, I'll have you know, my good man, that I paid good money for that elephant. If anyone should pay for that elephant, it should be Dinty. The tusks are the least remuneration I can expect. Do I make myself clear?"

Hazel made fists in her lap, but Roy never lost his equanimity. He even smiled. "That may be as you say, Mr. Frank, but what you did was far worse."

"What I did?" Jonas looked puzzled. "What did I do?"

"You redlighted his brother."

Jonas's sleepy eyes suddenly flashed. "That's a lie! That's a shameless lie, that is! That was years ago, that was, even before I bought the circus. They were employees then of the Griffin Bros. Circus."

Roy shook his head. "If I understand correctly, sir, it was only just before you bought the circus, and I understand Alf was the only hand unfortunate enough to get killed, but there're plenty of others who'd be willing to testify in a court of law, if necessary, that they were redlighted—whether by you or by the Griffin Bros. might be for a judge to decide."

Hazel nodded vigorously. "That's right. We can get in touch with Speedy and Silas—and they can get in touch with Ham and Skerrit and Joby. They lost out on I don't know how many months' pay."

The names meant nothing to Jonas. He pursed his lips. "That was years ago, that was. No court of law would take their word seriously today. You should know that, Mr. Bluey, if you are half the lawyer you appear to be—and, in any case, I am innocent. That was before I bought the circus."

Roy raised his hands to calm Jonas. "You're right, Mr. Frank, you're absolutely right. It's much too long ago and time has a way of playing tricks with people's minds. A good lawyer could easily discredit the memory of any number of old roustabouts—but the question, surely, is whether you can afford the publicity. The newspapers would print pictures daily of yourself next to Dinty, pictures of the Imperial next to the Abbott, the Capitalist versus the Common Man. Can't you see the headlines? It'd be a natural. The question is whether you'd be willing to take that risk."

Jonas got up. "I would—and I shall. I am an innocent man, I am, and I'll be damned before I let you threaten me. Let me tell you, Mr. Bluey, I consider this interview concluded and would be much obliged if you would leave my premises."

Hazel got up, but Roy motioned her down again, speaking as if there were no disagreement between them. "I'm sorry to have bothered you, Mr. Frank, but I wish you to consider one more thing."

Jonas stood glaring before Roy. Janet had reentered the room.

Roy raised his face. "I want you to consider that when this gets to the newspapers—and, make no mistake about that, it will—they will say that a man killed an elephant not only to avenge his brother, but to avenge his wife. I think you know what I mean, Mr. Frank."

Janet was the first to speak and she addressed Hazel. "Hazel, I cannot believe you would use the memory of your dearly departed ma so shamelessly. I thought you had more pride than that. How you can allow this ... this jigaboo to make you stoop so low I cannot understand, I shall never understand."

Roy's eyes flashed, but he knew he'd won. Slurs thickened when arguments thinned. Racism was the first refuge of the loser. He nodded to Hazel. "Let's go, Miss Bailey. We've said our piece."

Hazel got up, but Jonas spoke again, and again in his soft sad voice, again with his sleepy reproachful eyes. "Hazel, you know it. You know Janet is right, you do. You know in your heart you should not use the memory of your ma so shamelessly, you do. Now, in the memory of our long communion, I shall let Dinty go—and I shall let Siri go because to all intents and purposes he is a member of your family—but the tusks must remain. You can see that, can you not?"

Hazel appeared unsure, but looking at Roy she gained strength. "Mr. Frank, with respect, I thank you—but the tusks belong to Siri. I wish you could see that, and I will do what I can to see he gets what's his. You know how it is: a woman's got to do what a woman's got to do."

Jonas stared, shaking his head as if he couldn't understand where she had gone wrong. Roy allowed her to precede him out of the room. She walked carefully, unaccustomed to the heels, unaccustomed to the pile, not wanting to wobble at the last minute. Before they exited, Roy turned and spoke calmly again. "Mr. Frank, we have said much today that needs to be digested more fully. You can reach me at the Abbott through Hazel. I will be in Kendall Green for as long as it takes. I will wait five days before taking any action on Dinty's behalf. I give you my word of honor on that as a gentleman."

He bowed lightly, tipping his hat to Janet and following Hazel outside.

THREE DAYS LATER there came a brief note from Jonas for Roy: *You are wrong, but I acquiesce to your demands. I have spoken with my own lawyers, and while they assure me of victory in the litigation with which you threaten me, I have known the Baileys too long to conclude our acquaintance on a harsh note. If you will call me, we can arrange for a time to draw up the terms of an agreement.*

Shortly after their subsequent meeting with Jonas, Roy sent Hazel and Dinty a bottle of champagne and extended an invitation to celebrate the occasion with him in Cleveland. It was also to be his last day before returning to Chicago. Dinty grinned. "You go. I know he don't mean me."

Hazel was more relieved with their victory than in any mood to celebrate. Spike had left for New York and would soon be embarking for Bombay! She was sorry, feeling she had driven him away, but accepted Roy's invitation, as much to be courteous as consoled.

TWO — ABOARD *THE GARDENIA*

I knew as little about the sea as I knew about anything unrelated to the circus, but I was learning, and thrilled by my learning.

> Red sky at night,
> Sailor's delight.
> Red sky in the morning,
> Sailor's warning.

Jimmy Adamson was my cabinmate and fellow steward, and he was showing me the ropes in exchange for juggling tricks. A red sky at sunset meant fine weather the next day, or so the ditty went, and the last twilight had been the reddest.

It was four bells into the second watch, or 2 AM, aboard *The Gardenia*, and while a couple of thousand passengers lay abed, the ship's company of a thousand officers and men was ensuring their security and comfort. The second officer and quartermaster kept an eye on the automatic pilot in the wheelhouse on the bridge; engineers kept watch on turbines belowdecks; radio officers on the boat deck watched for messages sending news reports to the printer (two thousand copies of the ship's newspaper were served everyday by cabin stewards with morning tea and coffee); laundrymen fed roomfulls of linen into the mouths of giant washers and dryers in the bowels of the ship, while the ghost of a cleaning crew hovered constantly, and cooks, bakers, and butchers made early appearances in the galleys.

The ship was no less a city than the circus, with its own language no less than the circus, a caravan on water instead of wheels, but I liked it better. You might say the circus had chosen me, but I had chosen the sea. The decision to join Lumsden was the first major decision I'd made about my life and I didn't take the responsibility lightly. The way of the world was wider than the way of the circus, and I was looking for the widest world I could find. I had never known Elbo, never cared to know him; there had been no reason, and I'd had my hands full repairing my own life—but Roy was different. You had to notice Roy. He did not handle himself like any coloreds I'd known, keeping to themselves, speaking only when spoken to. Roy knew what he wanted and knew how to get it. In a single audience with Mr. Frank he'd secured Dinty's release. Hazel said he'd threatened a scandal over Alf's redlighting, but she'd become suddenly silent and I understood that our ma's death had also been a factor. Even Roy knew more about our ma than I did. I was glad Hazel had found an ally, but also resentful that Roy appeared more important than her own brother—but I'd made my own plans, my own choices, and I wasn't complaining.

Awaiting *The Gardenia*'s departure in New York, I'd missed Hazel, missed even Dinty and Siri, missed Eileen most of all. Hazel hadn't wanted me to leave, and had upset me at the last minute asking if I was running *from* something or *to* something. She'd fastened doubt to my departure like a gorilla to my back, but with the ship casting off I'd cast off doubt as well. I might as well have cast off into a different world. The band, the streamers, the confetti as we'd left the dock, all contributed to wellbeing; the world of the ship provided a camaraderie as cozy as the world of the circus; and the world of the sea provided a palimpsest of divine origins: the brow of the horizon over the belly of the ocean, the midnight vault of the sky with constellations like chandeliers, the salt in the air like a constant spray, refreshing as a shower. Jimmy had taught me to differentiate gannets and cormorants and albatrosses from bosun birds and frigate birds and petrels. I had seen flying fish in silver streaks glide across the water, heard them bump into the side of the ship. Jimmy had explained that they could fly as far as a mile at a time, reaching altitudes of twenty feet, and had occasionally flown onto the lower decks of ships.

Best of all, my sleep improved, dreams full of hope for the future, letting me know in no uncertain terms I'd made the right decision.

> Sixteen men on a dead man's chest.
> Yo-ho-ho and a bottle of rum.

The silliest things made me grin. My luck since I'd seen *The Gardenia* appeared to be powered by the same 90,000 horses which could whip the ship to a speed of 26 knots, almost 30 mph. There'd been more than a hundred applicants for each steward's position, but my timing had been impeccable: someone had died, someone else had canceled, a performer's sister had fallen sick. I could not only do beds and set tables but also juggle, they'd been too preoccupied with my skill not to believe me when I lied about my age, and two nights a week I merged my act with the cabaret performers. If not for my dream of joining Lumsden I might contentedly have pursued my new life at sea at length. The tarbooshes, chadors, and dashikis at the ports stirred memories of Saturday morning serials, as did humming bazaars with narrow streets and narrow faces with pointed beards. There was so much world to see and what better way than to get paid to see it, but I planned to jump ship when we reached Bombay. I wouldn't be paid, all remuneration was kept until the end of the voyage, but I'd saved enough, and I'd made almost as much again in tips. Jimmy had not exaggerated: including tips, stewards made more money than the captain.

With Jimmy, my luck had crested. A boy when he'd left Hoboken for New York, Jimmy was six years older, knew the world, knew Bombay, could advise me, and in exchange couldn't get enough of my circus life. Besides, even the smallest trailer was a palace relative to our cabin and each of us gloried in the luck that had bunked us together. Otherwise, we might not have been as cozy. We worked long hours, but the work left me exhilarated and I often preferred to talk into the night with Jimmy than to sleep. We might have been talking even at 2 AM, but Mrs. Hedda Alfven in 203 (one of Jimmy's cabins) was having a baby and he'd been summoned. Mrs. Alfven, I had noted, blood surging like the tide, had the same flamingo hair, the same coral highlights, as my ma.

> I must go down to the seas again, to the lonely sea and the sky,
> And all I ask is a tall ship and a star to steer her by.

Approaching footsteps foretold Jimmy's return. The door opened and his broad silhouette filled the narrow frame. I expected him to say something, but he shut the door behind him and sat quietly on his bunk. I opened the conversation, imagining Jimmy didn't want to wake me. "Hey, so what was it?"

"A boy."

"Wow!"

Jimmy said nothing.

I leaned over the bunk. I could barely see in the dark, but Jimmy appeared to be sitting, elbows on knees, hands covering his face. I turned on the reading light. "Hey! You all right?"

Jimmy removed his hands. His face appeared longer than I had ever seen it, the face of an old bloodhound. "She died. Mrs. Alfven died."

My mouth dropped. "Shit!"

"They couldn't stop the bleeding."

"Shit!"

I could think of nothing else to say. Jimmy took off his uniform. I turned off the light. Jimmy fell asleep first; otherwise, he might have wondered about my bunk shaking above. Look again at this sad sack, this toddling man, this boy in swaddling clothes, adrift on the ocean, as lost in himself as in the world, orphaning himself to get away from his half-orphaned self. Eyes, dry as the moon, dry for months and years, flowed like a river till his pillow was soaked like a rag in the sea. He sobbed into the dawn for his lost life, his utter helplessness, his boundless guilt, and his doubt returned, sheeted in lead.

THREE PANTHER AMONG LIONS

Hazel was so glad to see Roy's sedan that she forgot her annoyance. She hated being rushed, hated even more being secretive, but Roy had said it would be easier. She'd enjoyed their day in Cleveland. They'd had dinner, seen a picture, *The Bishop's Wife*, a comedy with Cary Grant, David Niven, and Loretta Young. She'd been too surprised to protest when they'd snuck in after lights out, sat in the back row, and snuck out before lights on, but she'd still enjoyed the picture. She'd voiced her protest later, Roy had nodded, and she imagined he'd registered her objection though he'd been too silent for her to be sure.

He had picked her up blocks from the Abbott when they'd visited Cleveland, and now she waited on the outskirts of town to be picked up for their picnic. She was tired of the subterfuge and had explained as best she could—"It don't matter to troupers who you are, only what you do in the ring, and you beat Jonas on his best day"—but Roy appeared to understand something beyond her ken. "It's not troupers I'm concerned about. It's Kendall Greeners. All small towns are alike—and so're the cities. The only difference is folks in cities're too damn busy to give a damn what anyone thinks or does. The only reason they seem more tolerant is they're more anonymous."

He was cautious on her account, but she was still annoyed. He was driving to Chicago the next day; she didn't get off from Salt'n'Peppah until two; they'd planned to meet at three. She was early and looked for him down the road, but he surprised her coming the other way. More precautions, she was sure, throwing her cigarette to the ground, dismissing her annoyance with a shake of her head.

He leaned over to open the door and smiled. "Hi."

"Hi." She was almost shy. He'd barely touched her, hardly even said goodbye when he'd brought her back from Cleveland, and stayed on his side of the seat as she got in.

"Been waiting long?"

"Nope, just got here."

"Good." He turned the car around, heading away from the town.

The Elephant Graveyard

She rolled down her window and up again. It was a cool day for a picnic, and she had worn a coat over her sweater and jeans as Roy had suggested. The cooler the weather the better their guarantee of privacy and it wouldn't hurt to be prepared. Roy wore, as always, dress pants, shirt, sweater, and coat. All he needed was a vest instead of the sweater, and a tie, and he'd be ready for business. She'd been impressed with his ability against Jonas, she was sure he could have got Dinty his job back at the circus if she'd wanted, but she was happy to leave trouping in her past. Hero was dead, and it would be a long time before she could develop a similar act with another elephant. She looked across the seat at his profile. "Pa's real grateful. I don't know what we'd have done without you."

"He's welcome."

He didn't look at her, didn't smile. She was afraid of his formality, afraid he was tired of her already, that he needed an educated woman to hold his interest. "He's jus' beginnin' to understand what's happened. Pa's slow like that, but he's gettin' better—thanks to what you did."

He still didn't look at her. "It was nothing, just your basic lawyer's trick. Let your opponent think you know more than you do, let him stew in his own juice, give him enough rope –"

She interjected quickly: "Dig his own grave!"

He laughed. "Precisely."

She relaxed a little, glad she'd made him laugh, settling into the wide springy seat. She loved the luxury of the car, the chromium dashboard, needles quivering in various gauges, numbers changing as miles passed, farms changing as they passed, farmers sowing corn, wheat, oats, alfalfa. On the trip to Cleveland she'd played with the windows, winding them up, winding them down, locking the doors, unlocking the doors, a child again, but a child such as she'd never been, without responsibilities for the first time in her life, and she loved it, secure in Roy's care, her unlikely Galahad. "Where're we goin'?"

They were traveling south through Lorain County and into Ashland County, home of Johnny Appleseed. "I thought we'd just drive for a while. The countryside's beautiful right around here—creeks, orchards, woodlands. Then we could turn into a backroad somewhere, give ourselves some privacy for the picnic. How does that sound?"

"Jim dandy." She wished to get his attention, but he kept his eyes on the road, spoke as if he were reciting theorems. It was the very attitude which had prevailed with such success against Jonas, but she wasn't Jonas, and she wanted to shake him from his lawyerliness though without appearing too much of a hellraiser. She crossed her arms, staring ahead at the road herself. "You know, Roy, I can't make up my mind whether you really wanna be alone with me—or you jus' don't wanna be seen with me."

He looked at her finally. She smiled, but coyly kept her gaze from his, enjoying the flirtation.

He spoke slowly, as if he'd given the matter much thought. "I want to be with you, but I don't think it would be wise for us to be seen together."

Her smile widened, but she continued to stare at the road. "Well, that's just peachy! How're we supposed to be together if we ain't to be seen together?"

He didn't like talking about it and took his time replying. When he did, it was as slowly as before. "I thought you understood. It's just the way it is. You know how folks are. It's not worth talking about."

She knew the subject made him uncomfortable, but was determined to talk it through. "But it *is* worth talkin' about. Why don't you think it's worth talkin' about?"

He believed she was sincere, but couldn't believe that she could be. When people stared, she ignored them—not that she didn't care but that she didn't notice them, or noticing believed them as innocent of malice as herself—not that she didn't understand but that her understanding was toothless because she had not yet been bitten. He was less oblivious of the looks himself, but he'd been aware of the looks for a long time, an awareness greatly enhanced during his years at Chicago's Kent Law School where he'd graduated fourth in his class. He could ignore the looks, but was always aware of them, of his difference in the white world. Suddenly, he grinned. "I'd explain it to you, but I'm afraid I'd corrupt you."

She looked at him then, but he turned his eyes to the road again. "Corrupt me? How d'you mean, corrupt me?"

"You want me to draw you a diagram?"

Her brow furrowed with puzzlement. "Yeah."

He continued to grin. "You want me to corrupt you?"

She grinned back. "I'm an old maid of thirty. About time I got corrupted, don't you think?"

She was a year older than him. "All right, then, but don't say I didn't warn you."

"I won't."

"Okay, as you wish." He squared his shoulders as if he were about to lift a heavy burden. "In case you haven't noticed yet, I'm different."

She listened silently, unsmilingly. He spoke of being different because he hated all the other words that defined his difference, not just the pejoratives but also Negro and Colored, not because the pejoratives were never far behind, not because he wanted to be white, but because the words implied that not being White he was less than white: he was American, but always with qualification, always with modification, where others were absolutely and unrepentantly American. "Let me put it this way."

He appeared to be thinking each word before he said it, as if he couldn't emphasize enough the gravity of what he said. "Think of me as a panther, a black panther living and working among lions." He raised a finger and brought it down on the wheel to emphasize each point. "Now, we all know I'm a panther, all the lions know I'm a panther, and they let me be a panther among the lions because I'm wearing a lionskin. They can see it's a lionskin, we can all see it's a lionskin, not the real thing, but no one cares as long as we all pretend it's real. They imagine they're doing me a favor, allowing me among the lions, when in truth they're only giving me what's mine. They allow panthers in their midst as long as the panthers can make the kills—but they don't acknowledge that it's harder for a panther to make kills in a world of lions than it is for a lion, especially keeping the lionskin in place. Am I making myself clear?"

Hazel felt he made too much of his difference, wore it like a badge, wore it on his sleeve. He reminded her of all the other coloreds then, either defiant like himself or subservient like Elbo, unlike when she'd first met him and he'd appeared to understand her like an old friend. She looked at him steadily, narrowing her eyes to make her point. "Roy, you're a man. I'm a woman. What else is there?"

He smiled at her simplicity. "Right. You know it and I know it, but out there," he pointed out of the window, "out there, in the world, where it matters, they don't know it."

Hazel shook her head. "But it don't matter what's out there, Roy. Only what's in here."

Roy shrugged. "If only that were so."

"It *can* be so. If we make it so, it *can* be so."

"We'll see."

She made no response but stared out of the window and they drove in silence for a while, passing hills of pine and hemlock, forests of oak and hickory.

Roy glanced across. "I hope you're hungry. I've got enough food in the back for an army."

She was glad he'd bridged the silence. "Starvin'. I skipped lunch 'cause I wanted to show my appreciation properly for your picnic, for all your trouble."

He smiled, unaccustomed to such ingenuousness. "All trouble becomes a pleasure when you want to take the trouble."

He was rewarded with a smile as pleased and guileless as a child's. She pointed to a turning ahead among the trees. "Why don't we stop over there?"

He slowed the car for the turn. "Why not?"

Roy drove along the side road through the grove until they came to a creek in a field separating them from orchards of apples. He parked the car by a row of oaks. "No one will bother us here." The grove was far enough to hide them from the road, to hide even the car.

IT WAS SIX-THIRTY when they headed back to Kendall Green, neither knowing when they would see the other again—or if—neither willing to broach the subject. He had brought a blanket, a cooler, a thermos, chicken and ham and roast beef sandwiches, Swiss and cheddar and goat cheese, mayo and mustard and ketchup, chips and pickles and tomatoes, and wine and cider and coffee. They had eaten and drunk everything, smoking cigarettes and talking about themselves, about Elbo and Prize who had never known their father, about Spike who had barely known his mother, and were comfortably silent and sated on the way back. The fields were flat on either side, the sun low, but the way Hazel felt it might have been a ring of fire over an African veldt. Less of a romantic, Roy would have said there was a glow to the evening unrelated to the sun even he couldn't deny, but he'd kept his eye on a state trooper's car which had been following them almost as soon as they'd turned onto the main road. There was little traffic, but he couldn't have been more cautious navigating an oceanliner among icebergs.

Hazel wasn't aware of the troopers until they drew alongside and flagged them down, but Roy could have predicted when they would make their move. Hazel was surprised. "What's wrong?"

Roy slowed the car, brought it to a halt on the shoulder of the road. "Don't worry. I'll handle it."

"What'd we do?"

"Nothing."

The troopers pulled up ahead. The trooper riding shotgun got out, a long gaunt man, with a long gaunt face, throwing a long gaunt shadow in the fading sun, squinting even in the gathering dark. He swaggered more than walked, slowly as if he were conserving energy with each step, hand caressing the gun around his waist, not stopping until he'd almost put his face through Roy's window looking past him at Hazel.

Roy spoke respectfully. "Is something the matter, Officer?"

The trooper's voice did not match his gait, not low, not drawling, almost a woman's voice, almost a whinny. He stared past Roy at Hazel as he spoke. "Out the car, boy."

Roy made no move to get out of the car. He couldn't, the trooper's head was almost in his face. He continued to speak respectfully. "I trust, Officer, that you will let me know if something is the matter."

The trooper thrust his face further through the window, addressing Hazel directly, speaking slowly. "I trust, miss, that this here nigger ain't botherin' you none."

The trooper's head was so far into the window Roy spoke almost into his ear. He spoke slowly, softly, still with respect, but a respect increasingly suspect. "The lady is with *me*, Of-Fi-Suh!"

Hazel took Roy's hand across the seat, staring back at the trooper. It was the first time she had touched him. "I'm with *him*, Officer."

The trooper held her gaze a long time. Roy squeezed her hand to give her courage, but it was unnecessary. Hazel stared back as easily as she was stared at. She had outstared Princess Ada who had outstared the big cats; she had outstared elephants in musth. The trooper blinked first, backing out of the window. "You should be more careful, missy. This here could be a stolen car for all y'know."

She felt Roy's hand tremble in hers and squeezed his hand herself as much to give him courage as to restrain him. Her eyes never wavered, crystalline as icebergs. "That's somethin' I know more about than you, Officer."

"Hmmph!" The trooper blinked again, backed away, and walked as slowly as before back to his car. Roy waited for them to leave. Getting in his car, the trooper appeared to be answering a question from his partner, but spoke without looking back loudly enough for Roy and Hazel to hear. "False alarm. Just a fuckin' niggerlover."

Neither Roy nor Hazel said anything until they were on the road again. Roy's voice trembled with indignation. "You see what I mean? That's what I have to put up with all the time, day in, day out, and that's what you'd have to put up with if I let you be seen with me. Do you see now what I mean?"

He'd let go her hand when he'd gunned the engine, but she'd moved closer, put her hand on his knee. "I don't care. They're the ones who should be ashamed, not you. I feel ashamed for them. They ain't lions. They're a hyena and a jackal, that's what they are, and you shouldn't care what they think."

Roy appeared oblivious to her touch and words, but couldn't have been more proud. She was teething so well she was beginning to fang. "You were terrific! Absolutely terrific!"

She grinned. "Thanks, but it was nothin'. He was a wimp. I enjoyed starin' him down."

He shook his head in wonder. "I'm glad this happened. It had to happen sooner or later, and better sooner than later. Now you know firsthand what I've been talking about."

She spoke without levity. "My corruption."

He spoke with deep satisfaction. "Precisely. I'm sorry, but that's the way it is. Even when they're smiling you don't know what they're thinking. You can never let your guard down—and if we're seen together you'll be in my camp, you won't be in theirs. You won't know what they're thinking either."

Hazel understood that Roy's friendship meant a constant penance. She smiled, lines Jack had recited occurred to her, *Kill a king and marry with his brother*, but Elbo had been no king. "I don't care what they're thinkin'. It's more important what *I*'m thinkin'."

Roy pursed his lips. "You'll find out. You can't *not* care. They have all the power."

Hazel slid next to him, hid her face in his shoulder, nuzzled him until he put his arm around her, and snuggled against his chest. "We got to show them. We got to show them we also got power."

They drove the rest of the way in silence, their proximity louder than words. *She loved me for the dangers I had passed, and I loved her that she did pity them.* The lines comforted him. What she didn't know she appeared willing to learn, and what she knew was more than the troopers would ever learn.

When they reached the Abbott neither wanted to disentangle from the other. It was dark, Roy parked where the streetlamps were dimmest and they did no more than hold each other as they'd been doing driving into town. He could have held her all night, but he knew they couldn't stay indefinitely.

Hazel was even more confused. Had he not been leaving for Chicago she might never have accepted his invitation to the picnic, but she no longer wanted him to leave. She kissed him finally because there was no other way to say what she was thinking. He was startled and cut short the kiss, but she made mewling sounds and he initiated his own kiss.

Their kisses were fluid for the next fifteen minutes, but they finally stopped, breathing deeply. She spoke into his ear. "When will I see you again?"

"I don't know. I wish I could say—but I know I'll be back to see Mama."

She wished he'd said he'd be back to see her. "I wanna see you again, Roy. I had a swell time."

"Me too. I'll call you."

"Please do."

She kissed him again. He held her gently by the back of her head, hair cascading down his hands, surprised she was crying. The night turned radiant; her eyes multiplied and melted in dreamlike images around him. "You can count on me, my dear. You can count on me for anything in my power."

She disentangled herself, turned her face away, and left the car without another word. He gripped the wheel tightly to keep from crying himself.

FOUR   ARRIVAL IN BOMBAY

The sunrise was pink and orange on the morning *The Gardenia* docked in Bombay. The sun bobbed in the mist like a Japanese lantern, leaving the coverlet of the sea in a gentle meniscus, the last lingering kiss of a lover. Bombay appeared in the east, first like a gleaming ribbon across the horizon separating sea and sky, then sharpening into ranges of hills speckled with islands and fishing boats at its foothills as the ship drew nearer, finally into rows of palms swaying in the wind. As the sun rose, the heat descended like a soggy blanket—and no wonder. Not only is Bombay a peninsula, but an amalgam of seven islands, created when the swamps and watercourses between them were filled and land was wrested from the sea.

Jimmy and I never saw the sunrise. The steward cabins, deep in the ship's hold, had not even portholes. By the time we descended the gangplank at two in the afternoon, taking time to collect tips from debarking passengers, the air clung like a bodystocking, an oily film of sweat gluing shirts to backs and pants to legs.

The ship was to depart at nine in the evening for Colombo, Singapore, Hong Kong, Yokohama, San Francisco, Acapulco, Cartagena, St. Thomas, Fort Lauderdale, and back to New York, the entire circumnavigation to take a hundred days, but I wasn't returning, and when I learned Jimmy had a friend in Bombay I'd told him my plan. He'd suggested leaving a note. It would help the purser, one of whose responsibilities was to make sure everyone was on board before they departed, and I'd agreed. *Not coming back*, I'd scribbled, *Sorry*. I'd signed the note, *Dan Bailey (Spike)*, and tucked it under Jimmy's pillow for him to find later.

The air was thick with heat as an oven, and so thick with moisture you could smell the water, you could smell the sea, you could taste the salt. It clung to the hair in your nostrils and made rubber of your bones.

In the waiting area a tall white westerner bobbed like a buoy in a sea of Indians. Beside him a tiny brown woman jumped and waved. Jimmy waved back. "There they are."

Jimmy introduced us and we shook hands. Will Gardner was American, a steward like us before marrying Zarine Dadabhoy (now Zarine Gardner, a doctor) and becoming her receptionist. He was tall, she was short; both wore white, he a cotton shirt and baggy pants, she a loosely wound sari; he was still as a sculpture, she bounced on her toes and fidgeted with the sash of her sari.

Will grinned. "Hey, Jimmy Jimmerino!"

Jimmy slapped his shoulder. "Hey, Wee Willie Winkie!"

They hugged each other, looking enough alike to pass for brothers, and Jimmy hugged Zarine before introducing me, saying it was my first visit. Zarine couldn't stop smiling. "Welcome. Welcome to India. Welcome to Bombay."

I shook hands. "Thanks."

Zarine stood on her toes. "Come on, come on, come on, let's go. How much time have we got before your big boat leaves?"

Jimmy grinned, shaking his head again. Zarine had hated the single voyage she'd made, spending most of the time in bed, dosing on Dramamine—though Will insisted her sickness had been a ploy for his attention (he'd been her steward). "Our big boat leaves at nine o'clock sharp. We've got plenty of time."

Zarine shook her head. "Not so much time with all the traffic. Comecomecomecome, let's go, let's go. We can chitchat in the car."

Naked brown children accosted us with open palms, a leper squatted by the side staring from a gargoyle face, but Zarine warned us to give them nothing or we would never get away. The car was an old black Morris Minor with running boards and a stickshift as long as a cane between the front seats. Jimmy and I crawled into the back. Zarine drove expertly with her hand frozen on the horn barely making a dent in the ringing and honking around them; all hands appeared frozen on bells, horns, and klaxons. Victorias, bullock carts, bicycles, pedestrians, cows, goats, and dogs eddied on the roads with buses, lorries, cars, and scooters. Vendors spread fruit, flowers, foodstuffs, jewelry, glassware, books, magazines, and toys on pavements, and peddled wares to the windows of cars stopped at traffic lights. Men wore white shirts, kurtas and dhotis; women colorful cholis and saris, hair braided and bright with oil, entwined with ribbons of marigolds. Sweatstains yawned from all armpits.

In twenty minutes we turned onto a road with four lanes, one side bordered by a crowded promenade separating the road from the sea, the other by residential buildings in Art Deco, four and five storeys tall. Zarine played tourguide. "Marine Drive. You must see it after dark, after the streetlights come on, from Malabar Hill. Queen's Necklace it's called, because of the way the road curves."

Will nodded. "It's a lovely sight. Maybe next time, when you have more time, we'll do Bombay properly as they say around here."

Jimmy looked at me as he spoke. "You may not have to wait that long. Spike's staying. He's jumping ship."

"Oh, my God, is he really? Then he's got more brains than you, Jimmy. That's for sure."

Jimmy laughed. "It's too bad you can't marry us all, Zarine. Then we'd all stay for sure."

Zarine laughed back. "That is very good, Spike, that you are staying. We will show you Bombay, Will and I."

I found her excitement infectious, as if she were providing a doorway to a new life. "It's a dream of mine. I'm gonna join Jordan Lumsden's party—if he'll have me."

Zarine's voice rose. "Jordan Lumsden? I think he was in Bombay recently, there was something in the *Times*, but I think he's gone now. Do you remember the article, Will?"

"He was on his way to camp—somewhere near Mangalore, I think. He'd contracted for two gaurs, I think—and elephants, and God knows what else. I remember thinking it was going to take some heavy lifting—the elephants, I mean."

"So Mr. Lumsden is expecting you?"

"No, I'm gonna persuade him somehow to take me on."

"OmiGod! So you are going to jump ship on the offchance that he will take you on? What is your experience with animals?"

Jimmy laughed. "Most people I know dream of running away to join the circus. Spike here's running away from a circus."

Hearing the story, especially learning Spike had worked with elephants, Will made the O.K. sign. "Perfect! Dollars to doughnuts Lumsden'll take you on."

Zarine's voice rose. "But how will you get there? I don't think there is transportation to his camp—at least, not direct."

"I ain't figured that out yet."

Zarine flicked fingers in the air. "Not to worry. We will make inquiries tomorrow."

"Thanks. I was gonna make some myself. There's an import-export place I wanna visit. I thought they might be able to help."

"What import-export place?"

I showed them Prem Gupta's card. "I found that in Kendall Green. I kept it as a good omen."

Will looked at the card. "How strange, but it's not far, actually. We could take you there tomorrow if you want on our way to work."

"Swell!"

Zarine turned into the driveway of Ganga Vihar, parked in a garage in the back, and fished keys out of her handbag as we stepped out of the elevator leading us to apartment 3B. A small foyer with a hat, coat, and umbrella stand led into a dark living-room, a brighter verandah beyond. Will switched on lights and ceiling fan, also a freestanding rotating fan which panned the room slowly. "Make yourselves comfortable. What'll you guys have to drink?"

Jimmy and I sat on the settee, wiping sweat from brows with handkerchiefs. "What've you got?"

"Lemon squash, orange squash, nimbu-pani, Coca Cola, beer, whatever you want."

Jimmy smiled. "Ah, I'd almost forgotten. Nimbu-pani for me. Nothing to beat a nice cold nimbu-pani when you're in Bombay."

I nodded. "Me too—whatever that is."

Will shrugged. "Just lime with water and sugar, but worth a try if you're going to spend any length of time in India—and you might as well try it here. The water's not safe except in private households, not even in restaurants. And the same goes for fruits, salads—anything uncooked."

Zarine nodded vigorously. "That's right. Take my word as a doctor. You can't even trust them to boil the water, but stick with Coca Colas and you will be all right. At least, you know they're safe—and I've cooked a safe nonspicy dinner tonight because I knew you were coming. Bhindi with mutton and plain jhinga curry and rice—and kulfi."

Will translated. "That's okra with lamb, shrimp curry and rice, and ice cream. We're eating on the verandah. It's cooler."

Zarine nodded again. "Dinner is almost ready, actually. It's early, but it will give us time for a drive when it's cooler when we take Jimmy back. I just have to heat it up a little bit. Might as well go to the verandah now. Much nicer, don't you think, Will? with the view?"

Will looked at Jimmy and me. "Might as well. It's cooler."

Jimmy nodded. "You just said the magic word. Wherever it's cooler."

Will moved toward a console with a Murphy radio and gramophone. "I'll put on some music. What'd you like? I've got Jo Stafford, Tommy Dorsey, Basie, Ellington, Crosby, Sinatra."

Zarine yelled from the kitchen. "Oh, please, not Sinatra again. If you're going to play something, play that Andrews Sisters record."

Will pulled the record from its rack. "You guys go on. I'll bring the nimbu-panis."

The verandah was lined with plants; creepers wound around a trellis along the walls and ceiling. A square wicker table had been set for dinner with a view of people promenading and the sea beyond. Strains of "Rum and Coca Cola" sounded behind us. I gripped the wooden balustrade, breathing the sea air, gazing at the strollers below, and lit a cigarette.

Jimmy joined me, lighting a cigarette himself, exhaling slowly. "Well, what do you think?"

I chased his smoke with my own. "I can't believe it. I can't believe I'm in Bombay. This has just got to be a dream."

Will appeared, with tall glasses of a misty liquid and ice and straws. "No dream, I assure you, but I know what you mean. I remember how I felt when I first got to Bombay—but it's no dream, no dream, except for Zarine."

He spoke quietly, so differently from his wife, but I could see they were both shy. He covered it with silence, she with noise. He smiled as he spoke, staring at the sea as if with memory. "I fell in love with the city from the first, and after Zarine … well, there was no going back—not that I had much to go back to in Jackson."

"Mississippi?"

"Nope, Texas. My family's kind of disintegrated. I wanted to start over—and Zarine gave me the chance. Bombay just became my home."

Zarine came out with a basket of rolls in linen and butter. "And now my family's kind of disintegrated also. They can't stand Will. Can you imagine? Bad enough we had to throw out the English from our country—but I had to bring an American into the family, a yankee."

She laughed. "But that's not the point. They would love him if he was a doctor or a lawyer or something, but he's a waiter, a servant. As far as they are concerned a steward is a waiter. That is the real reason they won't talk to us—but I don't care. Their loss, not mine, if they won't even bother to get to know him." She laughed again. "Actually, when we first met he was the doctor. I was so sick on that stupid boat, and he kept checking to see if I was all right. So sweet, he was."

Will smiled. "She looked so miserable I was afraid she was going to jump out of the porthole."

"As if!" She laughed. "And now he's good for my business. I have so many more patients now because he is my receptionist, mostly young women patients who come because he flirts with them."

Will responded mildly. "I do not flirt with them."

"You don't even know it, but you flirt with them."

"How do I flirt with them?"

"If you smile at them, you are flirting with them." Will grimaced and she turned to me. "It's true! They all think he is so goodlooking, so tall and so white, and with his blue eyes and his American accent they are all sick with love—and he cures them by flirting with them."

Will just laughed.

"I don't care, actually, as long as they keep coming, and as long as they pay their bills—but listen to me, talkingtalking, while the buns are getting cold—hot cross buns. I kept them in the oven fresh from the bakery before we picked you up from the docks. Eat them while they are still hot."

Jimmy looked at me, nodding. I knew what he meant, put down my cigarette, picked four buns, and juggled, eating one as I juggled, one bite at a time, chewing quickly, until I was juggling just three.

Zarine and Will watched in amazement. Zarine clapped first, cheering loudly when she realized what I was doing. "Shabash! Shabash! Well done! Well done, indeed!"

Will joined in. "Bra-Vo!"

Jimmy grinned. "Sorry. I've been trying to teach him some manners, but you know how it is. You can take the boy out of the circus, but ..."

Zarine shut him up with a wave of her hand. "Manners, schmanners! This is like having the circus in our own home. You can say Spike has earned his keep—but what I want to know, Jimmy, is what are you going to do for that bun you are eating with such relish?" She grinned, turning to him. "Will you do the dishes? We gave Morar a holiday, you know, for his daughter's wedding."

Jimmy grinned. Morar was their servant. "Whatever it takes, and with pleasure."

FIVE   3RD PASTA LANE

At eleven the next morning, after a night on the sofa and a breakfast of scrambled eggs on toast (spiced with ginger and coriander and flavored with onions and tomatoes), tea with milk, and mangos, Will and Zarine drove me through Colaba Causeway (a crowded thoroughfare lined with shops and restaurants, hotels and residences) to 3rd Pasta Lane. Traffic and pedestrians and animals blended as multifariously as the day before, even the night before when we had driven Jimmy back to the docks. More than just crowded, the streets were populated, people lived on the streets, cows owned the roads. Turning into 3rd Pasta Lane, Will was first to spot a placard, HANDICRAFTS OF INDIA, posted over a third floor balcony of Prakash Mahal and they dropped me off, wishing me luck, heading for Zarine's dispensary. I had everything I needed including rupees they had changed for dollars. I was suddenly afraid Mr. Prem Gupta would recognize the juggler from

Toledo, associate me with the loss of his wallet, even the death of the boy—but a moment dithered was a moment lost and I had come too far to turn back.

Steep stone steps pulled me into a small flagstoned foyer with a wooden directory posted on the wall displaying tenant names on brass plates: two apartments on each floor, including the ground, Peters and Banerjee, Saathe and Desai, Taraporevala and Mehta, and Gupta (HANDICRAFTS OF INDIA) who apparently occupied both apartments on the top floor. Narrow wooden stairs, sagging in the middle, drew me upward. The stairwell was clean, thick with the sweet smell of frying onions. The door was open on the top floor and I entered the showroom.

Glass showcases displayed merchandise, barred windows let in light, fluorescent lamps hummed from the ceiling, fans rotated lazily. Walls held rugs, tapestries, paintings, and masks. A boy rose to his feet from a desk as I entered. He might have been my age for his size (larger than me), but looked younger for short pants, an earnest expression behind hornrimmed glasses, limbs smooth and firm as a baby's, and he sounded younger yet for his politeness when he spoke. "Hullo? Yes?"

"Hi. Is this the place with the handicrafts?"

He nodded, spreading arms to indicate the wares. "Yes. Come in, no?"

The room smelled of curry. There was a noise of children giggling and whispering deeper in the apartment. A woman's voice sounded from another room. "Kown hai, beta?"

"Only someone to see the handicrafts."

I took a deep breath, unsure of myself. "The other apartments looked like private residences."

The boy nodded again. "Yes, it is also that. My mother is just cooking, my father will be home any minute, but it is also our place of business. We have got two flats because of that. This is mostly our, you know, our showroom, to show what we are selling. If you are interested in buying wholesale we will also take your order."

The closest showcase displayed an ivory papercutter, a papier-mache Hanuman, a bronze figurine of Dancing Shiva, and a wooden box inlaid with filigree. "Can I buy just one item? I don't wanna buy wholesale." I wanted to get something for Will and Zarine.

"Oh, yes, of course, you can buy. These are only for show. My father goes all over the world, England, America, with our brochure for people who are setting up showrooms in other countries. He has just come back from America, just these past two months. Anything in particular you are looking for?"

"Nope. Just lookin'."

"Looklook, no rush, no hurry, take your time."

There were cushions with mirrorwork, paintings on heartshaped pipal leaves, Shivas, Krishnas, Ganeshes, Christs; there was woodwork, weavery, stitchery, pottery. He smiled for the first time, shy and sly. "You are from America. I can tell. My father has got many American customers. He has got many business contacts in America. He has come back from America only two months past."

"You just said so."

"I am correct? You are from America?"

"Surprise, surprise."

He kept his smile. "Oh, believe me, it is no surprise. We get many American visitors. Only last month we had someone from America for dinner. Mr. Jay Jordan Lumsden was here for dinner only last month—famous, like Frank Buck—brings 'em back alive. You have maybe heard about him?"

I was too surprised to speak.

"You have heard about him? Yes? No?"

"Sure, I've heard of him. Who hasn't? What d'you mean he was here for dinner?"

"What I said. He was here. He is my father's friend. Both are members of the Bombay Natural History Society. Sometimes they are partners in business. My father is just on his way to see him in two-three days. He is going to his camp."

I stared, dumbstruck again.

He rushed back to the desk, returning with a framed photograph. "Look, here is a picture."

The picture showed Lumsden with a comradely arm around someone's shoulders. It was a grainy, black and white photograph, but I knew Lumsden's trademark drooping moustaches well enough to recognize him easily. "That's Lumsden all right. Hot diggety!"

"The other man is my father, see?"

"Hot diggety!"

"You know him? You know Mr. Jay Jordan Lumsden?"

I shook my head. "I know *of* him. I know his work. I wanna work with him. That's why I'm here. If not for him I'd still be in Ohio."

The boy brought his hands together in a single loud clap. "Well said! Well said, indeed! This is capital! Capital! You must meet my father. He will help you. He will be here soon now, any minute."

I couldn't help grinning. "Jeez, I can't believe it! That'd be swell! That'd be just so damn swell! I can't tell you what it'd mean to me if he could introduce me to Lumsden!"

"My father will be here in five-ten minutes."

I held out my hand. "I should introduce myself: Dan Bailey."

He was suddenly formal again, taking my hand. "Hullo. My name is Avinash, but my friends call me Babu—just a nickname."

I patted the hair down on my head. "My friends call me Spike, 'cause of my hair. It just won't stay."

Babu laughed. "From Ohio, you said? You are from Ohio? Toledo, Ohio?"

"Nope. Kendall Green, Ohio."

Babu smiled again. "My father was in Toledo. He had a bad experience. His pocket got picked. His wallet got stolen. He lost a lot of money, but money is not so important. Money you can always make back—but he also lost business contacts, also so much time. It was veryvery inconvenient."

I spoke carefully. "Sorry to hear that. That must've been a blow." I turned away to focus on a wooden jewelry box.

"Let me show you that." Babu dashed back to his desk, pulled out a ring of keys from a drawer, opened the case with the box, brought it out as gently as if it were a baby, and opened it. A melody tinkled. "Bithoven. For Elisa."

I nodded, taking the box, setting it on the showcase. "Very nice."

Babu grinned as if he'd been complimented. "Yes, very nice, and you can smell it. It is sandalwood. Just rub like this a little bit, see? Releases the fragrance."

I rubbed and sniffed. I liked the look of the box, the filigree was fine and intricate, and the melody and fragrance put an end to any doubts that might have lingered.

"Veryvery cheap, four hundred rupees only—but for you, coming from America, knowing Mr. Jay Jordan Lumsden, only three hundred rupees, twenty-five percent discount."

I did a quick calculation. Three hundred rupees was about eighty dollars, but even with the discount the price seemed outrageous and Zarine had warned me to purchase nothing without first bargaining. "Thanks, but I'd like to look around a bit first."

He might have read my mind. "Look as much as you want. Over here we have got some things, very cheap—but very nice." He unlocked another showcase. "Just some bits and pieces, odds and ends, this and that, fake ivory, scrimshaws, some broken pieces—veryvery cheap."

"Fake ivory?"

"Walrus tusks, pig tusks, hippo—even of narwhals, but that is a little bit different. Elephant tusks and pig tusks and hippos and walruses are all incisors, but narwhal tusks are canines—but only elephant tusks are real ivory."

"How can you tell the difference?"

"You can tell by engine-turning. You know what is engine-turning?"

"Nope."

"Look. I will show you." He picked up what looked like a shell of raw ivory. "This is a piece of an elephant tusk. Look closely at the cross-section. Look where the striations cross. Look how they look."

I had imagined, scratching the skin of ivory, that I would find woodgrain in white, or the mist frozen in marble, but this was different. The cross-section of the tusk revealed a pattern of diamonds—like those formed by ripples crossing one another as they radiate from pebbles dropped in a pond, turning to gothic arches among the outer ripples.

"This pattern is called engine-turning. Only elephant tusks have engine-turning. Others don't have the same tone, like comparing an athlete's body with a clerk's, one so clearly defined, the other not. See this? This is a pig tusk. See? No definition. See? And see this? This is a walrus tusk. See again? No definition. Flaky, flabby."

The striations were clear to the naked eye, the engine-turning was beautiful, like fossilized information, a peek into the heart of ivory. "How much for that piece?"

He waved his hand as if it were a trifle. "That is nothing, absolutely nothing." For a moment I thought he might give it to me. "You can have it for just fifty rupees. Fifty rupees and it is yours."

I knew it was worth less, but the piece had developed sentimental value already: it had revealed its heart. I nodded. "Done—and how about two hundred dollars—I mean, rupees—for the music box?"

Babu smiled ingratiatingly. "It is already discounted twenty-five percent, already down to three hundred. What can I say?"

"Two hundred and fifty?"

Babu sighed, looking one way, then the other, but nodding reluctantly. "Only for you, because you are coming from America." Someone was coming up the stairs, we could hear steps, keys jingling. "My father! He will be so happy to meet you."

I RECOGNIZED MR. GUPTA from the picture with Lumsden though he appeared older, moving with a hesitant gait. I recalled the short dark man from the prophetic day in Toledo, the tusklike stain on his left temple. I recalled him because there had been no one else like him—and dreaded he might recall me for the same reason. Babu didn't give us a chance to speak. "Daddy, this is Mr. Dan Bailey. He is called Spike because of his hair. He has come to Bombay from America to meet Mr. Jay Jordan Lumsden. What a great chance, isn't it, that he came straight to us only?"

The old man nodded without looking at his son, focusing on me, holding out his hand, smiling. "Hullo. Mr. Prem W. Gupta at your service. How do you do, sir?"

He spoke slowly, with a thick accent and a sucking sound, as if his sunken cheeks impeded speech, but his most curious feature was his eyes. They appeared perpetually closed, the lids so heavy that he raised his head instead of just the lids to see better. I shook his hand. "Dan Bailey, sir. It *is* a helluva coincidence, you knowin' Mr. Lumsden."

"You have come here to meet with Mr. Lumsden?"

"Not exactly. I came to India to find Mr. Lumsden—but you might say I came to your showroom by accident."

Gupta seemed puzzled. "From America you have come, is it?"

"Kendall Green, Ohio. Have you been there?"

Gupta's smile spread though his eyes remained heavily lidded. "Oh, no, Kendall Green I have not been, but I have been to Ohio, lovely state." His eyelids remained lowered, but a sharper gaze seemed to peer from within. "Lovely country, your America. So big, so vast, so much industry, so much comfort."

I lowered my eyes to affect humility. "Thanks. I hear you just got back from the States—but I heard you had some trouble."

Gupta raised his finger. "Yes, I had some bad luck in Toledo—just this last December."

I tried to look sympathetic, but succeeded only in looking at the ground. "Yeah, Babu told me—about your wallet. Sorry to hear it."

Gupta nodded slowly, speaking with the ease of a practiced businessman, still holding me with his gaze. "These things happen. That is life. You have been in Toledo?"

I could not have said whether I'd been recognized. Gupta's eyes, from which there was no release, released nothing. "It's been awhile."

"I have been to Cincinnatti, Columbus, Cleveland. I have seen many of the east coast states—mostly, you see, for my business—but, forgive me, I have not yet seen Kendall Green."

I ventured a laugh. "I wouldn't waste my time. If you've seen Cleveland, you don't need to see Kendall Green."

Gupta nodded, still smiling, apparently absorbed by everything I said. "If you are saying so—but forgive me again, my curiosity, but how is it that you are hearing about my little shop in Kendall Green?"

I raised innocent eyebrows. "But I didn't hear about it. I was just explorin' when I saw your sign in the window."

"Ah, yesyes, I see, I see."

Gupta's smile began to lose its width, his gaze seemed harder and uglier. I imagined he'd seen through me and decided to lie as little as possible. "I wanted to get somethin' for the people I'm stayin' with, just somethin' small to say thanks."

"Ah, yes, and with whom you are staying?"

I spilled my story: I'd dreamed of working with Jay Jordan Lumsden, taken the job on *The Gardenia* to get to Bombay, befriended Jimmy who'd introduced me to the Gardners, who'd left me to explore Bombay for the day.

They listened attentively. The old man smiled, apparently impressed by my initiative. "That is a very nice story, but Mr. Lumsden is a very busy man. So many are wanting to work with him. Why he should take you under his wing when so many are wanting to work with him?"

I risked a smile. "I'll jus' have to convince him when I find him. I can't believe he'd send me back when he sees how far I've come."

Gupta raised his finger again. "But what about Mr. Lumsden? What about the position you are putting him in? You have come a long way, yes, but for one moment put all that on one side. What about your qualifications? This is, after all, a business, not a charity. He has got something that you want, but what have you got for him that he wants?"

I played my trump. "I have some experience with animals. I was born in a circus –"

Babu couldn't stay quiet. "Arre! I say! Really? You were born in a circus? What circus?"

His father held up his hand, keeping his eyes on me. "Babu, let him talk!"

The voice was harsher than before and I spoke again with humility. "Not much to say. It would be an honor to work with Mr. Lumsden. I ain't askin' for wages. Board and lodgin' would be enough, and the chance to learn somethin' about trappin' animals."

"But what circus? What circus you were born in?"

Babu's father looked at him sternly, releasing me from his gaze for the first time.

"The Great Frank Bros."

Gupta appeared to be considering my story. "And what did you do in the circus?"

I resisted the temptation to say I juggled. "I worked with the elephants. I worked with Hero. He was pretty well known, the blackest elephant in the world."

Gupta spoke with renewed interest. "Ah, yes, I heard about the black elephant. He was poisoned, no, very recently?"

"Right, someone lookin' for revenge on the circus—but it was pretty much the end of my act, and I decided it was time to join Mr. Lumsden."

Gupta raised his head, peering again from lidded eyes. "This is a fascinating story, and how were you going to join Mr. Lumsden?"

"Well, the first step was to get to Bombay. My friends, the Gardners, said they'd find out what they could about routes to Lumsden's camp. It was just by accident that I found you."

Gupta's head remained raised. "There are many ways to Mr. Lumsden's camp—car, train, bus, whatever you want. Car is best if you can get it because you have better control of where you are going—but there are many ways."

I spoke hesitantly, as if I hated to impose. "If you could help in any way—a recommendation, I mean, or a hint on how to approach him, I'd do anythin'—I mean, *any*thin'!"

Gupta held my gaze in silence, speaking finally just as I had given up hope. "Give me your telephone number. I am going to meet him soon in Nandi—it is a drive of about seven-eight hours—but details are still being firmed up. I am coming back, but he will go on to his base camp. I will give you a ring about it."

"Are you sayin' you'd take me?"

"I'm saying details are still being firmed up, but if you will give me your telephone number I will give you a ring and we will see what happens."

I was afraid if Gupta talked with the Gardners my lie about finding his place accidentally would be uncovered and bit my lip feigning disappointment. "Darn! It's so stupid of me, but I left the number at home." I looked from one of them to the other. "Maybe I could call you if that'd be all right?"

Gupta's lids remained lowered. "I will give you my card, but I want you to think about one thing."

"Of course!"

"This is not something to be undertaken lightly. Let me tell you something. What is happening in our country is not unlike what has happened in your own country, in your America, more than one and a half centuries ago now. Both countries were under the English yoke. Both countries have now asserted independence. But what has happened in India is this. Indians became so happy to throw off the English yoke, they threw off everything to do with the English along with the colonialism, including the old shooting regulations. They began shootingshooting wildlife everywhere—on estates, in sanctuaries, everywhere. Everything the English said they could not do, now they did. Because of food shortages the government of India gave them guns for protecting crops, but this meant only more animals were getting shot. The government of India gave them jeeps and they went hunting in the night, shootingshooting all the animals that came in their headlights. The government of India gave them poison for insects, but the farmers poisoned also lions, tigers, leopards, cheetahs because they raided their farms in the night. Our Indian cheetah is almost extinct. Next year, this time, mark my words, he will be gone, poof, kaput, not there, no more Indian cheetah. Are you following me, Mr. Spike, what I am saying?"

I nodded.

"Then there are people like Mr. Lumsden who are trying to help us. They are trying to save our wildlife. They are not shooting them, but they are doing a riskier thing, a more brave and a more noble thing. They are catching them alive, for both Indian zoological gardens and foreign. They are helping us in spite of ourselves, in spite of our stupidity. What I am saying, Mr. Spike, is anybody who plays the fool with our Mr. Lumsden, any tomfoolery with our Mr. Lumsden, any jiggery-pokery, and he has to answer to me. He has to answer to me because he is playing the fool with my country's future. Are you reading me, Mr. Spike? Are you reading me loud and clear?"

"Yes, sir. Loud and clear, sir."

"Good. Now listen, what I am saying. I have got business to do, and I am going by car. In two-three days I will be visiting our Mr. Lumsden's camp. I am leaving early, day after tomorrow. Anything I can do to help our Mr. Lumsden I want to do, and I am thinking maybe with your elephant experience you can be of service. He has commissioned, I know, for elephants. If you are wanting to go, give me a ring."

Babu almost jumped. "What I told you, Spike? What I said? Capital, this is, no? Capital!"

I nodded, humble again, allowing a brief smile. "Yeah, capital. I will *def*initely call you."

Gupta nodded his understanding. "Give me a ring—but do not forget that I am leaving the day after. Babu, make sure you give Mr. Spike my card."

Babu almost dove back into the desk drawer, drawing out a stack of the familiar cards and offering one. "Here, here, I have got it."

I joined him at the desk, accepting the card. "Thanks."

"Take, take. Take more. Take for your friends."

"Thanks." I took more and put them in my pocket.

"You are still also wanting the music box, no? And the ivory piece?"

"Oh, yeah, sure."

"Only three hundred rupees."

I pulled rupee notes from my wallet, careful not to reveal Gupta's original card, but one of the photographs of myself as big game hunter astride dead Hero caught Babu's interest. "I say, not to be a nosy parker or anything, but that is a picture of a shikar, no?"

"What?"

"A shikar—a hunt. I say, is that you, Spike, in the picture?"

I laughed. "It was a joke. Lemme show you—but lemme put these away first." I stashed the cards quickly away before displaying the pictures of myself with Hero and explaining the circumstances.

The old man's eyelids didn't move, but his gaze hardened. His voice grew stern. "We are having more respect for life in India, Mr. Spike."

"He was dead. Hero was dead."

"There is no difference, Mr. Spike. Respect for life is respect for death. Especially we are having respect for elephants. We are not even killing them now for ivory. We are only taking ivory from dead elephants, who die naturally. Do you get what I am saying."

I hung my head.

"You get what I am saying, Mr. Spike? Respect for the living is respect for the dead, and respect for the dead is respect for the living. It is the same thing. Do you get me?"

I remained contrite. "Yeah, I get it. I jus' wasn't thinkin' … it's jus' … it's jus' all so different…."

Gupta stared, still as stone, but finally nodded. "Yes, of course, you are only a boy. Things are different in America. Still you have got very many things to learn."

The words were conciliatory, but I shivered: a cold finger, reaching into my mouth, had grown into a mist flooding my chest. Chastised by Gupta, I recalled Siri's curse, castigating me for the same transgression. It was the beginning of the long freeze, my entry into the graveyard. My end was close, or maybe I should say my end as Spike was close—because, as you know, I went on, but Spike did not—and Hazel, sister in my first life, mother in my next ... but once more I get ahead of myself.

SIX SURROUNDED BY MIRACLES

Early in the morning of the second day, I descended the elevator of Ganga Vihar to wait for Gupta. I had returned from his showroom a conquering hero, grinning like the man in the moon, all misgivings eclipsed by the photograph of Gupta with Lumsden. Providence had led me, providence would follow. Zarine had loved the box, continually inhaling it's perfume. "Thank you so much, Spike. Such a lovely box it is. Sandalwood is my favorite fragrance—and I love 'Fur Elise.' How did you know?"

I had called Gupta and we had made arrangements. The Gardners had provided a whirlwind tour of the city in the single day we had, but we had made it an early night. Gupta planned to leave at six in the morning. Zarine had nodded agreement. "Good thinking, best way to beat the heat—also the traffic."

I was surprised to find Gupta's large green Hudson waiting, my host smiling through an open window. "Good morning, Mr. Spike. How are you?"

"Mr. Gupta, sorry to have made you wait. I thought I was early."

He waved my apology aside. "Not to worry, Mr. Spike. You *are* early. I am just a little bit earlier. It is just my way. I like to beat the heat as much as I can." He wore a kurta and dhoti revealing bony brown legs, and chappals.

"Just what Zarine said."

He opened the door. "Give your bag to my driver. He will put it in the boot. Tickery, bag lay lo."

The driver wore a white captain's uniform with a hat and brass buttons. "This is swell of you, Mr. Gupta. I mean it. I can't believe I'm gonna see Mr. Lumsden!"

Mr. Gupta smiled, patting my knee avuncularly. "Most welcome, Mr. Spike. Most welcome. I told you I am going to take you to Mr. Lumsden in Nandi, and that is what I am going to do. From there I will come back after I have concluded my business, but you will go on with him to his base camp. We should be in Nandi—one o'clock, two o'clock, something like that—but there is something else I want to show you first, in Boregaon. It is on the way. As an elephant man, you will be very much pleased I think. We will stop there for lunch about noontime. They have the best sheekh kababs."

The blush of dawn over the Arabian Sea dissipated as the sun climbed the vault of the sky. Gupta fluttered his fingers, pointing to bottles and thermoses in the front seat. "We have got Coca Cola, nimbu-pani, of course water, also chai."

The heat rose with the sun and I squirmed in my efforts to miss nothing. There was little traffic on the road, but clusters of charpois were upended as we passed, walls dropped like drawbridges into storefronts, chaiwallahs roamed and squatted with streetdwellers by the road, stray animals were never far (dogs, cats, goats, cows), nor nutbrown children with swollen bellies.

Gupta sipped tea poured from a thermos. "You know, Mr. Spike, in one way your America was responsible for our Bombay's first industrial successes. You see, the first cotton mill was established in Bombay in 1857—and because of your American Civil War, from 1861 to 1865 I think it was, because of your American Civil War there was a great boom in Bombay cotton. After the war, prices fell—but then the Suez Canal opened in 1869 and again trade prospered."

"Yeah. Amazing how these things hook up."

"Yes, amazing—but maybe not so amazing when understanding becomes more complete. A bad thing happens in America, but it is a good thing for Bombay cotton. That is the big picture—but even in the small picture bad things give rise to good things, is it not? Tell me, Mr. Spike. What is your philosophy of life?"

I was surprised by the question, but recalled something Brown E had sometimes mumbled. "The way I see it, if chance will have me king, chance will crown me without my stir—something like that."

Gupta stared as if he were seeing me for the first time. "Aha, *Macbeth*! Mr. Spike, you are surprising me, and that is a good thing—but you see chance did not crown Mr. Macbeth without his stir, and he paid the full price for his stir, did he not? Later on, he said what? Life is a tale told by an idiot, full of sound and fury and signifying nothing. Much better, do you not think, if he had listened to Socrates, the unexamined life is not worth living?"

I knew less about Socrates than about Shakespeare. "I guess."

"You guess? But what do you think? I am asking what you think."

This was unlike any conversation I'd had, but impressed by his intellect I was flattered by his interest. "I guess I'd say life's for livin'. You got to see things, you got to do things—you got to, you know, experience things."

"Yes, of course, for living and seeing and things like that—but I am saying to you, most important of all, life is for understanding. What is the point of experiencing if there is no understanding? We are otherwise just like donkeys, seeing things and experiencing things, but understanding nothing."

"But even a donkey has to experience things first."

"Right you are, Mr. Spike, but what I am saying is that many Americans are going everywhere, traveling around and around the world, here and there and everywhere, spinning the world with their feet—and they are very rich, and they are very generous, and they are very good—but if you ask them what they are seeing and experiencing they will say only that America is the best country in the world. They will see dirty roads and they will say in America we do not have dirty roads. They will see beggars and they will say in America we do not have beggars. They will see lepers and they will say in America we do not have lepers. They are only interested in comparing, like little boys saying my daddy can, how do you say it? my daddy can lick your daddy?"

"What d'you think they should do?"

"Why not just see what there is to see? Why not just take what is there for what it is, not for what it might be in America—but they are seeing Stonehenge and they are saying Empire State Building is bigger, they are seeing Taj Mahal and they are saying it is only a tomb, they are seeing Acropolis and they are saying they should put an amusement park over here. God bless America means what? God is not going to bless the rest of the world? You get what I am saying?"

"All I'm sayin' is I wanna live my life to the fullest 'cause tomorrow I could be dead."

He winked. "Yes, but that may also be only the beginning, is it not?"

I remembered I was in India. "What d'you mean? Reincarnation?"

"Yes, maybe, reincarnation—but even reincarnation may be an illusion, like everything else."

"You sayin' *e*verythin's an illusion?"

He took a deep breath, smiling as he spoke. "Why not? In Einstein's world A can be nonA, the son can be the grandfather of the great grandson—*lit*erally, Mr. Spike, *lit*erally. In Einstein's world, maya, what you call illusion, becomes reality."

I said nothing. I knew even less about Einstein than I knew about Socrates.

"Think about it like this, Mr. Spike. It takes the light of the sun 8 minutes to reach the earth because, A, the sun is 93 million miles away, and, B, light travels at 186,000 miles per second. So, C, we are actually seeing the sun as it was 8 minutes ago, not as it is at this moment. We are seeing the sun in space *and* in time. We are seeing what is in the *past*, but we are in the *pres*ent. So, we may say, we are living in *two* times, is it not? but which is the correct one? We may say that time is an illusion, is it not? This is not some mumbojumbo I am talking, Mr. Spike. Do you get what I am saying?"

"I don't know. I guess."

"You don't know? You guess? Nono, it is so. The sun is 8 light minutes away, the moon is one light second away—and, tell me, Mr. Spike, do you believe in ghosts?"

"Ghosts?!!"

"Not ghosts of men, Mr. Spike. Ghosts of stars. There are stars that are so far away that by the time their light is reaching us they are dead.

We are seeing them alive sometimes after they have died. We are seeing their ghosts. Is that not a miracle?"

I could think of nothing to say.

"Think about it like this, Mr. Spike. We are like drops of water in the ocean, but it is not possible to separate drops of water in the ocean. Each of us is the ocean itself. Those who do not understand this are lost in the ocean—but those who understand become the ocean itself. You get what I am saying?"

I remained silent.

Gupta chuckled. "Your John Steinbeck said the same thing in his great book, *Grapes of Wrath*. He said each of us has got a little piece of a soul, but it is no good unless it is with all the other little pieces. Same thing, is it not? Ocean, soul: what is the difference? Also, if we are all part of one big soul instead of little pieces by themselves, then it is clear as geometry, is it not, that we are paying for one another's sins. I do something wrong, you are paying for it; you do something wrong, someone else is paying for it; because we are all One. Q.E.D., is it not? It is also in your Bible, is it not? Last shall be first and first shall be last? Theoretically, at least, it is explaining why bad things are happening to good people, why good things are happening to bad people, is it not? Cause and effect, is it not? A question of balance, is it not? Matter cannot be created or destroyed, energy cannot be created or destroyed, and it is the same with karma, is it not? What is karma if not the end product of matter and energy? the great balancer?"

I looked away, long out of my depth, but it only spurred him further.

"Think about it like this, Mr. Spike. We are surrounded all the time by miracles, is it not? We talk about walking upon the water as if it was a miracle, but walking upon the earth is also a miracle, is it not? Breath is a miracle, death is a miracle, everything is a miracle, we are surrounded by miracles. We can plumb the depths of the ocean, we can plumb the depths of the space, but the depths of the human psyche is a mystery, and as long as it is a mystery life is a miracle, is it not? but we are taking it for granted, we are ungrateful for what we have got, we want more than we need, and we have to pay the price. It is like the elephant graveyard, is it not?"

"Huh? What?"

"The elephant graveyard. It is myth, is it not? You must know it, working with elephants, no?"

"I only work with them. I don't know about myths and graveyards and stuff."

"It is a mythology. The graveyard is a mythology. The elephants are not making pilgrimages to the graveyards, they are not following mysterious summonses like the mythologies are saying, but sick and dying elephants are migrating to swamps and rivers. This is your famous graveyard. They are not going there to die, but to live, to find water, but they are dying, most especially during the droughts when they are failing to extract themselves from the swamps. Then, sometimes, hunters are herding elephants into gorges for slaughter in one fell swoop, and sometimes herds of elephants are succumbing to deadly gases seeping through the soil, erupting from the lakes. All become your graveyards, but they are not going there to die, is it not, Mr. Spike?"

I shook my head to clear it of the dark thoughts. "I don't know. All I'm sayin' is even a donkey has to see and experience things first. That's all I'm sayin'. That's why I'm here, to see and experience everythin' I can—jus' like a donkey."

Gupta laughed, patting my knee again. "Right you are, Mr. Spike. It is easy to talk, but the thing is to act. You know what Confucius said: a wise man is acting before he is talking, then talking according to his actions." He laughed again. "Alas, Mr. Spike, but I am not a wise man. Otherwise, I would not be talking like this. You must forgive an old man, Mr. Spike, for getting on his hobbyhorse. When you are old, philosophy is all you have left—but I am forgetting my manners."

I changed the subject. "I think I'll have that Coke now."

"Of course. Please. Help yourself." I leaned over the front seat for the Coke and Gupta unrolled a map to show me the route we'd be taking, towns we'd be passing through. "There will be some forts along the way, you will see. I think they will interest you greatly."

"Forts?"

"At least three hundred forts in Bombay State—sea forts, land forts, hill forts—maybe even four hundred—built by many dynasties. Best known is the Maratha hero, maybe you have heard, from the seventeenth century? Shivaji?"

I shook my head.

"Shivaji was a guerilla warrior against the Moghals. This was his territory. He built many forts."

He would have said more, but I stared out of the window. What was he thinking? I didn't know then, but I know now. There are no secrets in the graveyard. He could afford to be patient. Mr. Spike was in his power. His memory had been jogged by my mention of the circus in the showroom as clearly as if I had juggled fruit in his face.

America was a dangerous place for the wrong kind of person. He had seen the negro boy sundered and trampled and made himself scarce. Loss of wallet was secondary to loss of life. He hadn't reported the theft. An article in the newspaper seemed to have been all the justice the dead boy had received or required. His own color did not recommend him to America, but no more could he overlook the business opportunities, and as long as he played his cards right he stayed ahead of the game.

Mr. Spike was guilty of murder, at best of manslaughter, but in America, almost a century after emancipation, the slaughter of a negro counted no more than the slaughter of a pig—a flick of the finger and his own slaughter would have counted no more. He was on his way to see Mr. Lumsden, by which time he would long be rid of Mr. Spike—nothing so drastic as an eye for an eye, or even a wallet for a wallet, but a lesson Mr. Spike would do well to learn.

There was more that not even Gupta knew at the time. I had been delivered into hands greater than his, he was himself as much a pawn as I in the game of my comeuppance. Unknown even to him, I was being driven to my doom, the end of my sixteen-year-old self. Be warned. The sad sack's time has come, take your leave, say your goodbyes. Spike will not be with us much longer.

SEVEN   THE CHAMBER OF ELEPHANTS

Bombay was soon behind us, the countryside reduced to the ghost of a countryside by the inferno of the hot season at its hottest, before the first rain of the monsoon. The heat beat the earth cracking it like an eggshell, revealing ribs in the shallow river basins and rice paddies, reducing trees to skeletons. The car became an oven baking us to a crisp. Animals appeared occasionally, roasted half their size, phantoms of their former selves, foraging in the dust which covered the landscape like ash. Kestrels and crows hovered in the sultry sky. Gupta apologized for every inconvenience, even the weather, promising lusher vistas soon in the hills of the Western Ghats, the mountainous region lining the west coast, promising even the monsoon which was soon to arrive.

First we traveled north, escaping the Bombay peninsula through Salsette and over the Thana Creek, then south into the mainland, into the hills, toward the hill station, Nandi. Hill stations had been modeled by the English on English towns, patches of England on the Indian quilt, for the English memsahibs when the weather boiled over, where English clerks and shopgirls became maharajahs and maharanis, rulers of all they surveyed. Gupta was the best guide. "These hill stations are now all resort areas. Everybody is having a bungalow for the hot season, or they are going to hotels."

The landscape remained dry and dusty but less scorched, cooler as we gained altitude despite the rising sun, and villages tumbled unexpectedly into view around bends in the hills, mud huts clustered behind groves of rubber trees, banana trees, coconut trees. Villagers around a banyan, sheltered by its veil of vines, waved as we passed. Forests carpeted the hills. A tea plantation sprang into view as a comet of langur monkeys blazed through treetops ahead.

By noon we were driving through Boregaon's marketplace, a single winding street of shops, selling vegetables, jewelry, saris, trinkets, handicrafts, chappals, crowded with shoppers and bicycles. We had developed a comfortable camaraderie, Gupta and I, alternating between talking and staring out of the window. We passed through a clean residential neighborhood of narrow streets and gaily colored houses of wood and brick before Gupta stopped the car beside a vendor barbecuing sheekh kababs over an open brazier, and sent Tickery to get us two skewers each. He tapped my knee for attention. "You know, Mr. Spike, people are not knowing very much about Boregaon, because there is not very much to see, but there is one very amazing thing I want to show you just outside the village. As an elephant man, I think you will appreciate it." He spoke to Tickery again, taking the sheekh kabab skewers wrapped in newspaper, "Chalo, bhai, chalo-chalo," and we were once more on our way.

The road inclined as we left Boregaon and moved onto a promontory. The countryside dipped on either side to be replaced by walls enclosing us with what appeared once to have been a fort. A tower loomed, about sixty feet tall, the focus of the ruin, a lookout chamber crowning its head. The Hudson rumbled over the rubble. Gupta stopped the car just yards from the tower. "This is Hathi Minar—Elephant Tower, some are calling it also Tower of the Elephants."

I stared in wonder at foundations laid bare, walls thrust into air, chambers burrowed into the hill, cannon overgrown with shrubbery, encrusted with dirt. The ruined ramparts were twelve feet thick, thirty feet at their highest. The cannon was almost twenty feet. "Why elephants?"

Gupta smiled. "Everything in its time, Mr. Spike. First, let us have lunch."

I wanted to explore the fort, but Gupta unwrapped the skewers saying it would not do to let lunch get cold. We ate in the car leaving the doors open for the breeze. Tickery ate squatting outside, captain's hat perched on his knee.

Gupta spoke as we ate. "It is actually a funny story, why they are calling it Hathi Minar. The fort was built by Shivaji, but the name comes from a later period. There are some chambers that have been excavated from the hillside, maybe even just refurbished caves, no one is knowing for sure—but there is one in particular, a round chamber—with a mural of elephants. The whole round wall is a mural of elephants, all around you, one row upon another, elephants and elephants and more elephants, in full battle regalia—elephant cavalries, you might say."

Gupta smiled, nodding slowly, approvingly, at my spellbound interest.

"It is said that the artisan was from the eighteenth century, maybe the seventeenth century, no one is knowing for certain. The funny thing is that the minar itself, the tower itself, was not touched, no paintings, no elephants, nothing, but the place is now being called Hathi Minar, Tower of Elephants."

Gupta hadn't stopped smiling. He raised an open hand in question, shrugging at the mystery.

"The mural itself is not so good, but if you look closely, and if you concentrate, the elephants are moving. They are coming towards you. I have seen. It is fascinating. I thought with your background with elephants you would also find it fascinating."

I raised a skeptical eyebrow.

Gupta raised a hand to acknowledge my skepticism. "Say nothing. Just look, no preconceptions, and tell me what you see."

"All right."

After we'd finished Gupta passed me a canteen of water. "Drink, drink. Coca Cola is good, but water is better. In the hot weather better to drink lots of water. Do not worry, it is boiled. My wife only boiled it last night."

"I'm not hot anymore. It's cool up here."

"Never mind. Water is good, the more the better, flushes the system. Drink up at least a little bit."

I drank two long drafts and returned the canteen, but Gupta shook his head. "Keep, keep. I have got my own." He slung the other canteen over his shoulder. "Give it back when you are finished."

I slung the canteen over my shoulder.

Mr. Gupta opened a round tincan. "Cigarette?"

I took one, "Thanks," and Mr. Gupta lit it.

Gupta nodded satisfaction as I drew on the cigarette.

"Come. Let us go. Let me show you." Gupta led the way. "You know what is another funny thing, Mr. Spike? After you left the other day I was thinking about that poem, you know, by your Mr. Rudyard Kipling?"

I wanted to say he wasn't *my* Mr. Rudyard Kipling, Kipling being British, but I let it pass. My head felt heavy for no reason I could fathom as I stumbled in Gupta's wake. "What poem?"

He spoke over his shoulder. "You must be knowing it. 'And the end of the fight is a tombstone white with the name of the late deceased, And the epitaph drear, "A Fool lies here who tried to hustle the East."' You must be knowing it?"

An icy finger touched the base of my spine. Gupta walked as if he were sailing through a garden while I continued to stumble behind, wanting to hide my ignorance. "Oh, *that* poem."

Gupta seemed almost surprisingly jovial. "It is a funny thing, I was thinking, because I am the one who got the hustle in Toledo. I am from the East, and I got the hustle in the west. Is that not a funny thing, Mr. Spike?"

"The funniest." The icy finger stroking my spine was turning hot. I didn't understand, but took another drink of water. My comprehension was getting worse. Gupta's ears appeared incredibly long as I followed, even to be getting longer and wagging as if they might trip him as he walked, or bear him aloft like Dumbo's. I didn't understand what was happening and it made me tense. Gupta's hands appeared webbed and I wondered why I hadn't noticed before. I felt hotter and took another swig from the canteen.

Gupta entered a chamber which appeared in the side of the hill, a chamber which led through two other chambers into a cave. The temperature dropped, the natural coolness of a cave, but a cave much refurbished. Walls met floor in a gentle curve, a manmade curve. Gupta led me through chambers talking about the construction of forts and their materials. "As surely as B is following A, advance in fort design followed advance in weapons technology."

I wished he would shut up. The air felt thick with cobwebs and I followed him blindly, blood like a river in my temples, muscles flexing and unflexing until it seemed they would lose elasticity.

Gupta stopped suddenly and I almost bumped into him. "This is the place, Mr. Spike, from which Hathi Minar got its name. What do you think?"

I looked around. We were in the middle of a circular chamber, about twenty feet in diameter. I would have sworn we were in the heart of the hill, we'd walked far enough, but the chamber was lit from above through an opening revealing the sky.

The wall appeared covered by a pattern more than a mural—columns of gold flanked by pairs of red wings and white crescents—but looking more closely I saw the wings were eyes, the crescents tusks, and the columns trunks covered in mail. The elephants averaged three feet in height, four counting the mahouts on their heads, the howdahs on their backs. Behind the phalanx of elephants the hills were lit by the salmon sun of early morning. The pattern was broken at the entrance, but a wooden door had been affixed which Gupta swung closed and the pattern was continued on the back of the door. Gupta was still smiling and repeated himself. "Well, Mr. Spike, what do you think? Are they moving or no?"

I shook my head. "Nope."

"I will tell you what I will do. I will leave you here for five minutes, five minutes only. If they have not moved in that much time they are not going to move for you, but I hope they will move for you. It is indeed a sight to see." He pushed me down by my shoulder. "This is the best place. Keep your eyes open and tell me afterward what you see."

I sat on the ground without resistance as Gupta left the room. I was afraid to be alone and would have stopped him from closing the door, but my head felt heavy and I closed my eyes letting my head sink into my chest. Something was happening inside me that I didn't understand, something was moving, something inside me. I wished I were back in Kendall Green with Hazel, I wished I were in Eileen's bed, I wished I were being held by my ma. Hearing a noise I imagined Gupta was returning and opened my eyes again. I didn't want Gupta to see my despair. If you'd asked me what I felt, I'd have said my guts were writhing. If you'd asked me what I saw, I'd have hesitated. One of the elephants was trotting toward me, out of the wall, four feet tall, waving its trunk.

EIGHT ELEPHANT GRAVEYARD

The scientific American frowns, the blinkered Briton shakes his head, the businessman yawns, the economist groans, the accountant looks away, but I saw the elephant come out of the wall as surely as you're reading about it now, and Siri's words haunted me as surely as I imagined Hero was haunting me at that very moment: *His ghost will get you! He will not forget! Elephants never forget! He will get you!*

I stared without comprehension, waiting for the elephant to reach me, but it never did. Instead, the panorama widened, the indoors spread into the out, the chamber appeared to vanish into the landscape, into an arena, and the entire ring of elephants appeared to be trotting out of the hills, closing in on me, clouds of dust at their feet, the mountain coming to Mohammad, intent on punishing the desecrator of their dead.

I got to my feet. The elephants were too far for alarm and appeared to be trotting in place, treading earth, securing no ground—but the ground shook and I had to dance to keep my balance. I tried to be lucid. I knew I was not dreaming, not having a nightmare. The spectacle had to be a mirage, a hallucination, but it was affecting me physiologically. My head felt like clay and someone was molding it. I held my head in my hands to massage it back, but stopped when I felt it give.

When I looked again the elephants were closer all around, their trot sped to a canter, the earth trembling with their advance, the salmon sun filling with blood. They began to gallop and I lost my feet on the shuddering ground. Strangely, despite the gallop they appeared not to be covering ground, only getting larger—but just as they began to appear larger than life they began to shrink—not merely to shrink but to take to the air, retracting legs like birds of prey, ears transmogrifying to batwings. Rays from the sun, swollen with the color of blood, streamed through the slits of their eyes like lasers. These were not pink elephants, not gay blue Disney elephants, but the real black brown grey wrinkled baggy things, proboscides like faces in gasmasks, tusks glinting like spears, mouths gaping like plush pink pouches under raised trunks.

The first elephants swooped close enough to reveal networks of leathery veins in their ears, sacks under their eyes large enough to hold babies, and the wind in their wake brushed me like a giant hand. Elephant skeletons followed, white elephants with black tusks, golden elephants bursting into flame. I got up to run, but got in the way of an elephant—and, mercifully, lost consciousness. Was this what Gupta had conjured with his talk about the graveyard, this arena of fabulous elephants? but he had said there was no such thing as the graveyard!

This appears strange, but what's truly strange has yet to appear. I swear to what I saw, but you would do well to consider another perspective. If you'd been in the chamber you would not have seen the phantasmagoric armies of elephants aloft because you would not have been under the same influence. You would have seen me instead avoiding, unsuccessfully, three fruit bats. You would have seen me running at and bouncing off the elephants on the wall until I couldn't get up. Bats press and fold and hang themselves by day like coats on a rack—but they'll flap and fly in lesser darkness if necessary, if disturbed as they'd been that morning. You would have seen me next, lying on my back, blood on my brow, Tickery standing by, Gupta, anxious and kneeling, ear to my chest, fingers on my pulse. You would hear Tickery say: "He got heart-fail, sahib. American sahib got heart-fail."

Gupta's thoughts would be more complex, but you would know them as surely as I knew them. He had meant to teach me a lesson, punishment for my disrespect. He had never meant to introduce me to Lumsden, only to discomfort me enough to put me on a bus back to Bombay. He had meant to play me like a cat a mouse, like a Stradivarius—but he had dropped the instrument, the mouse was dead, and he had been the instrument of death, the puppet master had become the puppet. He was not meant to play God, a greater power had taken over, and a greater responsibility had been thrust on him, for which he would do penance for the rest of his life: the supremest court demanded no less.

The life of a man and the plan of his life did not always coincide. He was culpable, he, Gupta. He had made the solution too strong, pressed the canteen on Mr. Spike one time too many, a mild hallucination would have been punishment enough, but he had induced one too severe, and the boy (no older than his own Avinash, his own little Babu) had been constitutionally unsuited for its potency. It made little difference that the boy had been responsible for the death of the negro trampled that ugly Toledo day. By insinuating himself in the mix he had assumed a grand ungodly godlike status, and his heart buzzed with the responsibility like a hive.

For me, the strangest moments were just beginning, the beginning of my double life, living in a dream from which I could never awake. Dead, I could see myself dead, lying on my back between Gupta and Tickery. I could divine Gupta's thoughts, I could see a crucifixion in his face, but I couldn't attract his attention. My body appeared to expand, my hand as large as formerly my body, Gupta fit into my finger, into my littlest nail, before disappearing altogether with the chamber. Hathi Minar erupted momentarily before me before shrinking to insignificance, merging with the jade of the land, the horizon with the curvature of the earth. The

Bombay peninsula protruded like a finger from the torso of the country before clouds obscured the divisions between land and sea.

Manifold impressions followed: orchestrations of winged beings; cloudscapes crowned with turrets and spires; earth, moon, and other planetary bodies, like toys for children; constellations like kaleidoscopes of diamonds and pearls; the silver spiraling arms of nebulae like the vanes of windmills or the golden orbits of electrons. Dust to dust did no justice to the phenomenon; it was stardust to stardust. I might as easily have shrunk as expanded, as easily have slipped through the cracks of the earth, through its molecular structure, myself an electron in orbit, as allowed worlds to slip through my own molecular structure. Encompassing multitudes, I was no less encompassed myself. Wildhaired Barnum appeared in my thumb, I in Bailey's fist; Gargantua the Great in my palm, I in Hero's trunk; Hero smaller than a bear cub, my elbow larger than Elbo. Beyond Elbo, a point of light, Mary Eileen O'Donnell, thighs thick as hydrants; and beyond Eileen, the brightest sun, my ma, Myrtle.

She was smiling, like everyone was smiling, like I was smiling, about to obtain what I'd never stopped wanting—but I was no sooner beside her than I felt myself heavy again, filling with lead, feet of clay, shrinking and expanding, hot as Satan's hoof. It was what I'd wanted, but not like this, it wasn't my time, it couldn't be, I was just sixteen, thank you but no thank you, I'd be ready when I was ready.

I was being put in a box, the lid slid shut, nails hammered like anvils clanging in my head, and lowered into the bowels of the earth. Light, air, earth, mobility, none were to be mine. Rocks and trees and other sightless things were more visible and free. Gupta stood by, bowed with remorse, Tickery at a respectful distance among a group of somber townfolk. I shouted: *No, Gupta! No! Not my time yet! Not my time!* to no avail. I understood there had been an accident, Gupta had made a mistake, but I did not understand why I was paying for Gupta's mistake. I did not understand then, but it was one down and one to go. Some learn their lesson the first time, some never. I killed a man, more boy than man, and died myself more boy than man. No quid pro quo could have been more clear, no eye no tooth more justly repaid, but for the longest time I refused the rationale. In death I was redeemed, but knew it not then, stupid savage bullboy that I was, pissdrinking peabrain, killer to the core, deserving all I got and more.

I rushed in panic to regain the region of light and air I'd just fled, but in vain. For the next three and twenty years, mine was the fate of the living as much as the dead, the realm of the fabled graveyard. I was the poltergeist, the ghost of Spike, the fetch, the hant, the bhoot of Spike, the hide and hadow, shade and shadow, phantom and phenomenon, wraith and revenant—the soul, the spirit, and the specter. I was the spook of Spike. You can count on a ghost for a fancy prose style.

I couldn't have said when the sky became overcast, time had lost meaning, but the first cloudburst of the monsoon packed the land, sweeping its debris into the gutters of the earth. Children danced with elders in the street, welcoming the waters, soon to be hustled indoors. Day turned momentarily to night, rain poured like a river, lightning cracked the sky, thunder slapped the earth, wind lashed the trees, washing away the old, welcoming the new, teasing flowers like splotches of paint from the wet canvas of the earth.

NINE   A JEZEBEL, A DELILAH, AND A PANDORA

Roy called Hazel the day after the picnic. He would have called her the same night, but there was no telephone in her hotel room and he didn't want the lobby attendant wondering who might call her in the middle of the night. He called her early the next morning at the diner, again after his ten hour drive to Chicago, and everyday for a month. When she mentioned she was saving for a jacket for Dinty he sent her thirty dollars inviting her to buy something for herself as well. She bought the jacket for Dinty, but also a jacket for Roy which she sent with a photograph of herself asking for one in return of himself which he sent. They talked about their daily routines, saying nothing about how they felt, but when she accepted money from him she was telling him what he wanted to hear, and when she spent the money on Dinty and on himself she was telling him more than she could have told him over the telephone or in person. When he returned to Kendall Green a month later the details of their engagement remained in flux but the outlines were fixed in granite.

The Elephant Graveyard

He drove all Friday night to save time, he could stay only the weekend, but you wouldn't have said if you'd seen him that he needed sleep. Catnaps and coffee along the way served him well, but they couldn't account for the beam of a lighthouse in his gaze. They had arranged to meet, at Roy's insistence, in a strange part of town—at seven, but he was there by six, and Hazel half an hour later. He couldn't stop smiling, neither could she, but he didn't kiss her, not her cheek, not even her forehead, but his words were enough under the circumstances. "You look lovely."

She beamed, if possible, brighter than him. "Thanks."

"If we were in Chicago, we could go to breakfast."

She knew what he meant. She closed the door behind her, squeezed his hand on the seat between them. "Then let's go to Chicago. I ain't had breakfast yet."

He laughed. "We will, soon, but not today. I'm too hungry, and Chicago's too far, but I think I could hold out until Cleveland. What do you think?"

"If you promise we'll go to Chicago next?"

"I promise."

She smiled, but said nothing, settling in the seat instead, preparing for the drive to Cleveland. Ten minutes later they were on the road outside Kendall Green. She had released his hand but sidled closer, her hand on his knee. "Roy, I'm hungry now. I can't wait till we get to Cleveland."

He knew she was no longer talking about breakfast. Cautious as ever, he checked his rearview mirror. They were alone. He made the next turning into a copse of pines. They resumed their journey to Cleveland fifteen minutes later, and three hours later they were on the same road again, headed back to Kendall Green, to Bronzeville, to visit Mrs. Blue. Roy said his mama couldn't possibly feel differently about her than he did. Hazel couldn't stop smiling, but was less sure.

Parking the car in front of 34 Cumberland before the newly sturdy gate, heading past the newly landscaped yard, and up the newly straightened steps of the stoop, Hazel lost her smile. Roy knocked, smiling, on the door. "I'd get the doorbell fixed, but I'm still trying to get Mama to move to Chicago."

Hazel didn't think his mama was going to move after all the changes she'd made to the house, but said nothing. Roy appeared distant, less sure of himself, a smile fixed on his face, his gaze on the door, but he wouldn't look at her and stood in front as if to block her from view.

The door opened on the chain and Mrs. Blue peered out. "Hello, Mama. Guess who."

Mrs. Blue undid the latch, appearing no different from before, grey worn scarf wrapped around her head, grey worn housecoat draped around her body, eyes so narrow she might have been blind. "You late. You wrote you were comin' in the mornin'."

"I know, Mama. I'm sorry. We got delayed."

He stepped forward to hug her. Mrs. Blue raised her arms to enfold him and got her first glimpse of Hazel. She appeared to step back involuntarily and her arms returned to her side. "You didn't say nothin' 'bout company."

Roy stepped into the house to reach her again. "I said I had a surprise for you."

Hazel had assumed she'd been expected and felt unwelcome standing on the stoop, but forced a smile. "Hi, Mrs. Blue. How're you doin'?"

Mrs. Blue had not returned Roy's embrace. She took another step back, out of his reach, and raised her nose as if peering at Hazel through closed lids, but said nothing. She was taller than Hazel, and her long nose pointed like a finger.

Roy's smile was becoming no less forced than Hazel's. "You know Hazel, of course, Mama."

Mrs. Blue kept her nose on Hazel, but spoke to Roy. "I know more'n you. She say her name Hazel, but her name Jezebel. If you still got sense in you, boy, you'll listen to your mama. Her name Jezebel."

Mrs. Blue walked into the living-room as if making her pronouncement she was finished. Hazel recognized again her own tiredness in Mrs. Blue's shuffle, a tiredness she thought she had forgotten. Her mouth dropped, she stared at Roy who stalked after his mama. "Don't be talkin' foolish, Mama. You talkin' 'bout the girl I love, the girl I'm gone marry. Have a thought befo' you open your mouth at her—or you gone lose me just like you lost Elbo."

His mama's eyes opened wide for a moment at the mention of Elbo's name. "Don't you dare say that to your mama, you hear? Don't you dare!" They appeared to have forgotten Hazel on the stoop as they carried their argument indoors. The door remained open, but she remained unsure of her place.

Mrs. Blue's voice rose. "Don't you threaten me, boy—an' don't you call your mama foolish. I didn' raise my sons to be niggerish. Have a thought befo' you open your mouth at me. She a Jezebel, just like I said, an' she makin' you an Ahab. She bringin' damnation an' ruination upon your head, ruination an' damnation like a deluge 'pon your shoulders."

"Mama, I cain't talk to you when you talk like this. I cain't understand what you got against her."

"You cain't understand? What kind of devilment she put in you that you cain't understand? Elbo ain't in the ground a month an' you talkin' love an' marriage? What cain't you understand?"

There was silence. Hazel was taken off guard as much as Roy. She had been without the affection of a man for so long that she'd turned selfish, taking what she needed from Roy regardless of what he needed himself. She stepped into the house, closing the door behind her, staying outside the living-room.

"Beside', she a waitress, an' you a lawyer. In the Springers' home she the maid."

Roy found his voice again. "Mama, you still their maid. What you got 'gainst maids?"

Roy's voice was harsher than Hazel had known, but more surprisingly his diction was that of a colored man, and he was suddenly a stranger. A psychologist would have said Roy was regressing under stress, but Hazel understood it differently. He was reverting to type, a panther among panthers as he would have said himself, and she had seen him only with his lionskin.

"I was a maid so's you could be a lawyer. I was a maid so's you could rise among your own people, so's you could help your own kind—not the enemy."

Hazel stepped into the living-room. Mrs. Blue was seated on the couch, but Roy remained standing over her, hands on his hips. She was beginning to see him differently herself. She had never seen a colored man behave as he did, not just like a white man but an educated white man, as if there were no difference between them, the way he had dealt with Jonas—but his mama was right: an educated white man, a white lawyer, would never have given her the same consideration.

Roy watched in silence as she entered. Even his mama didn't see him as purely as Hazel. His mama saw him as a colored man, one of a race. Hazel saw him not as one of a race but of one race with herself because she saw herself of one race with everyone. He couldn't have explained that to his mama who would always see him first as a colored man, however exalted, but Hazel was one in a million.

Hazel was surprised to hear her own voice in the mix. "Mrs. Blue, you're right. There wasn't no rush. We shoulda thought about Elbo. I'm sorry."

"Now, Hazel, listen here. You ain't to blame. This ain't yo' fault. So don't be actin' like it was."

When he used the strange diction with her she couldn't tell whether he was a different man—or the same man finally comfortable enough to be himself in her presence, the same man telling her he saw her as one of his own race. "But it *is* my fault, Roy—and it's yours, too. Your mama's right. What's the rush? We shoulda waited. We shoulda thought about Elbo."

There was a hissing sound as Mrs. Blue inhaled sharply through her teeth, turning her head from Hazel. "Boy, that there's a Jezebel and a Delilah and a Pandora all rolled in one, but she ain't foolin' me. I ain't fallin' for her tricks. She don't care about you, nor about me, nor about Elbo, an' you can tell her damn straight I see right through her."

Hazel looked directly at Mrs. Blue who kept her head turned resolutely away. "Mrs. Blue, I'm sorry. I didn't mean no harm."

Mrs. Blue looked again through the crack in her eyes, raising her nose so she appeared to look down at Hazel even seated. "Listen up, Jezebel, an' listen good 'cause I ain't gone say this but once. You done took two of my sons. One you killed, the other you stole—you done stole his soul from under my nose, you done stole his soul from befo' my eyes, and that's the truth. Don't be tellin' me you sorry, an' don't be tellin' me you didn' mean no harm."

Hazel's eyes turned colorless. She blanched as she looked away, wondering if the old woman knew the truth, if mothers sensed these things, if her guilt about Elbo would cripple her as powerfully as her guilt about her ma. Her legs felt weak and she slumped against the doorway behind her.

The old woman wasn't finished. "If you keep my boy it won't be jus' me you got to worry about. Coloreds will hate you. White people will hate you. Everybody will hate you. You won't have nobody."

Hazel stared soullessly at cracks between floorboards, understanding even Roy had been rendered briefly speechless, but when he spoke she hardly heard what he said though he shouted loudly enough for the neighborhood.

"Goddammit, Mama, this is the stupidest goddam thing you done said yet in your whole goddam life. Hazel ain't stole nothin'—but you pushin' me away with this foolish talk the same's you pushed Elbo. If I don't come back, so be it, let it be on your own goddam head. Now you apologize to Hazel—or you take the consequences."

Her mother raised her eyes again at the mention of Elbo. "Don't you tell me about Elbo. This got nothin' to do with him. This between you an' me. You hear?"

"Mama, I'm only gone say this once more. You apologize to Hazel—or take the consequences."

The old woman crossed her arms. "I done said my piece. I done told the truth."

"You wouldn't know the truth if it bit you on your nose, ol' woman—and I'm bein' po-lite when I say that. You don't know Hazel an' you owe her an apology."

"I may not know *her*, but I sho's death know people. People got to stay with their own kind or they ain't no kinda people—specially colored people 'cause they ain't got no one else."

Hazel didn't know what Roy would have said next, but she knew he'd said too much already, she'd heard too much already. She'd waited only to regain strength in her legs. "I think I should go." She left the hateful room, the hateful house.

"Hazel, wait!"

Roy followed her onto the street and walked alongside trying to persuade her at least to let him drive her home, but she refused him everything. "It ain't right, Roy. Your place is with your mama at a time like this. She's right. We shoulda been thinkin' about her. We shoulda been thinkin' about Elbo. We weren't thinkin' rightly. You shouldn't have talked to your mama like you did."

"Hell, Hazel! She shouldn't have talked to you like she did."

Hazel shook her head. "Your place is with your mama, Roy. She needs you more than me. I don't feel right bein' with you at this time."

Roy realized he wasn't going to change her mind. They were a block away from his mama's house already, and he was walking fast to keep up. "When will I see you again?"

"I don't know."

"Are you saying you don't want to see me?"

"I don't know, Roy. I don't know what I want. I need to think. I need time alone."

"I'll call you tonight. We can talk then."

"No! Don't!"

Roy hesitated, holding her back by the arm, his voice fracturing into a hundred pieces. "Hazel, please let me call you."

Hazel was surprised because he'd never touched her in public. She didn't look at him and shook her head, but gave him an ambiguous answer. "You can do what you want."

THERE WAS A LETTER FROM BOMBAY awaiting Hazel when she got back, from Will and Zarine Gardner, news about Spike. When Roy called in the evening Dinty gave him the news, but Hazel wouldn't talk with him, nor with anyone except Dinty and Siri. Roy came to the hotel, but she wouldn't see him. Dinty was sorry, grateful to Roy for what he'd done, but there was nothing he could do. He shared Hazel's grief, but not her guilt. She'd felt abandoned by Spike, but it hadn't been his fault, only hers for losing patience with the difficulties of a sixteen-year-old.

Siri was sentimental, rolling tears like beads down his cheeks at the hint of an audience—not that he didn't care, but his own trials had gone too long unnoticed. To his credit, he became sole breadwinner in the family (bussing tables, shining shoes, running errands) for three months before Hazel returned to Salt'n'Peppah—not that he made enough to cover their expenses, but he provided a cover for Roy who gave him money for the family making it clear Hazel was not to know, and he found himself twice blessed, for helping, and for appearing to help even more.

Roy returned to Chicago, but came back the next weekend though she gave him no reason. He commuted every weekend for two months before he gave up his job and moved into his mama's home again on Cumberland though Hazel still refused to see him. He wrote to her, letting her know he was in Kendall Green, not to intrude but to be nearby. He wrote a dozen times in four weeks, saying the same thing, before she replied to say Thanks but she wanted her privacy. He sent her a Bible, then a book about elephants, and was gratified enough when she didn't return them to send more books. He also sent a jacket, a hat, a winter coat, but for Dinty, not to frighten her with gifts she might find too personal.

Hazel read everyday from the Bible he sent, not comprehending everything she read, but reading itself became a meditation, and turning the parchment pages a sacrament. Gradually, she read with more comprehension, and she read the other books, by Dostoevski and Tolstoy, which appeared to speak to her personally. If redemption could come to Raskolnikov after seven years, and to Ivan Ilych on his deathbed, it might yet come to her—but in its own time. She could not force it. Jack was in New York, the circus was on the road, she had only Dinty and Siri, and she was determined to seek their comfort before her own, to make their happiness her own. Dinty appeared to have grown smaller, more timid, shy even with her, and she loved his smile when she took him and Siri to the pictures, when she kissed him goodbye on his way to the YMCA where he'd made friends, when she bought him things—or when Roy bought him things. Siri needed even less, a game of cards, conversation, mostly her presence was enough.

She bought other books on her own, mostly philosophical, to understand better what had happened. She would never understand entirely, however much she read, but she read enough to understand that the sufferance of ages dwarfed her own trials, and the endurance of the dead prevailed over the transience of the living.

PART TWO / SIMON
SUMMER 1971

PSYCHEDELIC ELEPHANTS

Down in the alley where the garbage grows,
A flea jumped up on an elephant's toes
The elephant cried with tears in his eyes,
Why don't you pick on someone your size?

UNKNOWN

ONE   TWO PINK FAT FUCKIN' PIGS

One down, one to go. The narrator is dead, long live the narrator. Years went by, three and twenty to be precise, years of limbo, years of ennui, years of spookdom, years of festering in the graveyard. I could look but could not touch, I could look but not be seen, I could look and looked for ways to corporealize again, before the conjunction of gods and stars made for a moment propitious, tweezered me out of oblivion and materialized me into my second skin, from essence to ape again, my second birth foreshadowing my second death.

Three and twenty years accounted for many changes. Pants with rolled cuffs gave way to bellbottoms, crewcuts to longhairs, shirttails to haltertops—most importantly, the tanbark rings in our story gave way to gravel walkways, walls of canvas to walls of steel and glass, circus midway to college campus.

On Friday of finals week at CU, Chicago University, the last day of the spring semester, the ranks of students had thinned, but the twenty-year-old loping along one of the walkways would have been easily visible even among the throngs on Registration Day for his height, over six feet, three inches of it hair. Simon Blue wore a white t-shirt sporting bold black letters on his chest: DICK NIXON! On the back: KISSinger MY ASS! His jeans were striped yellow and black, flaring into red bellbottoms. He was lean, skin the color of honey, lips thick as thumbs, hair like a hive on his head.

At first sight he was a black man, but a great deal of milkwhite blood flowed in those blueblack veins. Second sight opened the door to his parentage: he had Hazel's Nordic blue eyes and Roy's hair of peach. He was, at best, half black, a bi-roon in the eyes of namecalling elements of the population, failing to recognize that so-called bi-roons and quadroons and octaroons and sixteentharoons and thirtysecondaroons have more blood in common with themselves than do races in distant Africa, that so-called bi's, quads, octs, 16ths, and 32nds are closer cousins to countryclubbing white suburbanites than to African tribes, literally their brothers in blood more than Africans.

His attention was drawn to a woman best defined by what she was not: not blond, not tall, not pretty, but not unattractive in a blue miniskirt and pink shirt sheer enough to outline braless nipples. A hawk nose nestled between rabbit cheeks. A peace medallion rested in her cleavage, a button shouted over her right nipple: GIRLS SAY YES TO BOYS WHO SAY NO! She was the secretary of the Engineering Department and sunk in reverie. Simon, concluding his junior year, was also her junior by five years, and duckwalked in her direction, tapping ash from an imaginary cigar. "Hey, Polly! Why the long face? It's Friday! Semester's over!"

She shook her head at his idiocy and punched his arm, showing seeds of a smile, dimples in its wake. "Cut it out, Si. You're, like, freakin' me out."

He bobbed out of reach. "It's okay to be freaked out if it makes you smile. You had a face long as a crocodile, eyes full of water as an aquarium."

"You're a poet, Si, and I bet you knowit." Barely managing highschool, she imagined college beyond her reach, but liked matching wits with Simon. She had the advantage: he liked her too much.

He grinned "... and I hope I don't blowit." He reached one long bony arm past her guard, long bony finger to the button over her right nipple. "I like your button. I said NO, you know."

She punched him again, but her smile flickered as the reverie resurfaced momentarily and her dimples disappeared. "Will you stop jumpin' around, Si? You're, like, makin' me nervous."

He didn't bother to bob from her second punch, but stopped bouncing and slid into a walk beside her. "Sorry—wasn't thinking. You looked like you'd lost your best friend."

She was grateful he'd noticed and sighed.

"Want to talk about it?"

"You may be sorry."
"Try me."
She remained silent.
"Did something happen?"
"Yeah—last night."
"We could discuss it over a beer."
She grimaced, shook her head. "Nah, that's, like, how the trouble started."
"Coffee?"
"Okay."
"Dungeon?"
"Okay."

The Dungeon was the campus coffee house, renowned for chocolate chip cookies big enough to break your heart. In keeping with its name, the walls sported broadswords, rapiers, cutlasses, scimitars—every primitive killing instrument was on the wall, even a gladiatorial net. Buried as the Dungeon was in the bowels of the Bowman Auditorium Building (Babs to the students), the tables were lit by candles, even at noon.

As they mounted Babs's wide cantilevered concrete steps, a man waved from within the tinted glass doors—almost as tall as Simon, almost as lean, also an Engineering junior, but there the resemblance ended. He sported a pale indoor pallor, brown boyish crewcut, dressed in a white shirt and grey pants, and was the first to speak as the electric doors slid open. "Hey, Simon! Hey, Polly!"

Polly smiled. "Hey, Chuck!"

Chuck and Simon were roommates, sharing a four-bedroom apartment on the north side of Chicago with two women: Tess (at thirty, the oldest of the four), who managed a clothing store, and Naomi (next in age, younger than Tess by four years), a tennis instructor, ranked ninth among women players in Chicago. Chuck was older than Simon by a year, but smiled with the benevolence of an uncle. Polly smiled, Simon waved. "Hey, roomie!"

Polly knew the Engineering students. As secretary, she had access to their files. There were too many to remember, but some she couldn't forget. She liked Chuck, always considerate (his height didn't hurt, nor his smile), but Chuck was unavailable. She knew. She'd tried. He was friendly, but uninterested.

Chuck smiled at Polly. "Are you joining us?"

Polly stared. "I donno." She looked at Simon. "You didn't say nothin' about joinin' no one."

Simon's jaw dropped. "I didn't get a chance. I was on my way to meet Chuck when I saw you—and, well, you know how it went—but all's well. I mean, I knew we'd meet him on the way to the Dungeon—and we did."

Polly rolled her eyes. "But, Si, I don't wanna, like, mess up your plans with Chuck."

Simon turned to Chuck. "Polly needs to talk about something. I didn't think you'd mind."

Polly countered with unmistakable irony. "Yeah, like it's real important."

Chuck understood Simon wanted time alone with Polly and shrugged. "Hey, no problem. You guys go ahead. It's okay, Polly, really, no big deal."

"See?"

Polly looked away, speaking suddenly. "Okay. Let's go."

She headed for the steps descending to the Dungeon. Simon looked at Chuck. "Sorry, buddy."

Chuck shrugged again. "No sweat, palomino." He winked. "Why don't you invite her?"

Simon winked back. "I was going to."

Chuck nodded. "You better hurry if you don't want to lose her."

"I read you, buddy. I owe you one. Check you later."

"You bet, alligator."

"Hey, Polly! Hold on! I'm coming!" Catching up, he gazed sideways. "Hey, you know the joke about Chuck Thompson's name?"

She wouldn't look at him. "No!"

"It's Thompson with a P—as in psoriasis, as in ptarmigan."

She looked at him.

He persisted with a smile. "You know, P—as in phalanx, as in phooey."

The corners of her mouth twitched. "I get it! I get it! You mean, like, *not* like in Thomson with*out* a P—as in pigeon, or in partridge."

He laughed out loud. "Exactly, without a P as in pelican."

"Without a P as in pea-*cock*?"

His smile twisted. "Right. Without a P as in penguin."

"Without a P as in *pee*-nis?"

He laughed more loudly. "That's right. Without a P as in por-poise, puff pastry, player piano."

She was enjoying his discomfort. "Without a P as in prick, as in *puss*sy?"

"Right." He took a deep breath, grateful they had reached the Dungeon.

The ritual of ordering and seating themselves helped him regain equilibrium. A caltrop and crossbow adorned the wall above their table. She ordered the trademark chocolate chip cookie smothered in vanilla ice cream, he a cappuccino. He was as excited by the possibilities as he was intimidated by her boldness, but Polly smiled. "I feel so ashamed."

There was no shame in her smile, the smile of a cat with a mouse, a snake with a rat, and Simon stared into his cappuccino. "What happened?"

"I was in a bar—like, I was havin' a really good time, if you know what I mean?"

"Yeah, sure—been there, done that."

"I was, like, feelin' no pain, you know."

"Yeah, I know."

"I mean, like, I was havin' a good time—a *real*ly good time."

"You were plastered."

"I was smashed. I don't usually go to bars, but I was, like, you know, lookin' for someone."

"Ah! Who were you looking for?"

"It didn't matter, just anyone, a man."

"Ah!" Simon's eyes dropped to the table.

"I, like, didn't care who it was, you know. I just, like, didn't wanna spend the night alone."

Simon remained motionless. "I take it you found someone."

"*Two* someones. I went home with *two* guys."

"*Two* guys!"

"It was like, freaky—like I'm still freaked, you know."

"Two at once!" Simon's grin was toothless. "That must've been one crowded bed."

Polly laughed. "Shit! The bed was, like, you know, too small. We were, like, all over the place, turnin' over chairs and tables. It was like a madhouse, you know. I'm still, like, freaked, you know."

"How did you manage it? I mean, did you just walk up to two guys one after the other or what?"

She laughed. "I didn't have to do a thing. They just, like, came on to me—together."

"It might have been dangerous. They might have been … oh, I don't know, gangsters, murderers, rapists—Republicans!"

She laughed. "Nah, I'd seen them before. They're, like, regulars at this bar."

"I guess that's okay then."

"We did, like, everythin', you know. You just don't know what it's like, until you've been, like, with two guys, you know—like, how much better it can be—you know, like, so many sensations at the same time instead of one after the other—if you know what I mean."

Simon's head filled with blood. "Hell, that must have been something!"

"But I feel like shit. I feel, like, cheap, you know."

Simon spoke without conviction. "You shouldn't. It's just something that happened. You didn't plan it."

"But what gets me, Si, is like how much I dug it. I *really* dug it, I can't tell you, like, how much—but now I feel cheap." She smiled again. "You don't know what it's like, Si, with one guy up your ass and another in your mouth? It's like heaven!"

Simon's voice was a whisper. "I'm not sure I want one guy up my ass and another in my mouth."

She laughed. "You know what I mean. It was like we never stopped comin'. We just, like, kept comin' and comin' and comin'. We, like, lost count of how many times we came. Sometimes, I felt like I was with three guys. It's like one guy's never gonna be enough again. What'm I gonna do?"

"What matters is how you felt at the time. What matters is that you dug it." Simon had fallen in minutes from confidante to eunuch to peeping Tom, from man of the world to little boy blue. "If nothing else that was the lesson of Woodstock. You shouldn't feel cheap. You should feel … liberated."

Polly still smiled and touched Simon's hand. "I do, Si. Thanks for understandin'. I guess I just, like, needed to tell someone—someone who'd understand."

He sipped his cappucino. "Listen, Pol, not to change the subject or anything, but we're having a party at our place tomorrow—a Fifties party. Everything's to be like in the Fifties—dress, music, everything. I'm going to pick up some of my old Elvis records later today, also my old man's. He's got the real old stuff—you know, the Platters, Ink Spots, Crew Cuts, stuff like that. Do you think you can make it?"

The names meant nothing to Polly. She lost her smile. "Where's the party?"

"Here." He scribbled his phone number and address on a napkin, got hers in exchange. She didn't understand why he needed her address, but gave it easily. "It's kind of a special occasion for us all. There are four of us, you know. Chuck and me—and Tess and Naomi, and each of us is celebrating something."

"Like the end of the semester, you mean?"

"Oh, yeah, of course, for me and Chuck, but Tess just got a promotion. She works in a dress shop. And Naomi just got ranked ninth best women's tennis player in Chicago."

"Wow! No kiddin'!"

"And Chuck and I are going to Bombay."

"No shit! That's, like, somewhere in New York, isn' it?"

Simon smiled. "Nope! India!"

"India!"

"Chuck's been there before. His dad's a consultant for nuclear reactors."

She shook her head as if wonders would never cease. "Nuclear reactors? Chuck's dad?"

"In Trombay, just outside Bombay, and Chuck kept up with one of the families. He's sweet on the daughter. They've been corresponding nine years. He visited them three summers, when he was twelve, fifteen, and eighteen—and this summer he invited me."

Polly smiled, shaking her head. "That explains it. Chuck's got a sweetheart. I always wondered."

"Oh, yeah. You couldn't pry them apart with a crowbar—not even halfway across the world. Funny thing is, my mom doesn't want me to go. Turns out her brother died in India a long time ago—before I was born, my Uncle Spike—whom I never even knew about. She never told me about him because she says she's kind of superstitious about what happened—but, what the hell, you don't get this kind of opportunity everyday. I'm going."

"You and Chuck?"

"Yeah, me and Chuck."

"Of course, you should go. Like, I wish I could go."

Simon nodded. "It's pretty expensive. I couldn't go if my old man wasn't picking up the tab—and thank God for my old man. I couldn't have persuaded my mom on my own—but, anyway, you should come to the party. There'll be plenty of people. Between the four of us we know just about everyone."

"I'll, like, try to be there."

"What's to stop you?"

She drew herself erect, one corner of her lip curled downward as if it were none of his business. "I got a kid, you know."

Simon retreated, leaning back from the table. "No shit. I didn't know." He wondered if she expected an invitation for her kid. "Can't you get a sitter?"

"Maybe." She stared at Simon, wanting to punish him all over again for his advantages, his indifference to her kid, wanting to smash his stupid earnest solicitous rich face. "You know what really bothers me about last night?"

"What?"

"They were fat, both of them were fat and pink like pigs. I slept with two fat fuckin' pigs. Just rolls of fat, soft flab all around. Jus' fuckin' and suckin' whatever we could get into our mouths. I think it actually turned me on that they were so fuckin' ugly."

Simon's gaze lost focus again. He shook his head.

"It's like, the more disgustin' it was, the hornier I got. I'm, like, gettin' horny right now just thinkin' about it."

Simon stared, too dumbstruck even to shake his head, and she smiled, more satisfied with their conversation than she had been yet.

TWO — BODYPAINTING

Chuck grinned watching Simon run after Polly, but he wasn't grinning at Simon. He hadn't stopped grinning since the trip to India had been finalized. He'd invited Simon because Simon was losing his girlfriend, Brooke, to Sydney, Australia, where she was to teach highschool—and a visit to India would make Simon a little less wretched.

Brooke was Simon's girlfriend officially, but not exclusively. It was the ethic of the Woodstock generation and Simon reserved equal rights for himself though he never exercised them. He was tied to Brooke's apron strings, a blind man could have read his waves of anxiety, and Chuck understood that nothing short of a comparable adventure would comfort him. They'd been friends since the third grade, he'd known Kamal would be too tenderhearted to refuse, but of course he'd asked her first.

He pulled an envelope from his pocket and unfolded it ascending a flight of stairs. They had planned to attend a bodypainting competition before Simon had bumped into Polly. He'd lost count of the number of times he'd read the letter, but his grin widened as he unfolded it one more time, admired once more Kamal's cursive script. He was no correspondent, wrote one for every three of her letters, preferring to call on the phone, what she delightfully called trunk-calls. The calls were often unclear, and you had to be stupid to put up with the expense—but he was glad to be stupid to hear her voice even against the hiss and crackle of transoceanic cables.

The Elephant Graveyard

30-4-70 [even the date was mystical, a communication from a country with more than twelve months in the year]

My Dear Chuck,

I will keep this letter short because I do not want to run out of things to say to you when I see you again (as if!!!). I cannot believe how soon I will be seeing you again now, but it's only fair because I have waited so long already. It's a lovely irony that the longer I wait now, the less I will have to wait—or is that a paradox? You must not think I am just a silly schoolgirl (I am in college, after all), but I start breathing heavily just thinking about your visit, and my heart beats like a hammer. You are so tall now that I wonder if you are still within hailing distance let alone conversing distance. Six Feet, Four! Oh, my God, but my dear Chuck is a giant, and I am very afraid his Kamal will never be more than an ant. Even Ashok has grown, my baby brother is now taller than me, but he is only five feet, six. You are a redwood, he is a coconut tree, and I am just a stump. You could count the number of inches by which I exceed five feet on the fingers of one hand. Oh, all right, you won't even need a full hand, you can count the inches on one finger. My chappals are no help at all. Even high heels will do me no good. I will have to wear stilts just to talk to you and you will get a backache just from giving me a hug (but you must not let that stop you). Or we will just have to sit all the time when we talk, but even then you will be taller. I will have to sit on telephone books, at least two. And I will have to run to keep up when we walk, but you will still be so much higher you will not even see me. I think I will make sure there are lots of little footstools in the flat for me to climb up on. Or I will carry a footstool around with me everywhere for everytime you say something to me.

It is so very kind of you also to think of your friend, Simon Blue. The poor boy must be feeling horrible. How could his girlfriend dump him like so much bag and baggage and dash off to Australia if she loves him? You must tell him she cannot love him very much—or would that be too cruel a thing to say? I do not understand Americans—only you, because you always tell me so clearly how you feel.

Ashok keeps saying Simon must feel so blue, and he thinks he is being so clever, but I have warned him not to be so clever when

Simon comes, not to make such stupid jokes. Of course, we must—and we will—do everything we can to make him feel better. I am so glad you are bringing him. I cannot wait to show him around Bombay and introduce him to our friends. Ashok is just as excited even though he loves to make his stupid jokes. But for you, since you have already seen so much of Bombay and you already know so many of our friends, we also wanted to make different plans. Daddy has a friend who has a bungalow in Nandi, and he has arranged for us to stay there for four days. It will be just us kids because Daddy has to work and Mummy says we're old enough not to need a chaperone. This was very bold of me, and I hope not too rude, but I told her she was right! Nandi is a hillstation, very beautiful, very scenic, many hills and valleys as you can imagine, also lakes, so we can go boating, also riding. Granny used to spend the whole hot season there in a hotel every year, right until the year she died. I think you will like Nandi. I know I will like it best because you will be there.

I did say I did not want to make this letter too long, but you know me. I just love to yak-yak-yak with you whenever I can. Anyway, I want to say thank you again for the record you sent. I think "Bridge Over Troubled Waters" is a lovely song, but the whole record is lovely. I think Simon and Garfunkel are my favorite group. Ashok insists the Beatles are still the best, even though they have broken up, but they are not his favorite either. He likes Jimi Hendrix and Janis Joplin and Jim Morrison. I think the only reason he likes them is that they are all dead, but if you say Bach, Beethoven, and Brahms are also dead he will say that they are for old people. I say shouldn't Jimi, Janis, and Jim also be for old people then, but he doesn't have an answer. He falls back on his old standby: girls don't understand rock music. He is so stupid, but he likes the **Abraxas** *record you sent him very much. I like it also, but not as much as* **Bridge Over Troubled Waters.** *He also wants to say Hi, so I will end.*

    Hurry up, Chuck! I cannot wait!

    With love,

    Kamal

Chuck turned the page to Ashok's short untidy note:

Hi, Chuck,

How are you, man? I do not know what my sister has been saying to you, but she loves to yak-yak-yak. You know how girls are, they love to yak-yak-yak. Do not feel you have to pay attention, but since she has probably said everything already I have nothing left to say. Thanks, man, for the record. It was really gear. That Carlos Santana is one maha guitarist. Can you also bring me the new Led Zeppelin record when you come? That would be terrific, but do not tell my mom and dad I asked you. Do not even tell Kamal. I hate to ask, but I just cannot live without these records, and it is too bad but we just cannot get them in Bombay. God, I hate living here sometimes. I wish I could have gone to Woodstock. Thanks again. Hang loose and stay heavy, man.

See you soon,
Ashok

"Hey, Chuck!"

"Hey, Ig!"

"What the fuck're you waiting for? Come on!" Iggy was calling him from a doorway.

Chuck refolded the letter, put it back in its envelope, back in his pocket. "Coming."

Iggy scrutinized Chuck's face as he reached the doorway. "Hey, what's up?"

"Nothing."

"Fuck you, Chuck. You look pretty shitfaced for nothing to be up. What's up?"

Chuck was grinning again. "Never mind, Ig. None of your damn business."

"Ah, fuck you, Chuckaluck. Fuck you twenty times. You're such a fuckin' dark horse."

Chuck punched Iggy's arm as they walked into the room. "Where's Dahlia?"

Dahlia was Ig's girlfriend. "Peeled like a banana, bare as a baby's butt—well, almost. A clean slate for my dirty paintbrush. I'm painting her like a dahlia."

Plastic sheets covered the floor; wrestling mats lined two walls. Students loitered, lounged on the mats, some to gawk, some to paint, some to be painted. Articles of clothing lay on the floor, women stripped to bikinis, one guy to red bikini briefs, the only guy to be painted by his girlfriend.

"LADIES AND GENTLEMEN! MAY I HAVE YOUR ATTENTION, PLEASE?"

Jerry Brady, President of the Student Union, stood in the middle of the room, explaining the rules: no duplication, every medium was permitted, and they had thirty minutes. "Any questions?"

A woman in a white sleeveless tennis outfit stepped forward. "I'd like to join. Am I too late?"

Heads turned: not only was she a stranger, but unbuttoning her pleated outfit, smiling as it fell to her feet, revealing a bikini patterned in the silver scales of a trout. Her smile was eager as a child's, her thick long redbrown ponytail like that of any campus coed, but she seemed otherwise older.

Jerry Brady's eyes seemed to spring from their sockets. "Does anyone have any objections?"

The question drew laughter. Someone shouted. "I object to any objections."

Jerry Brady turned to the woman. "What's your name?"

"Mercedes Carlssen."

"What's your painter's name?"

"I don't have a painter. I came for the tennis, but couldn't resist when I found out. Can I get a painter?" She spoke excitedly, holding her shoulders back, her chin high, and clasping her hands behind so her breasts strained against her bikini top. Balancing on one leg, one foot nuzzling the other, she seemed to be presenting herself.

Jerry Brady looked around. "Can we get a painter? Are there any volunteers?"

There was silence. Guys looked at one another wishing for the courage to volunteer, but CU served mostly buttoned-down engineering students. Iggy spoke suddenly, sounding louder than usual in the silence. "Hey, what about Chuckaluck? He's not doing anything."

All eyes centered on Chuck who hated spotlights. He swore at Iggy under his breath, but his grin never deserted him: the prospect of painting Mercedes Carlssen was not without appeal. "Sure."

"All right, Chuck!"

"Let the games begin!"

Chuck introduced himself, offered a handshake for something to do with his hands, but was hardly as calm as he appeared. He registered a vision of a pretty face, amber eyes, and chestnut hair before turning to concentrate on the canvas of her body. It was easier than talking. She was older, perhaps as old as Tess, thirty. Her bikini was minuscule, but its pattern of scales inspired him. He imagined her as a mermaid, matching the silver scales with scales of seablue, seaweed green, and streaks of gold to resemble reflected sunlight—and caudal fins for feet. He explained his design. "What do you think?"

"Very imaginative! I don't suppose there are any Cimabues or Cavallini's in the room, do you?"

He assumed she was talking about painters. "Hardly. Not even a Warhol."

"Oh, I don't know. Warhols spring up every fifteen minutes."

Chuck laughed, proceeding to outline a row of scales around her torso, instructing her to continue the pattern on her belly while he continued the pattern on her back and shoulders. They worked without talking, except to match colors, making applications with brushes and spatulas—but fingers worked fastest. He was hardly immune to the strange smooth sensual sundark skin, downy gold in the small of her back, palpable heat of her flesh, but he visualized Kamal's pretty face, remembered her letter, and wrestled with the esthetics of his task, flattening thick worms of paint with his fingers, soldering them like veins into her body. Mercedes began daubing more moderately. "We're going to run out of paint."

Chuck grinned, not looking up. "No problem. We're going to run out of time first."

She laughed and they continued, more hurriedly, more haphazardly. The scales along her calves degenerated into stripes and the caudal fins of her feet to banana leaves, but there was no doubting the winner. Most contestants had worked without a plan, as if their canvases were blackboards, providing a melange of equations, peace symbols, geometric shapes, sunsets, slogans, psychedelia. Iggy's dahlia looked more like a Venus flytrap (he'd painted interlocking rows of teeth along her belly). When he saw what Chuck had done with Mercedes he shook his head. "Fuck you like a bastard, Chuck Thompson."

First prize was fifteen dollars and Chuck gave it to Mercedes. She wanted to buy him coffee and he suggested a visit to the Dungeon. She went to shower, but after waiting half an hour Chuck left. He had preparations to make for the party the next day, some girls had returned from the showers complaining of difficulty removing dry paint, and he could imagine how long it might take Mercedes because he knew how deliberately he'd marked her, but he left an apology with Jerry Brady for his disappearance and an invitation to the party including his phone number and address.

So came Mercedes to enter the maelstrom, beginning as canvas for worms of paint, finishing as worms of paint for the canvas of the earth—but for the last time I get ahead of myself.

THREE   ON THE BACK OF THE ELEPHANT

The more things change the more they remain the same, but you cannot step into the same river twice. We have been this way before, but three and twenty years later the scenery has changed. Siri, wearing a white loonghi, sat atop the head of an elephant, pink soles of his feet behind the elephant's pink stippled ears, hands resting on his thighs, black eyes vigilant, sticks of his ribs as visible as before but arched over a softer belly than before. The dome of his head was bald and the fringe of hair around it white as chalk, scraggly as if with rain, no longer neat in the ponytail.

Behind him, Hazel lay naked on her back on the back of the elephant, couched on a blanket in the curve from the elephant's neck to the hump on the elephant's back, her head pillowed on her robe. She was thicker in her belly, breasts, shoulders, and most especially in her thighs. The elephant, Raja, was an inhabitant of the Brookfield Zoo a few miles west of Chicago. Twice a week the two stayed after hours, bonding with the elephants, familiarity breeding contentment.

It was a hot day and Raja fanned his ears languidly to stay cool. Elephants flap their ears in step when they march, they spread their ears to intimidate intruders, they spread the odor of musth from their temples with their ears, and, of course, they trap sound, they hear with their ears—but their ears are also coolants, webbed with blood vessels spreading like deltas toward the edges. The difference in temperature between arterial blood from the heart and venous blood returning can be up to 20 degrees centigrade. In the wet or the cold or the night they hold their ears close to their bodies to retain warmth. Closer to the equator elephants have larger ears (woolly mammoths of the north had the smallest).

Around them were more elephants, even some Africans. Outside the elephant house, in houses of their own, were hippos, rhinos, and tapirs, and farther afield houses of primates, antelopes, and insects, islands of seals, baboons, and bears, shops and restaurants, all threaded by a narrow gauge railway track, the train itself docked at its station, the clock showing a few minutes past 6 PM (closing time).

The parking lot was emptying, except for a red Ferrari moving in. Roy got out and headed for the Pachyderm House. His brow was rigid with concentration, focusing on the task at hand. His mama's neighbor had called to say his mama had fallen, broken her hip, needed rest, but wouldn't rest. She hadn't even mentioned it when they'd talked, but he was determined to bring her back to his home with Hazel in Oak Park, Illinois, to drag her if necessary, to stay until she had healed. She still didn't approve of Hazel, but she would have to learn, and this was a fine opportunity.

He'd learned from Hazel himself. He'd married her because she was blind to his color, or so he'd believed, but that was just part of the truth. He'd married her as well because she was white; he would not have married a black elephant woman, he would not have married a black waitress. Circumstances had played a role, but so had color, a role he'd been unwilling to acknowledge and his mother was still unwilling to acknowledge. He'd embraced her color, his mother had not, but neither had been as blind to her color as she had been to theirs.

Hazel had loved staying home the first months after they'd married, minding Dinty and Siri, but not after Dinty's death (falling on a flaming barbecue grill in the backyard, suffering a heart attack in the hospital). She'd wanted to work with elephants again after Simon started grade school, but he'd insisted she apply for certification to teach high school gym, wanting her to leave the old life behind.

She'd agreed, taught for four years, but the opportunity at Brookfield Zoo had been providential, certainly for Siri who was family but needed to be among his own kind as well (elephants as much as other Indians). Brookfield provided elephants and Oak Park, Chicago's closest western suburb, known for its multicultural identity, included a burgeoning Indian community with Indian restaurants, Indian stores, even two Indian movie theaters. The families were too upscale for Siri (doctors and engineers), but restaurant staff and grocery clerks provided him with more society than he'd had since he'd come to Kendall Green from Kerala, and prowess with elephants elevated his status.

The employment proved just right. Zoowork was hardly as grueling as circus, but it was enough. The elephants were taught basic commands to keep them exercised, mentally alert, and tractable at the vet's. They were bathed, groomed, fed everyday, and during summer performed weekly for zoogoers, swaying, saluting, standing on stools, lifting and rolling logs, even rolling over to display their anatomies for the edification of zoogoers.

Roy waved to a couple of handlers who waved back as he marched toward the door marked AUTHORIZED PERSONNEL ONLY. He wrinkled his nose entering the Pachyderm House. He hated the wild pungent smell, hated it most on Hazel though he'd been surprised how swiftly it disappeared, the first whiff the worst. He shook his head to clear the smell and it began to dissipate. "Hazel!"

There was a brief silence before Hazel responded, her voice scaling the clef with surprise. "Roy!"

"Mister Roy!"

Roy looked toward the voices, past a half dozen feeding elephants, to Raja's stall. Hazel raised herself on her elbows on Raja's back. Siri kept his poise, back straight, face turned haughtily in Roy's direction. Roy said nothing, absorbing the unexpected tableau.

"Hi, honey." Hazel slid down Raja's side, putting on the robe she pulled down with her.

Roy said nothing until he was close, but then his eyes narrowed and he whispered fiercely. "Hazel, what's the meaning of this?"

She noted his features converging to the bridge of his nose. She'd never mentioned her trysts with Siri. She'd been doing it so long before she'd met Roy it hadn't seemed necessary. She knew what he meant, but didn't like his presumption. Her eyes narrowed, her voice got huskier. "What do you mean?"

Roy continued to talk under his breath and the whisper remained fierce. "You know damn well what I mean, Hazel. I want to know what the hell is going on."

Hazel sighed, bored already with the conversation. As extraordinary as she found Roy, there were ways in which he could not have proven more ordinary. Her voice turned cold. "Yes, I know what you mean. The question is: Don't you trust me?"

"Of course I trust you. That's not the point."

"What's the point?"

"Hazel, anyone could come in here. Are you saying that means nothing?"

"No one comes in here without my permission, not while we're in training."

"I came. No one stopped me."

"No one stopped you because you're my husband."

It was true: Hazel was Queen of the Stalls, Manager of Training for Summer Performances, and She Who Was Not To Be Disobeyed.

Roy could think of nothing to say. Hazel tightened her robe. "Why are you here?"

Roy pointedly ignored the question. "What about Siri? You must be putting all kinds of ideas in his head."

Hazel just shook her head. "Roy, why are you here?"

"You're not answering my question, Hazel. What about Siri?"

"Roy, I asked if you trusted me."

"And I said Yes."

"Then what's the problem?"

"Hazel ..." Roy swallowed, shaking his head. Much as he trusted Hazel, much as he thought he understood her, she continually surprised him. He was angry because she had shocked him, but now he felt stupid. He trusted Hazel. He'd been upset by the suddenness of the scene more than the scene itself.

"Roy, why *did* you come?"

"Hazel, sometimes I just don't know what to say to you."

She recognized his relent. "Good. Sometimes you just don't know what you're saying. Just tell me why you came."

Her pale blue gaze was irreproachable. He knew well enough to drop his indignation even if he didn't understand the situation. She would explain if she wished, and if she didn't it wouldn't matter. He wanted to borrow her Dodge to bring his mama back to stay for a while, he'd brought her the Ferrari instead which was too small for his mama's things, and despite the antipathy between the women he was pleased that Hazel voiced no objections, not even asking how long his mama might stay. They exchanged keys, kissed goodbye. She smiled watching him leave, glad he'd asked no more about Siri.

FOUR   WHEN BLACK WAS NOT SO BEAUTIFUL

Hazel pulled the Ferrari into the driveway next to Simon's psychedelic Mustang. It was the worst paint job she'd seen on a car, even a psychedelic car, splotches without order, shapes without symmetry. It wasn't meant to be esthetic, Simon said, it was making a statement about chaos. She was glad Roy was away. He hated the car, most of all in his driveway.

Siri cupped an ear toward the house. "Simon is home."

Hazel nodded; if it wasn't obvious from the car there was a record player blaring from an upper window, but not Simon's window, and not a song Simon would have selected, "Only You," by the Platters, one of their favorite groups from their earlier years. Even Siri knew the tune and sang along as he pulled out his keys. In the early days Siri had amused them by singing songs phonetically, making the Platters' breathless accents even more breathless, "Only Hugh can make this girl seem bright." Siri never understood why they laughed, but joined in the laughter, happy for the camaraderie. One of Hero's tusks stood in the lobby, roped into a small area like an exhibit or shrine. Siri genuflected before the tusk, obeisance to Hero, his sahodharan, his brother.

Hazel yelled up the stairs, picking up mail from the hallstand. "Darling! We're home!"

There was no immediate response, as if she'd surprised Simon, but he soon yelled above the music. "Hi, Mom!"

Siri yelled "Hi, Si," and went to his room in the basement.

Hazel went upstairs, looking through her mail, to meet Simon coming out of her bedroom. "Hello, darling. I wasn't sure it was you."

"Oh?"

"Wrong music."

"Oh, that. I hope you don't mind. We're having a Fifties party tomorrow. I was going to ask if I could borrow some of your albums, but there wasn't anyone home. I didn't think you'd mind."

She hugged him, her skinny son; if he weren't so tall he'd have no girth; even with his height she sometimes felt she was hugging air. Roy had always been brawnier in her memory. "I don't mind. Just don't take any of your dad's jazz records. You know how he feels about those."

"I won't. It's not that kind of party." She lifted her face and he kissed her cheek, after which he kissed the top of her head to annoy her. She was hardly as annoyed as he imagined, but she let him have his joke, pushing him away, following him back into the bedroom.

"How'd your finals go?"

"Aced them, all of them."

It was the way he talked, but he usually did well. "My genius son."

There was a stack of records on the floor from which he was making selections.

She wasn't paying attention, opening one of the envelopes, a letter from New York. Simon watched as her face slowly lifted, her smile broadened. "Who's it from?"

"An old friend, Jack Lewis. You've heard me talk about him."

"Oh, yeah, from the old days."

"The old days." Hazel almost sighed.

"The clown, right? I forget his name—I mean, his clown name."

"Brown E—but not anymore. He's been a businessman since before you were born—and doing well from what I understand. *Reader's Digest* did a profile on him."

Simon shook his head disbelievingly. "Brown E. Dumbest name I ever heard."

"He was a clown, Simon! and he was a sweet man. I don't want you talking about him like that."

"Sorry, I didn't know you were sweet on him. So what's he want?"

"He's coming to Chicago for a convention. He wants to meet for lunch." She didn't add what Jack had added: *Seeing you again will be sweeter sorrow than parting ever was.*

She scuffed off her shoes. "Will you be staying for dinner?"

Simon shook his head. "Nope, things to do, places to go, people to meet."

"My son, the Chairman of the Board."

"Sorry, Mom—but before I leave, for sure."

She knew he meant before he left for India. "Sure." She was briefly silent, wondering whether to say more. They'd talked about it before. "Darling, I still don't want you to go."

"Aw, Mom! I know, I know, but we've settled that—and it's too late now anyway! Where's Dad?"

She'd told him little about Spike, but she saw her brother sometimes in dreams high above earth, not quite dead, not quite alive, hovering, knocking on heaven's door among clouds and high mountains, never gaining admission. The dreams had become more vivid as Simon's plans had materialized, but she gave up the argument. "He went to get your granma. She broke her hip. She's going to be staying with us for a while."

"No kidding. I can't believe she agreed to come."

"She hasn't yet. He's going to convince her. He didn't think she would listen over the phone."

"She wouldn't."

"Exactly, so he went to get her in person."

"And she still won't listen."

"Well, we'll see."

"Crazy ol' Granma."

"Simon!"

"Well, it's true, Mom, and you know it."

"She's not crazy. She's had a difficult life."

"Aw, c'mon, Mom. She's nuts, and she's a bigot. She hates white people. She hates you for marrying her big black beautiful son."

She had never learned how to talk about race and found herself reduced to platitudes. "Simon, don't talk about your dad like that. It's disrespectful. It's … ugly."

"Wrong, Mom! It's the truth—and the truth is always beautiful, man, because the truth will set you free. Dad acts like he doesn't even know he's black. He never even talks about color—but black is beautiful, man, and he should know it, and he should show he knows it. He should be proud—like me."

She was suspicious of the slang to which Simon resorted when he became polemical, as if he were parroting someone. "Yes, well, black wasn't always so very beautiful. Your father was black at a time when it wasn't so very beautiful … man."

"Is that why you married him?" He regretted the question immediately, but she'd taunted him.

Hazel's eyes flashed. She knew Simon well enough to understand something was the matter, but he couldn't have stung her more sharply with a slap. "I think you should ask yourself instead why you've never had a black girlfriend."

A gamut of emotions alternated in quick succession across his face: astonishment, accusation, fear. Hazel felt, in turn, triumph, guilt, tenderness—but he quickly masked his discomposure with impatience. "Aaahh, Mom, you don't get it. You just don't get it."

"Well, maybe I don't get it, but you sure as hell can't give it to me either. That was a pretty stupid thing you said about your dad—and I expect an apology." She left the room abruptly. He wanted to stop her, but it was easier to let her go.

Descending the stairs, Hazel lost her pique. It wasn't Simon's fault. Roy had set the pace—but it wasn't Roy's fault either. Her life had settled into a comfortable humdrum since they had married, but the matter of race remained a muddle. Roy was right to call it a skin cancer for which no doctor would find a cure though the cure was under every individual's skin. Perhaps future generations would evolve enlightened enough to recognize that the darkness under which their forebears had labored had been darker than their pigmentation, enlightened enough to be blind—less an unlikelihood in a late browning America where diverse ingredients continued to find their way into the stew.

    She had heard the rationalizations for racism: insecurity, immaturity, insularity, illiberality—but there would always be insecure, immature, insular, illiberal people, and if racism were to be miraculously resolved it would be replaced with another difference, no less pernicious, height or weight or baldness or hairiness. The problem, at bottom, wasn't race. It was feeling so bad about yourself that you needed to make others feel worse to make yourself feel better. It was the attempt to compensate, however misguidedly, for feelings of unworthiness by imagining that wealth or beauty or youth or intelligence or class or pigmentation or some other such variable made a difference—but a perfect world was a dead world, a static world, as much as an imperfect world was dynamic. A perfect world rendered you extraneous, rendered everyone extraneous. It was the striving, not the strife, that mattered—the process, not the end result—the attempt to make things better. You were defined by the attempt, not the consequence. If there was one thing she had learned through her trials, that was it.

    Worst of all Hazel hated the condescension of men who approached her in Roy's presence as if he were invisible, who twisted their faces in disgust and anger when they understood. Roy derived satisfaction from the incidents, a harder man than the one who'd wooed her so tenderly, but she'd come to understand him better. Understanding was her great gift and she gave it continually because he showed his appreciation continually, unexpected gifts, unexpected love notes, consideration for Dinty when he'd been alive, consideration for Siri. Her whiteness had been an accident of birth, but she was grateful for her color because otherwise she might have been as invisible to him as he was to many in the white world. Padding across the living-room in bare feet she knocked on the basement door. "Siri!"

    "Yes? Door is open."

    She popped her head in. "What do you want for dinner?"

    "Hot dog! Let us have a barbecue!"

"It's late, Siri. It's almost seven."
"It is not late. It is still light. I will set up the grill."
"Oh, all right."

They were in the backyard, sitting in twilight, when Simon came down to apologize. Siri invited him to join them, but he had to go. Hazel accepted his apology disinterestedly, thinking about Jack.

FIVE   A CURIOUS CHILD

Simon marveled at the difference a day made. His head had been filled the evening before with equations for calculating stresses in beams and columns, but speeding along the Eisenhower back home his head filled with a different kind of stress. His mother's remarks had stirred an uncomfortable image: slowdancing with DeAhna Jackson, the crazy black chick at a frat party during his sophomore year. She'd perched on tiptoe, leaning against him, pressing big soft breasts into his ribs and stomach, gnawing his chest through his shirt, whispering: "Come home, baby. Come home, my big black brothah. You been starin' at that white pussy so long you forgot where your big black dick belongs. Come on home to mama, baby."

He'd enjoyed her proximity, but he'd also been embarrassed, laughed it off, laughed about it later with his friends. He couldn't have said why he'd laughed—but his mother had suggested an answer, an answer he'd resisted, an answer he was now forced to confront.

Brooke would not have minded, she would have encouraged him. She was upfront, almost too upfront. She said she was with him because he was black, her experiment in miscegenation, forbidden fruit—which was all right with him. He was with her because she was white, or so he liked to say, as if he were kidding, but he was also vaguely ashamed. She was the experimentalist, he the rat in the maze. It was still racism, however inverted the theme, however the variation appeared. He was included, but included for his race, not his personality. She saw in him color and acted on him, not he on her.

He wanted to say he loved her, and he did, why else would he be so upset she was leaving? but he knew what she would say: he was limiting her, stunting her, and she was right. He loved her for her boldness—but her boldness was taking her away. It was a muddle: she was doing the right thing—and he was doing the right thing going to India, exercising more boldness himself, but it remained a muddle.

He got off the Eisenhower, but instead of taking Clark or State or Michigan home he took the Drive and got off at the Wilson exit. He passed a chophouse advertising the best steaks, a Chinese restaurant advertising the best Chinese food, and a pizzeria the best pizza. It was not a section of Chicago with which he was familiar, the night was dark, there was no moon, but he found Polly's street, Malden, easily. The street appeared wide because streetlamps were widely spaced. Yards were shallow, but appeared deep in the dim light. Buildings were no more than three storeys, but loomed massively behind yards, squat and black and solid. Simon couldn't read house numbers from the car and parked the Mustang, wishing for the first time that it might have been less conspicuous.

The sidewalk was littered with refuse: paper cups, empty cartons, plastic bags, gum wrappers, broken bottles, used condoms, newspapers, cigarettes. He walked along the street checking numbers of houses. Three men hung around a gate ahead, perhaps in their fifties, greying hair greased back. One smiled as he passed. "Wanna blowjob, darlin'?"

Simon, ever polite, shook his head. "No, thanks."

One of them hawked noisily, spitting behind him. Another shouted: "Fuck Agnew, too." He still wore KISSinger MY ASS! on his back and felt more conspicuous for his black and yellow stripes swelling into red bellbottoms.

He was glad for the breeze because his head was hot as he reached the door to Polly's building. The security lock was broken but Simon buzzed anyway.

"Yeah?"

"Polly?"

"Yeah? Who's this?" The voice was impatient. A child screamed in the background.

"It's Simon. I hope I'm not interrupting anything."

"Simon? Like, so what is it?"

"Can I come up?"

"Did they, like, fix the door?"

"No—I just didn't want to interrupt anything."
"You mean, like, you're jus' waitin' downstairs?"
"Yeah."
"Jus' come on up."
"Okay."

He climbed two flights to a dim landing and waited a moment before knocking.

Polly opened the door, smiling shyly.

"Hi." He almost held out his hand, but bounced on the balls of his feet instead, hands on hips.

"Hi." She stepped aside to let him in. "You'll have to, like, excuse me. I wasn't, like, expectin' company." She wore a short faded green robe.

"No, no. Excuse *me* for barging in like this, but I had to see you again."

"It's all right." She closed the door behind him. "This is, like, a nice surprise."

Simon looked around. The door opened directly into the living-room. She picked up pantyhose draped over an old couch, blue lace underwear. He recognized the blue miniskirt and pink satin shirt she'd worn in the morning. She picked up a stuffed teddy bear from the floor, one beady black eye hanging by a thread, also a copy of *Cosmopolitan*, dogeared pages spread like a dead pigeon. He could see into the bathroom ahead, a towel on the floor, unrolled toilet paper. He could guess the rooms on either side of the bathroom, a bedroom, a kitchen. A child stood by the couch, pink face, blond curls. He remembered the screams, but she was smiling, a wide charming smile. Polly seemed almost shy introducing them. "This is Arabella. Say hi to the nice man, Ari."

Arabella's head reached Simon's thigh. He got on his haunches. "Hi, Arabella. I'm Simon."

Arabella kept her smile, spoke sweetly, the lisp of a child. "Are you gonna fuck my mommy?"

Simon almost lost his balance. Polly appeared embarrassed, shaking her head helplessly. "I donno where she gets it."

Arabella continued smiling. "Are you gonna fuck my mommy?"

Simon stood up again. "She's a lovely child."

Polly didn't look at him. "I jus' donno, like, where she picks up that kind of language."

"Are you gonna fuck my mommy?"

Polly spun suddenly on her daughter. "Arabella! Shut the fuck up! Go to the bedroom!"

Arabella stamped her foot. "I don't wanna shut the fuck up!"

She began screaming the moment Polly picked her up, flailing pink arms and legs, but Polly carried her determinedly to the bedroom, turned on the TV, and returned to the living-room. She had shut the bedroom door, but couldn't shut out Arabella's screams. "I'm sorry. She'll, like, calm down soon."

Simon nodded, but couldn't be sure. He was thinking about Polly's panties, pink lace, visible under her short green robe everytime she bent to pick up something. Arabella was crying more than screaming, and Simon could hear the Bradies squabbling in the background, a quarrel about the bathroom.

"I donno what to do about her. I gotta have my own life, but I can't with her."

Simon nodded again. "Of course—but she is a lovely child."

"Thanks—so, anyway, what brings you here?"

Arabella was quiet, but the Bradies kept squabbling. Simon shook his head in disbelief. "I'm not sure how to say this."

"Can I, like, get you a drink? I've got a Bud."

"That'd be fine."

"In a minute."

Simon took his time opening the can she brought back from the kitchen. He spoke finally, grinning self-consciously. "This isn't easy, but maybe I should just get to the point."

Polly nodded, looking puzzled.

"Well, the point is, to put it bluntly, I got so damn horny after you left this morning. All that talk about two guys just got me so damn horny I had to come over."

Polly smiled.

"I couldn't get you out of my mind all day. I've been thinking about you all day."

Polly's smile widened, dimples appeared. "I'm sorry. I didn't mean to get you horny."

"But you did."

"No, I didn't."

"I mean … you did, whether you meant it or not."

"But I didn't mean to. I'm really sorry. I jus', like, needed someone to talk to—to, like, get it out of my system, and you volunteered. That's all. I'm really sorry."

He said nothing, but lost his grin, drank his beer.

Her dimples deepened. "But I'm really flattered—I mean, that you want me."

"I can't say how much."

"I'm really flattered—but I'm sorry. I didn't mean to get you all horny. I was jus' talkin'."

Simon took a deep breath, put down his beer.

"I'm sorry, Si, really. I'd hate you to think I was, like, teasin' you. I wasn't."

"I don't think that."

"I couldn't anyway." She nodded toward the bedroom door. "You can see that, can't you?"

He nodded. "I understand."

"I'm sorry."

He drank his beer. "It's all right."

She seemed reluctant to drop the subject. "Even otherwise, I couldn't. I'm just not in the mood. I jus' masturbated."

Simon stared, saying nothing.

Her dimples flashed. "Twice."

Simon nodded as if he understood.

"And even otherwise, we couldn't."

He said nothing, but looked inquiringly.

"You know."

He shook his head, only dimly comprehending what she was saying, afraid to find out.

"I mean, I'm not, like, that liberated yet—if you know what I mean. I'm sorry, but I mean, like, I believe honesty's the best policy, if you know what I mean."

Simon nodded. "Right, I understand." He understood nothing, except that he should never have come. He picked up his beer again, but put it down without drinking.

"I'm sorry, really."

"I understand."

His voice was harsher than he'd meant. She dropped her gaze as if he'd chastised her, but never lost her dimples. She seemed to hate him though she repeated one more time. "I'm sorry."

He said nothing, nodding without looking at her.

Driving home he recognized the full extent of his humiliation. She'd confided the most intimate details as if he were gay, or a eunuch—or black—as if he should have known his feelings couldn't possibly enter the equation. He was also rich, she was poor; he was going to Bombay, she would probably never leave the country. Race provided her with a salve for her resentment, a weapon against her limitations, and Simon an easy target.

On the car radio Ronnie Dyson sang "If you let me make love to you, then why can't I touch you?" Simon liked the song, but turned it off, suddenly understanding what Polly had meant, burning with the implications: she had slept with two pink fat fucking pigs, but drew the line at a black man.

SIX   TRIPTROPPING

Simon, Chuck, Tess, and Naomi shared a four-bedroom apartment on Scott Street on the third floor of a brownstone in Chicago's Gold Coast. It was a short street embowered with greenery, bordered with brownstones crowned with turrets, cradling wrought iron balconies crocheted in ivy. The wrought iron was echoed in tall fences enclosing broad swards of green and narrow herringbone paths. Hedgerows and rhododendrons lined the sidewalks as did Benzes and BMWs. Honeylocusts adorned the corners, grand pianos preened from bay windows, and steeply sloping roofs presented dormers to the taller trees.

Setting up the party with Chuck, Tess, and Naomi, Simon had cheered up from his evening with Polly, but as the house filled and darkness fell his shoulders slumped. The party had started well, flowing within minutes into the stairwell and landings, even into Tess's and Naomi's bedrooms (Chuck's and Simon's went deeper into the apartment). Iggy had brushed up on old dances and was conducting classes in the living-room, the hand jive, the hully gully, the bug, the boogie, the bop. Danny and the Juniors sang "At the Hop." Tess accompanied them raucously on her boyfriend's tenor sax. The men wore leather jackets, drainpipes, ducktails, the women poodle skirts, sack dresses, crinoline. Simon perched at the top of the stairs, smiling and waving at newcomers, looking down the well for Brooke, when Dahlia tapped his shoulder. She wore a tube dress of blue and white horizontal stripes fitting her like a stocking. She winked. "Brooke's here. She's in your room."

Simon grinned helplessly. "No shit!" He hadn't done much with his own appearance, merely slicked back his hurricane hair, penciled in a thin Little Richard moustache, and worn a pink shirt. "Why didn't she just join the party?"

Dahlia shrugged. "Maybe you should ask her."

"Maybe I will."

A group was coming up the stairs. Someone wore 3-D glasses, someone had a hulahoop, someone beat a pair of bongos, someone wore a coonskin cap singing "Daveee! Daaa-vy Crockett!" Simon waved at the latest crop of guests and disappeared into the apartment. It was so large that the four residents couldn't always tell when they were alone. Simon's was the farthest room, the most insulated from the living-room and street, but the noise of the party followed him all the way. He shut the door behind him, leaving the room unlit. A streetlamp threw shadows of trees on the ceiling. A shadowy form moved in his bed. "Brooke?"

"Over here, Si."

He walked to the bed. She was on her back wearing shorts, halter on the floor. In the dim light her small breasts, slender hips, and bob gave her a boyish appearance. "There's a party going on, Brooke."

"I know. I just didn't feel like facing a whole lot of people—and don't tell me I shouldn't have taken the fire escape."

He'd guessed, and still wished she wouldn't do it. She scared the shit out of him climbing up the escape in the dark, sometimes in the middle of the night, hugging the side of the building along the narrow ledge, plopping through the window into his bedroom without warning. He hated the risk she took: a loose pebble, a false grip, an errant footstep, and she'd be splattered on the sidewalk—but you couldn't tell Brooke what to do. "You shouldn't have taken the fire escape."

"Oh, cease and desist, Si. Don't be tiresome. Who'd ever believe your mother was in the circus?"

"I wouldn't be so damn tiresome if *your* mother had been in the circus instead of mine."

Brooke held out her arms. "Si, let's not fight. It's our last time."

He parted her arms as if he were parting brush, exposing her slender torso. She and Polly were both white women, one wanting him, the other rejecting him, both for his blackness. He gathered saliva in his mouth and spat copiously on her belly.

She stared momentarily before smiling. "*Si*mon! *Kin*ky! I *like* it!" She dipped fingers in the pool of spit, drew a slimy trail upward between her breasts, and fucked her fingers in and out of her mouth.

When he kissed her she drew him into the bed, turning him around until he was on his back, she astride him, kissing him—and before he knew it she had spat in his mouth.

He tried to roll her onto her back, but she resisted. "Wait, Si. I want our last time to be special."

He froze.

"I want us to trip together."

He said nothing.

"I want us to make love while we're tripping. Tess asked me to get some hits for her and Derrick. I got some for us as well." She stared into his face, smiling. "You'll love it, Si. I wouldn't do this if I didn't want to give you something special for our last time."

He shook his head uncomprehendingly. "I thought you were leaving on Tuesday."

"I am, but this'll be our last night together. Everything's going to be so hurried after tonight."

"I don't know, Brooke. You know how I feel about that."

Brooke got out of bed. "Ah, shit, Si, you're such a bore. Just about everyone I know trips, but not my own boyfriend."

They stared at each other in silence before Simon sighed. "You sure don't leave a guy much choice."

Brooke glowed. "Oh, Si! I knew you wouldn't let me down!"

He sighed again. "I still can't believe I'm doing this."

Brooke smiled. "I knew I could count on you." She kissed him, switched on the bedside lamp, rummaged through her purse, pulled out a cellophane bag, and handed him a tiny square of what looked like blotting paper. "Here, just put this on your tongue. Let it dissolve. That's all there is to it."

Simon examined the square carefully. "That's all? This is it?"

"That's all."

"What about you?"

Brooke pulled out another square. "Let's do it together. On the count of three. One. Two. Three."

They placed the squares on their tongues. Brooke grinned, proud as a mother with a toilet-trained toddler, and reached for her halter. "Good boy. I'll be right back."

"Where're you going?"

"I want to give Tess and Derrick their hits. Don't worry. You'll be all right."

"I'll come with you."

"No, Si, I don't want to baby you. You've got to find your own level of comfort. You've got to meet me on equal ground or it's no good—but there's no rush. We've got the whole night."

"Well, what should I do if … if I feel, you know … funny?"

She smiled and kissed his cheek. "Trust yourself, sweetie. That's what it's all about. Trust." She switched the light off again and left him sitting on the bed.

A poster of Dylan adorned the wall: silhouette of his face, knuckled nose, tendrils of rainbow hair. As he watched, the silhouette began to glow, muscles seemed to flex in his own head, and blood to gush like hot springs in his veins. Dylan's tendrils of hair streamed like snakes off the poster and onto the walls and curtains. Had he not known he was tripping Simon would have thought he was dreaming—or going crazy.

He began to sway, his head to swing from side to side like a metronome, and he held it firmly, afraid it might swing off his shoulders. He wanted to go downstairs, recalling stories of people on acid leaping from windows imagining they were birds, but he didn't want to be among people, not even with Brooke—especially not with Brooke until he'd found his level of comfort, whatever that meant.

He walked slowly from his room to the landing and down the stairs to the stoop, smiling and waving mechanically. There were fewer guests on the lower landings, there was no one on the stoop. He sat on the third step, feet on the ground, watching the empty street. His head felt like clay: he would have rubbed his eyes, but was afraid to rub them out of his face.

He couldn't have said how long he sat before the night was pierced by screams from Astor, the closest cross-street, but he wondered if he was imagining them. When the screams persisted he got up and walked toward Astor, but couldn't be sure, even turning the corner, that the screams existed outside his head. As he crossed the street, a woman stumbled toward him, wobbling on her heels, panting. "Thank God! Thank God you came!"

She stood six feet in heels, braided leather headband, hoop earrings, ivory necklace, and sleeveless denim shirt and shorts. Simon had difficulty separating what he saw from what he thought he saw, but she clung to him frantically enough to leave no doubt that she was real. His body beat like a single giant heart. "Were you screaming?"

She seemed not to understand the question, but nodded, eyes wide. "*Yes!*"

He was gratified the screaming had not been in his head. "Why were you screaming?"

Her breath came in spurts. "A man ... with a knife ... he ran when you came."

Simon raised his eyebrows, furtively watching the street. "Are you sure?"

"He grabbed my necklace"—she touched the necklace to reassure herself it was there—"thank God it held—then he grabbed my bag—but it got tangled in my arm—and then …"

Simon was listening, not without difficulty, his attention distracted by her necklace. "Are those … elephants? Little elephants flying in circles?"

His head bobbed as his eyes traced trajectories around her neck. "Yes. It's my necklace."

"Ah!" He smiled as if no answer could have been more satisfying. "They're like little white butterflies butterflying around your neck."

Her eyebrows rose, her mouth relaxed. "Are you tripping?"

He nodded, then shook his head. "Triptropping."

She laughed. "I thought so."

"So where're you going?"

"I had to park five blocks away, but I thought this was a safe neighborhood."

"It is."

"I was looking for 1223 North Astor—but there's no such address."

"There is—but the entrance is on Scott."

"Then why does the address say Astor?"

"It's a more prestigious street."

"Oh!" She still held his waist, but her breath was back to normal. "Please don't leave. He might come back."

"Actually, that's my place. We're having a party. You want to come with me?"

"Are you a friend of Chuck Thompson?"

"He's my roommate. You know him?"

"I met him yesterday. We won a bodypainting competition, but he couldn't wait while I was showering. It took the longest time to get the paint out, but he left a note about the party."

"Oh, yeah, he told me. Mercedes … something?"

"Carlssen—and you?"

"Simon Blue."

"What a lovely name! Thank you for rescuing me, Simon Blue!" She smiled, kissing his cheek. "I can't believe how tall you are!"

He liked her starstruck face peering into his, her appreciation, her warmth, her softness, her closeness, her disarray—he liked playing hero and wanted to show her off, no longer wishing to be alone. He greeted everyone as they ascended the stairs arm in arm, introducing her to Naomi as they entered the apartment. Mercedes waved seeing Chuck in Bermudas and a pink shirt. Chuck grinned seeing her snug with Simon. "I see you've met Simon."

Mercedes hugged Simon long and hard, kissing his cheek again. "He's my Perseus, my paladin. He saved my life."

Simon shrugged, grinning like an idiot. "And I didn't even know it."

The lights were low, reefer wafted in a sweet smell, Julie London sang "Cry Me a River," couples swayed in the middle of the room. A hand snaked, seemingly from nowhere, pulling Simon down and away from Mercedes. "If Simon's anyone's Perseus, he's mine—especially tonight." Brooke glared from the sofa, holding Simon's arm with both hands.

Mercedes raised her eyebrows, saying nothing. Chuck made introductions to Tess and Derrick among others. When he came to Brooke, she spoke for herself. "I'm Andromeda, the girlfriend."

Simon sat where she held him, basking in his level of comfort, a shitfaced grin spanning his face. "Yeah, but only till Tuesday. She's going to Australia."

Chuck smiled. "Her name's Brooke."

Mercedes nodded, but at Chuck, ignoring Brooke—but Brooke would not be ignored. "Is that ivory around your neck?"

Mercedes twitched her nose as if she didn't like what she smelled. "Yes. Why?"

Brooke ignored Mercedes, shaking her head pityingly instead at Simon. "Tch-tch-tch-tch! What's Hazel going to say?"

Chuck explained. "Simon's mother minds the elephants at the Brookfield Zoo."

Mercedes turned her attention again to Simon. "Does she really?"

Simon groaned. "Yeah. It's an old story. No big deal, really."

Chuck squeezed Mercedes's arm. "He'll tell you later, but let's get you a drink first. Then you can tell us what happened."

Naomi got Mercedes a glass of white wine and Simon let her tell the story, Brooke holding him firmly, Tess nuzzling him from the other side. "Si, you're so brave, such a Galahad. I love you."

Derrick ruffled her hair knowing how affectionate she got on acid, and was rewarded with a sultry gaze. "I love you, too, hon. I love everyone." She got up from the sofa, taking the sax from Derrick, blowing tuneless notes. "I love you, Chuck. I love you, Brooke—you, too, Naomi—and you, Mercedes."

Iggy swung into the room. "Hey, someone called the cops. Seems someone was screaming in the street or something. They're talking to someone downstairs. They're on their way up."

Naomi spoke ironically. "Right. Now that they're no longer needed."

Tess got up. "Let 'em in. I love coppers, sweet little piggies. Let 'em in."

Derrick nodded to Chuck. "I think we better go to the beach."

Chuck understood. "Go ahead. I'll take care of them."

Derrick held Tess close, looking at Brooke and Simon. "You folks want to come?"

Brooke adjusted her halter. "Where to?"

"Just down to the beach—until this blows over."

"Sure. You coming, Si?"

"Suuuurrrrre!"

They met the cops coming up the stairs. Tess greeted them with discordant notes on the sax. "I love you, coppies. I love little piggies in their starched white shirts. Don't ever change."

She would have kissed the cops had Derrick not pulled her along. Brooke and Simon followed, saying nothing, Brooke pulling Simon, Simon smiling.

They took the underpass across the Drive to the Oak Street Beach and sat on a bench, Simon's hand on Brooke's knee, Brooke's arms around his shoulders, Tess cradling the sax, Derrick cradling Tess. The sky was clear, bright with stars. "Look!" Brooke pointed to a star, and as they watched the star appeared to explode, disintegrating at its core, bursting into flame, only to be followed by another exploding star, the explosions appearing like so many flickering lamps on the lake.

Simon hadn't moved since he'd sat down, enjoying the fireworks, the garland of Brooke's arms around his neck. His head felt again like clay, but he didn't care. Brooke's face bloomed like a flower, and he felt blood gush in her knee like goldfish through arteries and veins. He wondered how it would be eating chocolate under the influence, listening to Hendrix, watching *Fantasia*, but he didn't want to move at all.

The couples remained silent, arms and legs intertwined, until the fireworks faded. It was four o'clock when they returned to the party. Some guests remained, some asleep on couches and chairs, some on the floor. Sinatra was singing "The Last Dance." Chuck was asleep. Naomi said the cops had taken a report from Mercedes and left. Mercedes had left a message for Simon, but she saved it for later: Brooke wouldn't give a damn once she was in Australia. Simon was tired, but restless; wanted to sleep, but couldn't. Brooke grinned; she felt the same, but knew what they needed.

Dawn found them still awake, Simon grinning. "I didn't know men could have multiple orgasms."

Brooke grinned no less. "I feel like a sperm bank overflowing."

"My life savings."

"Good."

They fell asleep finally after seven o'clock, waking at two in the afternoon to Cat Stevens singing "Wild World," hosts and leftover guests cleaning up. Simon poured orange juice for himself and Brooke as they munched pretzels and chips.

THE GHOST OF THE ELEPHANT

We don't know yet about life, how can we know about death?

CONFUCIUS

ONE ARRIVAL IN BOMBAY

Come we now to a second arrival in Bombay, three and twenty years later, by air as the first was by sea, past and present arrowing toward the singular point in the future, point of col*l*ision. The Air India jumbojet alighted at Bombay's Santa Cruz Airport at midnight. Simon and Chuck, flying for a day, were still on Chicago time, ten and a half hours behind, half past noon the day before—but though Simon imagined himself rested he was too tired to realize how tired he was. Darkness at noon perpetuated the deception, his daylight body at midnight.

He adjusted his shoulderbag, lugging his suitcase, waving away flies and mosquitos with his free hand. Like Chuck, he was dressed in shorts for the heat, but hardly prepared for the humidity greasing them with sweat, caking them with grime. Ceiling fans blew hot air, hanging from high rafters, spinning slowly on long spindles. Simon fanned himself with his free hand. "Shit—like walking into the belly of a beast."

Chuck grinned, but he'd been grinning since they'd left customs, eyes peeled for Kamal. "There she is!" Simon followed Chuck's gaze. Kamal stood smiling behind a gate. He recognized her from photographs, deeply dimpled round brown face, large black eyes, hair in a long loose braid behind. As they watched she drew her braid in front, combing its bushy tail with her fingers, standing tiptoe by the gate. She appeared in a trance, lips in a pale thin line, almost a dot. Her skinny brother, Ashok, next to her, shook long black hair from his eyes, grinning and waving and pointing and yelling. "Over there, Chuck! Go over there!"

Kamal wore a yellow print dress, Ashok bellbottomed jeans and a shirt patterned with flowers. Both wore chappals. She appeared to be choking and Chuck's face to grow larger to accommodate its widening grin. Past the gate he dropped suitcase and shoulderbag and opened his arms. The tiny woman disappeared into his huge embrace, showing only skinny brown arms like a vise around his waist.

A short sturdy man, thick black hair in a Nehru cap, muscled legs in khaki shorts, bobbed beside Ashok, grinning as Ashok stood grinning. Simon stared at them staring at him, everyone too polite to speak first. He put down his suitcase finally, holding out his hand. "Hi, I'm Simon."

"Oh, yes, of course!" Ashok laughed, taking Simon's hand, suddenly remembering his manners: he had not expected a negro. "I am Ashok. How do you do?"

Simon noted his long fingers, satin skin, eyebrows a woman might have envied. "Fine, now that we're here. I thought the flight would never end."

There was another silence. Simon looked at the sturdy man, but the sturdy man grinned and looked at the ground. They stared at Chuck and Kamal who remained oblivious to the world. Simon didn't want to interrupt, but Ashok had fewer qualms. "Come on, come on, Kamal! Come on, Chuck! Plenty of time for making out later."

Kamal loosened her arms, drew away. "Arre, where are my manners? How very rude of me! I'm so sorry, Simon. Hello, I'm Kamal, and Ashok you've met. Welcome to Bombay! Welcome to India! We have such a time prepared for you. I hope you will enjoy your stay."

Simon took Kamal's hand, graceful and delicate, almost enclosing it in his own, noting its fragility, like petals more than skin and bone. "Thanks! I can hardly believe I'm in India!"

Chuck and Ashok slapped each other's shoulders. Chuck salaamed the sturdy man who bowed, joining hands in namaste.

"Come on, come on, let's go." Kamal, still breathless, took Chuck's hand again. "I can't believe you're finally here. I can't believe it still."

He shook his head, still grinning. "Me, neither."

Kamal spoke to the sturdy man. "Arre, Gajar, chalo, chalo. Bag uthao, na?"

The sturdy man came forward, but Chuck picked up his suitcase again and so did Simon. "It's okay. We can manage our own bags."

"Nono, Chuck-sahib! I will take, no? I will take."

Chuck recalled his broken Hindi, holding onto the suitcase Gajar tried to take from him. "Theek hai, Gajar. Theek hai. It's okay." Simon followed his lead when Gajar approached him.

Kamal shook her head. "Just let him carry something. It's only a short distance to the car. Otherwise he'll feel bad."

Ashok slapped Gajar on the back. "He's strong as an ox. He eats his carrots."

Gajar grinned, but looked at the ground embarrassed by the attention. Ashok explained. "His name is Gopal, but we call him Gajar, the Hindi word for carrot, because he likes carrots so much."

They gave Gajar their shoulder bags and he hoisted them easily, grinning and waving them on.

The Indian car was like no car Simon had seen, a blue Ambassador, hardly small but squat. Gajar drove; Simon rode in front, Kamal in back sandwiched between Chuck and Ashok. They had barely left before Ashok's curiosity got the better of him. "I say, Simon, Chuck says your mother works with elephants? Is that a fact?"

Kamal glared at her brother. "Ashok! How rude! Give him some time, at least, to settle in."

Simon waved her protest aside. "It's all right. I'm used to it. Yes, she does, in the zoo."

"Wow! I swear we could hardly believe it. Dad thought Chuck was kidding, but Mom said he wouldn't kid about a thing like that. I swear I just didn't know what to think."

Simon was accustomed to the curiosity. "We have a lot of elephant jokes in the family. Did you know that you can't get ivory from an elephant—but in Alabama the Tuscaloosa."

There was a brief silence before Ashok laughed—so suddenly he snorted. "You get it, Sis? In Alabama the tusks are looser. Tuscaloosa is in Alabama."

Kamal was ironic. "I got it. I got it."

They moved quickly, Simon staring from his window, catching glimpses of people on charpois, some on sheets on the pavement alongside stray animals. Traffic thinned as they left the airport, driving over a creek, along meandering treelined roads, past a palmtreed seafront, past billboards of exotic movie posters. He had brooded about

Brooke in Australia during the long flight, measuring her adventure against his in India. Mercedes's message had helped, which he'd kept in his wallet. *Dear Simon, Thanks again for saving my life. I hope you had a nice night triptropping. I hope India is everything you might wish. Call me when you get back. I want to take you to dinner—and who knows what else!!!! Love, Mercedes.* She'd added her address and telephone number.

Gajar turned finally into the gate of Vasundhara, a six storey building. The lobby was dimly lit, but large enough for an elephant. They emerged from the elevator on the fourth floor into a long corridor lit at each end by a single dim lightbulb. Kamal whispered to Simon. "Be careful where you step. There are servants sleeping on the floor." Men slept on sheets by the doors of the flats of their masters.

Kamal put a finger to her lips, a key to the door. "Shhh! Mummy and Daddy will be asleep." A brass nameplate on the large, solid, paneled, wooden door bore a name deeply engraved: SIDDHARTHA GHATE. The door opened into a short hallway. A nightlight provided illumination. Kamal led them to her bedroom which was to be Chuck's and Simon's. She was to share Ashok's for the visit. Ashok yawned, Kamal told him to go to bed, but Chuck knew what he was waiting for. He unpacked *Led Zeppelin III* and Joplin's *Pearl* and the sleepy eyes widened again. For Kamal, he'd brought *All Things Must Pass*, also red hoop earrings which she inserted at once.

They took baths, first Chuck, then Simon. By the time Simon emerged in his robe Kamal and Ashok had retired. Chuck awaited Simon with a carafe of nimbu-pani in a tray with a plate piled with mutton, cucumber, and chutney sandwiches. Kamal's bed was much too short for either visitor and two mattresses had been laid side by side on the floor to accommodate them, the bedframe covered with a tablecloth to serve as a luggage rack.

MR. GHATE HELD HIS HANDS to his ears. "My God, Chuck, couldn't you get him a record with some music on it, at least? I woke up literally to a caterwauling sound—but I don't know what was worse, the caterwauling which I suppose passed for singing or the accompaniment which sounded like a locomotive running through our sitting-room.

They were at breakfast, a regular American breakfast of bacon, eggs, and toast, but with a milky tea rather than coffee, the table set for six, Mr. and Mrs. Ghate at opposite ends, Kamal and Ashok on one side, Chuck and Simon on the other.

Ashok grinned at Chuck. "'The Immigrant Song.' It's ab fab, yaar."

Mr. Ghate shook his head in wonder. "Ab fab? The boy's gone crazy. I don't even know what he's saying anymore."

"Oh, Dad, it's so obvious. Absolutely fabulous."

He shook his head again. "Couldn't you have got him something musical, Chuck? Pat Boone or Tony Bennett or something? At least, they can sing. These people can't even spell their own name, not even a simple word like 'lead.'"

"Dad, they do it on purpose—just like the Beatles."

"But what is the point of doing it on purpose? What is the point of being ignorant on purpose?"

Simon shrugged. "No point, Mr. Ghate. That's the point."

"I told you, Simon. Call me Siddhartha. It was the Buddha's name, and if it's good enough for the Buddha it's good enough for me."

"Sorry, Sid … dhar … tha."

Mrs. Ghate smiled. "Just call him Sid, like the rest of us—and call me Niru. Nirupama is even more of a mouthful than Siddhartha."

Mr. Ghate turned to Simon. "I still say, what is the point of having no point?"

Kamal smiled. "Daddy's a square."

"Why? Because I like real music?"

Ashok almost jumped in his seat. "I say, Dad, Simon says you can't get ivory from an elephant, but in Alabama the Tuscaloosa. Get it?"

Mr. Ghate smiled. "Yes, yes, but that's entirely irrelephant."

Ashok stared, momentarily silenced, before the joke ignited. "I say, how did you know that?"

"It's from an old Marx Bros. picture. 'One morning I shot an elephant in my pajamas. How he got in my pajamas I'll never know.' I forget what picture it was."

Mrs. Ghate smiled. *Animal Crackers.*

Kamal laughed and Mr. Ghate turned to his daughter. "See, your dad's not such a square after all."

"Oh, Daddy, the Marx Bros. are even older than Pat Boone."

Mrs. Ghate turned to Kamal. "What are your plans for today?"

"I thought we would drive around, show Simon the city. I thought we could do the standard tour, Hanging Gardens, lunch at the Naaz, Marine Drive. We should be back by three, plenty of time for everybody to take baths and get ready for the Bharatnatyam concert."

"Maybe you shouldn't be so ambitious. These boys have been traveling a long distance."

Simon shook his head, his twilight body deceived by daylight. "I feel fine. What's a Barat-what-you-said?"

"Classical Indian dance—absolutely superb. You will love it."

Mrs. Ghate spoke softly. "I'm not saying they will not love it. I'm just saying they may be tired still from the jetlag."

Mr. Ghate waved a disparaging hand. "Arre, Niru, they are no longer boys. Just look at them, big strapping young chaps, bigger even than me."

Mr. Ghate was tall, six feet, a freak for an Indian. Mrs. Ghate too was tall for an Indian woman. Kamal's size was a mystery to everyone, not to mention the constant butt of jokes. Mrs. Ghate spoke softly again. "Size has nothing to do with it—and even big strapping young chaps can get tired."

Simon scraped his plate. "If we get tired we'll sleep."

Chuck spoke with his mouth full. "If we get tired we'll come back."

"Okay, I suppose it's going to be a while before your bodies adjust, anyway. Nothing to do about it but wait. At least, you should be all right by the time you leave for Nandi on Saturday."

They were back at three-thirty, bathed and ready for the concert by four-thirty. Simon wanted a short nap, asked to be awakened at five; Kamal said that would give them enough time, but at five he woke on his own, Chuck asleep by his side, the room dark. He was up in an instant, yelling at Chuck. Kamal emerged in her nightgown from Ashok's bedroom, eyes lidded with sleep. "Simon, what is the matter? What is all this noise? You are going to wake everybody up."

Simon was bewildered. "It's five. Shouldn't we be getting on—for that Barat-dancing?"

Kamal couldn't stop laughing. "Look again. It's five in the morning. You fellows have been sleeping for twelve hours. You were sleeping so soundly we didn't have the heart to wake you."

IN THE EVENINGS, residents of Vasundhara sat by windows and congregated in verandahs at board games, carom, cards, and conversation. Ten flats per floor made for a lot of congregants and an apartment building was not unlike a neighborhood. Many families had grown up together and the kids hung out on the terrace in the evenings.

The terrace was large, crowded with the claptrap of buildings: pumps, tanks, pipes. Chuck knew the residents from previous visits: Minoo and Cyrus and Dolly, Anand and Nandita, Bomi and Rohinton, Asha and Kalyani and Sairam and Babu and Shama. A portable stereo had been set up, a rotating fan, cold drinks, snacks. That evening they played endlessly Zeppelin, Joplin, and Harrison. The talk centered on music, including concerts Simon and Chuck had attended. Kamal found a scrap of paper on the floor which she handed to Simon. "Simon, I found this. It's yours, I think, no?"

It was the note from Mercedes. He stuffed it back in his pocket. "Yeah. Thanks. I must've dropped it."

"Welcome. Sorry I had to read it to see whose it was."

"No problem. It's no secret."

"Good, because I'm really very curious. Did you really save her life or what?"

"She seemed to think so."

"And what is triptropping?"

Chuck and Simon related the story in bits and pieces. Chuck seemed apologetic. "We hardly know her—just met her a couple of times."

Kamal's eyebrows rose. "But hardly knowing her, still you painted her? Almost naked she was, and still you painted her?"

Simon had never seen Chuck so defensive. "I painted her, but Simon would have slept with her."

Kamal nodded. "I can see that! Already she's talking about doing What else!!!! with him."

George Harrison was singing "What Is Life?" Some sang along, some tapped their feet, some told jokes. When the group learned

Simon's mother had been in the circus they lost interest in Chuck. No one missed him when Kamal led him to the other end of the terrace, a corner made private by a water tank. "Chuck, why have you never kissed me properly?"

He lost his grin. He was a shy boy; the last time he'd seen Kamal she'd been just fifteen; their relations were complicated by cultural differences. He could have said all this and more, but led her instead to a row of pipes, raised her on one so she was a foot taller. She smiled, closing her eyes, raising her lips, parting her mouth. Chuck was suddenly unaware of the heat, humidity, flies. The first long kiss brought a sigh from Kamal almost as long as the kiss. Too soon they heard Ashok calling. "I say, Kamal, Chuck, where the hell are you guys?"

Kamal kept her perch on the pipes. "Damn, Chuck, I don't want to go, but I suppose we must. We have to be up early tomorrow for Nandi. I can't wait till we get there, with nobody to bother us."

TWO   NANDI

Kamal sat in the back of the Ambassador again between Chuck and Ashok on the way to Nandi, Simon in front, Gajar driving. "How long before we get there?"

"Seven-eight hours if we go directly—but we must stop at Boregaon along the way, we must see Hathi Minar and the Chamber of Elephants—also, they have the best sheekh kabab in Boregaon." Kamal was looking through a guidebook. "So much to do, so little time. So many sights: Elephant's Foot, Arthur's Point, Eleanor's Seat, Fulmala Falls. It's still quite wild out there, you know—not just deer and monkeys, but also panthers and tigers. If Lady Luck is with us, we might even hear the animals at night. We have a good chance. Serendipity Bungalow is on the outskirts of Nandi, practically in the wild."

They reached Boregaon at one o'clock. Kamal sent Gajar to get sheekh kababs for lunch. Chuck wanted to explore Hathi Minar, but Kamal suggested they eat while the kababs were hot. Gajar sat apart as they ate, Chuck, Kamal, and Ashok sat around the cannon, Simon atop the cannon fanning his face as if he were shooing flies.

Kamal smiled, amused. "What's the matter, Simon? Still hot?"

"Yeah, it's hot, but what's that smell, like the Chicago stockyards."

Everyone sniffed the air, Kamal taking a deep breath. "Smell? What smell? What are you talking about? This is the very best air for you, exactly 20% oxygen in the air, the very best percentage."

Chuck breathed deeply, following her example. "I smell the country, I smell sheekh kabab—also dung. Is that what you mean, Si?"

Simon sniffed again. "Are you kidding? It's *all* I can smell. I can't even smell the damn sheekh kabab in front of my nose."

Ashok sniffed delicately. "What are you talking about, man? The altitude's got to you, Simon. Come on down from that cannon."

Simon came down, sniffing, frowning. "You don't smell it? You really don't smell it?"

The three sniffed.

Kamal frowned. "Still you can smell it? Still?"

"Yeah. Can't you? Chuck?"

"Nope."

"It's getting worse. It's as strong as the damn Pachyderm House—only worse." The three stared at Simon who stared back.

Kamal knit her brows. "Simon, don't pull my leg. You're scaring me."

Simon looked at Chuck. "Maybe a flashback, do you think?"

Chuck shrugged. "Maybe."

Kamal kept her gaze on Simon. "Flashback to what? Triptropping?"

Simon nodded, looking away. "I must be more tired than I thought."

She nodded, smiling again. "We can rest when we get to Nandi. A long ride can do that sometimes—also, maybe you're still working off that jet lag. It can take a few days sometimes. Chuck is used to it now, but the first time he was here I thought he was such an idiot, falling asleep everywhere." She turned a benign look on Chuck. "Sorry, sorry. I was too young to understand then."

Simon wasn't convinced, but nodded. "Yeah, maybe."

"Let us just finish lunch and see the Chamber of Elephants. Then we'll go straight to Nandi and relax. I'm sure you'll be fine then."

They finished lunch. Ashok tried to describe the Chamber of Elephants. "It's like Cinerama, only better, makes you feel like elephants are all around you."

Simon still felt hot though Kamal and Ashok had put on sweaters before Kamal collected skewers, napkins, and paper cups in a brown paper bag. "Comecome, let's go. I guarantee you have never seen anything like it in America—anywhere in the world." Gajar stayed by the car as they left. "Bhoot hai, memsahib. Bhoot!"

Kamal pursed her lips. "He says there is a ghost, such nonsense, but let him stay if he wants."

Ashok explained. "There's a story that an American had a heart attack in the chamber—years ago—young man, perfectly healthy—but they said he had killed elephants for ivory. There was a picture—himself sitting on a dead elephant, and the elephants got their revenge."

Kamal remained loud and disbelieving. "Rubbish, rot, and old wives' tales—but people are so superstitious, especially in India. We will never join the modern world until we overcome our superstitions. People die all the time, even young people, of heart attacks. It doesn't mean a thing, but people like to find meaning in everything, and if they can't find it they make it up. That's all."

Ashok frowned. "But it's a good story, elephants taking revenge on an ivory hunter."

"Stories are stories."

They entered the first chamber, everyone remarking how cool it was, but the enclosed space made a furnace of the cave for Simon. Heat rose in fingers from the floor, turning his bones to rubber. The smell, which had never left, thickened. A dark sail seemed to waft closer from the distance, a brown unwashed threadbare sheet. Watching it, Simon was convinced he was hallucinating, recalling the tendrils of Dylan's hair swarming from the poster on his bedroom wall. There was no other explanation, it was a flashback and he was determined to put it out of his mind, but when the sheet descended to cover him like a shroud he felt his body grow slack. Barely able to stand, he felt himself lifted through the air as if by a giant hand and slammed against the wall from which he slithered to the ground.

The other three watched in horror, turned to stone by the Gorgon of events. Simon was whimpering, Chuck the first to move, getting to his knees, holding Simon in his arms. "Si, are you all right? Say something."

Simon was silent. Chuck looked at Kamal. "He's burning up. It almost burns me to touch him."

Kamal shook her head in disbelief.

"Speak to me, Si. Say something."

Simon remained still.

Chuck looked at Kamal again. "Will Dr. Petigara be in his dispensary?"

Kamal nodded. "Very likely."

"Ashok, help me get him to the car. Take his legs."

As Ashok took Simon's legs and Chuck moved to get a better grip on his shoulders, Simon opened his eyes, whispering. "Don't leave me, Chuck. Don't leave."

Chuck bent close, relieved Simon was conscious. "I'm not leaving you, Si. None of us is leaving. We're taking you to a doctor. You're burning up."

Simon shook his head. "Doctor's no good. Just don't leave me, Chuck."

"I'm not leaving you, Si, but we've got to get you out of here."

"Yeah, out of here—back to Bombay."

"First, the doctor, Si. We'll see what he says."

Simon shook his head, but closed his eyes again. Kamal followed as they carried him to the car.

Outside, Gajar was aghast. "Bhoot! Bhoot hai! There is a bhoot!"

Kamal frowned. "Choop, Gajar! Quiet! Simon seth fell down. He is not feeling well. We are taking him to Dr. Petigara. Now get in the car."

"I not driving, memsahib. Sorrysorry, but I not driving with bhoot in car."

Kamal was furious, upbraiding him in Hindi, either he could drive, or get in the passenger seat, or stay where he was, but he had better get out of her way.

Chuck and Ashok got in the back, Simon between them, Chuck holding Simon tightly around his shoulders again. Kamal got behind the wheel. Gajar hesitated, but when he saw they would leave without him he got in front with Kamal, sulking the rest of the drive to Nandi.

KAMAL DROVE TO DR. PETIGARA'S DISPENSARY IN NANDI along the winding roads through the Western Ghats, hills dressed in skirts of mist, hilltops rising like heads of submerged creatures, but the breathtaking glimpses were lost on the company. The doctor was making a house call when they arrived, and rather than wait at the dispensary they left him a note and made Simon comfortable in Serendipity Bungalow.

The bungalow, built along a shallow incline outside the town, was a fairytale cottage: red gabled roof, blue doors and shuttered windows, cloudy stucco walls quilted with ivy, and a verandah running the length of its facade. The front door led from the verandah to a hallway. Four small bedrooms lined one side of the bungalow, sitting, dining, bathroom, and kitchen the other. Prints of the Raj adorned the walls, Kashmiri carpets the floor, the head of a gaur overlooked the front door, a barasingha the living area, a blackbuck the dining. Chuck and Ashok walked Simon to a bedroom and lay him in a four-poster bed hung with a mosqito net. His eyes remained closed, but he clung to Chuck.

Kamal was relieved when the doctor arrived. Simon held Chuck's hand while the doctor examined him. "He must have fallen very hard. Difficult to tell the extent of the damage. He might be suffering from contusions." There were bruises on his face the size of quarters, his jaw was swollen. "I say, Simon, can you tell me what you're feeling?"

Simon's eyes stayed closed as he spoke. "We have to go back to Bombay."

"Yes, soon, but first tell me what you're feeling."

Simon shook his head, eyes still closed. "Tired, very tired."

The doctor looked at the others. "Can you tell me what happened?"

The three had not discussed what they had seen, not admitted it even to themselves. Kamal spoke first. "He tripped, I think. He wasn't feeling well. I wish now we had never gone into that chamber. He wasn't feeling well, kept complaining about a smell—a stink, actually, the way he described it."

"A stink?"

"Like the Chicago stockyards, he said."

Simon shook his head, suddenly opening his eyes. "Like a charnel-house."

"A charnel-house? Really? Can you tell me more?" The doctor's attention was fully on Simon, but Simon closed his eyes again.

Kamal was defensive. "I thought he was kidding when he said that. You know how these Americans are—always kidding. No telling when they are serious and when they are crying wolf—but Simon was serious."

"Hmmm."

"And he was burning up. I wish we had a thermometer, but his temperature must have been a hundred and four or more—he was that hot. The only thing that helped was Chuck. He wanted Chuck to hold him. If Chuck left he got restless—even sleeping he asked for Chuck."

Dr. Petigara took his temperature. It was a hundred point two. "You say it's come down?"

Kamal nodded. "He was much hotter before."

Chuck still held Simon's hand. "You could hardly touch him. I was burning up just holding him."

Dr. Petigara tried to get more information from Simon, but Simon only repeated what he'd said. "I'm going to give him an injection to relax him, bring down the fever. Difficult to say what the matter is without more symptoms—but it's a good sign his temperature has come down." He pulled a hypodermic from his bag. "Let him rest. Rest is the best thing. He should sleep soundly tonight after the shot. Tomorrow he'll be better."

"Hope so."

"Also put some eau de Cologne on his upper lip."

"Eau de Cologne? What for?"

"For the smell, to keep him comfortable. No unpleasant smells if we can help it."

"Yesyes, of course. Okay."

"Also on his forehead—to keep him cool. Also keep him covered. Nights can get cold and we don't want him getting pneumonia while he's in a weakened state—but if he starts burning up again apply cold compresses with the eau de Cologne. Don't let the temperature get higher than it is already. Keep checking every two-three hours or so."

Kamal nodded again. "I will send Gajar for a thermometer. My God, I feel so unprepared."

"I will leave you mine in case the chemist doesn't have. I have extras. You have my number. Give me a ring if anything gets out of hand—but I would say there is no cause for alarm. Most likely, I would say, just a bug he caught—and then he fell. He's going to be all right. Strapping young fellows like him have very quick recovery rates. I would say the chances are good he will be fine this time tomorrow."

Simon whispered. "Back to Bombay. Right away."

The doctor turned to him with the hypodermic. "Simon, you're not fit to travel. You have to rest—but I'll tell you what. I'm going to give you a shot to relax you. You should be all right tomorrow. Then, if you still want to go back, you can do what you want."

"Today! Go back today!"

Chuck took his hand. "Not today, Si—but tomorrow, if you still want to, it's a deal."

The doctor came forward with the hypodermic. "You've got a good friend in Chuck, Simon, old boy"—he gave Simon the shot—"but this should give him some rest also."

Simon had begun to relax, but immediately became rigid, eyes wide open. "NO! CHUCK STAYS! CHUCK MUST STAY!"

There was a moment of surprised silence, Chuck the first to speak. "I'll be right here, Si—in the next room."

Simon shook his head, but the shot was taking effect and he was unable to protest further.

NO ONE WAS HUNGRY, but Kamal thought they should eat and sent Gajar to Queen's Hotel for samosas. They played Monopoly, checking hourly on Simon who slept peacefully. The evening sun crept into the room, dimming and vanishing finally into night. Crickets and frogs provided a soundtrack. They retired to their bedrooms at ten. There was a cot for Gajar in the kitchen, but he insisted on sleeping in the car. "Bhoot hai. Ghar may bhoot hai. There is a bhoot in the house."

Kamal didn't argue. "Let him be. I don't know what kind of ghost he thinks it is if it will just let him drive away."

Chuck checked on Simon before retiring, squeezing his shoulder, "I'll be in the next room, Si, if you need me," tucking the blanket firmly, lowering the net. He had barely returned to his room and stepped into pajamas before someone knocked on the door. "Chuck?"

"Yeah, Kamal?"

"May I come in?"

"Of course."

She wore a nightgown and moved stiffly, face flat, mouth small, lips clenched, eyes large. "Chuck, you must not misunderstand. You know I'm not superstitious, no?"

"Yeah?"

"But I don't want to sleep alone tonight. Something is not right."

Chuck nodded. They had yet to discuss what had happened to Simon, the moment which had turned them all to stone; easier to imagine he'd fallen than been slammed against the wall, also more sane; but they could think about nothing else.

Kamal's voice was soft with fear. "I can't get it out of my head, what's happened. It makes me think how fragile life is, how precious, and how we shouldn't waste it. We should make every moment count."

Chuck nodded again.

"You must not misunderstand, Chuck. I want you to hold me, but only to hold me. I'm not quite American enough for anything more—not just yet, I mean. Would that be all right? You wouldn't think I was … a loose woman or something?"

Chuck spoke more tenderly. "Of course not, Kamal … honey. Come."

She came to him, raising her face for a kiss, when another knock sounded on the door.

Chuck put a finger to her lips. "Ashok?"

"Yah, Chuck. Can I come in?"

Kamal swore under her breath. "Damn!"

Chuck shook his head. "Can't blame him. We're all a little jumpy."

She nodded and opened the door.

"You, Kamal? What are you doing here?"

"What do you think? What are you?"

"I wasn't sleepy. I wanted to talk."

"What did you want to talk about?"

"I don't know. I was trying to sleep and I swear I heard a sound in the walls—like the house was settling or something."

"Arre, what nonsense! The house settled a long time ago. Otherwise, we wouldn't be here. You have too much imagination, Ashok. It was probably just mice. Go back to sleep."

"It *was*n't mice! It was a *suck*ing sound, not a squeaking sound—like walking in mud, a *squelch*ing sound! Something was settling, I swear!"

"Let him in, Kamal. None of us is sleepy. A talk might be just the thing."

Kamal stepped back. "Oh, come in, come in, then, if you're such a scaredy-cat."

Ashok closed the door behind him. "Man, if I'm a scaredy-cat, then what are you?"

Chuck sighed. "No one's a scaredy-cat. We've had a rough day."

Ashok nodded. "Right. I sure could use one of Simon's jokes now. Another Tuscaloosa!"

Kamal echoed Chuck's sigh. "We could all use a laugh. That's for sure."

The crickets and frogs had faded to white noise. A dog barked in the distance; another answered. A crow cawed. A car honked. The three were comforted by the familiarity of the sounds—but a scream, highpitched and descending, suddenly sparked the night like a bolt of lightning, and they froze.

A disconcert followed, raucous crows and whooping monkeys, frogs picking up their croak again. Kamal spoke, answering Chuck's raised eyebrows. "A leopard. Maybe he caught a monkey."

Ashok smirked. "Then why would the leopard scream? The monkey should scream."

"Maybe it *was* the monkey—in any case, nothing to worry about."

The leopard screamed again, if that was what it was. Chuck rubbed Kamal's arm. "Whatever it is, it has nothing to do with us. We're just jumpy, that's all. The key is to behave as if everything's normal."

Kamal held him close. "Normal or not, I'm staying the night with you."

Ashok nodded. "Me, too."

It seemed the most normal thing as the three got in the bed under the net, Kamal and Ashok first, holding the flap to keep out the mosquitos while Chuck switched off the light and joined them.

A green nightlight embedded in the headboard cast a glow within, making a luminous green cube of the mosquito net. Ashok sat crosslegged at the foot of the bed. Chuck snuggled with Kamal against the headboard. "So, what shall we talk about?"

Ashok shrugged. "I don't know. Anything."

Kamal shut her eyes. "I don't care if we don't talk at all. I could go to sleep just like this."

"I-have-got-a-bet-ter-i-de-a." The voice was a croak. Someone was standing beside the bed, casting an elongated shadow. "Why-don't-we-tell-ghossst-ssstoriesss?"

The trio turned with a single gasp to face the figure. The room wasn't bright, but each would have sworn the figure grinned like a joker. A dark hand snaked into the netting, gripping the flap like a claw. An oily finger greased Chuck's back; Kamal forgot to breathe; Ashok scurried across the bed to join them by the headboard.

THREE   JACK AND JILL

The Berghoff is a Chicago institution. Lanterns, mounted on its facade on Adams Street in the Loop, contribute to its turn of the century ambience. Brass and wood augment the appeal, so do photographs of Chicago streets during the Twenties. The food is German, so are the waiters, old and cranky, more old world charm. Jack waited for his Jill on the window seat in the lobby, hands splayed on bobbing knees. He was just fifty-five, but his hair, still thick and wavy, had turned white as bone. His handsome face had never lost its gaunt melancholy aspect, his green eyes their dullness, though business was good and getting better. BROWN E'S CIRCUS EMPORIUM was an institution among troupers as much as the Berghoff among restaurateurs.

He was his own best commercial: the suit was too large, the floppy polka dot bowtie now his trademark, and the baseball cap and sneakers didn't complement the suit any more than the bowtie—but therein lay his charm, too sad for women to resist, for men to be threatened. Soon to be with the only woman he'd ever loved after three and twenty years, his lip trembled, eyelids drooped. He'd left the rejected boy meaning to return the successful man, but she'd married, he'd lost his chance forever, and buried himself in his EMPORIUM. He'd written, she'd written back about Simon, then three years old, and Dinty and Siri who lived with them, and Roy. He was happy she'd written, but the news about Simon had thrown him. He'd wanted to congratulate, but hadn't, and as time got fuller congratulations got emptier. When he'd finally replied he'd included Simon in a big hello to be extended as well to Dinty and Siri, but she'd replied again with news of Dinty's death, which had thrown him again, and the fullness of ensuing years had rendered his unsent condolences no less empty than his unsent congratulations regarding Simon.

Letters froze events in time, engraved them in stone, made you dwell on them as telephones did not, as meetings in person did not, paper froze events in aspic—but you said things in letters you did not on the phone, nor in person, you thought out loud, at length and at leisure, you clarified as you might not otherwise even to yourself, and you allowed for a leisurely and considered response—but if you waited too long the correspondence became moot. He hadn't written again, hadn't called even the times he'd visited Chicago, but it had been long enough, he was successful enough, Dinty was long dead, Simon even longer born—and still his eyes darted anxiously with each turn of the revolving door.

He should have known better. Hazel no sooner saw him than opened her arms, inviting him in with a spontaneous smile, a dreamy cry, "Jack!" The years fell away with the rapidity of the big top being dismantled after a show. He entered her embrace light as air, entranced and trancelike, happier again than he could remember, dull green eyes blazing. She held him as if she would never let go and he knew there'd be no need for explanations—there never had been except in his imagination. Finally, she held him at armslength. "You look swell, Jack, just like I remember."

His voice was a whisper. "You look pretty wonderful yourself, Jilly." Her enthusiasm had reduced him almost to silence, to a neverending smile. Even the maitre d' couldn't stop smiling as he led them to a table.

She kept talking, he smiling, they ordered beer, she wiener schnitzel, he sauerbraten. She showed him pictures; Dinty, Siri, Roy, Simon; he was glad to see them, sorry about Dinty, drew on a cigarette, offered her one, she declined, no longer smoked.

She drew him into a confidence; he entered gladly, gratefully. "I'm worried about Simon." She'd received a postcard complaining about heat and flies, raving about his hosts, the Ghates, almost identical to one she'd received from Spike during his brief stay. Roy had said all visitors to India talked about heat and flies and wonderful hosts.

She was offering him a chance to reassure her, but his attention strayed. He'd lit another cigarette as soon as he'd finished the first, offered her the pack again as if he'd forgotten she no longer smoked, run his hand through his hair when she declined again as if he might pull it out. He'd smiled through the pictures, but they'd hardened the reality, each snap pitting no more than a pebble between them, but cumulatively building moat, ramparts, and battlements.

She saw his smile fizzle, recognized the tremble of his lip, recalled his tales of scrounging during the Depression, the reasons for their separation, none of which had been his fault, and understood he'd always be hostage to those days for which she was partly responsible. Her tone dropped. "Listen to me, babbling on like a fool about myself. I want to hear about your life, what you've been up to."

He was grateful for her recognition, which deepened the moment, elevated their chatter, but it was not as he'd pictured it. "I'm doing real well. I can't believe it myself—get written up in Who's Whos. They talk about me in the same breath with Emmett Kelly, Lou Jacobs, Otto Griebling."

"Jack, that's wonderful!"

"Sometimes they go back to Dan Rice and the Great Grimaldi."

"You deserve it, Jack! You deserve it all."

"*Time*'s doing an article on the Emporium."

"*Time!* Jesus, Jack! I'm so happy for you."

"The funny thing is that when I was a clown I was just a joey, but now that I'm a businessman I'm suddenly a great clown. Is that a hoot or what?" He laughed loudly, too loudly. She laughed in sympathy, but noted as well his bitterness.

He was no less aware of his laugh too loud and didn't wish to appear bitter, wished to appear large, but shrank as they talked. He didn't know what he'd expected: admiration, yes, but she gave it so willingly it was worthless. Most of all he wanted her regret for not waiting. He recognized his vanity, his stupidity, but couldn't help it. He had nothing she wanted.

She tried to compensate for his disappointment. "I read the article in *Reader's Digest*, Jack. I saved the copy. I read it out loud to Roy and Simon."

"That was good for business." He brushed off the comment as if the personal glory were secondary—and it was. They both understood now he wanted something else, something he could never have. "The *Time* article should be even better. They want to title it 'From the Depths of the Depression to Heights of Hilarity.'"

"When's it coming out? I can't wait to read it."

He continued to look away. "I don't know yet myself. I'll send you a copy."

"Thanks." Her enthusiasm dropped as her sympathy rose. "Be sure that you do, Jack, an inscribed copy. I'll never forgive you if you don't." He nodded and she wondered what he was thinking. "How're the Cuddihys?"

"They're swell. Edna's a beautiful woman. They still have me over on Thanksgivings and Christmases. I'm part of the family now—sort of."

Hazel risked a sly smile. "Any chance of a romance developing?"

"Ah, Jilly, there's no time." His grin was as ironic as his words. "Work's my wife and kids."

She didn't miss the irony and reprimanded herself for her slyness, wishing to compensate for her insensitivity. "It's so important to find meaning in your work—to find meaning in anything. If you find meaning in one thing you've found meaning in life. We have to infuse our lives with meaning. We have to find meaning wherever we can. If I've learned one thing in all these years, Jack, that's it."

He was grateful for what she said, the implied apology, for her understanding, and wanted to put her at ease. "I've had some ... romances. I just never fell in love again."

She wanted to say falling in love was for children. Adults found love in their work, in their friends, in their daily activities, as much as in their mates. They worked at love, they willed it, they found their meaning. She wanted to say all that and more, but didn't. It would have been condescending. It would have magnified her insensitivity.

Slowly, his smile turned to stone. He should never have got in touch, he should never have called, he could never regain what he'd lost and it hurt to remember. He smoked continually, insisted on paying for the meal, driving her home. She'd taken the CTA to avoid parking; he'd rented a car for his stay. She saw him slipping away like a wraith and suggested they visit Siri at the zoo, but he said he was short on time. She invited him to see her home. "There's only Granma in the house. I told you she broke her hip." Again, he didn't have time.

They were in her driveway. She knew he was lying. She was afraid she would never see him again. "Jack, it's been swell seeing you again, I can't tell you enough. I mean it. It's the loveliest thing that's happened in a long while. It brings back lovely memories—so many lovely memories."

He nodded, but his smile was a grimace. "Yes, so many memories."

She'd said the wrong thing again. His smile was painful to watch and he refused to look at her. "Oh, Jack, I worry about you."

He appeared pleased and looked at her. "There's nothing to worry about. I'm doing swell."

"Oh, I know, I know, but I worry. I can't help it."

It was good to hear her say it, the hiccup in her voice, but there was nothing to be done. He couldn't wait to get away. "Thanks. I'll be all right."

She leaned across to kiss the bitter mouth under the swashbuckling moustache. He held her for a long time and she didn't protest, didn't mind. She waved when she got out, but he didn't look back, didn't trust himself. She watched until he was out of sight before getting into the Dodge to pick up Siri.

Her premonition was right. She was never to see him again, never even to hear from him, not even for the *Time* feature a month later. This is becoming a morbid account, but we need to add one more exit to the tally to date. John Jack Lewis had been too long a broken man, success had only delayed the inevitable. It mattered less what he had gained than what he had lost, what he could never have. He had been the Depression's spoil and forever spoiled for better times. A length of hemp from the EMPORIUM was shortly to render him yet another casualty of that decade of irresponsibility and greed.

FOUR   HIS MOTHER TONGUE

Roy was preoccupied getting into the Ferrari, gaze unfocused, brow ridged with wrinkles. He had much for which he was grateful—lovely family, large home, good health, educated friends, cultural affiliations, six-figure salary—but the more things changed the more they remained the same. During the Forties, his apprentice years, fresh from Chicago's Kent Law School, he'd set up his own shingle, but blacks typically retained white lawyers then. White judges and juries were predominant, more attentive to white lawyers, blacks sought black lawyers only when they couldn't afford white, and Roy would have retained a white lawyer himself had he needed one—but he'd also felt betrayed.

He'd packed his shingle, joined Marshall, Justice, and Marshall, become their black sheep as they liked to say, their panther in lionskin as he preferred to say. They didn't give him his due, but they gave him more than his own kind and he'd stayed with them eleven years before the writing on the wall became embossed. Younger men had become senior partners while he'd remained a junior. He'd changed jobs, joined Stern, Stone, Stein, and Marmer; they had agendas in common, both stemming from a long root of oppression. Oh, the poetry, the theater, the exquisite touch, both of them brothers in distress, but after years of another junior partnership the moving finger was writing again on the wall. Oppressed or oppressor, the message was the same, a black sheep was for fleecing, and Stern, Stone, Stein and Marmur had fleeced him of his years as effectively as Marshall, Justice, and Marshall.

For a lawyer he'd been naïve, for a black lawyer even more naïve. Hazel had wanted him to stick with his shingle, she'd have stuck with him had the shingle plummeted to the center of the earth, she'd have followed it clattering to hell and brought it back. He'd have braved the inferno himself for Hazel—but he'd denied the problem instead, imagining that resolved the problem, imagining blacks kept racism alive by their acknowledgment of its existence. He'd even resented the Civil Rights gains because they reduced his own, made it easier for blacks to accomplish what he'd accomplished the hard way. He was only beginning to understand how they might benefit him, how they might render a new shingle profitable at last, but first he wanted to confer with Hazel.

He was disappointed not to see the Dodge when he parked the Ferrari in the garage, but understood the reunion with Jack must have gone well. Hazel had planned to take Jack to Brookfield to meet Siri, and he wasn't surprised not to see her, but still disappointed. He was always disappointed not to see Hazel. He'd come to rely on her judgment, her counsel, her presence—too much, his mama said, but he didn't care what his mama thought, what anyone thought except Hazel.

His mama was standing in wait in the foyer—sitting in wait, rather, in a Windsor chair. She spent her days on the windowseat in the living-room, cane in hand, television within reach, but mostly minding everyone else's business through the curtains. She must have rushed to the foyer, cast and all, when she'd seen the Ferrari—and now, raising her thin bony face, she almost gloated as she talked. "Royale, we got to talk." She still wore the housecoat, scarf, and slippers; age hadn't withered her as much as packed her more solidly; she was smaller, but harder, closer to the bone.

"Not now, Mama. I just got home."

"It's important, Royale—about that woman."

Roy might have spoken gently, but he was too tired. "Mama! You talk about Hazel, you use her proper name—or you don't talk about her at all! You hear? You show her respect in her own home."

He was putting his coat in the hall closet. "You listen to me, Royale. Don't be yellin' an' screamin' befo' you know what I got to say. You don't know what she done."

"Mama, I don't care what she done, but you got to show her respect after what she done for you."

"What she done for me? Nothin' but cause me worry. She don't give me nothin' but worry, Royale—about you, about Simon. What she done? She ain't done nothin'."

He walked to the stairs. "Mama, I don't want to hear it. I just got home. What I want's a bath. What I want's dinner. Anything you got to say can wait till I'm done."

She hobbled after him on longboned legs, pumping and rattling her cane on the floor, raising her voice. "Don't be walkin' away from me, Royale. It cain't wait. She come home befo' then."

"Then you can tell me after she come home."

"I cain't. I cain't tell you with her in the house—an' if you won't listen I'm gone leave your house this minute. I'm gone find my way back home by myself." He was about to ascend the stairs, but stopped, hand on the newel, knowing she would not be ignored. She took advantage of his hesitation. "Come to the livin'-room, Royale." She turned her back, hobbling confidently into the living-room.

Roy followed in her wake, protesting, "Mama, anything you can't tell me in her presence I don't want to hear, you hear? Anything you got to say to me you say in front of Hazel, you hear?"

"Royale, jus' you listen to me. I ain't blamin' her. It ain't her fault she ain't like us. There's a ol' song about why we got to be so black and so blue. She ain't never been black, an' she ain't never been blue—an' she ain't never gone be black. That's all. She ain't like us, she ain't never gone be like us, an' it ain't her fault—but we got to look out for our own."

"Mama, you don't got to be black to be blue. Hazel treats you like a princess, and you treat her like a house nigger. Fetch this and fetch that, take this there and bring that here. She gives you everything you want, but you don't give her the time of day, not even a thank you. Don't tell me it ain't so. I seen it myself. I seen it a hundred times." The angrier he got the more easily he slipped into his mother tongue, the language of his disenfranchised youth; and he was angry with himself for listening to his mama against his judgment, angry because what he wanted most was a bath and dinner.

"She don't give me nothin' I need, only what she want, but she don't know what I need."

"What you need, Mama? What you need that Hazel don't give you?"

"She don't give me the right food. She don't give me nothin' I can eat, jus' them sammiches, turkey an' ham an' baloney out a package. That ain't nothin' I can eat."

"Mama, that ain't even true. You eat what we eat."

"It ain't what I want."

"What you want, Mama? You ever tell Hazel what you want? All you got to do's tell her an' she'll get it. You know she'll get it."

"She should know what I want. She been your wife long enough. She should know."

"Mama, you never come round. You never want to see her. How she s'pose to know? You got to tell her what you want. You don't tell her what you want, you got no call blamin' her."

"I want turnip greens, an' I want cornbread, an' I want caramel cake. What so hard about that? Whyn't she know that?"

"Aw, Mama, don't be talkin' foolish."

"Royale, don't be tellin' me I talkin' foolish—an' I want fried chicken. What so hard about that?"

"Aw, Mama, Chicago's jumpin' with chicken joints. We can have chicken tonight if you want."

"That ain't the point. Whyn't she know that? That's the point. Whyn't Hazel know that?"

Roy was quieter. At least, she'd called Hazel by her name.

"Now I told you I ain't blamin' her—an' I ain't. I'm jus' sayin' it ain't her fault she don't know better. She white. It's how white folks be. Prejudice. They cain't help it, jus' like black folks cain't help bein' black. They jus' born racist. It's in their blood."

"Mama, Hazel ain't no racist. You an' me, we're racist, you taught me to be racist—but Hazel ain't no racist. If not for Hazel, I'd be more racist than I am already—but Hazel ain't no racist, no way."

"Now you talkin' foolish, Royale. What you mean I taught you to be racist?"

"Aw, Mama, it ain't your fault, but anythin' I did you didn't approve you called niggerish. If I was dancin' to the radio you said not to be niggerish. If I was singin' you said not to be niggerish. If I got into fights you said not to be niggerish. What was I to think? Bein' niggerish was bad, an' bein' white was good, 'cause bein' white was bein' not niggerish. You taught me that, Mama."

"I didn' teach you that. I taught you the difference between a nigger an' a good colored man. Tha's what I taught you. I cain't help it what you learnt."

"Aw, Mama, just lookit you. You wearin' a scarf—*in*doors—to keep your hair straight—like a *white* woman. I cain't rightly say when I saw you last without a scarf. What am I s'pose to think?"

She turned away. "I'm a ol' woman, Royale. Don't argue with me. I know what I'm sayin'."

Roy took a deep breath. "Whatever you say, Mama. I don't want to argue. What's done is done. Better leave bad enough alone before it gets worse."

"Royale, let me say what I got to say. Then you can do what you want."

"What you got to say, Mama? Tell me what you got to say."

"Well, I was mindin' my own business, Royale, just sittin' by the window mindin' my own business, about three or four in the afternoon it musta been, when I seen Hazel drove up by a white man—an' she kiss him befo' she get out. I swears it, Royale. As the Lawd be my judge I swears it. They was kissin'. Now you can do what you want, but I swears by the Good Book what I saw."

Roy laughed. "Aw, Mama. Is that all? That's Jack. She told me about him. He's an old friend. They had lunch. It ain't no big deal."

"They was kissin', Royale. I swears it. They was kissin'—an' it wasn' no friendship kiss."

Roy was tempted to say they'd once been lovers, but didn't. "I trust Hazel, Mama. She's my wife. She ain't given me reason to doubt her in all these years. I'm not gone start now."

His mama's narrowed eyes grew big and round and white. "If you trust white folks, you gone be one sorry nigger's all I got to say. Trustin' white folk is how colored folk been put down since they was first brung here."

FIVE   UNDER THE MOSQUITO NET

The smell had returned after the doctor left. It grew fainter when Chuck checked on him, almost vanishing when he touched him, but Simon could no longer call him. The sedative was too strong. He'd made a special effort the last time, when Chuck had said goodnight, but without success, and after he'd left the smell had continued to grow.

The mosquito net hobbled escape and compressed the smell. It held him helpless, hampered his vigilance, obstructed vision, rendered objects shadowy that were clear by day. The room remained still, but something fluttered like a sheet on a clothesline. It had followed him from the Chamber of Elephants.

The room got hotter. Chuck had tucked the blanket tightly, heeding the doctor's caution against pneumonia, but it strapped him like a straitjacket. The fluttering thing disappeared like a reflection sliding out of a mirror, and he realized he'd been watching its reflection in the full length mirror of the cupboard. Turning his head he saw the sheet fluttering beside the bed, as if it were watching him watch its reflection. He imagined a face in the folds and triumph in the face.

Then came the coup de grace. The sheet poured into his mouth, nose, ears, and skin, filling him like a balloon. Just as he thought he would burst he was lifted from the bed, slammed back, lifted again, slammed again, and shoved through the opening in the net off the bed to the floor.

Outside, the leopard screamed, twice; but Simon was oblivious. He rolled onto his stomach, hitting a wall in his scrabble to escape, picking himself up, crawling on hands and knees, but found himself slammed again headfirst into the wall, flat on his belly. He wriggled like a snake entering a burrow and lay on his stomach for some minutes before rising to his feet.

The first steps were like those of a child—more accurately, as if my legs were stilts, but I couldn't stop grinning. Walking was easiest if I stiffened my knees, spreading my arms for balance, tottering like Frankenstein's creature. The room was dark, but I could see perfectly: I'd been in darkness so long that darkness was light; years in the graveyard had rendered night to day.

I turned the knob, opening the bedroom door, delighting in my ability, shutting the door again, turning the knob so it wouldn't click, marveling at the mechanism of hinges and springs, opening and shutting the door again, opening again and I would have shut it again but for a disappearing sliver of light under Chuck's door.

The stone floor was cool under my bare feet, a puddle of moonlight a joy to wade, my shadow a joy to behold, the night air a joy to breathe. Already my hobble was improving. I could hear the three settling in Chuck's bed. I could hear Chuck's voice. "What shall we talk about?"

I slipped into the room and walked toward the bed. I could see them so clearly within the green cube of the mosquito net that I was amazed they hadn't seen me.

"I don't care if we don't talk at all. I could go to sleep like this."

I couldn't resist, standing beside the bed. "I've got a better idea. Why don't we tell ghost stories?"

The sound of my voice, however unstable, however raspy, however guttural, was a joy no less than the sight of my shadow, but within the net all breath came to a stop. Pulling the flap aside I grinned at the trio.

Ashok scurried to join the other two by the headboard. I crawled into the space he had vacated. I couldn't stop grinning, patting the space beside me. "Come, Ashok, sit by me. Why crowd young lovers?"

No one moved in the green light. No one said a word.

"A slumber party, Chuck? And you didn't invite me? You hurt my feelin's ... buddy."

Chuck finally found his voice. "Simon?"

"Who else?"

Chuck shook his head disbelievingly. "It's just ... the doc said you'd be out till morning."

"Aah! Doctors! What do they know?"

Kamal spoke loudly. "Why are you talking like that? You don't sound like Simon."

I ignored her, turning to Chuck. "You didn't answer my question, Chuck. Is this nigger heaven your idea of a slumber party?"

There was a hushed silence, broken first by Ashok. "I say, Simon!"

Kamal's face was impassive. "Simon, are you still not feeling well?"

Chuck was the most surprised. "Si, you don't talk like that. What's the matter?"

I frowned. "What do you mean? How do I talk?"

Chuck and Kamal exchanged looks, but again Ashok spoke first. "'Nigger.' You don't say 'nigger.'"

The Ghost of the Elephant

"Like hell I don't." I scowled at Ashok. "Tell 'em, Chuck. It's what we call 'em in America."

Chuck measured his words. "Not me, Si. I don't—and neither do you. Hell, Si, you of all people should know better."

"Me? Why me?"

"Man, Simon, you are a negro, no?"

"Shut up, you! I ain't no nigger!"

Chuck looked puzzled. "Si, what're you saying?"

"What do you mean, Chuck? I ain't no nigger. This damn nigger country's finally got to you."

The three just stared.

"Well, it has. It's the biggest fuckin' nigger country outside of Africa."

Chuck's mouth was a thin line. He spoke slowly. "Si, I know you haven't been well—and, believe me, I'm making allowances—but you owe us all an apology."

"An apology? Why the fuck an apology?"

My voice was smoothening, becoming more Simon, as we talked, but Chuck seemed puzzled. "Simon, you're black, a negro—I mean, just look at yourself."

I stared at my hands, first the palms, then turning them over the backs of my hands. "What's that smell? I can't stand it."

Kamal was almost afraid to ask. "Please don't start that again, Simon. I can't smell anything."

Chuck spoke carefully. "What do you smell, Simon?"

"It's like … perfume! I never use perfume! I smell like a dame."

There was an astonished silence before Ashok clapped his hands. His laugh was a bark. "The eau de Cologne! He's smelling the eau de Cologne"

Not without relief, Chuck and Kamal joined in the laughter, but I didn't understand until Chuck explained. "You'd been complaining about a smell—a stink, actually. The doc thought the eau de Cologne would keep your temperature down, keep the stink away. He said you needed rest. He gave you a sedative. He said you'd sleep until tomorrow. That's why we were surprised to see you. You should be sleeping."

"But I ain't tired."

They all seemed puzzled, and again Ashok spoke first. "'*Ain't*,' Simon? You don't say '*ain't*.' You never said '*ain't*' before."

I said nothing, as puzzled myself as they appeared, and Chuck spoke again. "You should rest anyway. We should all go to sleep. It's been a long day."

Kamal tightened her hold on Chuck's arm. "I'm staying with Chuck. You all go."

Ashok grabbed his other arm. "I'm also staying with Chuck."

I grabbed Chuck's foot. "Me, too. I'm also staying with Chuck."

Kamal was exasperated. "Oh, all right, all right, if that's how you all are going to be. Enough of this nonsense. I'm going to bed. Goodnight, Chuck." She kissed him lightly.

"Goodnight, Kamal."

She got out of bed and Ashok followed. "Goodnight, Chuck."

"Night."

I left last. "Night, Chuckaluck."

Chuck shook his head. "Night, Simple Simon."

SIX HALFLIFE

You see the point of convergence between past and present, time and place and blood in alignment, point of contact, point of col*l*ision—point, finally, of my entry, my reentry, even my intrusion into the world, lesser than Spike and greater, ghost of Spike past, ghost of Simon present. How these things happen, what actually happens, I cannot say. Why now, why Simon, I cannot say. How this transition from the graveyard, the blackest of black holes, into the ark, the oasis, the sanctuary, that was Simon, I cannot say. I may be a ghost, but no God; a drop in the ocean, but no ocean; I had a little piece of a great big soul, but no more—and, as a sage of the west once said: *There are more things in heaven and earth than are dreamt of in your philosophy.*

Let me spell it out: I was performing a balancing act, not merely putting on a body stocking, nor a clown's baggy costume, nor an elephant's sagging hide, but the toothpaste back in the tube, the genie back in the bottle. I was coming again into focus—but the balancing act had just begun, the test lay ahead: to keep the Book of Simon open enough not to close the Book of Spike; to appear to be Simon while remaining Spike; to talk like Simon while thinking like Spike.

I learned to keep my mouth shut, I was uncharacteristically quiet, but my sickness was all the explanation anyone needed, a variation on the theme of *in vino, veritas*—*in delerio, veritas*, if you wish. Gajar looked at me warily the next day; refusing to stay in a house with a bhoot, he had spent the night in the car; had Kamal not kept the keys he might have driven away when the leopard had screamed. I smiled. It wasn't to my advantage to rouse suspicion. I couldn't wait to get back to America, but used my time in India as a training ground. Chuck knew me best and suspected more than the others, but the truth was simply beyond comprehension and my sickness the easiest explanation for everything after I apologized for my behavior on the night of my recovery.

That was the start of my halflife. I may have seemed normal, but I was living a halflife: half in this life, half in that; half in this world, half in that; the dead as alive to me as the living. The first intimation that my life would be more different than even I had imagined came during our descent from Nandi, Gajar at the wheel of the Ambassador, Ashok beside him, Kamal squeezed between me and Chuck in the back. The vistas were grand enough for silent appreciation (deserted forts, valleys flooded with mist, hills like green elephants), sighs of surprise and pleasure, and silence was welcome after the hectic turn of events.

A bend in the road turned the peaceful moving panoramas to crimson, veiling the landscape in a red mist. Villages of mud huts, banyans like giant umbrellas, and vast swards of tea plantations gave way to a wide expanse of hillside, two men striding toward each other, the larger of the two walking with a swagger, smiling brightly, looming over the smaller, full sleeves of his cloak billowing as he opened arms in a welcoming embrace. The smaller man wore a peacock feather in a green turban, a svelte thick black handlebar moustache—and, most importantly, a ring on the finger of his clenched right fist. Each advanced with a posse of ten men in his wake in full battle regalia, and farther back, to my astonishment, stood armies, apparently awaiting the outcome of the encounter between the two.

The Elephant Graveyard

Neither man appeared armed, but the large man slipped a small dagger from his sleeve into his left hand as he held the smaller fast with his right arm. The smaller man seemed unaware of the dagger until the larger drove it into his back, only to have it deflected, the satin garb of the smaller man covering armorplate. Opening his clenched fist to reveal a wagnak (claws of the tiger, four hooks sharp as razors fastened to his hand by the ring), sweeping his hand upward, the smaller man disemboweled the larger—and the scarlet scenario got darker, filling with clouds of blood.

Once I guessed the identities of the men I knew what to expect. Gupta had told me the story of Shivaji, the Maratha guerrilla (who had built so many of the forts we had seen along the way), and Afzal Khan, the Moghal general. The Battle of Pratapgarh of November 1659 had been a rout despite Afzal Khan's superior numbers, 25,000 to 10,000, Shivaji's assault had been the signal for his forces to attack. My last image was of Afzal Khan holding his entrails, hurtling toward his palanquin, soon to be overtaken by one of Shivaji's lieutenants and decapitated.

Again, impossible to say how this works. Schizophrenics, epileptics, saints, speakers in tongues, madmen of the world, what are they but the possessed, shells for the lives of others, and so had I become, a seer of life, the one who saw, the only one who saw Shivaji disembowel Afzal Khan—and I kept my mouth shut. Archimedes spoke of moving the earth with a fulcrum from a point of vantage, Plato of the parable of the cave enlarging into the universe as each veil is removed, Socrates of the continuum of life and death, the Hindus of the cycle of life and death and birth. The point of all these philosophies is, in part, that sight is limited by perspective. Earthly justice, the kind we dispense in law courts, has no bearing on Divine Retribution. Mars may provide a point of vantage from which to move Earth, but not to view the universe. Only empiricists wonder why bad things happen to good people. Only egocentrics wonder why bad things happen to egocentrics.

We question the meaning of life when we may more profitably question the breadth of our perceptions—and while we may question the meaning of life, we may no more question its rightness than we may question the rightness of the universe. We act like a myriad separate entities, but the universe responds as the single entity that it is. Shakespeare was wise, but academics dispense everything about him but wisdom; Beethoven impoverished himself revolutionizing music, but dirigents make fortunes from pedestrian readings of his work; CEOs multiply their salaries a hundredfold while hundreds of thousands of workers tumble from their perches; children are born to luxury in the first world while millions die of malnutrition in the third; innocents are shot in Chicago ghettos while dogs are pampered in Beverly Hills salons. We become, in our blindness, miniature megalomaniacs when we might instead become the gods we are meant to be. To err is human—but we are all divine though we know it not.

During my long confinement I had seen my brethren cling to their halflives like misers to gold: Socrates turned half to stone, Hemingway with half his face blown, Bonnie and Clyde slimy with blood, Virginia Woolf bloated with the river, Hitler's toothbrush moustache overhanging a brace of teeth, King taking a bullet to go to the mountain, Gandhi leaner in death than in life, Cleopatra grasping the asp, Lincoln with a third eye, among millions of others taken against their will or before their time or by their own hand—and, as a sage of the east once said, *The Tao that can be named is not the absolute Tao.*

I HAD BEEN ABSENT THREE AND TWENTY YEARS, from 1948 to 1971. I won't bore you with my amazement at technological advances. More important were the things that had not changed, as eternal in Bombay as in Chicago, in India as in America—indeed, in the world. We were riding in a public bus for the experience instead of the car. Kamal and Ashok had windowseats, Chuck and I sat next to them in the aisle. We would have seen more from the window, but we needed the aisle for the legspace.

The bus was full. When two women boarded Chuck and I gave them our seats. Both women were fat, one fatter than the other, brown bellies overhanging the waists of their saris. Both were old, white hair in buns. Both said "Thank you" and sat with legs in the aisle, smiling at the two of us stooping to keep our heads from hitting the ceiling of the bus. The fat woman spoke to the fatter. "So fine he is looking, no? So fine."

Their focus was on Chuck and he turned crimson as the eyes of the bus focused on him. The fatter woman also smiled at Chuck though she had my seat. "Such whitewhite skin, no?"

They discussed him as if he were on display. "American, no, do you not think?"

"Yesyes—but maybe also English?"

"Nono, I don't think so. So tall, no? Must be American. In America they are playing basketball. Talltall boys they are having for basketball."

"But so red his cheeks are, no, like an English?"

"Yes, but his eyes are blue, no, like an American?"

"Yes, but English are also having blue eyes, no?"

Both women smiled brightly and neverendingly at Chuck, imagining their attention flattered him. Kamal and Ashok, flattened against the windows by the women, turned their faces away, choking on their giggles. I would have joined them; Chuck's neck was reddening, maybe even his chest; I no more wanted the attention of the women than Chuck; but I didn't understand why they had excluded me. My eyes were just as blueblue, the seat I had vacated just as goodgood. I was even tallertaller, but I might have been air for all the attention they gave me.

The barrage of encomiums continued after we got off the bus. Kamal nudged Ashok. "So redred he is, no? like a beetroot he is, no?"

"Like a tomato, I am thinking, no?"

"Yesyes—but maybe also like a radish, no, white inside, red outside?"

"Oh, yesyes, most definitely yes, radish—maybe even an apple, no?"

Chuck shook his head. "Cut it out, you guys. What I want to know is why they didn't lay into Simon."

I'd kept quiet as always, but took my cue from Chuck. "Me, too! I'm just as talltall as Chuck, tallertaller if you count my hair."

Ashok grinned. "But you are also a negro."

"You mean *Black!*—and even a black's an American first!" I'd spoken more harshly than I'd meant judging from Ashok's suddenly shrinking face.

"Yes, but Americans are still white Americans first. No offense, Si— just the way it is."

"No, they're not. Black Americans are just as American as white Americans."

Ashok spoke patiently. "Yes, but we are not used to thinking like that. No harm done, no offense intended—really, Simon. No offense intended."

Kamal frowned; I knew what she was thinking: she and Ashok were mocking the women's foolishness, they were mocking Chuck's embarrassment, but they were not mocking me. Why was I upset? She didn't understand that harm had been done; offense had been perpetrated; I had been excluded because I was black. Chuck was a hero for giving up his seat; my seat was taken for granted. Did even Chuck understand? "Believe me, palomino. I wish it might have been you."

Of course, he did, but that was not the point.

THE IVORY TRAIL

Slaves and ivory had followed the same routes out of Africa for centuries and, as Livingstone and the other early missionaries and explorers came to realize, it is more probable that slavery was a by-product of the ivory trade than vice versa. In the second half of the nineteenth-century the demand for ivory reached a new peak. The Arabs, long-experienced suppliers, therefore had to send their caravans further and further inland when the coastal herds of elephants had been eliminated.

IAIN DOUGLAS-HAMILTON

ONE   OAK PARK

Oak Park, Chicago's closest western suburb, was once part of Cicero, Chicago's farthest western municipality, which led some enterprising Ciceroans to claim one of Oak Park's favorite sons, Hemingway, for their own, since Hem was born in 1899 and Oak Park incorporated in 1901. You can't blame them for trying. Cicero's famous son, hardly a favorite son, is Scarface, aka Alphonse Capone—but even Hem was hardly a gracious son, calling Oak Park the town of broad lawns and narrow minds, revealing perhaps more about himself than about the village (as Oak Parkers call home). The villagers have long forgiven the slight and proven their minds at least as broad as their lawns. During the Sixties the black population in Chicago expanded westward at the rate of about two blocks a year, communities turned regularly from desegregation to resegregation, white to black, until its tendrils began tickling the toes of the village, flicking across the border.

    Oak Parkers wanted to share their village, but not give it up; integration, but not resegregation; and they adopted a policy of dispersal to fight the problem, welcoming blacks to live among whites but not separately, providing listings of homes anywhere they wished but not in enclaves. Village officials barred real estate agents from house-to-house solicitations, distributed brochures featuring blacks in photographs subtly inviting blacks and whites who wanted to live among one another while weeding out bigots, black and white. Roy and Hazel made it their home even before the new integration policies, moving from their west side apartment to the Oak Park house in 1965.

The trees along Harlem Avenue were so full and large they looked like a forest preserve as we approached, we couldn't see the houses for the border of giants on each side—elms, ashes, maples, and all the oaks of Oak Park. Chuck and I were in Simon's psychedelic Mustang, now my psychedelic Mustang. Simon and I had different tastes in cars, clothes, music. I'd taken down posters from the wall, bought new clothes, but had yet to repaint the Mustang—and the cultural dissonance was only the beginning. I was recalling memories of Simon's childhood. What else was I to believe when a robin hopping across a lawn flooded me with nostalgia? or a herd of bicycling teenagers dashing across the street ahead? or a balloonman standing by Scoville Park? as if I were snug once more on a blanket on Hero's back in his trailer bound for Bad Axe, Michigan, or Bird in Hand, Pennsylvania?

There was more. I was comfortable with Chuck—but others avoided me, particularly at Inventive Electrics, Inc. where I had begun my internship. Politely attentive, having once encountered my difference, having met the obligations of civility and formality, they avoided me, couldn't wait to get back to their real lives, relegating me once more to the periphery, the realm of Interesting Experience, as if I were a new food they had tried, making adventurers of themselves and a patsy of me—as if I were out of focus, as if I smelled, as if I were shit. I had been one kind of ghost and was now another.

"You okay?"

I looked at Chuck. "Yeah, why?"

"You just ran a red light."

"Ah, sorry. Bit tired."

"Want me to drive?"

"Nah, we're almost there. I'll be all right."

I wasn't tired, but nervous as hell—and excited, and confused, but most of all nervous as hell. I couldn't wait to see Hazel again, sister of my first life, mother of my second, but hardly the Hazel I knew anymore. It was four days since we'd returned, I hadn't seen her yet but we'd talked on the phone. She'd been recovering from a flu, my mettlesome mom who was never sick, but my trip had lowered her resistance, and my safe return had banished the flu, so she said. She'd invited us, Chuck and me, to a welcome home backyard barbecue. Just a small party—the family, the Triggs (Des and Elena, my godparents), and the Colfaxes (Tom and Geri, new neighbors whom I hadn't met, being welcomed to Oak Park). I was afraid she'd know who I was, afraid she wouldn't; afraid to tell her the truth, afraid to not; afraid the truth would make a difference, afraid it wouldn't.

I parked in the driveway, the front door was open, we walked through the house to the back. Hazel might have been a longlost lover for the way I felt, feverish and freezing at once, walking zombielike through a haze to the deck in the back. Daisies, dandelions, and buttercups fluttered with butterflies in the beds lining the yard. Bees hummed in the branches of two oaks standing sentinel at the bottom. Two cardinals added color, starlings whistled. Charbroiled smoke from the grill filled the air. Guests sat in deckchairs, Roy manned the grill, a picnic table held punch, condiments, foodstuffs. Hazel saw me first, Siri at her side holding paper plates. "There they are! Simon, darling, what took you guys so long?"

Heads turned, smiling faces, Chuck grinned, but I felt numb.

Roy grinned. "There's m'boy. There's m'Simon." He handed the spatula to Des. "Keep your eyes on the burgers a moment, will you, Des?"

Hazel put down the bottle of mustard in her hand and stood with open arms. "Simon, darling, it's good to see you again."

It was an idyllic moment, a cool fall evening—but the air got unexpectedly hot. The barbecue was yards away, but might have been blazing beside me for my arms prickling with heat. When the crimson mist descended I knew I was to entertain another vision from bygone days. In the halfworld I inhabited, from the scrapbook of my past, a long forgotten image took precedence: back in the ring, under the spotlight, roar of the crowd, the small white woman with the big black beast, her head in his mouth—snapping her neck with a crack! The lights went out, the band sped up, joeys jumped into the audience, and Miss Marianna's monkeys commanded the spotlight, but I could see her despite the tumult, broken body on the ground, Dinty beating his head on the tanbark, Hero's eyes full and glistening, Jonas cracking his whip in all directions, Siri invoking gods on his knees. What had happened? What had I missed?

I would have stared longer, but the temperature was getting unbearable. I felt too sluggish to speak let alone walk, but Chuck pushed me and the crimson veil dissipated. "Ha-zel?"

I'd barely whispered her name, but her eyes narrowed and I corrected myself, speaking with more authority. "Mom!" Her eyes broadened again, I was in her arms once more, holding her tight, not wanting to let go. "Mom!" I didn't know what to make of the ugly image, I had imagined Hazel dead, her neck snapped, the world gone mad around her broken body, but Hazel was alive, Hazel was unbroken, Hazel was well. *Be these juggling fiends no more believed!* "Mom!"

I hugged her for a minute. I would have hugged her longer, but Roy interrupted. "C'mon, Hazel. Don't be greedy. He's my boy, too, y'know."

Hazel held me at armslength by the elbows. "You've lost weight."

"I was sick."

"Oh?"

"Just an upset stomach."

Des nodded understandingly. "All that spicy food. I love a good curry myself, but it gives me nightmares. I can't stomach it."

Roy put his arm around my shoulders next and squeezed. "We'll soon fill you up with some good American food, m'boy. It's good to have you back. Welcome home."

Hazel hugged Chuck next, Roy shook his hand. Des Trigg spoke from the grill. "Hey, Simon, welcome back!" He held up his hand in a tight military salute, a short, balding, black man. He'd been in the service as he was always reminding you and was now an architect. I liked him, or should I say Simon liked him? and raised my hand in a return salute. Elena Trigg (tall, thin, white, also an architect) got up to hug me. "It's good to have you back, Simon."

Chuck knew them as well. "Hi, Mr. Trigg, Mrs. Trigg." He waved and Elena hugged him as well.

Next, we were introduced to the Colfaxes, Tom and Geri (Geri giggled: "you can laugh if you wish, we're used to it, it's our big joke"), both blond, bland, pleasant, pretty, white, corporate executive and housewife. He might have coached Little League, she might have conducted kindergarten. Geri smiled. "You seem happy to be back, as if you hadn't seen your mother in years."

"It feels like years."

Roy grinned. "The boy's seen the elephant. Of course it feels like years."

Tom raised his eyebrows. "The elephant?"

Hazel explained. "An old circus expression, from the days when elephants were new in the country. It meant you'd seen the world. Sort of like 'See Naples and die.'"

Tom nudged Geri. "Remind me to cancel our flight to Italy, honey."

Geri looked puzzled for a while, but brightened suddenly. "Oh, you see what I have to put up with? He's always doing that. He loves to pull my leg."

Siri stood smiling to one side, waving when we looked toward him. "Hi, Simon! Hi, Chuck! How you liked India?" He'd talked with Chuck about India though Kerala was the only India he knew, an India Chuck had never known.

Simon and Chuck waved to Siri, but Des interrupted before they could say anything. "Damn!" He lifted the burgers off the grill onto buns on the side. "I hope you folks like your burgers well done."

Hazel squeezed Simon's arm. "Simon, take Granma a burger. She likes them well done."

"Where is she?"

"Upstairs. She didn't feel like coming down."

"Isn't she well?"

Hazel shrugged, handing me the burger. "It's got everything, just like she likes them."

I took the plate she handed me and a coke. "I'll be right back."

"Don't rush. She'll be happy to see you."

The Elephant Graveyard

I didn't know the house, but walked to Granma's room as if I'd lived nowhere else.

"Whosit?"

"Just me, Granma. Simon."

"Well, c'mon in, baby. C'mon in. What you waitin' for?"

She was smiling, sitting by the window, cane in hand. "Hi, Granma."

"Well, well, well, well, hello, baby. C'mon in."

I held out the plate. "I got you some food, Granma."

"Well, set it down. It ain't goin' nowheres. Set it down an' let me lookit you, baby. It's been so long—an', Lawd, look how you growed."

I put down plate and coke. She leaned her cane against the sill, got up to greet me, and held me in a vise around my waist until I didn't think she'd let go—but I was comfortable in her embrace as I had not been in a while, not even in the backyard. I was fine with Hazel and Roy, fine with the Triggs, of course with Chuck, but the Colfaxes were like the people at Inventive Electrics, Inc., avoiding me while talking to me, giving me an itch under my skin I couldn't scratch. With Simon's granma I was no longer peripheral, I was the center of her world. I found myself tender, inhaling the sachet of her hair even wrapped in the perpetual screen of her scarf, marveling at the fragility of her head on my chest, her back and shoulders in my arms, holding her gently, afraid she might break despite the steel cordon of her arms.

When she finally released me, she stepped back as Hazel had done to look at me. "Lawd, Simon, but you do remind me of my babies, Elbo an' Prize, but I lost 'em both, you know. They was my babies, my darlin' twins—but you my baby now. You jus' like 'em, you know."

"Really? You got any photographs?"

"Photygraphs? I got photygraphs—plenty photygraphs—but they up here." She pointed to her head. "We was too poor for any other kind—but you jus' like 'em. I seen you from up here gittin' out the car, an' you walks jus' like my Elbo—like my prayers was answered in you."

"How's your leg, Granma? Maybe you should sit down."

"My leg don't matter none. I likes standin' with you."

"I could sit with you."

She smiled, sat again by the window.

I picked up the plate again, pulled up a chair. "Here's your burger, Granma—well done, with everything, the works."

"Just the way I likes it. How'd you know?"

"I didn't. Mom said so."

"Hazel? What she know? I ain't even hungry."

"You better eat something, Granma. You got to eat something."

"I ain't hungry, baby. Let it set awhile. Let it just set."

"Aw, Granma, it'll get cold."

"It don't matter. I ain't hungry. You eat it, baby, if you hungry."

"Aw, Granma, it's your dinner."

"It don't matter, baby. I told you, I ain't hungry. You ain't eaten yet, have you?"

"Naw."

"Then eat, baby. Jus' set right there and eat. It do me good to see you eat my dinner."

"Naw, Granma. I can get my own. I'll get my own plate and I'll be right back. We can eat and talk together then."

"No, baby. You stay an' eat. Eat my dinner, go ahead, eat. I want you to eat my dinner. I ain't gone eat it. I'd be happier if you ate my dinner than you got your own. They say a little starvation good for the soul, an' I be happy to give you the food out my own mouth, so to speak. Go on, eat."

She was smiling, pushing the plate at me. "Well, if that's how you put it …"

"That's jus' how I put it, baby. Eat it all up—everythin'. Eat. We can talk while you eatin'."

"Well, okay, Granma. Thanks." I offered her the coke, but she shook her head pushing it back at me as well. I set it down and took a bite of the burger.

She smiled, watching me, touching my knee. "Tell me about India."

I surprised myself. "Aw, Granma, they're prejudiced there. Even in India, with brown skins and black skins darker than yours and mine, they're prejudiced."

Her smile faded, she nodded. "I ain't surprised. I heard it's like that in China and Japan an' jus' 'bout ever'where. Ain't no burden heavier than what the colored man got."

I told her what had happened on the bus with Chuck and me. "It made me feel like shit, Granma. I never felt like such a piece of shit before."

She didn't wonder that I'd never felt like a piece of shit in America before, and she didn't object to my use of the word, but nodded again as if it were no surprise. "You got to be strong, baby. They want to be prejudice, let 'em be prejudice. They the losers—but it don't matter what they be, only what you be—an' you got to be strong."

"Right, Granma, I know it, but it gets difficult—even when they're the ones being the niggers."

She smiled. "That's right. That's what I tell your daddy all the time. There's a difference between bein' colored and bein' niggerish. Let 'em be niggerish if they want. Indian folks can be niggerish as much as white folks, but don't let 'em mess your mind. You just be what you want to be and don't make 'em somethin' they ain't—and remember they ain't nothin' but what you make 'em."

"Thanks, Granma. I'll remember." I'd finished the burger and glugged the coke. "Tell me about Elbo and Prize. What happened to them?" All I remembered about Elbo was his crazy walk.

"It was 'cause of Elbo, 'cause he died, that your daddy met your mama. She come blubbin' about how a elephant fall on Elbo an' killed him."

"An elephant fell on Elbo?"

"The same one whose tusks you got in your house."

We were talking about Elbo, but my body temperature had risen steadily since her mention of the twins, the world turning darker than blood, igniting the sorriest image of my life: the mob pouncing like a panther on the hapless helpless boy. I had seen the specter of Prize in Elbo—and I had died before I had died, in the Cleveland square before the chamber of elephants in Boregaon. I recognized belatedly my sordid place in the tapestry of history, my hand on the lever of the machinery of the world.

THE OTHERS HAD FINISHED EATING when I joined them again in the backyard. Siri had left, Chuck was talking about jetlag. "My mind's in Chicago, but my body's still in Bombay—so's Simon's."

Des was tidying the grill. "Is that so, Simon? Your body's in Bombay?"

I'd been sobered by what I'd learned at Granma's side and didn't even hear him until Roy prompted me. "You going to give us an answer, Simon?"

"Oh, yeah, but even when Chuck's body's in Chicago, his heart's in Bombay."

Geri looked questioningly at me.

"He's got a sweetheart in Bombay."

"Chuck's sweetheart? Chuck's got a sweetheart?" Geri stared at him. "Why didn't you say so?"

Chuck smiled, shrugged.

She stared at me next. "He's been telling us so many stories about India, and never once did he mention his sweetheart in Bombay."

"He's shy. She's his childhood sweetheart."

"His *child*hood sweetheart—in Bombay?"

Chuck explained.

"Oh, but that's so sad—that she's so far away, I mean. When will you see her again?"

"Next summer. She's coming to Chicago. I'm going to show her around Chicago, and I'm not sure where else just yet, but I'm planning a road trip, give her a feel for America."

"Oh, that sounds wonderful, so romantic! I'm so happy for you!"

Hazel touched Simon's hand. "I thought you were never coming back, Simon. Aren't you hungry? Aren't you going to eat anything?"

"I ate Granma's burger. She insisted. She said she wasn't hungry."

"She did?" Hazel's brow wrinkled. "Well, there's more if you want it."

THE PARTY BROKE SHORTLY AFTER. The Colfaxes left first, then the Triggs. I yelled goodbye to Siri in the basement and visited Granma again to say I was leaving. Chuck joined me in paying respects. I pulled Hazel aside for a big hug. Her hug in return left me almost breathless. I almost called her by her name again. "Mom, I'm so glad to see you. I was afraid something had happened to you."

She gripped my arms, pulling me down for a kiss. "To *me? You*'re the one who insisted on going to India no matter what I said."

I grinned, hugging her again. "I know—but I had bad dreams about you. I was afraid." The image or hallucination or whatever it was had lodged more deeply under my skin than I was willing to admit. In my relief that she was all right I said more than I would have otherwise. "Remember that act of yours—you told me about—with Hero?"

"Yes?"

"I dreamed you were on the ground—on your back, in the ring—and Granpa was beating his head somewhere—and Siri was praying. I thought something had happened to you."

Hazel's eyes widened; her hands on my arms lost their grip; her mouth dropped, but she said nothing. I hugged her one more time, long and hard, but her strength seemed to have left, her return hug reduced to reassuring pats as if she were dusting my back.

I hugged Roy again at the front door. "I hope you don't mind, Dad, that I didn't bring back your records yet. I want to tape some of them for myself."

Roy arched eyebrows. "Sure. No rush, but I thought you didn't like all that sentimental junk."

"I do. I don't know why."

Chuck shook his head in disbelief. "He's been listening to the Ink Spots and Nat King Cole all week—no Hendrix, not even once. Go figure."

Roy beamed saying goodbye, squeezing my shoulders again, shaking his head, walking us through the house to the car. "Man, Simon, I can't believe that posh neighborhood of yours puts up with this damn niggermobile. When're you going to get rid of it."

"Actually, I'm getting pretty damn tired of it myself. Soon's I get organized she's getting a new paint job—a dusty white, kind of a ghost white."

Hazel had walked slowly to the front door, her mouth still open, but saying nothing. Roy slapped my back. "Damn, Simon, if I'd known I'd have sent you to India ten years ago. First the music, now this."

Chuck got into the Mustang on the passenger side—and, again, I couldn't resist. I walked the Elbo walk the short distance to the car, swinging left limbs together, right limbs together, listing side to side like a ship on a stormy sea, loping like a camel, the greatest of Great Danes. Granma, watching from her upstairs window, smiled and whispered. "Elbo!"

TWO HURRICANE MERCEDES

I had just begun to explore the world when it had been snatched from me. I had circus etched on my bones and India splashed on my skin, but knew the rest of the world as I knew Melville, North Dakota—or Timbuktoo before Rene Caille emerged in April 1828, the first European to see the legendary city and live to tell the tale. I was getting to know Chicago as Simon knew Chicago, but I also knew what Simon did not, and learned what Simon could not. The best analogy I can provide of my experience is that of a psychic intuiting stories from auras and objects, losing contact when revelations vaulted the threshold of pain—like the surges of heat I experienced during the revelations in Oak Park with Hazel and Granma.

Simon, not I, had met Mercedes—but I understood his preoccupation the moment I laid eyes on her waiting for me in front of her Lincoln Park apartment building. She wore blue jeans, a matching denim jacket, and a braided leather headband holding her redbrown hair—but she looked as if there were a circus in her head and I wanted to be in the center ring. She bent smiling to the car window, blinking her eyes (amber in color, almond in shape), revealing tiny ivory elephants dangling from her ears. "Hi!"

The single syllable was a caress, traversing three tones, rising and falling. I leaned over to open the door. "Hey! Good to see you again!"

She got in to the crackle of ivory bracelets on her wrists. "Good to see *you!* I'm *dy*ing to hear about India!"

"Plenty of time. I see you like ivory."

Her eyes narrowed, her voice turned harsh. "I do—I like the feel of it, the color of it, the craftsmanship—in fact, there's nothing about it I don't like. Is it a problem?"

I swallowed. "No ... I just remembered the necklace from before, and now ..."

"I know. Is it a problem?"

"No, it's not. Why do you ask?"

"Well, I know how some people are, I know your mother minds elephants, and I wasn't sure."

"I'm not my mother."

She seemed not to hear, moving through a litany she might have recited a dozen times. "It's legal, it's legit … and we have as much right to it as to gold or diamonds or whatever else is hacked from the earth at whatever cost."

I took a deep breath. "Hey, take it easy! I said I'm not my mother! Have mercy!"

She laughed, surprising me again, regaining her composure as suddenly as she'd lost it. "Sorry. I've been known to overreact. Sorry."

"It's all right." I didn't say much the rest of the way to Alferno's, an Italian restaurant on Broadway distinguished by a torch flaming over its doorway after nightfall. The interior was dark and rustic: candles in cozy booths, wooden tables and chairs, and though I couldn't tell what she was thinking I prided myself on the looks she received. She removed her denim jacket and hung it on a hook beside our booth. Underneath she wore a sleeveless maroon blouse cut in a low narrow V-neck.

We ordered pizza, a pitcher of beer. We raised glasses, took long swallows, and gazed into each other's eyes. She looked momentarily away. "Listen, I'm really sorry for jumping down your throat earlier. It's just … well, let's just say it takes all kinds, and I wasn't sure what kind you were."

I shook my head. "Forget it. Have you heard the joke about Chuck Thompson's name?"

She shook her head, leaning forward, elbows on the table, the candle on the table shading her breastbone like the wings of a bird in flight. "No! Tell me!"

"He spells Thompson with a P—as in pneumatic."

She was momentarily silent before throwing her head back and laughing. "You mean with a P as in pharmacy?"

I grinned. "Right—as in pterodactyl."

"Or in phthisis."

"What?"

"Phthisis, p-h-t-h-i-s-i-s—you know, tuberculosis, consumption?"

I didn't know, but didn't want to admit it. "Oh, of course—as in pneumonia."

"Very good—and Phrygian."

"And ... phrenology."

"And phthalic acid."

"Psychedelic ... psychosis ... psychiatry ... psychology."

She laughed. "Psoriasis, psalm, ptomaine, Ptolemy—and ptosis."

I didn't know what ptosis was either, but didn't ask. She had reeled them off as if she were reading from a book. I raised open palms in a gesture of defeat. "I give up. You're too clever for me."

She laughed. "No, I just know more words." She took another swallow of beer and leaned forward again. "So tell me about India—*all* about India!"

Even beyond her sheer pulchritude, I found her vivacity inspiring, her intelligence impressive. "It's a magical country. Magical things happen there."

She laughed again. "Oh, I love it, I love it! Tell me more!"

"There are peacocks in every tree, snake charmers on every street."

She laughed again. "Houris in every house? Harems in every courtyard?"

"Yes, and monkeys drive taxies—and elephants are buses."

She choked with laughter. "Oh, you liar, you *li*ar, and, of course, there's no poverty, no disease?"

"Right! No poverty, no disease."

"No dust, no heat, no flies, no mosquitos?"

"Right!"

"No hunger?"

"Hunger has been banished by the law of the land."

"Oh, you make it sound like Camelot!"

"Camelot?"

She sang: "'And there's a legal limit to the snow here—in Camelot.'"

"Ah, yes: 'In Camelot, those are the legal laws.'"

"It all sounds lovely. I almost got to go once, you know."

"Oh, yeah? What happened?"

She shrugged, dropping her smile; her face shrank. "Sergei Ivanovich Atramentov happened."

"What?"

"A stockbroker I was going with, from the Soviet Union. He came to New York on a cultural exchange, as a dancer—and defected, but never stopped looking over his shoulder. He was paranoid, thought the secret police were after him, said there were cameras on him at all times. Sometimes, in the middle of the night, he would get up to check the hallways and windows."

"Wow!"

"Anyway, he gave up dancing as soon as he got here. It was no way to make money, he said. He went into commodities—and he was very good, made a lot of money. We made plans for a trip around the world. Everything was in order." Her mouth pursed in a moue of regret. "On the last day he …" her voice got lower, softer—"left with someone else." She shrugged.

"I'm sorry."

"I broke all the dishes in the house."

"Good for you."

She laughed. "Only they were mine. I broke my own dishes—but that was months ago."

"I *am* sorry."

"I'm all right now—really, I am. I've been having elimination dreams. They're very healthy."

"What are elimination dreams?"

"Sitting on a pile of shit. It's a recurring dream—I'm *lit*erally putting my shit behind me."

"Ah!"

"And I've found someone else—well, sort of—he's with someone." My eyebrows rose.

She laughed. "My best friend—don't judge me now. We're perfect together, but he met Adora first—when I was with Sergei." She shrugged. "You know how it goes."

"Adora?"

"For Theodora!" She laughed again. "God knows what her parents were smoking."

"So you're not seeing anyone now?"
"Well, just him."
"But I thought …"
"I know, I know, it's all wrong—but there it is."
"How does he feel about you?"
"The same."
"How do you know he's not leading you on?"
"He pays my rent—well, he owns the building in which I live, and he doesn't charge me rent. Adora knows, but she thinks he's doing it for *her*—because I'm her best friend. We've been best friends since childhood—but I live on the first floor. They live in the penthouse."
"He owns *that* building, in *that* neighborhood? What does he do?"
"Take a guess." She crackled her bracelets.
"Ivory?"
"Well, lots of things, actually, but it started with ivory. He has a store in Wilmette: *Outpost*. It's the best store. We should go sometime … and he dabbles in this and that, I'm not even sure myself what exactly." She laughed again. "He says I'm better off not knowing."
"What's his name?"
"Quint—Quentin Castleworth, actually, but we call him Quint."
"So what makes you so perfect together—I mean, that you would cheat on your best friend?"
"He *knows* things. I'm a sucker for a man who can teach me things. He's also very unusual, and I'm a sucker for unusual men."
"What makes him unusual?"
"Well, for one thing, ivory is his work, but his first love is snakes—not just any old snakes, but cobras—and not just any old cobras, but *king* cobras."
"I didn't know there was a difference."
"Oh, there is, there is! They're different genuses. The king's venom is actually less potent, but its bite delivers a larger dose, enough to kill an elephant—or twenty humans. The king is much larger, the largest of the venomous snakes. It can grow up to twenty-six feet—also, regular cobras eat rats, mice, toads, frogs, but the king eats other snakes—mostly nonvenomous snakes, rat snakes—but also kraits and cobras and even smaller king cobras. That's why its Latin name is *Ophiophagus*

hannah—snake-eater. It's a cannibal! In fact, the female leaves the nest—it's the only snake to build a nest for its young—when the eggs are ready to hatch because she might be tempted to eat her own young."

I shuddered. "Great dinner conversation this is turning out to be."

She laughed. "Well, you asked for it—but you see what I mean? And that's just *one* of his quirks. He also has what I call his Ahab Complex."

"What's that?"

"He lost his arm once on an elephant shoot. It was a white elephant and it almost killed him. He says he wouldn't have minded being killed. According to the natives, death by white elephant is a ticket to heaven—but, fortunately or unfortunately, it didn't kill him. It tossed him into a tree and he managed somehow to hang on, even as the elephant was uprooting the tree—until the animal was killed."

"Holy Smokes!"

She giggled. "Holy smokes, indeed! He has people in Africa who keep him abreast of the white elephant population. He wants his revenge on the white elephant."

"But I thought you said the animal was killed?"

"Yes, but that wasn't enough for Quint. He has a prosthetic arm and it reminds him constantly of his nemesis. He won't rest until *all* white elephants are dead—or at least as many as he can get at—an Ahab Complex."

"He sounds crazy!"

She laughed. "Yes, of course, he's crazy—but he's also a genius. All geniuses are crazy. He knows something about everything. That's what makes him so fascinating."

I sat back in my chair, drawing deep lungfuls of air. "Well, I don't know about that—but going back to the cobras for a moment, what fascinates me is why someone would develop an interest in cobras—I mean, here, in the US—I mean, why not rattlesnakes—at least, they're indigenous."

"Well, I should let him tell you the story sometime—but, oh, well, I might as well tell you myself. He's traveled a lot, and the cobra obsession started in India, when he was the guest of the Maharajah of Durgapura. The Maharajah had his own private zoo—but more than anything else he liked snakes—and, most of all, cobras. Cobras are sacred in

India—very different from the serpent tempting Eve. There's a story of a giant cobra spreading its hood over the Buddha to provide shade while he meditated. Images of cobras guard the entrances of Hindu and Buddhist temples."

"But, still—why?"

"Well, Quint's quite short, and cobras are the only snakes that can actually stand. They can raise their heads to about a third of their length—and he found himself, once, eye to eye with a king cobra. The cobra may even have been taller—of course, it was behind glass, but that's all it took. He has a pet king cobra now. Can you believe it? In the penthouse of that swanky apartment building there lives a king cobra. He calls it Hannah!" She laughed. "I can't imagine what the tenants would think if they knew!"

"I didn't know it was allowed—I mean, dangerous animals in residential quarters."

She laughed again. "That's not a problem for Quint. He knows all the right people—he knows Daley—and, as he likes to say, if you have enough money in your pocket, politicians will find their way into your pocket as well." She grabbed my hand and held my gaze. "This goes no further. He'd be furious if he knew I'd told anyone. I'm not usually such a blabbermouth. What do you suppose it means?"

"Maybe that you're not really over … what's his name … Sergei?" Her smile dropped for a moment, her eyes narrowed and I wondered if I'd offended her again. "I mean, if you're really over someone you don't talk about it—otherwise, it looks like you're trying to convince yourself."

Her eyes hardened. "This isn't about Sergei. It's about Quint."

"I know, but it started with Sergei. Quint's sort of a Sergei substitute, isn't he?"

Her eyes softened and she looked away. "Maybe you're right. I'm still having the elimination dreams. If I were over him I suppose I wouldn't have the dreams anymore. I just don't know what to do."

I squared my shoulders. "Well, let me tell you. You should find someone who's available—I mean, someone who's unattached."

She laughed. "Like you? What about your girlfriend? What did she call herself? Andromeda?"

I shook my head. "That was Brooke. She's in Australia, but that's over."

"It's always been my last resort—the obvious solution, I mean."

"If the old ways don't work ..." I shrugged.

She smiled. "You *are* easy to talk to, you know."

I shook my head. "You just needed an ear."

"Right—but how did you get so wise? How old are you anyway?"

I didn't know that I was wise, but I was part Simon, part Spike, and part something that was three and twenty years of age. "I'll be twenty-two next year."

She giggled, shaking her head. "Shit, I'm robbing the cradle."

"How old are you?"

She batted eyelashes. "I was thirty last year."

I laughed. "How old is Quint?"

"Forty-two."

"*Forty-two!* I think you need a younger man."

"Why?"

"So he can look after you as you get older."

She laughed, slapping my hand across the table. "You bad boy!"

THERE IS A TIDE AND MINE SEEMED AT ITS FLOOD. I regaled her with stories of the circus and India. She took my arm as we walked to the car and after I drove her home invited me in for a nightcap. Her apartment wasn't one of the rentals, but a suite that had once comprised service rooms, the glory of which was a small private garden in the back. The front door opened into a foyer. She flipped a switch bringing bright light into the room. I knew from the telltale singeing of my skin, the rosiness flooding the world, that I was experiencing yet another illusion, but I didn't understand what I saw: a sunset gilding a horizon, a beach sloping toward the sea littered with what seemed to be the detritus of the ocean. A second look revealed what the first had refused to acknowledge: the detritus comprised corpses of black men and women left to rot, bloat, decompose, float off to sea—and, as the image congealed, a deep red mist descended like a curtain over the panorama, the world encased in blood.

I must have been staring vacantly, unable to find the significance, when Mercedes shook me to my senses by the elbow. "From the *Outpost*. Aren't they amazing?" I was staring at upholstered elephant feet in the foyer, white toenails encased in black skin, one an umbrella stand, the other a flowerbed for poinsettia. Mercedes hung her jacket on a tree. "They freaked me out at first, but I love them now."

"They're Africans."

"What? Oh! How do you know?"

"Five toenails. Indians have fewer toenails."

She stared as if she'd discovered the new world. "Wow! I don't think even Quint knows that."

I regurgitated what Hazel had fed me since childhood about differences between Africans and Indians. The African, Loxodonta africana, measured from its shoulders, is sleeker and saddlebacked, with ears wider than its neck, more wrinkles, more ribs, more rings in its trunk (culminating in two fingers), and more toenails; some females have tusks. The Indian, Elephas maximus, measured from its crown, is more compact, with an arched back, a trunk culminating in a single finger, and depigmentation (occasionally rendering ears and trunk almost pink); no females have tusks, nor do some males. There are two varieties of Africans and three of Indians—but, most importantly, they are different species, Africans descended from the mastodon, Indians from the mammoth. Scientists will tell you Africans cannot mate with Indians, but Jumbolina, an African at the Chester Zoo in England, who didn't know any better, impregnated Sheba, an Indian who didn't care, and birthed Motty, a hybrid exhibiting the doubledome of its mother behind the single of its father, and the rear hump of its father behind the central hump of its mother. Unfortunately, it died eleven days later of a gastric ailment common to baby animals.

"I just knew it! You're older than you look! Oh, you know so much!" She led me into her living-room, switched on a wall light, kicked off her shoes. "Make yourself at home. What'll you have?"

The room was spacious, but even in the dim light I could see it was spartanly furnished. "Beer."

"More beer?" She shook her head. "No, it's got to be Scotch. That's a man's drink. I'll take care of it." She laughed as she left the room. "I knew there was something I could teach you. Why don't you put on some music?"

I selected an album by Julie London, drawn to the cover (sultry London, cigarette in hand, gazing from a grainy photograph, leaning against a pillow and the brass bars of a headboard, her trenchcoat low enough to indicate she wore nothing underneath) and the title: *Nice Girls Don't Stay for Breakfast.*

Mercedes returned with two glasses to guitar and rising strings, brush strokes swirling on skins, the smoky voice singing the title line. Her own voice was no less smoky. "What about nice boys?"

I took my glass, a hard swallow of Scotch. "I'm a bad boy, remember?"

She laughed, taking a swallow herself. "Yes, of course—just the ticket for a naughty girl."

Almost everything she said was accompanied by a laugh. I couldn't tell whether it was nerves, the Scotch, the conversation, or the contemplation of what was to come—not that it mattered.

I took her glass, placed it with mine on the coffee-table, and drew her to me by the hips, but she held back, hands on my shoulders exerting the barest pressure to let me know she wasn't ready. "I don't usually do this on a first date, you know."

I rubbed her shoulders, slipping my thumbs under the straps of her blouse. "It may be the first date, but … you know … I've already saved your life, haven't I?"

She laughed. "I haven't forgotten—my paladin!" She looked up, still holding back. "You're so tall. A girl could break her back just kissing you."

One strap fell off its shoulder. "If we lay down we'd be the same height."

She laughed again, taking a step back. She led me by the hand to the bedroom, laughing all the way. The room was dark, but she stood me very precisely where she wanted and pushed.

"*Hey!*" I was in freefall, but the bed was soft, springy, and kingsized.

She lit a candle before heading for the bathroom. "I'll be right back. I'm going to change into something more comfortable." She smiled. "You should do the same."

My arousal was unquestionable and not just for the three and twenty years I'd been waiting. I removed shoes, socks, pants, and shirt, and waited stripped to my boxers. When I saw her again she was naked, framed by the doorway, silhouetted against the light from the bathroom, one fat round breast jutting from her flat belly, swelling to a nipple like a bee sting.

I had expected a robe, a slip, a negligee—*some*thing—and her stark nakedness, her rootedness in the doorway, pulled me from the bed like gravity. She laughed. "You're so eager—like a little boy."

"No, a sailor—back from months at sea."

"Oh, good, I always wanted to be a sailor's whore."

It was a Bangkok night. Vaginal muscles moved subtly as tides and I swelled as I had not thought possible fighting the pressure of those sea walls.

She brought me breakfast the next morning on a tray wearing a short red kimono. "Hey, sailor! Hit any squalls last night?"

The tray held orange juice, a bacon-cheese-and-mushroom omelet, buttered toast, strawberry jelly, coffee, and a rosy apple.

I pulled her down for a kiss. "No squalls! Just Hurricane Mercedes!"

AFTER BREAKFAST, freshening up in the bathroom before I left, I saw a photograph of two naked women, one white, one black, standing so close they might have been one, faces glued together from forehead to chin, sharing one nose, one pair of lips, eyes from different faces, bodies glued so the left breast was strawberry, the right coffee, strawberry and coffee hands demurely covering her crotch, front legs splayed, rear arms and legs invisible, hair streaming red on one side, walnut dreadlocks to the shoulder on the other. Mercedes interrupted my admiration with a smile and a mug of coffee. "Haven't you had enough?"

It took me all of a moment to recognize the redhead. "Are you kidding?"

She laughed. "*Playboy*, July 1968, 'Models of Chicago.'"

"*Playboy*? No kidding. Wow!"

"Thanks to Quint. He knows Hugh."

"Hugh? Quint knows Hugh? You call him Hugh?"

"It's only appropriate once you've attended his parties."

I blanketed my astonishment, not wanting to appear too much the rube, too much the kid I was. "Of course—and who's the other woman?"

"Adora."

"*That*'s Adora? My God! You could be sisters under the skin."

More than sisters they could have been twins but for the difference in their coloring. Mercedes laughed. "That's what Hugh said. We do feel like sisters. We're very close."

I no longer questioned her affair with Quint, nor her relations with Adora, all part of a brave new world, and I had taken first steps the night before. "When do I meet them?"

She sighed. "Soon, I hope. Adora's not well—suicidal, actually, took a razor to her wrists. She's supposed to rest and recuperate for a while."

I took a deep breath. "Wow! Why?"

She shrugged. "Who can tell? Who really knows about these things? She's got everything a woman could want. You can't imagine how hard this is on Quint."

She turned to lead me out of the bathroom and I felt the heat rise again, a heat I was learning to recognize, red mist descending as the panorama changed. Before me rose a large house, fighting-men of mixed Arab and African descent lounging in the verandahs, courtyard littered with thousands of pounds of tusks, diseased slaves chained and rotting. Beyond the gate flowed a river and along a narrow strip of beach lay black men and women and children, seared with scars like barbed wires, skin pocked with pustules of blue and red, some dying, some dead, partly eaten by hyenas. A whiterobed Arab walked by them in amity with a khakied Englishman—clean, courteous, and perfumed host leading his adventurous guest to a repast fit for royalty within the house. The Englishman seemed bemused. "Why not cure the smallpox? Save the lives?"

The Arab smiled as if he were explaining to a child. "Not worth it. We have gone to the trouble and expense of bringing them from the Congo for nothing. Who will carry their loads of ivory to the coast now?" He shook his head, still smiling. "No one is to go near them. You see that guard?"

The Englishman nodded, seeing a soldier nearby with a rifle.

"He has orders to shoot if anyone comes near. They are beyond hope, you see. We have spent too much already. We have put them close to the water for the crocodiles. After sunset they will come."

Red sky at night,
Sailor's delight.
Red sky in the morning,
Sailor's warning.

THREE MYRTLE AND THE ELEPHANT

It was Sunday morning, not quite eleven when I got back home, at a loss to explain the gruesome image. Naomi was on the courts giving lessons, but she'd left a note to say Hazel had called and wanted me to call back. Chuck was at church, Tess out to breakfast with Derrick, and they appeared just as I called Hazel. "Hi, Mom. You called?"

"Yes. Listen, Simon, darling, Granma's been cooking up a storm. I told her she shouldn't be standing so much on her leg, but she wouldn't listen—and she wants me to bring it to you. Are you going to be around for a while?"

"Granma's been cooking? but, Mom, we don't need food. We've got plenty of food—and if we run out we can always get more."

"I know. Don't even ask. There's also something I want to tell you. Are you going to be around?"

"Yeah, I'll be around."

"Good. I'll be there in about an hour. Make room in your refrigerator."

Derrick was watching news on the television we'd fitted into our fireplace for the summer. Tess looked back as I hung up the receiver, her arm over the back of the peagreen sofa balanced on two legs and two sets of bricks. "Hazel's coming?"

I nodded. "She said to make room in the refrigerator."

"What for?"

"My granma's been cooking. I don't understand it myself."

Hazel was as good as her word, arriving before noon, unloading a large picnic basket, canister after canister: buttered biscuits, blackeyed peas, collard greens, smothered porkchops, fried chicken, apple pie. She shook her head as amazed apparently as everyone else. "Your granma must think you're starving. Cane and all, she insisted I take her shopping and she's been busy in the kitchen ever since. She insisted I bring it to you—'fo' Simon an' his frien's,' she said."

Tess's eyes bulged. "Holy smokes, Mrs. Blue! That's enough for an army! Thanks so much!"

"Don't thank me. Thank Simon's granma." She rolled her eyes. "I don't know why, Simon, but she seems to think you're her son Elbo come back to life. She seems to want to make up for everything she didn't do for Elbo."

"What? She didn't feed him?"

"Who knows? It doesn't matter. What did you guys talk about to bring all this about?"

"Prejudice—in India. There were these two fat old biddies we saw on the bus." I told them the story. "Granma said they were niggerish. She told me the difference between black and niggerish."

Hazel dismissed the matter with a shake of her head. "Simon, there is something else I want to talk about. It's personal. Can we go inside?"

"Sure."

HAZEL FOLLOWED ME TO MY ROOM, shut the door, and took an armchair under the Dylan poster. I stretched out on the bed. The walls sported posters as well of the Beatles, Woodstock, Zeppelin, Stones, Tull, a couple of *Playboy* centerfolds, and shelves of books and albums. "What's up, Mom?"

Hazel leaned forward, elbows on knees. "It's about your dream, Simon—what you said before you left—that you saw me dead."

My eyes shut in a grimace. "Aw, Mom, it was just a dream. I should never have told you."

"No, I'm not so sure it *was* just a dream. That's why I'm asking."

She was right, it had not been a dream, and I didn't know how she knew, but I didn't want to find out. "Mom, I really don't want to talk about it. Relax. It doesn't mean I want you dead or anything. It was just a bad dream. You'd been sick, and I was afraid, and I was glad to see you well. That's all. You don't have to go all Freudian on me."

"Simon, listen." I pulled a pillow over my face. "Darling, it's not what you think. Just tell me. Could you see my face?" She pulled the pillow away. "Simon!"

"Mom, this is stupid!"

"I know it is—but indulge me, darling, just for a minute. Yes or no. Could you see my face?"

I turned my face aside. "I don't know. It was a dream. You were on your back, Granpa was beating his head, Siri was praying—who else could it have been?"

"It could have been *my* mother—your other grandma, Grandma Myrtle."

"What?"

"I never told you the story, but I think you should know."

She returned to the armchair. I sat crosslegged on the bed. "What story?"

Now that she had my attention she lapsed into a reverie. "It was 1936. I was eighteen. I wish you could've seen Pa then, before Ma died—your granpa, Dinty, I mean. You were seven when he died, but you saw him at his worst." Her voice got soft with reflection. "You wouldn't have recognized him. He was six inches taller just from the way he walked when Ma was by his side."

Her voice got smaller. "The change started in Pa when Alf died, his brother. It was five years after the Crash. We were beginning to adjust ... but that was the beginning of the end ... for Pa."

She took a deep breath. "In those days, the act revolved around me—when I put my head in Hero's mouth. It was a big act, the crowds went wild, what few still came—but I wanted more—I wanted independence. I was eighteen. I felt the circus was holding me back. I traveled widely with the circus, but traveling with a circus is like traveling in a tunnel. Wherever I was I was always with the circus, and the circus in Florida was no different from the circus in Maine or the circus in California—and I wanted to see Florida, I wanted to see Maine, I wanted to see California. I had many admirers. I could have gone with any of them. Jack was just the last, Brown E—you know who I mean."

I nodded.

"Well, on that night I was with Jack. I'd had an argument with Pa—I can't even remember about what anymore. Before Alf died we never argued, but it got so we didn't even need an excuse anymore. A loud noise, a hot day, cramped quarters, a squalling baby—anything could set us off." She shook her head, her voice heavy with regret. "We'd just argued. I said I was damned if I was going to go through with the act. It was a big night. We were in New York—the biggest crowd we'd had in a long while. Jonas wanted the best show, all the acts, nothing left out of any of the acts—but *I* wanted a night on the town. I'd been in New York before, but on the road every city's the same: you get in, you do your act, you get out. I wanted to see New York, *re*ally see New York—and the way I felt I didn't care what anyone said. I was *go*ing to see New York. Jack had a friend we could stay with, and Jack would do anything I asked."

She took another deep breath. "You can guess what happened. Jonas wanted the act—if not with me then with someone else. Siri volunteered, but … Jonas wanted a woman, a white woman, because that's how we'd been billed—and he insisted. It was more glamorous with a woman, more daring—and Ma volunteered."

She spoke quickly. "She'd worked with Hero, of course, but never like that. Pa didn't want her to do it. He was afraid. It was too delicate a lift to be made without rehearsal—but Jonas insisted, and so did Ma until Pa felt he had no choice. It was either that or he'd have to find another circus."

She paused. "I don't rightly know what happened. I wasn't there and I didn't ask. It doesn't matter. She broke her spine. She died instantly."

Her voice shrank to a whisper and I rose to comfort her—but she shook her head, holding me at bay with an outraised hand. She seemed angry, as if resurrecting the story had defiled its memory. "That's what happened. Jack, Jonas, me, all of us, we all had a hand in it—I for staying away, Jack for helping me, Jonas for insisting. We all blamed ourselves, but Pa most of all."

She spoke slowly again. "Pa changed the most. In important ways he was paralyzed for the rest of his life. Jonas always made allowances. I think that was his reason for letting him off so easily even for poisoning Hero. Sometimes, I wonder, even now, if Pa didn't poison Hero for what he did to Ma—not consciously, of course, but by that time he wasn't thinking clearly about anything."

There was another long silence before she spoke again, her voice still lost to memory. "I wish you could have known him then, Simon. He was a strong man—even with the injury to his back, he was a strong man ... but after what happened to Ma he just gave up."

She sighed. "You see what I mean? I never told anyone except your father, not even your uncle Spike—but I always wondered ..." She paused. "If Spike had known he might have stayed—he might have been alive today." She looked at me, shaking her head as if shaking herself from the memory.

I hadn't understood the image myself, but hearing Hazel's story it couldn't have been more clear. Like everyone, she carried her most tragic memories in that netherland visited only by psychics and psychologists. "I bet it *was* your mom. I don't remember seeing the face. I just took it for granted." I had learned, finally, the mystery of my mother's death. I wanted to come clean myself, put myself at Hazel's mercy, bawl about the miseries of man, but I would only have disenfranchised myself. I couldn't bring Simon back without sacrificing myself, and she wouldn't have sacrificed Simon for anyone.

"There was never a need to tell you, but after that dream of yours ... it's uncanny—but I'm glad you know. We don't need to say anything about it ever again."

She spoke as if we'd just discussed a movie and it struck me all over again how terrific she'd always been, taking everything in stride. She made me want to be like her, be my best self. "Mom?"

"Yeah?"

"I'm glad you told me."

She got up, smiling. "Come here, Simon. Give me a hug."

FOUR — THE BRASS FLOOR

In that big book about a mammoth mammal, fully 28% of the pages are devoted to an encyclopedic account of the animal—more than a quarter of the book to what might be considered filler, cogging fact upon fact from book after book, growing fat on the fat of libraries. Among other things, an entire chapter is devoted to the ashenness of the animal, 3,639 words to the effect that as much as we may worship and revere what's white it remains no less a terror. The author is right, but how convoluted is the world? Darkskins bow to lightskins the world over, and the more they bow the more they get exploited—Africa, Asia, Australia, America, all fell before Europe.

Roy knew the score—finally. He had succumbed to the sickness while imagining he'd beaten the system. He'd expected the call and worn his darkest suit, wanting to appear his best. He straightened his tie in the men's room before taking the Brass Elevator, satisfied with the image in the mirror. He knew the stories; he knew the law. He had absorbed Jim Crow's passage from Emancipation to Black Codes, Slave Codes, Home Rule, and States' Rights so fully that he had lived the history. He had studied *Dred Scott*, *Plessy*, *Brown* and all the rest so compulsively that their writs were etched on his bones.

He knew the people: salty Sojourner Truth telling southern white men they couldn't get enough black pussy because they'd nursed at the tits of big black mammies like herself; Harriet Tubman, escaping the south only to lose count of the number of times she returned to lead six hundred more out of southern darkness; Gabriel Prosser, Denmark Vesey, and most of all Nat Turner among so many others, American heroes all, scarcely recognized today. Toussaint L'Ouverture drove colonialists from Haiti, Point du Sable founded Chicago, Jack Johnson tweaked the white world, Jesse Owens tweaked Hitler—and that was just starters.

That was his heritage, and he was proud, but in his quest for all things unniggerish, he'd slept with the enemy—with Marshall, Justice, and Marshall, and later with Stern, Stone, Stein, and Marmer, willingly becoming their bondman, congratulating himself on his foot in the door, imagining himself the camel commandeering his master's tent despite the lesson at Marshall, Justice, and Marshall—and now that the writing appeared as embossed on the walls of Stern, Stone, Stein, and Marmer, he felt snookered. The camel remained shivering outside the tent. More than a color, blackness was a weight, a smell. The more you denied it the more you smelled, the more it weighed you down. You could make a million bucks and still smell. You could be granted a hundred ways of access and still be unwelcome. You could win the Nobel as King had done and still be a nigger. No one, not even King, could save an entire race, but King had saved himself in the attempt. Right action counted for more than success.

Whatever the arguments, the bottom line never changed: he was a black man and he'd lived his life as if he were not, imagining like Booker T. that blacks could live with whites as the fingers of a hand—but the good Booker was wrong. Ralph Ellison was right: you had to overcome them with yeses, undermine them with grins, agree them to death, let them swallow you till they burst. Even an Irishman had shown more sense, advocating silence, exile, cunning. The Civil Rights Movement had enraged him, demanding pro bono what he had earned with sweat and blood—but he'd also begun to find his perspective, cheering silently for Rosa Parks refusing to vacate her seat on the bus and Daisy Bates organizing the Little Rock Nine, enraged by fools like Orville Faubus and Bull Connor turning the National Guard, fire hoses, and guard dogs on blacks, on black women and black children—and cheering, again silently, the freedom rides and sit-ins.

Despite his sympathy he had separated himself from the events, imagining they were isolated—but each incident had created a wavelet within, swelling to billow with other wavelets, and accumulated like a tide until a relatively undramatic incident had crashed the sea wall. He'd been watching the news with Hazel, President Johnson stumping for voting rights legislation. "Their cause must be our cause too," he had said, "because it's not just Negroes, but all of us who must overcome the crippling legacy of bigotry and injustice—and WE *SHALL* OVERCOME!" The last three words had taken him by surprise, President echoing King, and he had heaved silently, summoning tears that would not come, emotion long buried. Hazel had said nothing, stroking his face, cradling his head, understanding him as always better than he understood himself.

That had been six years ago.

The Brass Elevator went to the Brass Floor, both named tongue-in-cheek for the top brass who rode it. The elevator walls were lined with brass rails and dark mirrors making shadows of reflections. The floor was plusher than any other floor in the building, except the Brass Floor where the pile got deeper yet, the air more rare, the ceiling higher, the echoes fainter. To the left of the elevator stood the security desk in a large waiting area, club chairs upholstered in red leather, sunk in pile. Handsome volumes, leatherbound and giltedged, titles veined in gold, which no one ever read, languished on dark wooden shelves behind glass cases no one ever unlocked. Nautical panoramas in watercolors hung on the dark wainscoted walls. Roy recalled that Dr. No's reception room, in the James Bond novel, had been likened to the reception rooms of presidents of large American corporations. He imagined, not entirely facetiously, that only kings and criminals could afford such luxury. He waved to the desk. "Hey, Cliff."

The guard waved him on. "Hey, Mr. Blue."

"Mr. Gold's expecting me."

Cliff released the security door. "I know."

The hallway beyond was lined with antique chairs, tables, sideboards, Queen Anne style, that no one ever used. Recessed lights showed the way, hunting panoramas on the walls accompanied visitors. Roy entered the office of Dennis Gold's secretary, Georgina, and exchanged pleasantries before she announced and escorted him to the inner sanctum.

Gold's desk was oval, cluttered, mahogany. He got up as Roy entered, pushing back his chair. Tennis had kept him slender but could do nothing for his saucer eyes, mouth like a shark, hairs sprouting from the dome of his head, white wings fluttering over longlobed ears. He held out his hand. "Roy, good to see you."

Roy knew the office. Gold had sponsored his hire. Portraits of Stern, Stone, Stein, and Marmer, all of whom were dead except Marmer, stared from one of the wainscoted walls, bookshelves lined another, a living-room set occupied the wall across the desk, the fourth wall was a window overlooking Madison Avenue, sixty-two storeys high. The day was cloudless, a jet commanded the north sky, a crow flew past the window. Gold's family stared from a frame on the mahogany cabinet behind him: small, blond, pretty, smiling Melanie, his wife (often featured in the Lake Forest society columns); Cornie (for Cornelia), the oldest; and Bryce and Blair, the twins, in twin suits. Roy was glad the kids got their looks from their dad, but not even Melanie (now twice the size of the woman in the photograph) could hold a candle to Hazel, not even in the days of the photograph. The desk was wide enough for Roy to have to lean forward to shake Gold's hand, but he said nothing, merely nodding in response.

Gold barely leaned forward himself and patted his hair. "I'm glad you came."

Roy was glad to see he wasn't entirely at ease. "Of course."

They sat, Gold at his desk, Roy in one of the upholstered visitors' chairs, noting they'd stayed at the desk instead of adjourning as they sometimes did to the sofa.

"How's Hazel?"

"Couldn't be better."

"Good. Glad to hear it. I'll never forget that amazing demonstration she gave us. Mel still talks about it to our friends—so do the kids."

They'd visited the zoo together, Blues and Golds, Hazel had taken them behind the scenes to feed buns and baguettes to Raja, Rani, and Jabardasti. Roy nodded. He knew Gold was buttering him—keeping this nigger running to apply Ellison's phrase. "I'm glad she found it so memorable."

Gold shook his head. "She'll never forget—hell, *I'*ll never forget, shaking the elephant's trunk—and the hairs, we never imagined they'd be so prickly."

"They're very prickly."

"Just the thrill of it, standing next to such a large animal, touching its leg, like swimming with dolphins, so otherworldly, so weird and wonderful—but not for Hazel, of course."

"Of course."

Roy's mouth was a grim line. Gold changed the subject. "How'd Simon like India. I never had the chance to ask."

"It was an education he said."

"Of course." Gold realized the small talk wouldn't go much further. "You know why I've called you, Roy. Frankly, I was very surprised—no, I was shocked to get this." He tapped a file on his desk. "Have we had a misunderstanding?"

It was his letter of resignation. "No, no misunderstanding. It was my fault—entirely my own fault, for only beginning to understand myself."

"Understand what?"

"It's hard to explain, Dennis, and I'd rather not if I don't have to—and I don't have to."

Gold took a deep breath, playing again with his hair, pulling out a gold cigarette case, offering Roy a cigarette.

"No, thanks. I haven't smoked in three years—and neither has Hazel." Roy's voice was sharp, implying Gold should have known.

"Ah, yes, of course. You don't mind if I do?" He didn't wait for Roy's response, but extracted a cigarette, extracted a lighter, lit the cigarette, inhaled, blew out smoke, put away the case as if he were considering what they'd said, what to say next.

Roy might customarily have said something, he'd often felt he owed Gold a debt for his sponsorship, but said nothing, gritting his teeth to keep silent.

Gold blew a wreath of smoke. "I wish I could change your mind, Roy. We've been through so much. I'd like very much for us to carry on."

Roy remained polite. "Thanks. I appreciate the sentiment."

"Is it a matter of compensation?"

Roy shook his head. "I've been well compensated."

Gold took another deep breath, twiddled his hair with his fingers, but said nothing again immediately—and again Roy bore the silence gritting his teeth until Gold finally spoke again.

"I see you're going to make me play a game of twenty questions, Roy. You know how I hate that, don't you?"

"Nope, that's not it. I've said what I wanted to say. It's all in the letter. I've nothing to add."

"There's nothing in this letter, nothing about why."

"Let's just say it's personal."

"You can tell me, Roy. Hell, we're practically family. I got you the job. I deserve that much."

"Yes—but it's more a question of what I deserve."

Gold's face registered dismay. He held out his hands helplessly. "Help me, Roy. Tell me what you deserve. I'll see what I can do."

"Let's say it's a matter of professional mobility and let's leave it at that."

Gold smiled and nodded, his long thin mouth threatening to split his face in two. "I think I understand—but why the cloak and dagger routine? Why not just say what's on your mind? Juvenile of you, Roy, I must say. I didn't expect it."

Roy gritted his teeth. He'd said too much, given Gold the opening he'd sought, allowed him to play martyr while beating him with a stick—but the satisfaction of airing his dissatisfaction was not the satisfaction he'd wanted. He would not be drawn further. "Yes, of course, but that's the way it is."

Gold raised his finger as if he'd received inspiration. "It's Epstein, isn't it?"

Epstein was only the most recent attorney to receive a senior partnership, but the line stretched much further back. "Hardly. It's hardly just Epstein."

"He's a rainmaker divine, Roy." Gold raised admiring eyebrows. "I don't have to tell you, do I?"

"No more than myself, Dennis, I have poured like a monsoon myself, and you know it."

"Ah, I see. Not a question of professional mobility, then, is it, as much as professional jealousy?"

Roy took a deep breath. "You're doing me a disservice, Dennis—and yourself. I didn't ask for this discussion."

"Of course, Roy, of course. I'm sorry. Believe me, I was just thinking out loud—but, of course, I shouldn't have. I'm sorry."

"Apology accepted."

Gold's smile settled like the grimace of a predator. "Well, then, let me just call a spade a spade, if you'll pardon the pun. We have no need of blacks among our senior partners. It wouldn't reflect well, our clientele would be disappointed—a matter of politics, you understand, not prejudice—but of course you understand, you've always understood. That's why you've been with us so long."

Roy drew breath slowly between his teeth. "Let me correct you on a minor point, Dennis. *You* have always called a spade a spade, and *I* have always been too damn obtuse to notice—but no more. Thanks for lifting the mist so categorically—and goodbye."

He got up to leave, but Gold held up his hands, helpless again. "Again, I apologize, Roy. Again, I'm sorry. I had no idea this ran so deep. Please, for old times' sake, sit down a minute."

Roy sat. "A minute—for old times' sake."

Gold nodded, looking past Roy, appearing to be scanning for words. "Roy, I've said this before, you know. We're alike, you and I. A word against you is a word against me."

Roy knew where Gold was going. He nodded, saying nothing.

Gold's fingers were in his hair. "You know what I'm talking about."

"I want to hear you say it."

"You know what I'm talking about, Roy. Don't make me say it."

"The six million?"

Gold nodded.

At least, someone was counting, Jack, Roy wanted to say. *My people have been invisible for centuries*—but he didn't, he didn't want to play Gold's game, reducing vast historical tragedies to rhetorical flourishes. Besides, he was no more exemplar of his race than Gold of his. He got up instead, walked to the door. "Goodbye, Dennis. I didn't think you'd sink so low. My best to Mel and the kids." He shut the door behind him, gave Georgina a mock salute on his way out, strode down the hallway back to the elevator with a bounce that had little to do with the pile of the carpet, and waved to Cliff as he passed.

Justice Taney, deciding the *Dred Scott* case, had decreed: "Negroes have no rights which the white man is bound to respect." Frederick Douglass had responded: "The Supreme Court is not the supreme power in the world. Taney cannot bail out the ocean, or pluck the star of liberty from the northern sky." Roy wished he had more imagination, more of the poet, but couldn't stop grinning: he hadn't been too shabby himself.

FIVE — DINNER IN THE PENTHOUSE

The talk with Hazel had swept the mists like so many cobwebs from my mind. The road ahead was clear—but I had an angel on one shoulder and a devil on the other. I wanted to render unto Hazel the things that were Hazel's—but not yet. In the words of Saint Augustine: Give me chastity, but not yet. The devil infesting my days was Mercedes, whom I visited night after Bangkok night. The warnings were plentiful and palpable, a heat so high I should have burned, images so horrific I had to turn away—but, tumid as a rainforest, horned as a rhinoceros, I wanted more.

The images were confusing (slaves and ivory, ivory and Arabs, Arabs and slaves) because I was unfamiliar with the history, but the rationale was clear. Mercedes's apartment was caulked with elephantalia. The elephant feet in her foyer barely foreshadowed what followed. Her boots and briefcase were of elephant hide. Her jewelry boxes and much jewelry were ivory, also fans, letter openers, a seal with her name. A whisk was an elephant tail, a braided headband elephant hair, the skin of a drum an elephant ear. Ghastliest were elephant eyelashes, hanging from her mirror like dead spiders, a symbol of fertility (though she had no desire to get pregnant). Picture frames were ivory, intricately carved with elephant vistas: bathing, at play, on parade, in the circus, bearing howdahs on tigerhunts.

I didn't make the association right away, but a particular series of images finally answered my questions: a family of ten elephants feasting at leisure in the forest; men with kalashnikovs gunning them down; giants falling like houses during an earthquake; men with knives and hatchets leaping on their backs and faces to hack and chop and wrench free the tusks; the sucking sound of flesh turning inside out surrendering its treasure; pink glutinous jellies sliming the ground, oozing from sockets which once had held tusks firmly in place; a banquet of bloodied mountains for vultures, hyenas, and lions. They were poachers, descendants of the slavers. When I asked Mercedes about the origin of her treasures, she retreated to her mantra about legality and legitimacy. Her rigid back and the set of her lips said otherwise, but I was having too much fun to protest. Bottom line: none of my business.

My life was smooth: my internship at Inventive Electrics, Inc.; my classes at CU; my relations with Hazel and Roy and Siri; my home with Chuck and Naomi and Tess; my lovelife with Mercedes. The last surprised me more than the rest, but I was soon to learn how much I was her pawn. Meanwhile, aside from occasional images misted in red, my life was normal. I adjusted to everything. Just as a person given lenses to turn the world upside down learns to pour her tea upward, I learned to control what I saw. It became as easy as blinking. I could turn it on, I could turn it off. I could do it without thinking.

The honeymoon with Mercedes lasted six weeks. I never saw Quint or Adora, in that time though Mercedes never stopped talking about them. Quint was busy, Adora recuperating from her suicide attempt, but the more I heard the more I wanted to hear. Quint, a child of the Depression, born the day of the Crash into a wealthy Connecticut family in Westbrook, lost father and fortune the same day, father to the street which rose to meet him stepping off the ledge of his New York office building, following their fortune into the maw of the Depression.

His mother rejoined her penurious brother in New York, took Quint with her (though she blamed him for the date of his birth), and succumbed to a more prosaic depression herself. Her brother, Quint's uncle, spiraled into alcoholism and ten-year-old Quint took to the streets, stealing apples to sell, eating what he couldn't sell, juggling jobs from paperboy to junkman to honkytonk pianist. He was too young for the war when it ended, but old enough to take advantage of the opportunities in its wake.

Calling on family ties he found himself gainfully employed in Ivoryton, a single-industry factory town, within hailing distance of his hometown, Westbrook. Ivory had been worked in Ivoryton since the time of Thomas Jefferson, sailing from the Congo to the Connecticut via Zanzibar, around the Horn of Africa, up the Red Sea, through the Mediterranean, and across the Atlantic. Ivoryton children cut their teeth on ivory rings, as did children of neighboring Deep River and Essex. Outhouses of old houses sported ivory doorknobs.

Among other things they manufactured combs, brushes, billiard balls, knife handles, chessmen, dice—and, more than anything, piano keys. Three factories manufactured keyboards for all pianos made in the US, Canada, and Australia, making them the largest users of ivory in the world. Following a business lead, Quint opened a branch in Chicago where he met and married Harriet, his first wife, dead two years later when her Cadillac careened into a wall. He also branched into other businesses, and nine years later met and married Adora at a time when Mercedes was minding Sergei Ivanovich.

All had one thing in common, deadened by the Depression or warped by the War they were siblings in despair, offspring of men and women broken by the machinations of nations. Mercedes, born in 1940, was a year older than Adora, but both lost fathers to the War, Mercedes in Normandy, Adora in Iwo Jima, Adora suffering additional hits, her mother finding the final solace in pills when Adora turned twelve, her grandmother shot by a catburglar before her eyes when she was seventeen—precipitating her career as a dancer at the Moulin Rouge on Rush Street after a year of waitressing. Quint saw her dance, sent expensive gifts, promised modeling jobs, and finally married her.

As girls, Mercedes and Adora lived two blocks apart on Chicago's south side, bonding when they'd lost their fathers, sharing boyfriends when they were old enough (sixteen and seventeen), developing reputations as the fast girls of the neighborhood, Mercedes taking the lead from her own mother who fell in love with any man who showed the least interest, an everlasting line of stepfathers providing the model for an everlasting line of lovers—until she'd met Sergei, and then Quint, and now me. I knew about her affair with Quint because she'd told me. I knew neither how far it went, nor what Adora knew, nor what it meant for me, nor did I ask. She'd made no promises, but neither had she asked for any, and far be it from me to upset so rubious an applecart. When the dinner invitation came from Quint and Adora, a hurrah for her recovery, I was curious, I was eager—I was also stricken with panic.

THE ELEVATOR DOOR OPENED directly into the foyer of the penthouse. Mercedes held my arm tightly, pressed against her breast, willing my courage. She wore a black formfitting dress to her knees with a mandarin collar, black stockings, black satin shoes, topping everything with a black satin turban—also an ivory necklace and earrings. There was nothing in Simon's wardrobe to fit the occasion and I'd bought a black dinner jacket which I wore over a white turtleneck. Mercedes thought I looked smart and garlanded me with a peace medallion.

The bell was answered by Addison, Quint's manservant, sixty odd years showing in his grizzled closecropped head, but as bright for his white captain's uniform and brass buttons as for his smile. "Evenin', Ms. Carlssen. Lookin' mighty fine!"

Mercedes returned his smile, tooth for tooth. "Thank you, Addison! This is my friend, Simon Blue."

Addison gave a little bow. "Evenin', Mr. Blue, sir."

"Hey, Addison."

Classical music provided a ceremonial soundtrack as we traversed a hallway and entered the living-room through an archway. There was to be one more couple, the Currans (Quint's attorney and his wife), but the room was empty and Mercedes hallooed our arrival. "Yoo hoo! Anyone home?"

We had entered an atrium sporting two staircases at opposite ends and a balcony circling the space. Addison came around from behind us. "They still in the bedroom, Ms. Carlssen. They say to wait in the livin'-room. Shall I get you and Mr. Blue drinks while you's waitin'?"

"Thanks, Addison—two martinis please."

"Yes, Ms. Carlssen."

There was a bar along one side of the living-room under two four-foot tusks crisscrossed on the wall, but Addison left through another of the doorways. Mercedes drew me first to a window for the view. The panorama went beyond the park, beyond Lake Shore Drive, beyond the lake, to the curve of the horizon. On a clear day you could see Michigan, and to left and right spread the northshore of Chicago, from Belmont Harbor to the Lincoln Park Zoo. Mercedes needed a restroom and left, kissing my cheek for courage.

The room was huge, Regency furniture augmenting a sense of the old world. Large plush sofas crowded the floor, draperies dressed the windows, paintings and portraits adorned the walls, and showcases separated the living-room into three separate spaces. Elephant footstools were everywhere, as was much of the elephantalia I'd seen in Mercedes's apartment—and more. My first impression was of confusion: there was too much to absorb at once, enough artifacts to fill a museum, but my attention was soon drawn to a set of erotic sculptures in a showcase, each no more than a cubic inch, all in ivory. I bent over, lost in admiration, when someone snuck up behind me. "Hello, Simon?"

"Yes?" I unbent immediately, turning around. It was the woman with the coffee complexion I'd seen in the photograph with Mercedes in her bathroom. She was taller than Mercedes by a couple of inches, ropy dreadlocks fell around her head, and she shimmered with every movement in a satin gold sleeveless blouse and miniskirt made of white plastic disks linked by chains. She wore a black band around her neck and a thick ivory bracelet on each wrist. "Adora? Hi!"

She seemed brittle, as if she might have cracked with an unkind word, and I recalled she was a recovering suicide. In the long pause that followed I was afraid she would start crying, but she put on her best face and forced herself to speak. "Those are nice, aren't they?"

I nodded. "I was just admiring the detail."

Addison brought martinis, I took one and Adora took the other, requesting two more for Quint and Mercedes. She shook her head. "That's *just* Quint's style. Would you believe he once commissioned a golf bag made of an elephant's penis?" A thin laugh followed. "Here's another one he commissioned. It's his favorite." She led me to another showcase from which she removed a clamshell and a magnifying glass from an ivory box inlaid with white satin.

The shell was carved, like the erotica and box, in ivory, revealing a stark landscape, a cemetery marked by rocks and gravestones, a king cobra rising above the vista like a deity of the dead, its head splayed against the sky as imperious as it might have been before the Fall, resembling the arched neck and flat head of the brontosaurus of old or the Loch Ness monster of myth. Under the eye of the glass I could see bugs crawling on the treetrunk, toads on the rocks, writing on the gravestones, roots threading the ground, and the eyes, fangs, and forked tongue of the majestic magisterial malevolent monarch though its head was barely a centimeter long. I could even see the ribs in the flanges of its hood. "Wow!"

I shuddered recalling that a live Hannah lurked within, the name Quint had given his hamadryad, perhaps coiling and uncoiling that very moment. I was so overwhelmed that the red mist caught me unawares once more. A single row of slaves, naked men and women attached to one another by their necks fastened into the forks of six-foot-long poles, trudged along a beaten track between walls of jungle, so fragile in appearance that a sudden stop or fall might have broken their necks. They carried tusks on their heads weighing from twenty to seventy pounds, some women had babies on their backs, bodies caked with mud and shit, shoulders scarred by whips of hippopotamus hide, feet bloated with open sores, and shrouds of flies feasting on crisp drying blood.

The slave caravan filed out of the jungle into a camp to be met by a white missionary who greeted the Arab headmen politely and was greeted politely in return. The Arabs, clothed in clean cotton garments, carried rifles, knives, spears, and whips. The missionary shook his head looking at the bearers. "These men are not fit for such loads."

The Arab headman shrugged, smiling. "They can go or they can die. It is up to them."

"Are they all bound for Zanzibar?"

"Most—the rest will stay on the coast."

"Have you lost some already?"

"Oh, yes—many die of hunger."

"Any run away?"

"No—too well guarded—but there is nowhere to run."

"What if they become too sick to travel?"

The Arab held up his spear. "We kill them. Otherwise, all would pretend to be sick."

"What about women carrying babies? What if they are too weak to carry the baby and the ivory?"

The Arab shrugged, smiling again. "We lighten her load. We kill the baby."

"The baby? But the baby has done no wrong. Is that not a sin?"

The Arab shook his head. "Does not matter, baby or big. All are the same. All are unbelievers. Does not matter."

Someone shook my arm. Mercedes's voice penetrated the mist. "Simon! Are you all right?"

I put down the magnifying glass, shaking the image from my head, heat like a blanket around my shoulders. "Sorry—got carried away. I'm all right."

Adora looked at me curiously. "You look like you've seen a ghost. Would you like some water?"

She spoke sympathetically, no longer brittle, finding purpose in my fragility, a sibling in distress. "I'm all right, but thanks." I put the clamshell down carefully. "That's really something."

Adora nodded, pressing my hand in solidarity. "I know. I'm sorry. It's creepy. But that's Quint."

I was grateful for her commiseration, glad to have pierced her exterior.

Mercedes felt my forehead. "Are you sure you're all right? You're burning up."

"I'm all right—I'll be all right. It was just so astonishing—like looking into another world."

An amused voice resounded. "It's the altitude. Tall people are hazardous to their own health."

The voice came from the balcony, soft and insinuating: Quint. Despite what Mercedes had said I'd expected a booming ringmaster of a man, but I could see as he descended the staircase that he scaled barely five feet. It didn't help that he was balding, but the head was imposing, the head of a larger man. He compensated for balding by growing hair long enough along the periphery of the dome to cover his ears, a heavy black Dostoevskian beard, and a heavy black Nietzschean moustache. His nose overhung the mop of his moustache like a hood ornament, hypnotic mudbrown eyes were spaced far apart and framed by thick black round lenses. His torso swelled like a barrel, plainly outlined in a blue turtleneck and narrowed to tiny legs in tight black leather pants. A black leather glove extended from the sleeve of his prosthetic right arm, the original lost to the white elephant. His left hand was bare. He looked like a powerful dwarf, but I was reminded as well of couples long together and people long with their pets who came to resemble each other. So much does a long communion tend to make us what we are that in Quint's huge head and tiny legs I saw the splayed swaying head of a king cobra.

He remained unsmiling and fierce despite his joke. Mercedes kissed the top of his head in greeting. Adora struck his upper arm fondly. "Jealous!"

He narrowed his eyes. "Of course. Always." He spoke ironically, his voice still soft as he shook my hand. "Pleased to meet you, Simon. Let's see if you live up to your billing." The grip of his prosthetic hand was metallic, unnecessarily strong, and cold even through the leather. The doorbell brought a shout from him I would not have credited to the soft voice: "*ADDISON!*"

Addison strode by. "Yes, sir! Gettin' the door, sir!"

Adora followed Addison with her eyes. "That'll be the Cols. Good. They're on time."

Mercedes felt my forehead again. "That's funny. You're normal again. I could have sworn you were up to a hundred and four!"

Footsteps in the hallway announced the Currans, a chic conservative couple, Colleen in a kneelength bareshouldered whitelace evening dress and velvet shawl, Colin in a dark suit and solid gold tie. Colleen, in her midthirties, putting on weight, wore her dark hair in a bob; Colin was fairhaired, smoothshaven, in his midforties. When I was introduced he shook my hand, smiling, ironic. "Simon! Dear, dear, what have you got yourself into?"

I grinned. "I have absolutely no idea!"

Everyone laughed. Quint spoke in his soft voice again. "He'll soon find out."

Colleen shook my hand, grinning. "Call us Col. We always know which one's being called."

"Addison! More martinis!"

"Yes, sir, Mr. Castleworth!"

"And the trays!"

"Yes, sir, Mr. Castleworth!"

Quint was shepherding us toward one of the living-room sets when he saw me raise my martini again. "Simon, maybe you shouldn't?"

His voice and smile were so sly Colleen responded with surprise. "And why not, Quint?"

Quint spoke, eyes downcast. "He had an episode—right before you arrived."

Colleen's surprise turned to concern. "Oh, I'm sorry. What kind of an episode?"

Mercedes's voice, too, was rich with concern. "He was burning up—but he seems all right now—but, Si, maybe you shouldn't—just to be safe?"

I guzzled the rest of my martini and grinned. "There! I feel fine! In fact, I'd like another!"

Adora gulped the rest of her drink as well. "Down the hatch!"

Addison returned with a trolley bearing trays of cheeses and crackers, varieties of nuts, finger sandwiches (ham and cheese, roast beef, sausage, each with a paste to complement the meat)—and more martinis. Adora helped herself to another martini, and as she sat again the symphony on the turntable came to a close. I was closest to the player. "Shall I turn it over?"

Colleen looked knowingly at Quint. "K. 551?"

"Right—and now we'll have K. 550, please, Simon?"

I stood by the stereo, suddenly unsure what was expected, when Adora came to my rescue. "That's K for Kochel, Simon, in case you don't know what the showoffs are talking about—some guy who numbered Mozart's music."

Quint raised his eyebrows. "Catalogued."

Adora rolled her eyes. "Sorry. Catalogued."

Quint peered at me over his spectacles. "Ludwig Ritter von Kochel was his whole name, an Austrian scholar."

I nodded. "I thought they were called opus numbers."

"That came later—with Beethoven. Schubert, who came around the same time, was catalogued by another Austrian scholar, Otto Erich Deutsch, but was also given opus numbers—so the *Trout Quintet*, for instance, is catalogued D. 667 as well as Op. 114."

"Very enlightening." I turned the record over. "Why do you suppose they call it the Great G minor? Aren't they all?"

Quint meant to be helpful, but couldn't help being patronizing. "All what? G minor?"

"No—all great."

Adora spoke without inflection. "There's also a Little G minor."

"Even Adora knows."

Quint's smile was smug and I disliked him for showcasing my ignorance, but Colin grinned, at once ironic and sympathetic. "I can tell you haven't been around Quint long enough—or you'd know everything you always wanted to know about Mozart, but were afraid to ask."

Colleen laughed. "Not to mention everything you *never* wanted to know and never *thought* of asking."

Quint's smile broadened. "Am I showing off again?"

Colleen shook her head. "Not again, you silly man. You never stop."

It was comforting to hear the others treat him so cavalierly, but I couldn't set my caution to rest. I was his rival for Mercedes, and whatever Adora meant to either of them I remained unsure of my place in the mix. Mercedes seemed almost to read my mind. "Simon just got back from India. Ask him about it."

Colleen turned to me first. "Did you really, Simon?"

Mercedes laughed. "They ride elephants everywhere. Ask him about it."

Colleen kept her focus on me. "Did you really, Simon? Did you ride an elephant?"

"Not in India—but I have, right here in Chicago, at the Brookfield Zoo."

Colin frowned. "Brookfield? I didn't think they had elephant rides."

"They don't. His mother minds the elephants. She used to be in the circus. Tell them, Simon."

Colleen shook her head in wonder. "Do tell, Simon! Your mother minds the elephants?"

I sighed. "Yes. It's ancient history, but that's how she got started. She knows just about everything there is to know about elephants—and about the circus. Did you know George Washington attended the first American circus?"

Quint reclined further back in his seat, but the others leaned forward, Colin speaking seriously for the first time. "Is that a fact? What was the name of the circus?"

"Ricketts's circus—for John Bill Ricketts. It was mainly an equestrian show, but he also had a tightrope walker and a clown. He built his own amphitheater in Philadelphia—it was the capital then, of course—and he flattered Washington's riding ability to get him interested. In those days, horsemanship was a test of manhood."

"Of course!"

"It was great publicity, as you can imagine—but in the days before radio and movies and television *everyone* went to the circus."

Colin laughed. "Hey, Quint! That's something I bet you didn't know!"

If he meant to rouse Quint he didn't succeed. The response came in the same soft voice I was getting to dislike. "Did you know Mozart died during George Washington's first term?"

Mercedes laughed out loud, but Adora frowned. "Shut up, Quint. This isn't about Mozart."

Colin grinned. "Too bad Washington didn't use elephants in the Revolutionary War. We'd have won in a flash."

I shook my head. "Actually, we didn't get our first elephant until 1796—and he wasn't in the circus. He was the whole show. People paid just to see him. Nathaniel Hawthorne's father was a member of the crew that brought him from Bengal for $450 to be sold for $10,000 to a Welshman from Philadelphia, who made his money back touring the eastern seaboard with his elephant—and the second elephant in America, an African named Old Bet, arrived in 1815, in time to give the lie to the first elephant's billing as the only such animal in the country."

Quint shook his head. "Actually, the first elephants were in America long before that—by about ten thousand years. Specimens of mammoths and mastodons have been trawled by fishing boats along the eastern seaboard—also in the Rancho La Brea tarpits in California."

Colin grinned, winking at me. "Here we go again. Everything you never wanted to know about elephants …"

BY THE TIME WE GOT TO DINNER I was tired of Quint, but began to understand something of Mercedes's fascination. He was a walking encyclopedia, his experiences ranged from eating elephant stew in Ethiopia to attending a ball with the Queen of England (he'd enjoyed the stew better, chunks of the trunk and fibrous feet served in a thick gritty gravy with manioc). Adora was the least impressed, Mercedes the most responsive. The Cols had their feet in the ground and tongues wedged firmly in their cheeks, kidding Quint as much as he enjoyed being kidded by them, playing burra sahib to their bandar log.

Chandeliers in the dining-room were dimly lit. A candelabrum glowed on the table, sconces on the walls, mirrors multiplied the glow, providing an eerie illusion of stars in deep space, but the semidarkness provided refuge for my consternation. Quint and Adora faced each other across the length of the table, Mercedes and Colin to Quint's left, Colleen and I to his right. Baskets nestled rolls in linen and coins of butter floated on ice. Napkin holders were of ivory, champagne and wineglasses rimmed with gold, water glasses heavy tumblers of stainless steel, plates skyblue streaming with cumulus clouds.

Quint remained standing, clearing his throat as we seated ourselves. "Ladies and gentlemen, welcome! I will keep this brief. It is neither the best of times nor the worst. It is a solemn occasion, but also cause for celebration. We come to honor Adora's victory over her demons." His smile twisted as he raised his glass. "I would like to propose a toast to her courage, her recovery, her determination—and, most of all, to her middle finger held high in the face of adversity. Cheers!"

We raised glasses, showering cheers and smiles. Adora nodded, but seemed otherwise oblivious.

Quint sat. "You have before you a commemoration of the evening. Please, everyone?"

All plates bore boxes wrapped in red with blue satin ribbons—all except Quint's and Adora's. The four of us turned on cue to Adora who clacked her bracelets, clapping her wrists together, holding them up for show. "I opened mine already. I couldn't wait."

The table laughed and I realized as we tore into the wrappings that her bracelets were wide enough to hide her wrists. Each box held an ivory bookmark wrapped in tissue, shaved so thin you could read letters through its mist, engine turning plainly visible (the crosshatching of concentric rings capturing diamonds within its whorls). Each was topped by a perfect plump elephant in profile. Amid the expressions of wonder and gratitude Quint raised his hands and asked in his soft voice for quiet. "There is a greater point to be made about the bookmarks. A bookmark is for marking your place, but also for marking progress. Some are content to mark time, others move forward. The choice belongs to the individual. I wasn't born to ivory. It was thrust upon me. Some say they must bear the responsibility who are to the manor born. I say they have a greater responsibility on whom the manor is thrust."

His gaze scanned the table, all attentive except Adora who remained oblivious. "You see, I respect ivory—and when you think about how many elephants have died—in the *mi*llions—it is only right to respect their sacrifice. That is what I do. If you understand the carnage that has been wreaked in the name of ivory, you will understand that Africa will be better off when the last elephant has been killed."

The company seemed hypnotized by the mellifluous tone unrolling sentences like so many red carpets, I no less than the others, but I also felt the arguments were directed toward me, and wanted to say something in Hazel's behalf if not my own, loyal brother, son, and bullman that I was. "Are you saying we should respect the deaths of those elephants—by killing *more* elephants?"

I was surprised to hear myself interrupt, Mercedes no less than the others from the tilt and turn of her head. Quint's tone did not change. "That is *just* what I am saying. As long as there is ivory, Africa's other industries remain dormant. Ivory overshadows everything else, everything else remains undeveloped and fetal. The perfect solution would be a total ban—but that is not going to happen. The only alternative is to get that last tusk, and the sooner we do it the sooner we will have normalization."

"I thought your vendetta was against just white elephants."

"My vendetta is against just white elephants." He raised his leathergloved right arm. "A white elephant did this to me, white elephants must pay. Against white elephants, it's personal. Against other elephants, it's political. The sooner the elephant goes, the sooner Africa thrives."

Adora passed me the breadbasket, following with butter. I helped myself and passed the basket to Colleen. Quint was a certifiable megalomaniac, but it hadn't sunk in yet and I frowned attempting to sort his logic. "I don't see how you can blame the elephants for the problem. It's the dealers—and if you take ivory away from the dealers they will find something else to … to be abnormal about. You might as well say the problem will be resolved when the last of the dealers has been … killed—if that is the word you want."

Quint became condescending—though, to be fair, it had slipped my mind that he was one of the dealers I had so blithely condemned to death. "No, Simon, that is not the word I want, that is the word *you* want—but let me give you an example. A seventy-pound tusk provides forty-five keyboards. In 1910 alone three hundred and fifty thousand pianos were manufactured. Thousands of elephants were killed so little girls could delight their mummies and daddies. The piano came into its own in the nineteenth century and every bourgeois living-room in America and

Europe with pretensions to culture had to have one. Keyboards were the most extensive use of ivory—but here's the point I want to make. In 1958 ivory keyboards were replaced by plastic—less expensive, more plentiful, and driven by the will of an audience made aware of the butchery. The trade was consumer-driven, not trader-driven. The trader was just the middleman. You might as well say the problem will be solved when the last consumer has been killed."

I sat up. "No, you have just made *my* point, not yours. If consumers drove piano manufacturers to use plastic, they can drive other manufacturers to use other materials as well."

Quint frowned, but his tone didn't waver. "No, they can't. The change was successful only because there *was* an acceptable substitute. A total ban on ivory is simply not feasible. The only way to ban it completely is to destroy the source ... completely." He shrugged. "That may sound extreme, but that's the nature of the beast. We might as well accept it—and the sooner the better. Do you know what Stanley said—Sir Henry Morton Stanley?"

I didn't know who he was, let alone what he'd said, but Colin came to my rescue. "The speaker of the immortal words: 'Dr. Livingstone, I presume?'"

Ah, that Stanley! but I didn't know what he'd said. "You mean, aside from that?"

Quint was impatient. "Yes, of course, man, aside from that. He said, and I quote: 'Every tusk, piece, and scrap in the possession of an Arab trader has been steeped and dyed in blood. For every pound weight a man, woman, or child has been killed. For every five pounds a hut has been burned, for every two tusks a village has been destroyed, for every twenty tusks an entire district with all its people, villages, and plantations.' Why is this, you ask? Because there is ivory. Voila!"

"But that's like blaming the elephant for the greed of the traders—or even of the consumers."

Quint smiled again. "Pre*ci*sely. It is the fault of the elephant for being the elephant. That is why we need to remove the elephant ... to the last elephant. No elephant, no ivory trade, no problem."

I shook my head again, but couldn't have said what I was denying.

Quint went on. "The trouble started when the Arabs discovered treasure troves of tusks around the villages of Africa—just lying there for the taking. The natives hunted elephants for food, but had no use for ivory—and the Arabs bartered pounds of tusks for pennyworths of cotton cloth and coral.

"The Arabs willingly paid all taxes and tariffs associated with transit and trade because the quality of their lives depended on the quality of their relations with the natives. Armed with just daggers, swords, and spears, they were at the mercy of the superior numbers of the natives. They also needed the natives to carry the tusks since donkeys and mules and other pack animals were vulnerable to the tsetse fly—and they paid as willingly for the labor, sending the laborers back to their villages once the tusks had been brought to the ships.

"Thanks to the mutual good will, the nineteenth century saw Arab strongholds established with gardens and homes and harems. The trade had been peaceful for the first half of the second millennium, but concluded with the advent of the Europeans, beginning with the Portuguese, followed by the Dutch, the British, the French, the Germans.

"Once the Arabs obtained superior firepower they took what they wanted without even a pretense of barter. They enslaved Africans from whom they stole the ivory and forced them to carry the stolen ivory. One in ten survived the march to the coast and these were sold along with the ivory making the ventures doubly rewarding, a trade in white gold *and* black, ivory and slaves, the two were one. Once the gambit proved successful the slaughter commenced a hundredfold—and with the Europeans it continued a thousandfold. I won't go into details, but Tippu Tib, the best known Arab slaver, was responsible for the murder of a hundred thousand Africans. He was smart enough to recognize the power of the Europeans and saved many white lives following the rule that you kept your friends close and your enemies closer—but finally he was betrayed by Stanley himself working for King Leopold of Belgium, who was responsible for the murder of millions. See what I mean? No ivory, no slaughter. Simple as that."

Quint smiled as if there were no more to be said. I had to say something, surprised no one else seemed to recognize the flaw in his

The Elephant Graveyard

argument. "You can't blame ivory for the slaughter. If not ivory, it would have been something else. We're just as bloodthirsty for diamonds and copper and whatever else we want from whoever has it."

Quint stopped smiling. "But it *was* ivory. *That* is the point."

Emphasizing it was ivory, he implied other commodities did not matter. I could have argued further, but realized we were both wrong, he for insisting ivory was the problem, I for insisting diamonds and copper and the rest were no less a problem. The problem wasn't ivory, nor was it diamonds and copper and the rest. The problem was greed and vanity, plain and simple—Arab greed followed by European greed, the law of the jungle prevailing, the country with the most gorgonzola the victor.

I realized also that mine was the argument of the idealist, the extinction of greed even less credible than the extinction of the elephant. Mercedes gave me a smile so subtle she may have been daydreaming, everyone at the table understood what Quint could not. She was also warning me: I had won the battle, but if I persisted I would lose the war. I shrugged, letting go the argument. The Cols smiled their relief, Adora threw me a look of commiseration. Quint preened, grinning at Mercedes. "I'd strike the sun if it insulted me."

Mercedes returned the grin. "If the sun could do that, then could you do the other."

"I'll see how this plaguey juggling thinks over by daylight."

The others seemed unimpressed and unsurprised by the exchange. Adora couldn't have appeared more bored. "Don't mind them, Simon. The showoffs are just quoting at each other again."

Dinner was normal though hardly ordinary: a salad studded with escargot and a buttery dressing, curried salmon with lemon wedges, a saddle of venison with roast potatoes and stewed cherries and peaches, to be followed by an apricot souffle and baked Alaska. Quint had found his chef, Mesereth, in a hotel in Addis Ababa and been enchanted enough with her cuisine to entice her to Chicago.

QUINT'S MONOLOGUE rendered the images I had entertained behind the red mist more profound than I realized. Back at Mercedes's apartment I recognized Tippu Tib, the whitegarbed, goldturbaned, greybearded, blackfaced slaver. He sat on a lowseated, highbacked, thronelike chair, eyes gentle, smile benign, slender fingers linked in his lap—but not all the perfumes of Arabia could have sweetened those elegant hands. He complained to an English explorer, Alfred Swann, seated similarly beside him, that but for him Stanley would never have crossed Africa, but as soon as he had returned home Stanley had claimed Tippu's country for Belgium. Swann reassured him that both sides of the story would be heard because Europeans loved justice.

"Do you? Then how did you get India?"

"We fought for it!"

"So what you fight for is yours?"

"Yes! That is European law!"

"It is the same with us Arabs, but have we tried to rob you of India?"

"The jackal cannot rob the lion."

"Aha! There lies the truth! Do not let us speak of justice. The white man is stronger than me. He will eat my possessions as I ate those of the Africans—and someone someday will eat his!"

"Do you believe in one God?"

"Yes, all Mohammedans do—but you say there are three."

"But you destroy His work by catching and killing slaves, do you not? Did He make a mistake for you to rectify?"

"Slaves do not acknowledge Him. That is why they are slaves. Abraham, Isaac, and Jacob made many slaves and God did not punish them."

I realized Mercedes was staring again and brought myself immediately to the present. "I don't think Quint likes me very much."

She took my arm, smiling. "Of course not. You're with his girl."

"I thought you were my girl."

"I was his girl first."

"But not anymore."

"Oh, Simon, don't be silly. Don't spoil it now. We're so close. Everything's going so well. Aren't you enjoying yourself?"

"Yes, but …"

"Don't spoil it now, Simon, please. In another week, I promise, you'll have all the answers."

I didn't know what I might have spoiled, but I was beginning to understand: the horrific images revealed the price paid for ivory, gruesome visions for pretty trinkets, illuminating the bloody progress from the heart of Africa to the wantons of the west, bejeweled babes and monied manchildren with portraits more repellent than the portrait of Dorian Gray.

SIX OPHIOPHAGUS HANNAH

In the end, I lost the war. My victory, if so it could be called, was pyrrhic. That was the last time I saw Mercedes. We breakfasted the next morning at a neighborhood diner. She gave no inkling we wouldn't be seeing each other again, but when I called the next day there was no answer. Receiving no answer to my next two calls I was taunted by an image of Mercedes, a thought balloon clouding her head: *Don't spoil it now, Simon, please. In another week, I promise, you'll have all the answers.*

Quint had always been her quarry, I'd never been more than bait, but twenty-three years in twilight had whet my appetite for more seconds in the sun. I'd enjoyed Mercedes, and the suddenness of her departure left me alternately raging and blubbering, but I'd known all along what I needed to do: render unto Hazel the things that were Hazel's, her son for her brother, Simon for Spike. I visited Mercedes's apartment on Thursday, again on Friday, and getting no answer I asked the doorman to call the penthouse. When there was no answer from the penthouse I left a message with the doorman for Adora to call.

I lived about fifteen blocks south of Mercedes and walked back and forth because it took as long to park in that neighborhood. It was dark by the time I returned home, walking alongside the lake, bright blocks of the city on my right, spectral silence of lake and sky on my left. The shoreline of the bay gripped the black water in pincers of light, a halfmoon illuminated gulls flying in formation, a pinpoint of light from a motorboat moved silently in the distance. A chill in the air had cleared the lakeside of joggers, strollers, sweethearts, bicyclists, and dogwalkers. I wore a jacket, but huddled to stay warm, fists clenched in my pockets. I walked close to the lake, more my home now than the highrises, its sleeping breast rising and falling, consonant with mine, calling me to its deep dark bed, the deepest sleep. Overhead hovered the glittering jewelry of the night, shimmering mantles of stars, brighter for my distance from the citylights, also my home more than the highrises, calling me no less than the lake, stardust to stardust.

Home again, I turned sentimental as never before, recalling the unlikeliest memories: shadows of bare trees cast by streetlamps on my ceiling; lullaby of the night (rustle of foliage, crackle of crickets, hum of traffic on the Drive, surge of the surf beyond in the weeest hours of the morning); an elm that grew by my window, a tree like an inverted pear, shimmering in sunlight like a sequined dress, shedding red and yellow sequins through the fall, glistening by lamplight, pointing bony fingers at the sky.

Tess and Derrick were in Tess's bedroom listening to *Jesus Christ, Superstar*, Tess's new favorite album, Chuck and Naomi watched news on the rickety seagreen sofa. Fortunate as they were in the sweepstakes of the world, they appeared suddenly like children, optimistic and ambitious—but I was already in a different world. I wanted to hear from Adora, after which I knew what I had to do.

I joined Chuck and Naomi on the sofa, aware of a gulf between us never to be bridged. John Lennon's *Imagine* climbed the charts, Beethoven's 201st loomed, Pablo Neruda won the Nobel for Literature, India joined the war to liberate Bangladesh from Pakistan, Nixon set a deadline to remove 45,000 troops from Vietnam—the news droned on. The telephone rang. Naomi answered. "Simon! For you. Adora." The household knew my trouble. Naomi squeezed my elbow for comfort, also delivering a note of caution. "I think she's high."

I nodded. My heart raced. I took a deep breath. "Hey, Adora!"

Her first response was a giggle.

"Adora?"

She spoke slowly, slurring her words. Naomi had been kind when she'd said she was high. "*Shi*mon! I'm *sho* glad y'called. Y'wanna party?"

"Adora, where's Mercedes?"

There was a pause as if she were considering the question, another giggle. "*You* donno?"

"I've been calling, but she doesn't answer. I think something's happened."

"Yeeeah, shumthin's happened—but tha'sh not bad."

"Adora, please, do you know where she is?"

Again there was a pause. "*Shcrew* Mershades! No! Wait!" Her giggle verged on hysteria. "You did that already. Bad boy! Naughty boy! Naughty-naughty boy!"

"Adora, do you know? Please tell me."

Again a pause. "She's gone. Gone 'way."

"Where? Do you know where?"

Her voice descended. "Wi'Quin'. She went ... wi'Quin' ... Nairobi."

"Nairobi!"

"He heard 'bout a white el'phant."

I said nothing, shaking my head.

"They alsho gettin' married. I shigned a release f'Quint."

I drew a deep breath. I had the confirmation I'd wanted, but having it I was silent. Seeing the pieces fit, I knew what to do. The questions were no longer what or why, but how and where and when.

"Shimon? Y'there?"

"Yeah."

"Sho, y'wanna party or shumthin'?"

She was putting on a brave front, but sounded like a girl of five. "Adora, is anyone with you?"

"No ... shent 'em all home—Ad'shon'n'Mesh'reth'n'Mar'Lee. All the others."

Addison and Mesereth I knew from the evening of the dinner; Mary Lee was one of the maids; the others I didn't know. Considering Adora's history I wished Mercedes and Quint might have chosen a better time. "Adora, are you all right?"

"I'm fine ... but ... y'gonna come? I'm inna bituva ... shtate."

"Of course. Twenty minutes?"

I could hear the relief in her sigh, another giggle. "Great! I'll leave th'door open. Jush c'mon in."

Chuck offered to come with me, calling me Palomino for the last time, Naomi gave me a hug goodbye. I was conscious more than ever of what I was leaving behind, but not regretful. From Tess's bedroom came a line that ricocheted repeatedly through my head: *To conquer death you only have to die!* or, in my case, I only had to stay dead!

I TOOK A CAB. The doorman waved me to the elevator. I acknowledged him almost unconsciously, ascending in a tornado of anticipation, welcoming the closure I expected, unsure of its framework. She'd said she'd leave the door open, but not that she'd leave the lights off. I didn't realize it until the elevator door shut behind me and I was standing in a black hallway. "Adora! Are you there? It's Simon!"

I didn't need to shout: in the vaulted silence whispers carried like trumpets, but there was no answer. I stepped tentatively toward the living-room and stumbled immediately on what might have been a can from the way it clattered.

"Simon! Be careful! Don't fall!"

The disembodied words tumbled from the atrium, but I couldn't see the entrance. "What happened to the light? I'm afraid I might knock something over."

Her voice rose in pitch and volume. "No! No light! I don't want light! Just walk slowly."

The giggle had been drained from her voice. Not even a hint of alcohol remained. Something had happened in the twenty minutes since we'd spoken to scare her straight. "All right. No light." As my eyes grew accustomed to the dark, I saw the curve of the arch leading to the living-room and waded slowly forward, outspread hands like sensors. Reaching the living-room, I stopped. Newspapers and magazines littered the floor, pizza boxes, takeout cartons, empty cans of beer, empty bottles. "Where are you?"

"Here!"

I thought I'd heard a rustle in the black silence, but her voice came from an adjacent direction. She seemed to rise as I looked, not just up from her seat but *on* her seat, visible as much for her movement as her voice. "Are you standing on the sofa?"

"Yes."

"Why?"

She shrugged in answer, opening her hands in question, and I navigated the debris with care. As I got closer she dropped so heavily into my arms I almost fell, dreadlocks shrouding my head. She might as well have tripped or jumped, but I braced myself and pushed her back on her feet. She continued to cling, leaning against me, smelling of gin, but otherwise could not have been more sober. Standing on the sofa she was as tall as me, shivering though the apartment was warm.

"Are you cold? Are you sick?"

She shook her head, holding me so close we might have been one.

"Adora, are you all right?"

"Please … just hold me. Don't say a word. Just … for a li'l while."

Another red mist had threatened since the elevator door had closed, but I'd shut it out: the time for visions was past. She trembled in my arms for almost five minutes, breath against my neck, cheeks soft and damp and warm from crying, before she relaxed a little. "Adora, I'm so sorry. That was a dirty trick they played."

She shook her head again. "It was just a matter of time. They're so right for each other."

"That's not the point!"

She kept her head on my shoulder, warm wet ginbreath on my neck. "Simon, you're sweet, but that *is* the point. They're smart. They always have something to say to each other. I was just in the way."

"No, that's *not* the point—not after what you went through. What were they thinking?"

"Simon, you *are* sweet! Don't be so sweet. It makes me so sorry."

"Sorry? Why?"

She took a deep breath. "I was gonna … you know … off myself again."

It took me a moment to understand. "Oh, Adora, no, no … don't even think about it."

"Too late."

"Too late for what?"

"Simon … don't be mad." I felt her deepest longest breath yet on my neck, her voice shook and she swallowed. "After we talked … I left the elevator door open like I said … but … I just felt so shitty … I didn't want to see anyone … but I did such a bad job before …"

"What's that?" I thought I heard a noise amid the debris on the floor, but Adora remained silent. The red mist descended then too suddenly to be refused and an image rose above me of a flat head, beady eyes, high arched neck, grinning mouth tipped with fangs dripping poison. An icy hand gripped the back of my neck. "No, you didn't!"

She was shivering again, hiding her face in my shoulder, locks damp with sweat. "I thought he'd ... do a better job."

"Oh, *shit*, Adora! *Fuck!*"

I would have flung her from me, but she clung too tightly. I couldn't even back away without dragging her along. "Don't be mad, Simon! Don't be mad! I'm sorry. I'm sorry."

She trembled so violently her teeth chattered. I should have been furious at her thoughtlessness, but the writing had long been on the wall. Her immortal longings, never a secret, were also mine—and in her muddled fashion she was showing me the way. I took a deep breath. "Come on. We've got to get out of here."

"I don't wanna ... get off the sofa." She clung to me, raising her legs, clamping them around my waist. My own legs felt drained of blood, but I gained courage recalling what Mercedes had said about *Ophiophagus hannah*: it was passive unless provoked; it ate smaller animals; it ate once a week. The noise was a slither, easily recognizable among the papers and cartons and bottles, but far enough for safety. Inch by inch I slid one foot after the other toward the entrance.

I didn't recall the monarch could be twenty feet long. A noise at one end of the room didn't mean it wasn't at the other end as well. I didn't understand either why a congenitally shy Hannah would share a room with two others when it had a maze of rooms to roam at its disposal. That was hardly my concern, but the shallow jungle of refuse in the living-room may have made it home to the lost ophiophagus. My concern was getting to the elevator and I almost made it, but entering the hallway I stepped on something that moved under me, robbing me of balance.

I understood then in my head what I had known all along in my skin. The seed planted three and twenty years ago by Gupta sprang fullgrown in the matter of a moment, like Athena from the mind of Zeus, Ganesh from the loins of Parvati. Matter could neither be created nor destroyed—nor, indeed, energy, nor karma. A little piece of a soul was no good unless it was with all the other little pieces. It was not a question of good and evil, but cause and effect. An eye for an eye was the law of the universe, but the universe proposed and the universe disposed; man controlling nature led to nature controlling man. Taking a life, I lost my own; taking an eye, I would lose my own—to agents of justice ranging from the tiniest bacillus to storms of meteors, including, why not? an ophidian named Hannah. I was, indeed, as Gupta had said, surrounded by miracles, as are we all—and, again as Gupta had said: Q.E.D. My role was clear, I embraced my fate, my far far better thing, my moment, finally, of (there was no other word) *un*collision, and even as I lost my balance I regained a greater balance, one I had lost three and twenty years ago.

Adora screamed as we fell, rolling to lie on her back by my side. I heard a low growl mixed with a harsh sucking sound so loud it rattled. The head of the hamadryad rose in the distance and skated toward us propelled by a mad coiling and uncoiling of the body slapping the floor until it loomed over my face. The malign intelligence in its eyes glistened; its hood flared to its fullest; and parallel fangs grew large as spikes as the head descended.

THE SUN MOVES, not of itself, but as errandboy in heaven. The stars revolve, not of themselves, but spun by a hand too vast for visibility. Not one heart beats, not one mind beams, not one body breathes, but by a will beyond our ken. Heart and mind and body are lesser mysteries—dissected, vivisected, analyzed, and anatomized until they are mastered—but the soul is a centipede moving on a hundred legs. It had been a hey diddle diddle night, crazy as a cat and fiddle and a snake coiled around the moon. I gave up the ghost—finally—but Simon survived.

Concluding its mischief Hannah rose, swaying its head from side to side like a Bharatnatyam dancer, flicking its tongue, sniffing the air, evaluating threats before lowering its head and slithering away. Adora had lain still and silent as the dead beside Simon, welcoming the soft slither of retreat after the loud slaps of its advance, and without heed to the peril to herself she clambered atop Simon, undoing his shirt, uncovering the pinpoints of entry, sucking and spitting blood and poison from his shoulder—not that Hannah's bite could have been so cured, but that Simon survived, I did not, and the logistics don't matter.

This I had known: I had been this way before: lying on my back, I could see myself lying on my back; alive, I could see myself dead. My body expanded as before, my hand as large as formerly my body.

As Spike, I had risen from an eastern rib of the Arabian Sea; as Simon, I rose from the southwestern shore of Lake Michigan—but, as I said, I had been this way before. Expanding further still, I found the room smaller than my hand, the penthouse, the building, the Drive, the lake, all shrinking as I expanded, as I grew once more into the universe—but one final vision before I enter the empyrean again will drive home a salient point.

Across Lake Michigan, across the eastern seaboard, across the Atlantic, southeast to Africa, to Kenya, to a boma west of Nairobi, illuminated by the halfmoon, stood a white elephant, forelegs shackled by irons but spread wide, trunk swinging threateningly, ears spread to present its largest head, piss gushing like a hydrant raising dust like steam from the ground—and growling.

The elephant was more grey than white with salmon highlights, but its hair was white contributing, more than its pigmentation, to the illusion of whiteness even by night. Three-foot tusks, curved like scimitars, gleamed like pearls. The eyes were midnight blue, not the common pink of albinos. Long lashes fluttered, feminine and flirtatious.

The ammoniac smell of piss was predictable, but another smell of rot and sewage grew stronger: musth. The elephant was rutting for females in estrus, black liquid seeped from gashes in its temples appearing like makeup running in rain. The abundance of testosterone made it an impossible animal for the most experienced of mahouts, but facing the elephant was no mahout with the metal claw of an ankus, but a man with a rifle—Quint in khakis and cargo shorts—and off to the side, where the tall timbered wall of the boma met the ground, fallen on her flank, frozen with fear and shock, also in khakis and cargos, sola topi face up beside her, lay Mercedes.

A harsh brassy sound erupted from the enclosure, like an organ of a hundred pipes with all its keys jammed, blaring from the giant iron gullet of the white elephant, and heavy chains rattled as the beast tugged at its shackles—but more ghastly than the Jurassic sound was the sight of what followed as one of the irons broke: Quint impaled on a crescent of tusk as the white elephant raised its head and trunk, pouring sound from jaws so whiskered that the chin seemed bearded and gleaming with whiteness. Dark fountains gushed from the points of entry and exit,

The Elephant Graveyard

hovering like clouds in the air for one long paralyzed moment. Quint's screams, such as they might have been, were lost in the cacophony. The orchideous shadow grew more hideous yet as the abominable snowy mass turned its attention to the other body in the boma, trembling against its own volition but otherwise unable to crawl or roll or slither away.

Sad Mercedes, as sinned against as sinning, as betrayed as betraying, may mercifully have died of fear before the pounding began, graduating from Depression days and Bangkok nights to this African hell, from a Helen for the show and tell and gaze of the world to stew for the earth, pudding for worms.

More deaths, death upon death upon death, the universe working its will, its mysterious way, death by white elephant, the sacred white elephant—and, as such, a blessing as much as a curse, as if the pope had sanctioned the execution, wielded the fatal weapon himself, sending the pair to heaven or hell or back into the universe, one again with the elements of sun and sand and sea and sky, my own destination as much as theirs.

Forgive an old circuspoke, waxing philosophical, but not for nothing have I served my time. I know whereof I speak. Tit for tat is a metaphysical game, nothing matters but balance. The more we attempt to affect the balance, the more the balance affects us. The stiller we become, the more balanced we become. This rationale has been echoed in many faiths, the karmic principle of Hinduism, the yin and yang of Taoism, the dualism of Zoroastrianism, the detachment from attachment of Buddhism, the eye for an eye of Judaism, the sowing and reaping of Christianity, the Islamic belief that every human action is followed in direct proportion by a divine, the secular belief that what goes around comes around, not to mention Einstein's contention that God does not play with dice. Matter, energy, karma, none can be created, none destroyed. The universe cares only about balance, we reap what we sow—more clearly, since we are one soul, we reap what others sow as much as they reap what we sow, each of us a tiny Christ continually dying and rebirthing for the world.

In the words of the wise Greek, it's time to go, you to live, me to die, and God alone knows which is better, all of us orphans in the end—but let me leave with a brighter image: Simon, recovered, under Hazel's wing, memory lapse attributed to shock; Adora, also under Hazel's wing, for risking poison for her child; Granma Blue in the hinterland, gazing as benignly on Hazel as on Simon and Adora, imagining a new romance in the bud; Roy standing by, protective; Siri farther back, smiling; and, farthest of all, I, Spike again, again on Hero's broad black baronial back, negotiating again the long black tunnel, the curvature of the earth from a coign of vantage, beyond the reach of Indian ages, beyond all hum of human weal or woe, regaining all, finally, with a sigh, taking my leave once more, not merely dead, not merely unorphaned again, but returned home to that mythical place, the yard where the elephants go to die.

AFTERWORD

For the longest time my two cultures, Indian and American, merged only in dreams. I looked continually for links between the two in my writing, but the immigration theme had long been flogged to death (thirdworlders with one foot on a dirt track, the other on an escalator), not least by myself, and I wanted to find another way.

Strangely, or not so strangely, the elephant suggested itself as an option: an Indian elephant in America. It is the favorite animal of many, including myself, but only in an academic sense, a favored status that invites neither the risk nor sacrifice of a bullman, handler, or mahout. As a boy, I'd had elephant cufflinks, elephant bookends, elephant lamps, elephant patterns on curtains and bedcovers among other such elephantalia. For my Navjote (equivalent of a Bar Mitzvah or Confirmation) I'd asked for a wooden elephant two feet tall. The mother of a friend once called my mother to say that I'd spent the entire afternoon of a visit drawing pictures of elephants. My first published novel was called *The Memory of Elephants*, but the title was a metaphor for longterm memory, nothing to do with the great grey beast itself—with which I'd had little contact except at the Bombay zoo where I'd ridden the mighty animal on one of two benches strapped back to back on its back, and of course at the circus though only from a distance.

To begin, I had little in mind except to have an elephant feature in the novel, following which I read as much as I could on the animal, researching for facts as much as ideas. I had planned to place it in a zoo, but the circus soon suggested itself as a more colorful alternative, following which I researched the history of the circus. I visited zoos and circuses scouting the grounds to get a feel for the places. Best of all was a personal encounter at the Brookfield Zoo near Chicago. Three African elephants performed in the paddock for children, pushing logs, showing off parts of their bodies, standing on stools, first on four legs, then on two. Most of the children wanted to know how much the elephant ate (400 pounds of greens a day), but an imaginative kid twisted himself into a pretzel and asked if the elephant could do that!

The Elephant Graveyard

One of the handlers, Amy Kraus, was good enough to take me with her into the elephant house. Following her instructions I found myself alone, waiting in a long hallway separating the paddock from the individual stalls, standing in a great doorway, getting nervous as the first elephant ambled toward me. The sheer size of the animal was intimidating. I couldn't see Amy and had little recourse but to trust all would be well, and it was. She came around almost immediately with baguettes and hot dog buns which she gave me to feed the elephant, one baguette at a time, and buns by the dozen. It was an even bigger treat to touch the tusks, trunk, and thorny hairs, not to mention hearing its burps (like farts).

A photograph in a *National Geographic* of a man being lifted by his head in the mouth of an elephant gave me the central plot. The plot was further developed by another indelible image from *National Geographic* of a king cobra standing six feet tall in a graveyard: malevolent, magisterial, and magnificent.

My outsider status also played into the novel. I am fairskinned enough to surprise people when they learn I'm from India, but I was called the N word on a couple of occasions leaving me wondering how many times it might have been thought and left unsaid. I knew I wasn't being mistaken for a black, I also knew I was being verbally slapped. I don't mean to say my blues are bluer than the blues of blacks, they're not by a wide margin—but, whatever my advantages, I was disenfranchised in the US—and, for the longest time, too dumb to recognize it because I wanted parity with the majority. As a Zoroastrian Parsi, I am swept in the current of the American soup, too small a minority to be considered a minority—or, indeed (fortunately), oppressed as a minority—but enough of a minority to be isolated, different, other, alien, to be tolerated, even indulged, until day is done and it's time for the majority to return to the root, their aria of patronization drawn to a close. This is not a complaint; without my cross, I might never have written *The Elephant Graveyard*; it is the way of the world, but it is also good to be aware of the way of the world, awareness an advance in itself.

Afterword

Also, educated as I was in India, stranger as I was to American history, I had imagined racism as much a relic in Twentieth Century America as slavery. I was surprised to learn Civil Rights were not even a decade past when I arrived (1969), and my research uncovered events too heinous to mention let alone repeat. The hypocrisy covering the events alone was transparently racist. Thomas Pickens Brady, a Yale graduate who went on to become an associate justice of the Mississippi Supreme Court, said the *Brown* decision would set the cause of the negro back a hundred years because it transgressed the rights of "the loveliest and purest of God's creatures, the nearest thing to an angelic being that tread this terrestrial ball, a well-bred, cultured Southern white woman or her blue-eyed, golden-haired little girl." I wish he might have met Hazel Bailey. She would have told him only cowards masked their murders under cover of chivalry, only tompicbradies transgressed the rights of their women by pretending to protect them. She would have wished she could have married Roy ten times over if the sight might have blinded the tompicbradies of the world, she would have wished her skin ten times as white, her eyes ten times as blue, her hair ten times as gold—and she would have thanked God the circus had been her college and not Yale.

I won't dwell on my problems with assimilation, but a large difference between me and almost everyone I knew was that in America I was sans family, sans community, sans ground beneath my feet. This played well into the structure of *The Elephant Graveyard*, but more subtly than the common theme of a stranger in a strange land. The supernatural element is also a variation on the theme of the outsider, a specter being even more of an outsider than an Indian or a black. It also drew me to that most provocative of themes: metaphysics.

Moby Dick suggested itself almost immediately as a model for obvious reasons, as much for the mammal as the metaphysics. Rereading the book twice, I was moved to fillet my novel with some of Melville's incantatory prose, to rise to a more luscious prose of my own (*You can count on a ghost for a fancy prose style*, a sentiment I filched from Nabokov), and to revisit his themes of death and obsession—though the elephant lore sandwiched into *The Elephant Graveyard* is hardly as exhaustive as Melville's of the whale. I had not attempted paranormal fiction before—indeed, I realized it might be considered paranormal only after I'd written the book—but, like many, I have wrestled with questions regarding the meaning of life and the paranormal framework allowed me to explore the theme more lucidly. The closest I have come to understanding the conundrum of life is spelled out in Gupta's worldview (or otherworldview) on pages 133-137. The parallel between the religious and scientific conceptions that he explicates is striking. I don't say it answers all questions; I do say it answers more questions than other explanations. My childhood obsession with elephants had parlayed itself into an adult search for meaning.

It might be appropriate to say here why I found it necessary to supplement the epigraph I chose (the concluding lines of Alexander Pope's *An Essay on Man: Epistle I*) with a quatrain of my own. "Whatever is, is right" appears an invitation to resignation, an abdication of responsibility, an imperative "to suffer the slings and arrows of outrageous fortune" against all manner of egregious behavior. Only monks and rishis, whose duties are solely to God, have the right to absolute inaction. The rest of us, living in society, have a duty to Caesar as well as to God, even in this world where all roads no longer lead to Rome. Our duty to Caesar is to use whatever means we have at hand to overcome whatever outrages our sense of humanity. Our duty to God is to keep faith when our best efforts fail, to bear in mind (what Gupta did not) that God knows what He is doing even at His seemingly most incomprehensible. We may not all be in synch regarding the existence of God, whether we talk about the God of the Bible, of the dictionary, or of the many myths and legends and faiths of the world—but there has to be agreement among atheists and theists alike regarding the existence of forces beyond our ken, only a fool would deny what is beyond his power to know. My answer to Pope follows Hamlet to his alternative, "to take up arms against a sea of troubles, and by opposing end them"—and one step further: should opposing not end them, it might then be time "to suffer the slings and arrows," but only then, and not until then, and our duty remains to keep faith—most of all, then.

II

My story ends in 1971, but the greatest elephant slaughters reigned from 1971 to 1989, after which period the ivory trade was completely banned. Professor Henry Drummond wrote in *Tropical Africa* as long ago as 1889: "The truth is, sad though the confession be, the sooner the last elephant falls before the hunter's bullet, the better for Africa. Ivory introduces into the country an abnormal state of things. Upon this one article is set so enormous a premium that no other among African products secures the slightest general attention; nor will almost anyone in the interior condescend to touch the normal wealth, nor develop the legitimate industries of the country, so long as a tusk remains. The elephant has done much for Africa. The best he can do now for his country is to disappear for ever." I appropriated Drummond's argument for Quint in the novel, though morally the two are polar opposites.

Almost a hundred years later, Drummond's ugly meditation was almost brought to fruition. Iain and Oria Douglas-Hamilton provide an excellent account of the ivory wars in *Battle for the Elephant*: "With the price of ivory skyrocketing in 1978, Zairians were slaughtering elephants in unprecedented numbers using poison, traps, and even hand-made guns fashioned out of Land-Rover steering rods. The soaring price of ivory had caused entire villages to drop their agricultural activities in order to hunt elephants full-time. Even the diamond and gold smugglers had switched to ivory and the whole shady business of buying, collecting and transporting tusks had become a cut-throat operation. According to government officials around fifteen hundred tonnes of tusks were stockpiled throughout the country—a hoard of colossal proportions."

The high price of ivory was compounded, not surprisingly, by corruption. To take just one example: In 1986, Burundi, a country with no elephants, exported enough ivory for a herd of ten thousand with the connivance of the authorities, helping neighboring countries circumvent the restrictions of quotas. Exact figures are impossible to come by, but Iain Hamilton estimated: "In 1976, all ivory leaving Africa may have come from anything between 100,000 and 400,000 elephants." The solution, as Drummond had foreseen more than a century ago, was to choose between a total slaughter of elephants and a total ban of ivory—and a total ban was assumed impossible! Fortunately, the assumption proved false.

Armed with facts and figures—more trenchantly, photographs of faceless elephants and butchered herds—the pro-ban lobby appealed directly to consumers. The Douglas-Hamiltons say it best: "Support was instantaneous. Shocked by what they had heard, people gave generously. Their credit cards, they promised, would be returned to department stores selling ivory, and their Senators would be urged to close the trade. Our picture of Boadicea charging and Joyce Poole's poached faceless elephant appeared in massive advertisement campaigns and in the Press—asking people not to buy ivory.... Instead of going through the roof as critics of the ban had warned, the price of ivory to a poacher fell through the floor, from around $30 to less than $3 a kilo."

I learned much of the story myself as I researched the novel, and my predilection for ivory fell no less heavily through the floor. The elephant bookends of my boyhood had ivory tusks, my papercutter was of ivory, as was a bookmark, and a shell the size of a ladybug contained a dozen tiny ivory elephants. Reading a review of Edmund Morris's *Sound Factory; the Making of a Steinway Concord Grand*, I recognized the irrevocable change in myself. According to the reviewer, James Barron: "From the moment a Steinway piano begins its life, as various integrants of wood, cloth, metal, and (sigh) plastic ivory-substitute cohere under myriad hands, until the first outside player plinks a freshly polished key and listens to the sweet response; the piano is a product of the human body, designed to return to the body as music, with ample power to chasten and subdue." Very nice, but the plastic ivory-substitute drew no (sigh) from me, and wouldn't either from James Barron were he acquainted with the facts. There should be no sighing about the absence of ivory. It is only ignorance that separates sighers from slavers like Tippu Tib.

Afterword

Unfortunately, such memories have short lives. The war against elephants is heating up again, the Chinese insinuating themselves into the ivory trade (among other commodities) in 21st Century Africa, as had Europeans and Americans and Arabs in the 19th and 20th centuries. Additionally, another parallel, more difficult battle is also being waged in Africa, excellently portrayed in the movie, *Blood Diamond*, diamonds replacing ivory as the commodity in question, villagers replacing elephants as the victims. Sadly, while images of mutilated elephants broke the ivory market, images of dead villagers have no power to break the diamond market, first world elites too blinded by glittering rocks to care. Again, it is only ignorance—unfortunately, a willful ignorance— that separates baublebearing socialites from slavers.

III

The supernatural element resonates in my model for Hazel Bailey. For too long I was an office drudge, and riding home from work saw many of the same people daily on the bus, one of whom caught my attention sufficiently for me to strike up a conversation, a woman who appeared to enjoy my company—but not enough to accept my invitation to dinner.

I didn't ask her out again, but continued talking with her on the bus, using her as my model for Hazel. She was an attractive blond blueeyed white woman—and, about a year after I'd first approached her, I saw her walking arm in arm with a black man. I said hello, and we talked, and I learned they were engaged to be married—but she'd said not a word to me throughout our conversations about her engagement, and I met them *after* I'd written the section about Hazel and Roy. I won't say I do or do not believe in ghosts—but I do believe, as did Gupta, that we are constantly surrounded by miracles.

To wit: Walking on water is a fantasy, walking on earth is a miracle; magical realism is fantasy, realism is magical; those who ignore history may be doomed to repeat it, but you cannot step into the same river twice; the only constant is change, and even that cannot be the last word.

GLOSSARY

Arre: exclamation of surprise
Ayoo: oh (Malayalam)
Bandar log: monkey people
Beta: son
Bhai: brother
Bhindi: okra, lady's fingers
Burra sahib: big master, top man
Chai: tea
Chalo: let's go
Chappals: sandals
Charpoi: rope cot
Choli: blouse worn with a sari
Choop: quiet, silent
Dharamsala: rest house, motel
Dhoti: formal white garment tied around the waist, covering most of the legs
Ennte: my (Malayalam)
Gajar: carrot
Ghar: house
Hanuman (great monkey-god of the *Ramayana*)
Hath: hand
Hathi: elephant
Jabardasti: obstinacy
Jhinga: shrimp
Kown hai: who is it?
Kulfi: enriched ice cream
Kurta: light cotton collarless shirt
Lay lo: take it
Loonghi: like a dhoti, but informal, not necessarily white, for indoor wear
Maha: great, large
Memsahib: madam
Minar: tower
Nimbu-pani: lime-water
Oolloo: idiot, uneducated, unschooled
Sahib: sir
Sahodharan: brother (Malayalam)
Samosa: spicy deepfried triangular snack, with vegetarian or non-vegetarian filling
Seth: sir (same as Sahib)
Shabash: well done, congratulations
Shantih: peace, quiet
Sheekh kabab: spiced cubes of lamb or beef, skewered and barbecued
Shikar: hunt
Sola topi: pith helmet
Uthao: lift

Boman Desai was bound for a career in market analysis when a chance encounter with Sir Edmund Hillary, his first hero, turned him back to writing. He had his first break when an elegant elderly woman submitted half a dozen of his stories for publication to *Debonair* (in Mumbai)—all of which were published, but the woman vanished and her identity remains a mystery to this day. His second break came when another elegant elderly woman, Diana Athill, published his first novel, *The Memory of Elephants*. Desai is best known for that novel, published subsequently by the University of Chicago Press, and for TRIO, *a Novel Biography of the Schumanns and Brahms* which was awarded the Kirkus star and listed among their Best Books of 2016. The book was subsequently transcribed into an opera, *Clara*, and may now be seen on youtube. More recently, he revised and republished two novels which were available for distribution only in India: (1) *A Googly in the Compound* (a novel of the Raj), its plot ranging from 1910 to 1945, from rural Navsari to cosmopolitan Bombay to 1930s London to wartorn Burma and Mesopotamia, both world wars playing a role in the plot. (2) *Portrait of a Woman Madly in Love*, in which a vivacious, intelligent, beautiful, talented, rich, spoiled, and selfish woman, pays the price for her indulgences, spanning the years from WWII to the 1980s, illuminating themes of love and marriage, feminism and friendship, art and academia. Desai has won about a dozen awards and taught fiction at Truman College and Roosevelt University (both in Chicago), and the University of Southern Maine. He is also a musician and composer, with among other things a symphony and piano concerto to his credit (though yet to find performances). You may learn more about him at bomandesai.com. He may be reached at boman@core.com.

The Memory of Elephants

BOMAN DESAI

A novel

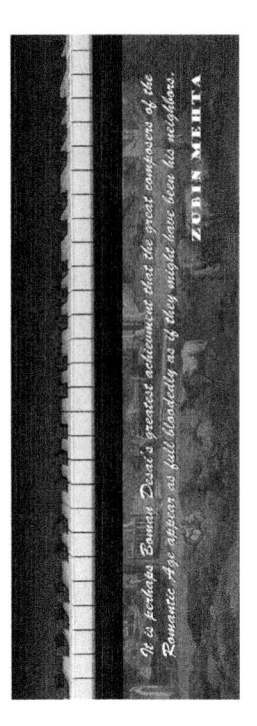

TRIO

THE SCHUMANNS AND BRAHMS
(A NOVEL BIOGRAPHY)

BOMAN DESAI

It is perhaps Boman Desai's greatest achievement that the great composers of the Romantic Age appear as full-bloodedly as if they might have been his neighbors.

—ZUBIN MEHTA

A Goosly in the Compound

Boman Desai

a novel of the Raj

The tiger cub grows as dangerous as the British Raj for India. Both have tasted blood and both demand more. Desai spins a fascinating story of Parsi bloodlines, romance and intrigue, counterpointed by the events that made WWII such a watershed in the history of both India and the world.

—*Anjana Basu*

A family's long-simmering tensions boil over during a trip to the old homestead in this literary novel... The result is a wide-lensed meditation on power dynamics—within countries and within families.
—*Kirkus Reviews*

Portrait of a Woman Madly in Love

An unhurried but immersive tale of ambition and love.
—*Kirkus Reviews*

BOMAN DESAI

A splendid foray into the initiation rites of the modern fearless woman ... brimful of erudition, some age-old wisdoms and a more recent one that everyone seems to have forgotten: the meaning of gender equality.
TARA SAHGAL, *India Today*

Excerpts from

THE MEMORY OF ELEPHANTS

When Homi Seervai, a whiz kid from Bombay, is dumped by his first love in Aquihana, Pennsylvania, he invents the Memoscan, a machine designed to scan his brain to make a record of its memories. Isolating the memory traces covering his time with his inamorata, he sets the Memoscan on a repeat cycle to relive continually the most ecstatic hours of his life. Unfortunately, the machine goes haywire, dipping into his Collective Unconscious, the Memory of Mankind, including his own racial, familial, and ancestral memories. Seeing the dead and the living juxtaposed in a jigsaw of history and biography, he imagines he is going crazy—but, instead, as he comes to realize, he is only beginning to live, his first love no more than a flicker in the panorama of possibilities that beckon him into new life.

FIRST EXCERPT

Let me be clear: It wasn't a movie as much as a single scene, a single scene which I had played repeatedly through the memoscan—at first, and for countless times, successfully, to its conclusion—but, increasingly, the memory disintegrated into hallucinations. Yes, hallucinations. There was no other explanation. Back in the room, I saw naked Candace; back outside, camelbacked Arabs; back and forth, back and forth, Candace and Arabs, Arabs and Candace, both hostilely glaring at me. When the images began to merge, my command finally slipped and I surrendered to the madness. The lips of her vagina grew larger, more wrinkled, grey, an elephant's trunk and tusks emerged from the folds, elephant ears sprouted like wings on her back. I think that was when I started to scream.

What was happening? A vagina was flying on elephant ears, dragging trunk and tusks behind. Worse, I saw the dead (Bapaiji, Granny, Dad) and the living (Mom, Jalu Masi, Sohrab Uncle, Soli Mama, Rusi, Zarine—Myself!) as if they were acting out the scenes of their lives by my bedside. Worst of all, I saw armies, hordes and phalanxes of warriors, Arabs and Iranis, on foot, horseback, camelback, elephantback, engaged in battle, showers of descending arrows, a constant swarm of adverse activity as might be witnessed when rival ant colonies or galaxies collide. The fantastic merged with the real, the ancient with the modern, naked Candace, airborne on elephant ears, mounted on an elephant's trunk and tusks, split into a hundred similar images, and the flight of Candace angels soared to meet squadrons of flying monkeys approaching from the distance. The landscape was littered with rhinestone jackets, gold ballet slippers, blue miniskirts, and red panties, all to the accompaniment of a relentless atonal symphony. No wonder I felt in terror of imminent insanity.

SECOND EXCERPT

They were not far when they heard Dhunmai call. Adi threw everything into his sack and jumped into the tree, Bapaiji on his heels. They didn't mind being found together, but didn't want to give Dhunmai the satisfaction of finding them. Too late they realized they'd left one of Adi's whittling knives on the ground. Behind Bapaiji, in the thick foliage, hung the tails of three monkeys. She would have ignored them; there were hundreds of monkeys in the trees, tails hanging like furry brown ribbons; but not this time. She grabbed all three tails and yanked—hard. The idyll of the forest was slashed as if by lightning: the monkeys shrieked oop-oop-oop-oop, setting other monkeys shrieking, birds screaming, a wolf howling in the distance as if it were night; and woven into their screams, as brilliantly as the centerpiece of a peacock's fantail, was Dhunmai's screech as she turned and ran. The monkeys continued to shriek, oop-oop-OOP-OOP-OOP-OOP!!, baring their teeth, whooping around Bapaiji and Adi as if the trees had suddenly grown too hot to touch. Bapaiji bared her own teeth, whooping back. Adi laughed so hard he fell out of the tree; when Bapaiji reached to catch him he pulled her down with him; the fall knocked the air out of them and they choked, unable to stop laughing.

THIRD EXCERPT

The summer came to an ugly end: Penny, descending the schoolbus, flaxen hair flying as she turned her head for a final (too prophetic) goodbye, flashing her last big happy sweet last lover's smile before the rush across the street to meet Erica, her English speaking ayah whom she called Nanny; a screech, a thud, a scream, Miss Bean (responsible for the children on the bus) shouting, "Do not look. Nobody is to look out of the window."

How does a six year old cope with the loss of his sweetheart? He puts himself in quarantine, he lowers his resistance, he searches out toxins as if they were grail, he dreams of a reunitement (pupal angels cocooned in a Hansel and Gretal heaven). In the two years that followed I contracted mumps, jaundice, chicken pox, typhoid, two kinds of measles, three kinds of flu; I underwent a second tonsillectomy, an appendectomy; I had yet to run through cholera, small pox, tuberculosis, and whooping cough, but something I read and someone I met so exposed the selfindulgence of my quarantine that even the most benighted eyes (mine) began to see.

Excerpts from

TRIO; a Novel Biography of the Schumanns and Brahms

The trio comprises three musical geniuses: Robert and Clara Schumann and Johannes Brahms. Clara married Robert with whom she fell in love when she was just sixteen, though it meant challenging the iron will of her father who wished her to marry an earl or count, certainly not an impoverished composer. The Schumanns had eight children and Robert's greatness as a composer was never in doubt, but he was also mentally ill, attempted suicide, and finally incarcerated himself in an asylum where he died two and a half years later.

Johannes Brahms entered the picture shortly before the incarceration and fell deeply in love with Clara, but was just as deeply indebted to Robert for getting his first six opuses published within weeks of their meeting. Clara was forbidden to see Robert in the asylum because the doctors feared she would excite him too much. Brahms became a go-between for the couple, ferrying messages to and from, but both loved Robert too well to abuse his trust. Brahms learned instead to associate deep love with deep renunciation—and, coupling this love with early experiences of playing dance music for sailors and prostitutes in Hamburg's dockside bars, he became a victim to the Freudian conundrum: Where he loves he feels no passion, and where he feels passion he cannot love.

Firmly grounded in fact, the book unfolds like a novel, a narrative of love, insanity, suicide, revolution, politics, war—and, of course, music.

FIRST EXCERPT

The rule in Paris was to play first at soirees, and if and when the newspapers mentioned you to follow up with a concert. Her uncle arranged for invitations to soirees and the first at which Clara played, the Princess Vandamore's, was notable as much for what happened as what did not. The chambers were upholstered, hung with tapestries and portraits, stuffed with porcelain, figurines, vases, cups, and stuffed animals and birds; dogs had the run of the rooms as did parrots and canaries—as, to Clara's delight, did a monkey, with whom she shook hands, though Wieck warned that she could not trust such an animal not to bite—alongside princes, ambassadors, and priests arrayed in their finest. Wieck shook his head in disbelief; the French were children pretending to be adults; how Bonaparte had conquered Europe he would never fathom.

A young man approached the piano for which Wieck was relieved, more comfortable listening to music than making conversation, particularly in French. The man was short, stooped, and frail, his eyes were heavylidded, and the long fair hair covering his ears was exquisitely combed. He smiled, appearing to enjoy himself, but looked beyond the walls and once he sat at the piano he appeared beyond the weal of the world himself. Wieck, more concerned with seating himself comfortably, paid little attention until the man began to play, one note in the high treble, so clear and commanding that Wieck became still. A configuration followed, more single notes, first descending, then ascending, but what a configuration! With an uncanny use of the pedal he had blended the individual notes into one great blooming undulating chord.

Clara gripped his wrist with a whisper. "Chopin!"

SECOND EXCERPT

He sighed, sitting again at the piano. Willy wouldn't be back until late in the evening and he was faced with the prospect of the long day ahead. He had work to do on the *Zeitschrift* and the *Fantasiestucke* he was writing for Robena, but he sat at the piano instead, doing nothing—or so it appeared, but something was spinning in his head that he needed to let out and he could let it out only on the piano.

He couldn't explain how it worked: had he not pined for Clara there would have been nothing to release; had he not sat motionless at the piano there would have been no conduit for release. He couldn't have said how long he sat, but something congealed in the time, the red blood, the hard bone, of the new composition, a strident melody, roiling harmony, interspersed with tender interludes, pulled from the collision of the thunder outside, the purr of the rain, and the noise in his head. He held his hands over the keys and under them the landscape of his nerves, blood, and bones sprang to life, little kingdoms growing under his fingers.

THIRD EXCERPT

On March 7, 1897, a shrunken Johannes Brahms, suffering from cancer of the liver, attended a performance in Vienna of his Fourth Symphony.

The symphony glides so smoothly into its first theme that the listener finds himself deep in its wake before he realizes it has even begun.

The second movement showcases a plaintive melody hovering around a single note like a hopeless lover. A friend had said that only Brahms could have written that symphony, and even Brahms had had recourse to certain locked chambers of his soul for the first time—but he had finally run out of locked chambers.

At the end of each movement the conductor turned to Brahms's box to acknowledge the composer, the audience stood, and the composer stood to acknowledge the downpour of applause, knowing the symphony would not otherwise commence.

With the conclusion of the symphony, the downpour swelled to a monsoon, all eyes turned to the tiny man, hollows in the back of his neck, skin discolored to bronze, trembling with tears, the auditorium awash with light and color in his blurry eyes.

Twenty minutes later the emaciated old composer still stood, the audience still applauded.

He was tired, but remained standing, clinging to the rail, buoyed by the love in the hall, wishing no more to sit or to leave than they, his lovely Viennese, wished to let him go, their eyes no less damp than his own, cheeks no less bright, manly beards aglitter with tears like diamonds, all of them knowing it was the last time they would be seeing one another.

He died less than a month later, but what remained—the residue, the essence, distillate of his life, gold from straw—remains impervious to fang and claw, at once the heart of the riddle of life and medicine for the heart.

Excerpts from

A Googly in the Compound; a Novel of the Raj

The Sanjanas planned to enjoy the tiger cub and surrender the adult to the zoo, but no plan had been made for the adolescent. The family is breakfasting in the compound of their bungalow when the cub gets its first taste of blood from a cut on Sohrab Sanjana's hand. Also in attendance are Daisy (Sohrab's English wife, married when she was stranded by WWII in India); Rustom (Sohrab's brother, back from the war in Burma); Dolly (their mother, afraid the rivalry between her sons might erupt into violence echoing the rivalry between the two brothers she had married in succession); and Phiroze (Dolly's second husband, younger brother of her first). Their story spans the years from 1910 to 1945, and the globe from rural Navsari to cosmopolitan Bombay to 1930s London to wartorn Burma and Mesopotamia.

FIRST EXCERPT
The crowds had thinned when many British and Indians had turned west, some in the party suggesting they too should turn west, but Stilwell had continued north, transferring loads from sedans to trucks when the terrain had proven too rough for sedans, and from trucks to jeeps when

they'd had to ford a stream and sacrifice most of the trucks. They'd had one narrow escape already. Taking two wrong turns they had lost miles when they couldn't afford to lose yards, and having corrected their path they had stopped to confirm their direction and found themselves overlooking a valley of roiling humanity.

At first it resembled nothing so much as a large snake coiling and uncoiling, but grew worse as details came clear: gray-uniformed Chinese dragged a Burman from the cab of his truck, slapped him with a pistol, bloodying his face, breaking his nose, commandeering his truck; blond Britishers struck unarmed families with the butts of their guns for bags of rice; tall gaunt Punjabis with long black beards snatched food from toothpick children; tribespeople looted bodies of the dead; heat waves magnified the disaster like a glass; the smell rose to grip them like a giant hand; someone fired a rifle, someone replied with a tommygun, then came screams, then more gunfire, then silence, first to fall were first to be trampled, women and children the fairest game of all.

They had hurried back to their convoy to find families of skeletons, grey with dust, holloweyed and leatherskinned, foul with shit and blood and flies, beyond the shame of their nakedness, crawling and rising from the ground, cracked cups and broken bowls in outstretched hands, babies sucking from dry dugs, children picking grains of rice from piles of shit. Stilwell had walked into the midst toward his jeep, shouting his concern out loud. "Hold it! Don't give them anything or we'll be mobbed! Crank up and get moving and don't stop for anything!" They had started engines, honked horns, and hurried away.

SECOND EXCERPT

Alphonse took two steps forward. He was close enough to touch Victoria when he steadied the gun, took aim again, and fired. In the wake of the blast there was once more the howling of monkeys, the screeching of fowl in the forest, but in the compound there was only a wide white silence, the sentient stillness of cemeteries awaiting the advent of ghosts, followed by an awful vibration riding the air, sweeping the grounds like a grating, atomizing all it swept, the savage roar of the tribe of tiger, Victoria erupting in an orange flame as if the ground were a bed of lava.

THIRD EXCERPT

"It was on Christmas Eve, the Turks attacked our makeshift fort, and Rajan ... at one point ... he simply threw himself at me. I didn't understand, I hadn't seen the shell whistling its way toward ..." Phiroze was once more speechless. Rajan had thrown him on his back and spreadeagled himself to cover him like a second skin—before growing suddenly weightless. His back had ripped open releasing fluids coagulating around Phiroze, encasing him in a gelatinous mold. He had tried to hold Rajan close, tried to hug him, but he had hugged bones, a ribcage clawing his chest, a skull like a lover's head lolling over his shoulder. The smell of shit was overpowering, but in that moment of sacrifice everything pertaining to Rajan became sacred, and he had breathed the odor as if to make it part of himself, wallowing in the clay that had once been his friend.

Phiroze swallowed, but still could not speak. Daisy squeezed his hand again, gripping and rubbing his arm, seeming to understand what he couldn't put into words. "My God, Phiroze, I'm so sorry. I'm so glad ... I'm so grateful you're still here."

He shook his head, eyes glistening, speaking again though his voice still trembled. "I am the one who is sorry. All this happened so long ago, more than thirty years—and here I am, an old soldier, blubbering like a baby."

Excerpts from
PORTRAIT OF A WOMAN MADLY IN LOVE

Farida Cooper is too shocked by her husband's treachery even to talk about it, but in hiding her shame succeeds only in denying the damage to herself and making casualties of others, among them an infatuated 17-year-old boy. Farida is vivacious, intelligent, beautiful, talented, rich, spoiled, and selfish, but her life is hardly as rosy as it appears. Her father's affairs render her mother frigid, leaving her effectively parentless. Her saving grace is her Kaki with whom she lives after her sixth birthday, but this also heightens the sense of her parents' indifference and she learns to show nothing of her feelings, allowing them instead to erupt years later in a series of disastrous choices. Her story shuttles between Bombay and Chicago, spanning the years from WWII to the 1980s, illuminating themes of love and marriage, feminism and friendship, art and academia, as she learns what it means to become a woman in full.

FIRST EXCERPT

She was a woman in love, and a woman in love lived on an exalted plane, in a world where even inanimate objects palpitated with life like the creations of spring, her very pores seemed to expand and contract with each heartbeat; her nightly dreams were full of flight, arms like rudders propelled by a helium heart, but even by day she felt unbound by gravity, every move bursting with grace, every step a leap into ether. It had been almost a month since Darius had returned the socks with which she had mocked him for his cold feet, they had met three times a week for lessons, she had seen him just two days ago—but every separation was bearable, even charming, only because she knew she would be seeing him again soon. She shuddered to think of life once more without him, a lacerated landscape bearing beings of cracked skin and brittle bones, a world lacking a center not knowing what it lacked, the pulsing oceanic galactic radiant heart of love.

SECOND EXCERPT

It was not quite four o'clock when they returned to Blue Mansions, but seeing Darius's bicycle standing in the compound Farida barely acknowledged Ratan's goodbye, slamming shut the door of his Plymouth, dashing up the stairs like Cinderella in reverse, bursting into the sitting-room to find Darius on the sofa. "Sorry, I'm late."

He got up. "You're not late. I came early." The clock chimed four in corroboration, but neither noticed. "Did you run up the stairs?"

Her face remained anxious. "Yes, but that's not why I'm out of breath. Silly of me to think a minute would make a difference, but I saw your bicycle downstairs and didn't want to keep you waiting."

He shook his head. "No place I would rather wait."

His voice had developed a vibrato through which you could shove a cello. She saw nothing but her lover standing in a void.

Sofa, floor, ceiling, walls, all disappeared. There is a way people move when in love, they glide with preordained grace, floating through obstacles, becoming the other's compass, rudder, wind, and star. It is a state of grace and they had joined the select club, could have danced all night and still have begged for more. "Have you been waiting long?"

He shook his head again. "Just got here." The sitting-room was a goldfish bowl, Kaki and Sashi and other servants in dangerous proximity. He pointed to the studio door. "Shall we get started?"

She had issued orders they were not to be disturbed at their lesson. "Of course." Behind closed doors again they coalesced into a single egg, a single beating heart. Minutes later they remained entwined. Farida whispered. "My darling, how are you? How have you been?"

THIRD EXCERPT

The night following Horace's visit was no different from the others. Rohini mitigated Farida's fears by day, as did the hundred and one cares of daylight, from brushing her teeth to cooking and cleaning and showering among so much else, but under cover of night her tears ran like a river. Night was the realm of solitaries and ghosts, rippers and prowlers, mists bearing tooth and claw, when helping hands appeared like hammers of doom, and encouraging words like the growls of beasts, and not even Rohini could hold at bay the hound she had unleashed upon herself.

Printed in Great Britain
by Amazon